PERSPECTIVES OF VIOLENCE

JACOB GROVEY

global
genius
society

Global Genius Society Publishing
www.GlobalGeniusSociety.com
www.JacobGrovey.com
Ordering Information:

Printed in the United States of America
First Printing, 2023
ISBN 978-0-9910633-7-6

CONTENTS

This book does not set out to glorify violence, nor guns. The purpose is simply to have a conversation about something that has heavily impacted so many of our lives.

Proverbs 3:31

Do not envy the violent or choose any of their ways.

BEFORE THE NARRATIVES

What is the meaning of life? Why are any of us even here? Do we have a purpose, or are we just taking up space? We have all had these questions at some point, but unlike most, these are questions I've had since the first day of my existence.

When I arrived in this world, I wanted to know what I was called to do. I know most people find it almost impossible to believe what I am saying and I understand your skepticism. You may be thinking there's no way I could have had such questions on the first day of my life, but unlike you, I'm not confined by the restrictions of the common man because I am not like the rest of mankind.

I know how that may sound, but trust me, it is not meant to be braggadocios because I honestly have no right to brag. However, those like me have always been involved in the history of mankind and there is no denying that. Who am I? Well, it's not a matter of who but more of what. To put it simply, I am a gun, and to better understand the circumstances of those around you, you may need to look at things from a different perspective. This is your chance to do so.

The following pages consist of a collection of narratives presented by those like me. At times, our stories are told as if we are able to see the world around us the exact same way you do. There will be other times when our ability to see will not come from sight, but from the overall experiences of the situations we're in.

Many of our stories are told from the time we were introduced to a specific human, but sometimes you will be treated to learn how things were before we got to meet anyone. Either way, our telling of the stories won't be convoluted by humans trying to recall what they think may have happened. What we say happened is what happened; it's as simple as that.

Our stories end when our connection to our humans do. We can't tell you what happens to a person once we are no longer around them, this is when your human ability to draw conclusions and use your imagination will come into play. Remember, you know how the human world works much better than we do. We are limited to the facts, you are not.

From my interactions with people, I have learned that many of you like to fool yourselves into thinking you are much smarter than you actually are. This means, you may feel like you already know all there is to know about your fellow man. I have witnessed some of you judging the people you do not know while making wildly inaccurate assumptions about those you do. You have always told yourself (and anyone who would listen) that you know exactly what would cause a person to react the way they do. No matter what the situation is, you have convinced yourself that your actions would not have matched those you disagreed with. Perhaps you're right, but then again, there's always a chance you are not.

I may not be the best when it comes to statistics, but I do know there has to be millions of connections between humans and various relatives of mine that are not dramatic, exciting, or eventful. For the most part, these are not the stories we are going to tell. Instead, the majority of the following narratives involve violence in some way. These acts are not romanticized because they don't need to be.

When you read our stories, you will notice that we do not add gore just for the sake of including it because we know that would be pointless. The events that we recall are not made out to be bigger than what they were because we don't believe in fabrication.

When it comes to tales of violent acts, you are used to hearing a story based on what was said by the victim (or someone close to them), the one who allegedly committed the crime, or even by someone who had the opportunity to witness the act for themselves. In between all of that is a jigsaw puzzle known as the truth. For those intent on finding it, they must piece this puzzle together.

Since we have the unique experience of being involved without ever having the ability to be in control, we are able to provide the unadulterated truth that people seem to be incapable of telling by themselves. You may think you understand your world now, but after you've had the chance to hear what we have to say, you may view your world quite differently. When it's all said and done, you may actually gain a new perspective (of violence).

NARRATIVE 1: INNOCENCE LOST

*M*y story starts on a cloudy and gloomy day. That may sound cliché, but it's fitting because I've heard many times that gloom tends to follow me. On the day of my 'birth,' I was pulled from the assembly line for a routine quality check. When an unknown person looked me over to see if I had any birth defects, I was able to see many of my siblings for the very first time.

My family was incredibly large, and even though we were similar in appearance, it was easy for me to see our differences. Each of us had a shimmer of hope, at least that's how I felt—at first. I wanted to introduce myself to everyone, but that seemed like an impossible mission.

"Well, it looks like you're ready to go number ten."

Those were the first words I ever heard, and I didn't understand them. Where exactly was he saying I was ready to go to, and why did he call me number ten?

The questions remained unanswered, at least one of them did. I quickly learned my name was simply a part of my identification number. It was a little disappointing to realize no thought had been put into what I was called, but I guess that person didn't feel my name deserved any reasonable consideration, but I digress. After hearing my name and seeing my family, I thought I would get an opportunity to meet everyone, but I was incorrect. I was shown how unimportant I was when I was thrown into a box with a few others. From there, it felt like we were added into a larger shipping container, but I couldn't be sure.

The box I was in was dark. I wanted to speak, but I couldn't. So, I just sat there. I had no real concept of how much time passed, but every once in a while, I would hear different voices speak as our temporary mobile home moved. Soon, I stopped feeling the motion I grew accustomed to. The boxes we were in were finally opened by an older man who smiled from ear to ear as soon as he saw us.

"There's nothing like the smell of new guns!"

He made it very obvious he was happy to see us. After quickly wiping us off, he put us on display. He used the sheet of paper that was included in the box to enter our identification numbers into his computer. As he did so, the bell that hung above his door rang to let him know he had a potential customer.

"Good morning to ya! What brings you in?"

"To be honest with you, I don't even know what I'm looking for. All I know is, my wife and I have been in our new home for about a week or so, and I want to make sure I'm able to protect her," the potential customer said.

"I can certainly respect that. Do you already have your license?"

"Yes, sir. Do you need to see it?"

"I will, but not right now. Let's go ahead and find the perfect product for you."

The two continued to speak. As they talked, the person who seemed to be the owner of the store handed me over to the potential customer.

"I guess this'll work."

The lack of confidence he had was made even more evident with each word he spoke.

"This is a gun. You can't be guessing if it'll work for you or not, you have to be sure. If you don't know what you want, maybe you should take some time to research what will be best for you and your wife. One thing I know, guns will always be big business. We've been here for over thirty years, and we don't plan on going anywhere. Take your time and come back when you're ready."

The customer didn't say anything, he just stood there and stared.

"The more I hold the gun, the more I know it's for me. Let's go ahead and get the process started."

"Now that's what I like to hear."

The customer pulled out what appeared to be a license, some paperwork, and some cash. He handed it all over to the store owner. This was the first time I was able to witness people showing I had value to them.

"Here you go, Kevin," the old man said as he handed everything—except for the cash—back to him.

"What about bullets?"

"Check the bag. Here, just like your favorite bar, the first round is always on us. I appreciate your business, and I hope you have a good time with your new friend."

It seemed like a strange thing to say about a gun, but those words were the last ones exchanged between them. After the purchase, I sat in a discrete bag accompanied by a small box of bullets as the person I was introduced to, Kevin, carried me to his car.

We sat outside of the store for a few moments. Kevin, almost immediately, began to question his decision.

"What are you doing? Why do you think this is even necessary? Is our neighborhood so bad this is the only way I can make sure my wife is safe? This....this can't be life."

He placed me on the passenger's seat.

"She doesn't even want you. She told me that before, but that was a while ago. I'm sure she won't mind. Yeah, she'll be okay with this, right?"

He acted as though he was waiting for me to respond. Of course, I said nothing. He let out a sigh, seemingly in angst, as he relocated me from the seat to the cluttered darkness of what he referred to as the glove compartment. The car started to move shortly afterward.

The ride was bumpy and it seemed to take forever for us to reach our destination. When we finally did, I was unsure if I was going to leave the car. My non-verbal concern was soon addressed when the bag I was in was grabbed. Kevin walked us slowly into what had to be his home. The place was silent, except for the echoes of Kevin's footsteps. From the sounds they created, the home seemed to be quite large.

"Kevin, is that you?"

I hadn't yet been introduced to the woman with the happy tone, so I didn't know who she was.

"Yeah, babe, it's me," Kevin replied nervously.

"I've been waiting on you to get back. I bought this new rom-com everybody's been talking about, so I want us to watch it together."

Her voice came closer and closer with each word. By the time she finished what she was saying, it sounded like she was standing right next to us.

"Yeah, that's a good idea," Kevin replied.

His voice trembled a little when he was speaking. More than likely, he said what he said not only to appease the woman, but also to soften the blow of the response she would give once she found out what he had purchased.

"What's that, Kev?" she asked.

The bag closed in on me a little bit more as Kevin tried to act like neither I, nor my bullet companions, were even there.

"Oh, this? This is nothing. Don't worry about it."

She giggled as if they were playing some type of game.

"Quit playing, Kevin. What's in the bag?"

She continued to reach for the bag while Kevin tried his best to keep it away from her. Soon, his efforts meant nothing as she became victorious in the game of keep away.

"Nah, babe, don't look in there," he said in a last-ditch effort to keep her from getting upset.

"Boy, stop," she said as she moved away from him a little bit.

She reached inside the bag and slowly pulled me out. For a few seconds, the house was filled with silence. She carefully placed me on the nearby counter and stared at me. The look she had on her face was one I hadn't seen in my limited interactions with humans. She picked me back up and held me as I became acquainted with the tears that fell from her eyes.

"I can explain why I bought that," Kevin stated.

"We had several discussions about it, and I begged you not to get one. Are you telling me you can explain why you got one anyway? I'd like to hear that!"

"We need it! I can't risk something happening to you!"

"Kev, babe, will you please take a look at this home. Think about the neighborhood we're in. And then, think about the places we grew up. Is this anything at all like that?"

Her questions and comments caught Kevin by surprise. What she said grabbed ahold of his tongue and made him unable to respond for quite some time. After moments of silence, his words were finally able to once again break free.

"I can't risk it, Phoebe. We have way too much to lose."

Phoebe. The woman's name was Phoebe. That was the first time since I had been brought into the home that her name had been mentioned. It wasn't until then I felt we had been formally introduced.

"Kevin, we don't go to sleep to the sounds of gunshots anymore. Why are you inviting that energy back into our home? Our family doesn't need that."

Kevin moved closer, and rudely took me out of Phoebe's grasp. What she said truly made me understand the feeling of being unwanted for the first time. I had quickly become the child my parents never agreed on having.

"Yeah, I see where you're coming from, but..."

"But, what?"

Kevin fell to the ground and took me with him. I sat still as his eyes started to overflow with emotions.

"I'm scared, Phoebe. I'm so scared."

Although she had just expressed feelings of anger, sadness, and disappointment toward Kevin, she still wanted to let him know she was there for him. Soon, she sat right next to us.

"What are you afraid of, Kevin?" she asked with genuine concern.

"I'm afraid our past will haunt us. I'm scared envious family members will attempt to take what we've worked so hard for."

"Don't even speak that stuff into the atmosphere. Your words have power, and the more you talk like that, the more likely it is to come true."

"I know you're right, but I can't help it."

"No, Kevin, not only can you help it, but you also have to. All of us are depending on you."

I hadn't been around humans long, but her phrasing sounded a bit out of place.

"I know you're depending on me, but....wait, what do you mean by all of us?"

Phoebe got up and stepped back.

"I meant just that. All of us are depending on you."

Kevin stood up and left me on the ground as if he no longer cared about me.

"Babe, do you mean...."

"Umm...let's just say there's a reason why I haven't been feeling well lately," she replied.

I was lost. I didn't have enough experience to be able to put together what was going on. I would've remained confused if the next part of the conversation hadn't cleared things up for me.

"Phoebe, are you telling me I'm going to be a father?"

"That's exactly what I'm saying," she replied as she started to giggle.

A child, huh? By the sounds of their apparent glee, I could tell they were happy. I, on the other hand, could not say I shared in their sentiment. I had just been brought home, and they were already talking about bringing someone else in to inhabit the space we shared. They left me on the ground as they expressed their excitement.

I helplessly watched them, feeling continuously worse and worse. Were my best days already behind me? I questioned the promise I had for my life. I thought my destiny was one of greatness, but perhaps my thought process was faulty.

"Maybe you're right, babe. Maybe I was kinda looking at things the wrong way. I get paranoid, Phoebe," Kevin said as he finally picked me up from the ground.

I was placed on the counter as they talked about their future addition. They didn't know who their child would be, but it didn't stop them from wasting time throwing around names. It seemed pointless to me, but I learned humans didn't necessarily value their time the way I felt they should have.

More time passed, and I just sat on the counter, unnoticed. I was no longer part of any of the conversations they had and it made me restless. I didn't know what was going to happen to me, but I didn't think my future would include Phoebe and Kevin. The sun rose and set many times without me being moved. I wished I could have just gotten up and walked away, but I couldn't.

One day, Kevin finally decided to pick me up again after so much blatant disrespect and neglect. Instead of finally preparing me to leave the house with him, I was just placed in the top drawer of a nightstand. Even though it was larger than the glove compartment I came home in, it still didn't feel good to be there. Kevin didn't care. He just locked the drawer and left without saying a word.

A lot more time passed without me seeing the light of day. Phoebe hadn't mentioned me in quite some time, which led me to believe she was under the impression I was no longer there. I didn't know if that assumption came from lies she had been told, or if Kevin just made sure to avoid me as a topic of conversation. Whatever the case was, I had become like a ghost, an ever- distant memory.

This was one of the many times I had to consider if, as a machine, my life actually had a purpose. Maybe my only purpose was simply to exist. That pill was a little hard to swallow, but I had to come to terms with it. Then, it all changed very suddenly when Phoebe laid down in bed one night.

She and Kevin followed through with their nightly routine. I thought it would be another night of the same thing, but a loud noise in the house interrupted the couple's slumber.

"Kevin! Kevin! Wake up!"

In a tone that was almost slurred, Kevin replied.

"What? What's going on?"

"I heard a loud noise. I don't know what it was! Please, can you check it?"

He didn't say another word, but I soon heard the drawer being unlocked. I was soon free again. Phoebe gasped when she saw I was still there, but for a brief moment, her perspective on my relevance in their home was different than it had been before.

No words were spoken as Kevin and I searched the house to see if anything was out of place, or worse if there were uninvited guests inside of our home. We moved slowly to ensure everything was inspected properly. I could feel Kevin's anxiousness as his body quiver a little bit more with each step he took.

When it seemed like everything was clear, Kevin started to head back into the bedroom. Then, he stopped.

"Something's not right," he said quietly to himself.

He continued very slowly as he made his way into one of the rooms near his bedroom. For a moment, I was moved closer to Kevin's chest where I could feel his heart racing. Each new move was incredibly methodical. He paused momentarily in the room. I could only assume he either heard or saw something that was out of place.

Suddenly, the floorboards creaked as something moved toward us. Out of nowhere, someone hit Kevin hard enough to knock him down. I fell out of his hands and hit the ground before I slid across the floor. Even though I was no longer close to Kevin, I could hear him panicking. It felt like something bad was about to happen, but I didn't know if my feelings were warranted until I heard a new voice in the room.

"I guess you lookin' for this, huh?" the voice asked as I was lifted into the air.

"Come on, man! If you're in here for money, you can have that. You can have whatever you want! Please... just take what you want and leave!"

The stranger laughed.

"Are you giving me permission to take what I want, Kevin? Do you not want me to hurt you, Kevin? What about Phoebe? Do you care about her?"

The man made sure he mentioned Kevin's name several times. It was as though he wanted to make sure Kevin understood they had crossed paths before and that his house wasn't chosen at random, it was targeted.

"Don't you mention my wife again!"

I had heard Kevin briefly get upset before, but it wasn't until his wife was threatened that I heard him truly get angry.

"Oooh! Do you feel better now, Kevin? Did yelling at me again make you feel like a man, huh? Did it?"

"Quit playing games, man. Who are you?" Kevin asked.

"Oh, so you don't even recognize me? Hold on, I think I can help you out with that."

I was lowered from my position in the air so that I could be used to hit the light switch.

"Can you see me now? Do you know who I am?" the stranger asked.

Kevin didn't say anything as the man took his mask off.

"Velt? Is that you? What are you doing?"

"Yeah, it's me, but don't act like we're friends. Don't call me by my nickname like we're cool. We weren't cool when you became the boss and had security escort me out of the building I had worked in for ten years! Did you know, without a job, my wife told me she had enough? She left me and took my daughter! What you did started a chain of events that destroyed my life! Tonight, karma has come to destroy yours!"

And without me being warned, I was forced to hurl a bullet I didn't even know I had, toward the first person who had given me a home. I didn't necessarily like it, but I had no choice. Luckily, the bullet missed Kevin, but it started another domino effect.

Phoebe was able to remain quiet until she heard me yell out. She screamed for her husband to help keep her out of harm's way, but her fear was like music to Velt's ears. He let out an evil chuckle as he ran through the house as if he lived there.

Kevin tried his best to keep up with every step Velt took. Sadly, he wasn't able to do that. Soon, Velt ran into the couple's bedroom. As Phoebe realized the first person who entered the room wasn't Kevin, she let out several blood-curdling screams. Kevin couldn't take it anymore. He created a distraction by throwing a book that happened to be by his feet.

Velt ducked to avoid being hit, and when he did, Kevin lunged toward him. A tussle immediately ensued. Once again, I hit the ground, and when I did, I could hear several punches being thrown between the two men.

Kevin begged his wife to leave the room, but her lack of movement let us all know she was frozen with fear.

"Phoebe, please get...."

As Kevin spoke, I was picked up from the ground. At first, I couldn't tell who I was with, but when I was used to hit Kevin, I got my answer. One punch did a lot of damage, but that wasn't enough for Velt. He had to make a point, so he continued to use me to fight my adopted father until he wasn't able to fight back.

"What do you want from us? Please, take what you want and leave!" Phoebe said.

Velt stood up and turned the light on in the couple's bedroom, just as he did in the previous room.

"It's funny how you and your man tried to offer me the same deal. He took a lot more than money from me, and I want to return the favor."

As if he could sense what was about to happen, Kevin somehow found a way to get up. He spat out a mouthful of blood before he started to speak.

"I'm sorry, Roosevelt, but you losing your job was not just on me. I don't make those types of decisions alone."

"Nah, you don't make those decisions alone, but you had something to do with it. I know you didn't fight for me like you could have. We've known each other for way too long for you not to respect me. There was no respect, Kev. You have to learn to respect people, no matter what their position is."

"I do respect you, Roosevelt."

For the first that night, Kevin called Velt by his full name, Roosevelt. It also was the first time it sounded like Velt had some reservations about what he was doing. I had hopes I would no longer be used as a tool of anger, but my hopes were quickly shown to be pointless.

"That's a lie, Kevin! And the fact you'd lie to me after I just told you I felt disrespected is like slapping me in my face. I'm not takin' that anymore!"

Without saying another word, Velt aimed me toward Phoebe and pressed the trigger a few times. Kevin reacted as quickly as he could to try and jump in front of the bullets that were headed directly toward his wife. The room became silent for a moment. The steady hand Velt had a few seconds prior, disappeared. Both of his hands now shook, almost uncontrollably.

"You see what you made me do? You brought this on yourself!"

Velt's voice broke the silence, but neither Kevin nor Phoebe said anything. That moment was when I felt an intense amount of the human emotions known as nervousness and fear.

"You deserve whatever happens, Kev!"

Velt told Kevin he deserved whatever happened, but I could tell he didn't actually believe it. It wasn't long before Velt grew tired of hearing his own voice, so he quit speaking. He soon felt the brief time he spent trying to convince the non-responsive audience his reason for disrupting their peace should not only be understood, but also forgiven. This was when his emotions changed from nervousness to something I had become more accustomed to—anger.

"Y'all don't have anything to say?"

With his hand still shaking, Velt took me and beat me against the wall several times. I felt myself getting scratched and scarred. I hadn't seen a reflection of myself, but I knew there was no way I still had the same shine and gloss I once sported.

"You....sorry....no good...."

Kevin finally began to speak again, but his words were incredibly low and hard to understand.

"What? Are you trying to say something to me, Kevin?"

I expected another verbal sparring session between the two, but it didn't happen. Instead, Kevin, the man who was just barely able to speak, once again found the strength to jump up. This time he threw himself toward Velt.

"What do you think you're doing? Don't you know I still have a gun in my hand?"

I was jarred back and forth as Kevin suddenly began to unleash a flurry of punches on Roosevelt's face, completely disregarding my presence.

"You must be ready to die!" Roosevelt yelled.

"If I die tonight, I'm gonna make sure you do, too. My wife is hurt because of you. Do you feel good about that?" Kevin asked as he continued to throw punches at Velt so quickly, he didn't even have time to fight back.

Before I knew it, one of the punches caused me to fall out of Roosevelt's grasp. Once again, I slid on the hardwood floor, but nobody seemed to care. Kevin continued to beat Roosevelt until the sounds of police sirens began to approach.

One of the neighbors must have heard all of the commotion and took it upon themselves to call the police.

"If you think I'm going to prison for you, you're wrong," Roosevelt said as he broke away from Kevin.

While Roosevelt made his way out of the house, the police were making their way into it. Kevin's breathing immediately began to change, which indicated he was feeling different than he was just moments before.

"I can't let this happen! Get it together, Kevin!"

I wasn't sure exactly what he was talking about, but I soon found myself being thrown back into the nightstand as Kevin grabbed his cell phone and made a call. I guess he wanted to call just so there would be a record of him trying to get assistance after the attack.

"I need help! Someone just broke into my house and tried to

kill me! They shot my wife and...we need an ambulance over here now!"

I faintly heard the person on the other line tell Kevin to remain calm because they police were almost there. When he ended the call, the police were breaking the door down as they announced their arrival.

"Police! If anyone is here, you better announce yourself!"

The sudden entry of the police into the home changed the environment. Kevin focused on the footsteps of the officers who sounded like they were drawing near.

"I'm in here. My name's Kevin and this is my home. Someone broke in and shot my wife."

He repeated what he had previously said on the phone while the cops quickly made their way into the couple's bedroom.

"Sir, we need you to stand up slowly. Do not make any sudden moves. Now, slowly put your hands where we can see them."

"I'm gonna do exactly what you tell me to do, but I need for y'all to know my wife is hurt, and she is in desperate need of medical attention. I just called 9-1-1, so hopefully they're gonna send an ambulance. I love that woman, and I tried my best to protect her when we were attacked. Please make sure she's okay."

By the way he spoke, I could tell Kevin was being taken away, not only from his home, but away from Phoebe. She hadn't made a sound since Velt made me shoot her, and I was uncertain if she was still alive.

"Do you want to tell us what happened here, or do you need to come with us to the station?"

"Sir, I have no problem telling you what happened again, but please get some help for my wife."

Kevin's request was granted. One of the officers used their radio to make sure medical assistance was on the way. A short time passed before more sirens wailed in the background. It didn't take long before the room was filled with EMTs telling the officers to stay out of the way.

"She's already lost a lot of blood. If there's any chance of saving her, we have to go right now," they said.

The tone of the voices I heard confirmed, once again, how serious the situation was. That's when I had to take a moment to think about my actions. Sure, I wasn't the only cause of what happened to Phoebe, but I certainly played a major role in it.

"We'll be taking her to Parkland," one of the voices said.

"Can you please allow me to follow them? I need to make sure she's okay," Kevin yelled out, sounding as if he was only a few seconds away from crying.

The medical team left and the officers' attention went back to Kevin.

"You can forget about following them because that's not about to happen."

"Sir, can we please go with them?" Kevin asked again.

There was no response to Kevin's question. Instead, I heard what sounded like some kind of struggle that ended very quickly. After that, there was nothing. That loud sound of nothingness filled the room for quite some time.

I kept anticipating hearing Kevin or Phoebe, but it didn't happen. I was locked up in a drawer, alone. Was this how the rest of my life was going to be? If it was, I really couldn't do anything about it. And just when I was about to give up, I heard the door slam. Again, I don't know how much time had passed, but at that moment, I knew I was no longer alone.

Each step I heard seemed to have more intensity than the one before it.

"You think this is how it's gonna go down?"

Before those words were spoken, I wasn't sure who was in the house. Even though I hadn't heard him in a while, as soon as I heard him speak, I knew Kevin had returned. I didn't, however, know who he was speaking to.

"Nah, you won't win!"

I only heard Kevin's voice for a little bit, and that was incredibly strange to me for some reason. I wondered what was going on, but I didn't expect to find anything out.

"And my stuff better not have been moved, either!"

He was now in the room where I was. After walking for a few more minutes, he unlocked the drawer I had been kept in.

"Hello, little beauty. How are you?"

He held me in the air. I checked to see if anyone else was in the room, but we were alone. Although I appreciated the compliment and being asked how I was doing, I found it to be strange.

"I hope you were able to get plenty of rest because we may have to go to work soon."

His words grew stranger, and I got concerned about the work he was talking about. I was soon placed on top of the nightstand I had just been freed from. Then, Kevin decided he needed to speak with someone on the phone.

"Hello, Roosevelt. How have things been for you since we last saw each other?"

His tone was eerily calm as he pulled the device away from his ear and put it on speakerphone. He placed the phone right near me. It was as though he wanted to make sure I didn't miss a single word of what was being said.

"Who is this?" the person on the other end asked, almost as if he was holding back laughter.

"I'm not calling from a different phone number, so you know exactly who this is."

Roosevelt let out a slight chuckle.

"Yeah, I know it's you, Kev, but I don't know why you're calling me."

"You accomplished your goal, Velt."

"What do you mean?"

"The night you were over here, you said you wanted to ruin

my life. Well, you did that. You got me, Velt, and I have to make sure I pay you back."

"Am I supposed to be scared or something, Kevin?"

"No, you're not supposed to be scared at all. I just don't want you to be surprised. I want you to be informed, and even though I'm no longer your supervisor, I still feel obligated to make sure you're prepared for the obstacles that may come."

"Prepared? Prepared for what?"

Roosevelt spoke very dismissively, but Kevin kept his composure.

"You told me I ruined your life when you lost your job and your woman left you. Even though I apologized and explained I wasn't the only one responsible, you still decided you wanted to disregard how your actions were ultimately what caused your dismissal. You weren't man enough to accept the consequences of your actions. No, you couldn't take any responsibility for it because you'd rather just blame others. You decided you wanted to do to me what you felt I had done to you. You wanted to eliminate things from my life, but that's not what you did, Roosevelt. No, that's not what you did at all."

"What are you talking about?" Roosevelt asked, sounding concerned.

"You didn't take a thing from me. Velt, you did far worse than that."

"Quit trying to sound threatening, and just get to the point."

"Okay, I'll do that. Velt, you didn't take something from me, you took someone from me. See, you didn't know it, but my wife was carrying our first child. The bullets you fired caused my wife to lose so much blood, she lost the baby. And she...she is laying in ICU, trying her best to fend off the reaper."

"Oh...I..."

"Whatever you're thinking about saying, just save it. Just so you know, I didn't tell the police you broke into my house because I didn't want them to arrest you. Nah, jail would've been getting off easy. I want you to suffer like I have. So, do whatever you have to do because I'm comin' for you. If you wanna get it over with, come on. You know where I work, and you know where I live. I dare you to do something," Kevin said.

I was shocked at what I heard. Not only had my parents lost the child they had yet to meet, but Kevin also now seemed ready to throw his life away for revenge while Phoebe was in the hospital. I was as close to feeling shame for what I done as I could possibly get and at that moment, Kevin and Phoebe's initial difference of opinions about me made sense. Sure, Kevin may have had the best intentions when he brought me home, but Phoebe knew the problems I could potentially cause.

After the phone call, Kevin picked me up and stared at me.

"The last time you had to go to work, it was unexpected. The next time will be very different. Are you ready for that? Are you ready to make up for what you and Roosevelt did?"

I couldn't believe he thought doing something bad would correct the negative actions that had already taken place. Going after Roosevelt would not bring their child back, nor would it help Phoebe recover. If I understood this, I didn't know why Kevin didn't. If I had been able to, I would've yelled at him for wanting to do something so stupid.

"We have to go!"

He didn't tell me where we were going, but leaving the house as quickly as we did, let me know Kevin wasn't thinking clearly.

Soon, I found myself with my safety clicked on as I was thrown into an old backpack. He zipped the bag up and we left. I wasn't sure if we were going to find Velt, but it only took a little while before I found out where we were headed. Kevin's phone started going off. I didn't know he grabbed it before we left, but humans can't seem to go anywhere without their phones, so I should've known.

"Hello."

He turned on speakerphone once again.

"Kevin, how are you?"

The woman's voice was unfamiliar, but her concern for Kevin seemed genuine.

"I'm okay. How are you?" Kevin asked.

"I'm just concerned about you, and so is your father."

"You don't have to worry about me, Mom. I'm good."

That was the first time I ever heard any mention of Kevin's parents. It was refreshing because I thought if anyone could talk some sense into him, it would be his mother.

"Kevin, you're acting like nothing happened. Son, it's okay to take some time and grieve."

"Mom, I'm good. Thank you for your concern, though. I'm about to go see Phoebe, so I'm trying to be strong."

"Oh, I understand. Do you want us to go over there with you?"

"I appreciate it, but I just want to spend some time alone with her."

"That's a good idea, Kevin. Let us know if you need anything, okay?"

"Yes, ma'am, I will. And Mom, no matter what, I want you to know I love you and Pop. Y'all are the best."

"Thank you, Kev."

"You're welcome. Since I'm almost at the hospital, I'm about to let you go. It's always good to hear from you. "

"You, too."

There was a bit of unusual silence before Kevin ended the call. It seemed as though he had more to say, but for some reason, he forced himself not to say anything else.

When the phone call ended, Kevin chose to keep the car silent. There was no radio station playing music in the background. There were no conversation between Kevin and himself discussing his future plans. There absolutely nothing.

The silence broke when the dinging sound from the car let

me know Kevin opened the door. With hardly any hesitation, I knew Kevin was ready to make his next move. Since he told his mother he was going to see Phoebe, when he grabbed the backpack I was in, I assumed we were going to the hospital.

I have never claimed to fully understand the rules and regulations of the human world, but I didn't think I would be a welcomed guest inside a hospital. This didn't matter to Kevin, though. We moved around the hospital without Kevin saying a word to anyone. Then, we just stopped moving.

There were a lot of unfamiliar noises. The sounds were somewhat distant, at first, but they kept getting louder. This led me to believe we had made it to Phoebe's room.

"Hey, babe. How are you feeling today?" he asked as if he expected a response.

I sat in the bag, hoping to hear Phoebe's voice again, but she didn't say anything. The bag was placed on the ground as Kevin continued to speak to his wife.

"Stuff has been crazy, and I know it's all my fault. Babe, my thoughts have been running 'round and 'round in my head trying to figure out what I can do to make things right. I just hope and pray whatever is done, you can forgive me for all of this."

He paused momentarily before releasing what sounded like nervous laughter.

"Did you hear me, Phoebe? I used the word 'pray.' Out of all of the times you wanted me to pray and have a closer relationship with God, I waited until this situation to listen to you. I'm sorry. Please just open your eyes and talk to me. Be mad, yell, complain...anything. I need to hear you. I need my wife back. Phoebe, please...I can't make it without you. Do you hear me? I love you, and I cannot make it without you. So I need you to fight. Fight as hard as you can. Please."

Since I had been brought into Kevin and Phoebe's home, I was able to witness many human emotions. I had seen disappointment, sadness, intense anger, and love. Hearing Kevin pour his heart out to a wife who was unable to respond, showed me how loving someone unconditionally could make another person vulnerable and open to expressing themselves in their moments of weakness. This also made me wonder if love was more of an asset or a liability.

As I pondered the value of love, Kevin began to cry until someone else entered the room.

"Hello. Are you Mr. Vincent?"

"Yeah."

"Mr. Vincent, my name is Dr. Johansen. Would it be possible to speak with you outside? I would rather not put any possible negative vibes into your wife's room."

"I don't know what you want to tell me, but I would like to stay in here with my wife."

"I understand. Have you been told about the full extent of your wife's injuries."

"No, I haven't. Just tell me the truth about what's going on."

"Okay, let me get to it. Your wife is not doing very well. Her injuries are far worse than they initially appeared to be and with the loss of the baby..."

"Yeah, I know it's looking bad, but she's a fighter. She'll pull through."

His words caused me to once again question my understanding of humans. Only a few minutes before, he was crying and begging Phoebe to stay alive. Then, all of a sudden, he spoke as if he had no doubt she was going to make it. It was baffling.

"Mr. Vincent, your optimism is encouraging, but I need you to understand the severity of the situation. It is my opinion that if she makes it, her quality of life will be nowhere near what it was before the incident."

"What do you mean?"

"If she survives, it's very possible her brain may not be functioning fully. She lost a lot of blood and oxygen. We have been running tests, but we don't know how her brain was impacted. I know you want her to live, but I need you to think about the possibility of losing her or living with a wife who will be totally dependent on you because she can't talk, walk, or possibly be able to move. Picture having to provide care for her twenty-four hours a day. Will you be able to handle that?"

"Are you serious?"

"Yes, I'm very serious."

"I will do anything for that woman. I will die for her if I had to."

"I commend you for accepting the possible responsibility of taking care of her. Now that you know how serious things are, I'll leave you alone with your wife. If we get any new info, we'll be sure to pass that along to you."

The conversation ended, the door closed gently afterward, and I assumed only Kevin, Phoebe, and I were left in the room. It had to be difficult for Kevin to hear what the doctor had to say about Phoebe. Even though I couldn't feel the same pain Kevin did, it was almost as though I could understand it.

Although I was manufactured, Kevin was like my father, and even though she didn't like the idea of me being in their home, Phoebe was like my mother. I did not want her to be taken away from me. The ironic thing was, if she didn't make it, it would be because of something I, her unwanted child, had done.

Would it have been easier if Kevin would have just pulled me out of the bag I was in and set me on fire so that I was destroyed? Perhaps sensing me burn in her presence would be enough to wake Phoebe up. If a few bullets released from my grasp had the doctors questioning if my mother was going to live or die, then maybe I shouldn't have been around; at least not around them.

I tried to yell out loud enough for Kevin to hear me, but I had to face the reality of being voiceless. I had no control over what I did, or what I did not do. At that point, it seemed like I was made only to hurt those who may not have deserved it, while helping those who deserved to be in pain. Whether or not this was the case didn't matter. Again, I was simply a machine designed to do what I was told.

"Babe, I know you heard what the doc said, but I don't want you to pay attention to it. It's not your time. Do you hear me? It is not your time."

As Kevin continued to beg his wife to fight for her life, I could hear him pacing in the room. I was convinced he was losing control of his emotions.

"Phoebe, I have to step out, but I'll be back a little later."

At the time he spoke those words, I felt the backpack being moved. There was no mention of where we were going, but I had an idea. I felt Kevin was on his way to use me to make a dumb move that would change the rest of his life. As we got in the car, I already knew Kevin wanted to kill Velt for altering his family, and nobody could blame him for having those thoughts.

However, if having an injured wife and losing a baby had already caused him to be in pain, how did he think he would be able to handle the feelings he would have to carry if he killed Velt? I knew he hadn't thought about that, but there was nothing I could do. I just waited until we stopped moving, which didn't take long.

We had not gotten out of the car, but we seemingly hadn't been traveling very long, either. Kevin also hadn't said anything since we left Phoebe's room, so I couldn't be sure where we were. I soon heard what sounded like a door being locked. Then, I heard the zipper of the bag I had been trapped in, which let me know I would possibly be set free again.

"So, what's up? Do you just wanna keep talking about what you're gonna do, or are you gonna do it?"

A single voice generally meant Kevin was talking on the phone, but as the bag I was in was unzipped, and I was pulled out of it, I saw Kevin wasn't on the phone. Instead, he was speaking to a reflection of himself in the mirror of a public restroom as he locked the door.

"Oh, so I see you with the nine, but are you really ready to use it?"

Although I was once called #10 by the person who first inspected me, I was a 9mm, and right then was the first time I ever heard Kevin refer to me as such.

Kevin continued to swing me around as he questioned and argued with himself. An internal battle ensued. The real Kevin, the one I knew, was engaged in conflict with a persona his mind had created to carry out a plan of revenge. The more he talked, the more the real Kevin seemed to fade away. As his speech and demeanor continued to change, there was a loud pounding at the door.

"Hey! Open up," the person on the outside yelled.

"What?" Kevin replied.

"Open the door," the person said again.

"Bro, it's best you step away quietly. I promise you don't want me to open this door!"

I thought I would be placed back in the bag, but I ended up leading the way as we moved toward the door. He waited for a moment to see if the guy would be quiet, but he continued to make noise.

"Hey, quit playing and open the door now! This restroom ain't yours!"

"Okay, I warned you, but you didn't want to listen," Kevin responded.

He unlocked the door and pushed the door open. I was forced to introduce myself to the guy before he even knew what was going on.

"Wh-what are you doing, man? Is it really that serious?"

Kevin pointed me at the guy's face and he started sweating immediately.

"I tried to get you to leave, but you wouldn't do it. I told you it was best for you to just let me have some time to myself, but you thought it was a game. Now, you see how real it is, don't you?"

The guy was so frightened he could no longer speak.

"That's alright, you don't have to say anything. When you got up today, did you think it could end like this? That's a rhetorical question. I know there's no possible way you could have imagined this, but that's not even important right now. You felt it was important to disturb someone's peace when they were practically begging you not to. Now, I just need to talk to you man-to-man."

"I'm sorry, man. I-I don't want any trouble. I have a family, so I'll just go."

The little laugh Kevin released was unlike anything I had heard from him before. It was devious, and I could see the person found it to be frightening.

"Quit wasting time and let me talk. Let me ask you something. Where are we right now?" Kevin asked.

"In a restroom."

"True, but where is the restroom located?"

"Umm...in the hospital."

This was when I found out we had gotten in the car, and it felt like we had moved, but we hadn't traveled anywhere at all.

"Yeah, we're in the hospital. Generally, people who don't work here, come here because something is wrong with them, or something is wrong with someone they care about. So, you telling me you have a family doesn't mean anything to me because I do, too. What's your name, man?"

"It's Julius."

"Julius, why are you at the hospital today?"

Kevin was speaking as if he was concerned, which was strange. Even though I was silent and not being talked about, I was still impacting the conversation.

"I'm here for my little girl."

"Really? What's her name?"

"Her name is Autumn."

"That's a beautiful name. What happened to her?"

The guy paused, but he finally answered the question.

"She was playing on the swing with her cousins. Since they were a few years older than her, she wanted to impress them, so she decided to jump out once the swing reached its highest point. Her cousins said the jump itself was great, but the landing wasn't. She ended up landing on her arm, breaking it in three places. So, she's getting looked at now."

"I'm sorry Autumn hurt herself, but I'm sure she'll be okay."

Kevin's tone was somewhat comforting. The more they talked, the more it was like I wasn't even there.

"Thank you. Yeah, she'll be fine. Hey, why are you here?" Julius asked.

The man was now speaking as though he had forgotten he had just been threatened. Perhaps it was all part of a plan to ensure he was able to leave safely.

"Well, a former co-worker broke into my house, got ahold of this gun right here, and he shot my wife."

Just when I thought forgot about me, Kevin reminded Julius I was still there.

"I'm sorry. How is she?"

"She's in the ICU right now, so, I wouldn't say she's doing good."

If I had the ability to feel guilty, that feeling probably would have kicked in right then. It's bad enough that I was involved in the incident, but when Kevin told someone about my involvement in Phoebe's injury, it just made things worse.

"For real, I'm sorry."

"I appreciate that, but I didn't tell you about her to get any sympathy. I did it because I want you to know other people are going through things in their lives, too. Sometimes, the things other people are dealing with are worse than anything you have going on in your life. Sometimes, instead of pounding on a door and yelling for someone to open it, you may want to start thinking about why that person may have the door locked in the first place."

"You're right, and I apologize."

"It's okay. I guess you had no way of knowing," Kevin said.

"No, I didn't, but I do need to show more patience. This wasn't the first time my short fuse has gotten me into trouble. Hey, this may seem like a strange question, but do you mind if we pray? It seems like we both could use some prayer."

The concept of prayer was something new to me. I had only briefly heard about it when Kevin mentioned it in Phoebe's hospital room.

"I don't really do that very often," Kevin said.

"I can't pretend I'm spiritual enough to do it all of the time, either, but like I said, I think we both need it. I'll talk, and if you have something to add, just join in. Is that okay?" Julius asked.

"Yeah, I don't see anything wrong with that."

"Okay, let's bow our heads and close our eyes."

"Julius, please don't try to be a hero. I'm willing to do this praying thing, but I promise you, if you try to run out, take my gun, or anything else that's stupid, you'll regret it."

"Trust me, I understand. Now, can we pray?"

Kevin didn't say anything. He just breathed deeply as he waited for Julius to begin.

"Heavenly Father, this is a situation beyond explanation or logic. I don't know this man's wife, and I don't know him, but today, I am praying for healing for all of us. His wife needs physical healing, but he seems to be in need of mental and spiritual healing. Please help him let go of whatever is causing him to be so angry. Let him release any thoughts that are not of you. Let him realize you are the only one who can truly pass judgment. I pray that I learn consideration and patience. My words get me into trouble, so God, I ask that you help me learn how to speak more positively. I pray for Autumn's quick recovery, and I pray my family will be able to enjoy each and every moment we have together because it all can be taken from us at any moment. I pray for these things in the name of Jesus. Amen."

That prayer was unlike anything I had ever heard. Julius was speaking to someone who wasn't physically in the room, but neither he nor Kevin questioned if that someone would be able to hear them. Julius referred to the person as Heavenly Father and God, which let me know whoever they were speaking to, went by different names. Also, Kevin and Julius hadn't met before that day, but they still seemed to know who God was, which meant they were somehow connected.

"This may sound crazy, but I needed that, Julius. Thank you."

"You're welcome. As strange as all of this has been, I think it happened for a reason."

"Yeah, you're right. And let me sincerely apologize for everything I put you through. This ain't really me. I've just had so much on my mind lately; I've just felt like I'm losing it. I haven't had anyone to talk to. Well, that's how I've felt. You reminded me I can talk to God, no matter what. Again, I'm sorry."

"Hey, we all mess up. We've all asked for forgiveness and hoped we didn't keep making the same kind of mistakes over and over again. It's all good, though. I forgive you."

"Thank you, Julius. I needed to hear that. I don't even know who I am right now. You know what? You're good, bruh. Just go ahead and leave," Kevin said.

"Are you serious?"

"Yeah, man. Go ahead and leave. I need to clear my head. You just better not say nothin' to anybody. You hear me?"

"I won't say a word. Before I go, I just have to say something to you."

"I'm listening."

"Just remember, regardless of how you feel, and regardless of how things may seem, you are not alone in this world. You are not in this by yourself."

"I appreciate that, Julius. I really do. Now, leave before I change my mind."

I never would have thought the interaction would end the way it did, but predicting the nonsensical actions of humans is nearly impossible. When Julius left, Kevin chose not to lock the door. I guessed speaking and praying with him made Kevin feel it was no longer necessary.

I thought there may have been a chance Kevin felt good enough to put me away and go back to the room with Phoebe, but once again, I was incorrect.

"Do you think he was right? Do you think prayer will help everything that's going on? God knows I don't want to kill, or even hurt anyone, but at the same time, I'm supposed to be Phoebe's protector. What kind of man would I be if I just let the person who attacked my wife get away with it?"

All of the questions and concerns were spoken while Kevin sat in one of the stalls. Everything seemed to be directed at me, but even if I could have spoken, I would not have known what to say. Then, seemingly out of nowhere, I began to feel those tiny waterfalls fall from Kevin's eyes. I knew if they were around, Kevin was not feeling good.

"Buying you was a mistake, and I'm an idiot for not listening to her," he whispered in my direction.

He said similar things before, but for the first time, I started to agree with him. I knew I would never truly understand the dynamics of human relationships, but I was beginning to realize relationships were far more than just two people being together. It was becoming very evident that people could find themselves being together for a multitude of reasons, but the couple's ability to survive has a lot to do with them communicating and making sacrifices for each other.

Granted, I had only been able to witness one couple, but

their major issue happened because Kevin wasn't willing to sacrifice what he felt was necessary for his family, which was me. He refused to believe, even though his wife tried on many occasions to convince him, I wasn't needed. Bringing me into their home went against what she wanted, and because of that, the outcome, up to that moment, was not a positive one.

After a few moments of Kevin talking to himself, I heard the door open. I briefly pictured another situation similar to what happened with Julius, but Kevin didn't want another conflict. He barely moved as he remained silent in the stall. It seemed like he was pondering his next move, but I had no way of confirming this.

As Kevin sat there, I was put back into the bag only to be pulled right back out. Kevin was so confused, he didn't know what he wanted to do. I was placed back in the bag yet again before Kevin finally decided to move. When we left, I didn't know where we were going, but the familiar sounds of the machines beeping let me know when we made it back to Phoebe's room.

"Babe, one day you'll look back at this moment and you'll realize how strong you are. I just know it."

He was back to being the confident and caring Kevin. Although I preferred his more natural persona to the one he recently exhibited, both were starting to feel equally fraudulent. How would Phoebe feel if she knew her husband had just threatened a man's life? How would she react to the person Kevin was pretending to be? And would she find the feelings she had towards me had changed, or would they still be the same? I mean, not only would some consider me to be a bad influence on Kevin, but I was also the child she never wanted, who caused her to lose the child she did.

I wanted to leave, but I was constantly faced with my limitations. I just knew the longer I was around Kevin and Phoebe, the more harm I would likely do to them.

"Can I ask a favor, Phoebe?"

Kevin stood up and carefully placed the bag on the floor.

"I need for you to trust me, and I need for you to promise, no matter what, you won't stop loving me. I'm a flawed man, babe, but I only wanted what I thought was best. I hope you understand that, and I hope you know I love you."

After those words, he picked up the bag, and we were on the move again. His tone and the words he used told me he had once again convinced himself to make a move that wasn't in his best interest.

"So, it's 3:00. That means..."

He started to mumble and slur his words. He sounded different than I had ever heard him sound before. This was just another reason I questioned his mental stability. Then, out of nowhere, he started the car, turned on his radio, and squealed the tires as we peeled away from the hospital's parking lot. He was on a mission to get somewhere, and he wasn't going to let anything get in his way.

Only a few songs had the chance to play on the radio before we stopped.

"This is what you've been waiting for," he told himself.

He opened the bag and let me out. I was about to have to go to work, whether I wanted to or not. He didn't try to hide me as we ran up three flights of stairs of an unfamiliar apartment complex. He stopped and knocked on a door.

"Who is it?" the person on the other side asked.

Kevin stood to the side of the door and forced himself to laugh as he answered.

"Man, it's me. Just open the door and quit playing."

The person Kevin spoke to was probably very confused, but for some reason, he decided to open the door anyway. When he did, that's when I was re-introduced to an old 'friend.'

"What's going on, Velt? I know you're not just gonna stand there. Don't you wanna invite me in?"

Velt wasn't given a chance to answer because it didn't take long for Kevin to use me to get inside of Roosevelt's home.

"You ain't just gonna walk up in my home and…"

Velt spoke as if he was ready to fight, but his voice seemed to be telling a different story.

"Calm down, Velt. I know you're scared, so don't waste your energy pretending. I just need for you to sit down and listen."

"Yeah, man, whatever you say."

"I'm glad you said that. If we were in the movies, this is where one dude would spend all day telling someone how he's going to carry out his ingenious plan. I usually think that's corny, but I find it necessary to tell you why I'm here."

There was a chance that every word Kevin spoke was bringing me closer to doing something that probably shouldn't have been done. If he put me to work, he would have to be the one to deal with the repercussions of his actions, not me.

"Bro, I know why you're here. Just get it over with. I'm tired of looking over my shoulders anyway. I already told you, you took everything from me when you took my job! I ain't got nothin' to live for anyway. Do it already!"

Roosevelt had truly given up. He didn't care if he lived or died.

"Don't act like you know what's gonna happen, Velt. Now, be quiet, and let me say what I need to say."

Roosevelt did exactly what he was told and Kevin continued to speak.

"You killed my baby. That ain't no exaggeration, you literally killed my unborn child. And you put my wife in the hospital. The people there can't even tell me if she's gonna make it. This stuff has been weighing on my heart for a while now. Truth is, I wanted to pull the trigger a few times, like you did, so I could stand over you and watch you breathe your last breath. I tried to convince myself I was ready to do it, but that ain't me. Getting revenge ain't my job and ending your life might make me feel better for a minute, but it won't bring my child back, and it won't help Phoebe."

"So, what are you saying?" Roosevelt asked tentatively.

"I'm saying, I'm done with this stuff, Velt. This act we've both been putting on needs to end. Look, I'm truly sorry for you losing your job and your relationship. As a supervisor, I had a responsibility to do what was best for the company."

"So, it was the company over your friend, right?" Roosevelt asked.

"Friendship had nothing to do with it, and you know that. You knew your behavior would have consequences. I even warned you, but you acted like you were untouchable. Bro, none of us are untouchable with these companies. We are all a negative action away from being thrown to the streets."

"If that's how it is, why were you willing to do whatever they asked you to do?" Velt asked.

"I have obligations to my wife. No friendship will go above what I need to do to make sure my wife is taken care of."

"So, if that's true, how is this over without you killing me?"

"Like I said, I have a responsibility to take care of my wife. Killing you gives me momentary pleasure, but it doesn't allow me to take care of Phoebe. It'll ultimately make things worse. I can't do that to her because she's already been through enough."

"So, is that really it, Kev?"

"As far as I'm concerned, it is. I know you resent me. You may still want to kill me, but I won't have anything to do with that. Coming here, apologizing to you, and clearing the air has lifted a huge weight off of my shoulders. I know you still hate me and you may still try to harm me. If that happens, then, so be it, but I'm done. I refuse to keep doing this."

It was a long conversation, but it ended there. I was no longer pointed in Roosevelt's direction as we left his apartment. What took place in that apartment was not expected and the restraint it took to not use me to settle their dispute was commendable.

I didn't know what was going to happen after that, but when we got back into the car, Kevin felt the need to have a discussion with me.

"I have to talk to you," he said.

Having a discussion with a gun was not smart, but doing so close to the area where something bad could have easily happened was borderline idiotic.

"I was wrong. I was dead wrong. I thought Phoebe and I needed you, but we don't. You've done nothing but bring turmoil our way and I'm tired of it. It's over for you. It's too late to take you back to the store, but I have to get rid of you."

This was an example of how quickly humans put the responsibility of their actions on somebody or something else. Here I was, just a gun, and I was being blamed for the actions of people. If I were able to get mad, that's exactly how I would have felt right then. How could he blame something that could only do what it was made to do, for any trouble that came the handler's way? It was ridiculous, but I just had to stay there to hear his lecture.

"I got you for protection, but I suppose there was a reason I second-guessed your purchase before I even brought you home. You're no good, and you can't be around me anymore."

The audacity of this man. If that's how he felt about me, then he needed to quit wasting time talking and figure out what was going to happen to me. He let me know he no longer wanted me around, so I had to make myself ready to leave the place I called home.

While he talked, he finally put me back in the bag, and we left the apartment complex. As we went to yet another unknown destination, his phone rang. As was the case with pretty much every phone call he took while we were in the car, his conversation was put on speakerphone.

"Hi, is this Mr. Vincent?"

"It is. Who is this?"

"This is Krystal from Parkland Hospital."

As soon as he heard who it was, he momentarily lost control of the car. The slight opening in the bag allowed me to see the look of concern on his face as he gripped the steering wheel very tightly.

"What's going on with my wife? What happened?"

"Don't worry, Mr. Vincent. It's nothing bad. I'm calling to let you know your wife has opened her eyes and has managed to speak a few words," she said.

"Ma'am, please don't play with my emotions. The doctors told me there was no hope for her. So how could her condition improve out of nowhere?"

"I wish I could explain the full details of what happened, but I can't. All I've heard is that her current condition is nothing short of a miracle. The doctors are still running tests, but you should be able to see her in the morning."

"Thank God!"

"We just wanted to make sure you knew your wife is truly a fighter, and we are all so glad to be able to witness her strength."

"Yeah, she is amazing! I'm very blessed to have her. Trust me, I'll be there first thing in the morning."

"Alright, and if I can just add something; we have some great doctors and nurses here, but I believe this was the result of not only their work, but of prayer. God is good and he always makes a way. Have a excellent evening, Mr. Vincent. May God continue to bless you and your wife."

After he finished speaking to the person from the hospital, Kevin was in a much better mood. Joy replaced the concern on his face and I noticed he had loosed his grip on the steering wheel.

"Did you hear that? As soon as I made the final decision to get rid of you, I got some of the greatest news I ever had in my life. You bring darkness, and like I said, it's over," he said with a look of sincerity in his eyes.

Then, we stopped. When he grabbed the bag, I knew my time with the Vincent family was coming to an end.

"Hey, how are you?" Kevin asked someone.

"I'm good. What brings you in today? Are you looking to buy anything in particular?"

"Nah. Actually, I have something in here I would like to get rid of."

Kevin passed the bag over to the person he conversed with. The transition to a new home officially began at that moment. The stranger pulled me out of the bag and looked me over.

"It's a beauty. Why are you getting rid of it?" he asked.

"I thought I needed it, but it's been more trouble than it's worth."

Kevin said I was more trouble than I was worth as if he didn't have a hand in everything that went wrong with our relationship. I empowered him when he felt like he couldn't protect his wife and this was how he chose to repay me.

"Are you looking for cash or something new to take home?"

Kevin took a brief look around to think while I was left in the hands of someone I didn't know. I almost felt violated.

"Yeah, it looks like you have a lot of good stuff, but I'll just take the money."

I witnessed the stranger getting Kevin's fingerprints and a copy of his license just in case we had caused harm to anyone. Kevin assured him nothing happened, but it didn't stop the stranger from completing the process. As the deal was finalized, Kevin left without even having the decency of saying goodbye to me.

Right then, I learned humans didn't believe in loyalty, so I knew I couldn't, either. Since Kevin and Phoebe were the first people I ever really knew, I foolishly expected them to keep me around. Knowing that wouldn't happen taught me not to get attached to any of these people. I was made to do a job and that was it. Humans were not my friends and they were not my family. They didn't care about me, so it was good I couldn't care about them.

Right then, I may have ended my chapter with Kevin, but I had no doubts another human would take me to a new home at some point. As I was locked away in a case with some possible relatives of mine, I thought about the likelihood of seeing Kevin again in the future under different circumstances.

It was funny how he continuously found ways to blame me for the obstacles he was forced to face. He pointed his fingers at me as if I caused him to lose his innocence. All I knew was that if I ever had the chance to see him again, I would be obligated to show the same level of respect he showed when he got rid of me. I promise if that happens, I'll do my best to make sure he loses far more than his innocence.

NARRATIVE 2: DAWN OF A NEW DAY

*H*umans are emotional creatures. They are always feeling some type of way about something. I've seen them wake up mad for no reason, and go to sleep laughing as if everything in their world was going exactly the way they wanted it to. As machines, guns are not supposed to have anything to do with emotions, but somehow, each one of us has been altered by the emotions of the people we are around.

When I met my last human, she was a young lady, who was about twenty-one years old. I already had the opportunity to live with a few other humans, so I had a bit of an understanding of how they were. This young lady wasn't like any of the other people I had interacted with. From the moment I met her, she seemed to have a positive energy that was different than everyone else. If there was a such thing as a typical gun user, she wouldn't have fit the description. In fact, I'm pretty sure we would have never met if it hadn't been for her father.

I had known her father for quite a while, and we had been on a lot of adventures together, but one day, he told me it was time to meet the person who would be responsible for the next portion of my journey. When a person chooses you for the first time, you think you're special. You think the person will be with you forever, but as the years go by, you realize that's not always the case.

People are able to do whatever they want to machines without any guilt because they are used to doing the same thing to other humans. They use each other until they've had their fix, then they get rid of them. For the most part, that's how they do us. The day the first human decided to give me away, he pulled out a leather box that was just large enough for me to fit in.

As I was placed inside of the box, I wondered how things were about to change. I wondered if my previous interactions would be similar to the ones I would have in the future. I waited for what seemed like forever before I felt the box move, which let me know I was being relocated. Then, I heard a loud shriek.

"Daddy, is this for me? What is it? It's not even my birthday or anything!"

"Well, every day with my little girl is special, so I just want to give this to you. Once you open it, I'll explain why."

She grabbed the box and started to shake it around as if that would let her know what was waiting inside. Her squeals of delight indicated how excited she was. I didn't know exactly how she was going to react when she finally saw me, but I was ready for whatever was about to come my way.

"Daddy....is this a... but...why?"

I was confused by her words. I thought I had missed some of what she was asking because her fragmented thoughts didn't make sense to me.

"I know you may be wondering why I'm giving you a gun, but I think it's well past time for you to have it."

"But why? It's not like I hang out in bad places or anything. I'm the stay-at-home-type, you know that."

"That's true, but the way this world has become, any place can become a bad place before you even have time to blink. Plus, you're living on your own now, and as your father, that scares me. And let's not forget, you've been getting close to that guy."

"What guy, Daddy?"

"I can't remember his name, but I'm talkin' about that one guy you talk about all of the time. You know, that one who you tried to bring to meet your mother not too long ago."

"You mean, Clarke?"

"Yeah, that's the one."

"Why do you think I need a gun for him? He's one of the nicest people I've ever met."

"That may be true, but I don't trust him. When it comes to you, I don't trust any of these young guys. I pray nothing ever goes wrong, and you never actually have to use this gun, but you'll have it just in case. Now, go ahead and hold her."

I knew she didn't want to pick me up, but she did it anyway.

"She is cute, though. This handle is dope!

"Yeah, that's high-end pearl."

"So, that's what I'm gonna call her."

"What, high-end?" her father asked as he started to laugh.

"No, Dad. I'm gonna call her Pearl."

"Pearl? Don't you think that's an old lady's name?"

"Maybe, but I think it's cute, just like her."

Giving me a name would indicate there was some type of connection between us, but I already knew she would possibly get rid of me one day, so I didn't think much of it. It didn't take long for the excitement the young lady displayed to vanish, and she just put me back into the box. Then, one day, she told me she was putting me inside of her car. I didn't know where I was going, and I still didn't even know this person's name, but I figured I would learn more about it all in due time.

"Pearl, we've made it to your new home."

Being named for my handle wasn't creative, but I did appreciate the effort. And even though my new owner told her father I wasn't needed, she seemed to find a reason to pull me out of the box nearly every day. It had been a while since I had been given so much attention, but it quickly became boring. Prior to meeting this young lady, I thought I would be okay with a quiet life, but that was not the case.

Each day felt like we were just repeating the one before. I remained in the box until she decided to grant me momentary freedom. When she did, she just talked to me for a few minutes, cleaned me up, and then she would put me right back into the box. One day, there was an unexpected change to the routine.

"Hey, Pearl! How are you today?" she asked.

I wanted to answer her and tell her how pointless I thought my existence had become since I was given to her, but I couldn't. I wanted to ask her if we could at least go to a shooting range just to get out. I wanted to do a lot of things, but in reality, all I could do was just listen to what she had to say, and hope things would eventually change.

"I know you get tired of being in that box so much. I can only imagine what you were doing before you were given to me. At first, I thought I wouldn't need you. I mean, I like pretty things, and your handle is just so modern, yet retro, but being pretty isn't a reason I should have you. Maybe my dad was right, though. Maybe I had the world all mixed up. Who knows? You think you know everything when you reach your twenties, but the older you get, the more you discover."

As she spoke, her doorbell rang. Normally, when she had a guest, she hid me as if I embarrassed her, but our idea of normal was quickly evolving. This time, she held onto me as she went to the door.

"Hey, what's up, Dawn? Wh-what's that in your hand?"

This new person's moment of nervousness provided me with the young lady's name, something I still hadn't known until that moment.

"Don't be silly, Clarke, you know exactly what this is."

"Yeah, I know, but I'm wondering why you have it."

"She is not an *it*. Her name is Pearl, and she's here because... well, you just never know these days."

"That's true, I guess. Well, Dawn, it seems like you have some things on your mind, so I'm just gonna go home. I'll talk to you later."

"Boy, don't be crazy. Have a seat. I think we need to talk," Dawn said as she started laugh.

I don't know if Clarke wanted to sit down or not, but me being around made him feel like he didn't have much of a choice.

"What's up, babe?" he asked.

"What do you think is up, Clarke?"

"I don't know. You're sitting here with a gun in your hand. That's not you. A gun doesn't even fit with your personality."

"Are you saying I shouldn't have this because I'm normally a happy person?"

"That's exactly what I'm saying."

"I don't know if you've noticed or not, but I still have a smile on my face. I'm still Dawn. It's just...something has to change."

"Like what?"

"Like our relationship. I mean, what are we doing? Do you still want to be with me, or are you just staying around so I won't talk to anybody else?"

"Babe, what are you saying?"

"Do you really want me to spell it out, or are you gonna be a man and admit the wrong you've done?"

She waited for Clarke to respond, but he didn't speak. We all just sat in silence as he tried to come up with something to say. This was another thing about humans that didn't make sense. It was obvious Clarke did something wrong. It was even more obvious Dawn knew what it was. It would have made sense for him to just tell the truth and deal with the conse-quences, but that's not what he wanted to do. Instead, he pretended he didn't know what she was talking about. It was sad that I understood the concepts of truths and lies, yet he acted like he didn't.

"I haven't done anything, and I don't have to sit here while you create some type of story about me."

Dawn laughed again. This time, it was as if Clarke had just finished telling the funniest joke she had ever heard.

"Actually, you do have to sit here, but I won't have to make anything up about you. No, baby. I'm just gonna state the facts. See, I saw you the other day when you were with that girl."

"Nah, Dawn, you have it all wrong!"

"Please don't do that. And don't think getting all loud is gonna help you make a point because it won't. We will both behave like adults so we can have a conversation. Is that okay with you?"

"Yeah, it's cool, but..."

"Please, just let me say what I need to say. So, before I was interrupted, I was talking about seeing you with that girl. I wasn't following you or anything crazy like that because I never would have imagined I would have a reason to. I just happened to be visiting that new coffee shop down the street when I saw you two holding hands and kissing. Clarke, that hurt me like I've never been hurt before. I know we're young, and I'm smart enough to know there's no such thing as a fairy tale love story. I knew there was a chance we would break up, but I never thought you would disrespect me like that. And contrary to what you may be thinking, I'm not going to talk bad about her because she probably doesn't even know I exist. I'm not even gonna go off on you because evidently, you're too stupid to know what you have. I wish I could say I hate you, but I can't lie to myself. I love you too much to say anything different."

"What do you want from me? You already know what it is, you saw me. I'm human, and I messed up."

"Yeah, we all mess up, but why? What happened in our relationship that made you step outside of it? No, let me ask a different question. What's going on inside of you that made you want to cheat on me?"

Dawn remained calm. She tried to keep an upbeat tone even though she was presenting serious statements and questions to someone she thought she had a deep bond with. She tried to smile through her pain, but eventually, the tears she didn't want to release fell. Each tear that meandered down her face made me hope she would put me to use, but a conflict also started to set in.

I'm a machine that was designed to do one thing. We want to prove our worth by doing what we were made to do, but as I said before, we are sometimes impacted by the feelings of the people we're around. I wanted to do my job, and I wanted Clarke to get what I felt he deserved, but if I was ever used against him, I didn't know if I wanted Dawn to be the one who pulled the trigger.

"The truth is, I don't even have a reason why I started talking to her. I just saw her one day and I wanted to see if I still had it. Obviously, I do."

"That's your answer? That's what you have to say to me?"

"You can't get mad because I told you the truth; especially since you said that's what you wanted."

"You know what? You're absolutely right. You gave me exactly what I asked for, and I thank you for that. Now, I need for you to leave."

"Is that it? You don't wanna talk anymore?"

"Not really. You just gave me a lot to think about."

"Are you for real? You mean you had me come over here for that?"

"Do you see my friend, Pearl, in my hand? I had her out because I had certain ideas of how I would deal with you. Honestly, the more you spoke, the more I wanted to formally introduce you to her. Then, I started to think about life. I thought about how things would turn out if we stayed together. Then, I imagined how things would be if I just ended your life today. You know what? If either of those things happened, your ignorance would have a negative impact on the rest of my life. I can't have that. That's why I need for you to leave."

"That's stupid! All of this was pointless! See, this is that kind of stuff that makes me glad I'm messing with that girl."

Clarke's arrogance made Dawn lose her composure. She didn't use me to shoot him, but as I came in contact with his face, he was quickly given a lesson on how strong Dawn was with me around.

"Now, will you leave like I asked you to?" she asked.

I'm sure he didn't want to end the conversation, but he probably didn't want to see what would happen if he didn't listen. He jumped up, said a few explicit words, and slammed the door as he exited Dawn's apartment. For a moment, she tried hard to act as though she was okay, but feeling her increased pulse as she put me down on the table let me know she wasn't.

"Why would he do that to me? Why?"

We were the only two in the room, and although she asked questions aloud, I knew she wasn't speaking to me. She just needed a little while to vent about the frustration her boyfriend had caused.

"I'm way too good of a person to have to deal with this kind of foolishness! Plus, this dude's got me going outside of my character. I'm giving him the power to take away my joy, and there's no way in the world he should have that much power!"

She stopped talking to herself and started talking directly to me.

"Can you believe him? We almost had to take him out today, Pearl, but I have way too much to lose. I can't go off on him and end up in prison. I'm only twenty-one. I would literally be throwing my life away. I can't do that, right?"

She knew the answers to everything she asked me, but it was

as though she was seeking validation. Since I couldn't respond, she just held me tightly as she paced around her apartment.

After a few paces, she stopped and took a look at me.

"Did that happen because of Clarke? I'm sorry, Pearl. I didn't mean to mess you up like that. You're way too pretty for that."

I had no idea what she was talking about, but I felt fine.

"I didn't even hit him that hard. I can't believe he bled that much from that little hit."

I wasn't concerned about having a little blood on me, but neither of us knew what type of consequences would come because of Dawn's momentary loss of good judgment. I understood things could have been much worse than they were, but I also understood how sensitive humans could be when their egos have been hurt.

Even though Clarke didn't say anything about it, my previous human interactions let me know getting beat up probably didn't sit well with him. Based on how he acted when he was confronted by Dawn, I was all but certain Clarke would try to retaliate in some way. Dawn, however, didn't seem concerned at all. Almost immediately after she asked me if I was okay, she seemed to quickly transition back into the person who just seemed happy about her life.

I had been around a few different humans, and none of them could move from one emotion to another as quickly as Dawn. A day after she ended things with Clarke, it was almost as though they had never been anything more than just friends. This made Clarke extremely upset, and he let it be known each time he called. Dawn found it quite entertaining to hear his pain.

"Hey, Clarke. How are you doing?" she asked gleefully.

"So, you're just gonna act like nothing happened? What's wrong with you?"

"Nothing's wrong with me. I've just been able to accept the reality of what's going on in my life. It all comes down to me being with someone who didn't love me. No, scratch that. I was with someone who didn't even respect me enough to be faithful, and that same person couldn't put on his big boy pants and tell me how he felt. It's cool, though. I was hurt for a minute, but I'm good now."

"So, you're just gonna throw away everything we had and all the years we spent together?"

"I might as well because that's exactly what you did," Dawn said as she started to chuckle.

They were speaking as cordially as you would expect up until that point, but hearing Dawn laugh pushed Clarke to the edge.

"You just gonna laugh at me while I'm trying to be real with you?"

"I'm not laughing at you, per se, I'm laughing at the situation. I'm laughing at myself because you turned me into one of those females on reality TV and social media who everyone else clowns. You made me be one of the ones people make fun of because they were too blind to see what was happening right in front of them. It's hilarious, but it won't happen again."

"You must have a new man or something. Is that what it is? You must have one of those sensitive, lame dudes to cater to everything you want."

"Boy, bye! We just broke up. In order for me to have somebody else that fast, I had to be creepin' like you were, but I wasn't. Only one of us was messin' around, would you like to guess who it was?"

"Are you trying to make me mad?" he asked.

"Honestly, I'm not trying to, but if that's what's happening, it is what it is."

When she said that, Clarke yelled and screamed out of frustration, but he didn't say any additional words before he hung up the phone. I don't know why, but I was glad Dawn had decided to put the phone on speaker so I could hear every word they were both saying.

Similar situations have caused other people I had been around to become embarrassed. When people get embarrassed, they try their best to forget about the situation as quickly as they can, or they'll go out of their way to try and make someone else feel just as embarrassed as they were. I was sure Clarke would do the latter. When you combine a person's sensitivity with heartbreak, ego, and embarrassment, you tend to get a very volatile human.

People can be confusing. Clarke caused the issue that led to the breakup with Dawn, and then he kept calling her once they were no longer together. Eventually, the rate at which he called slowed down a lot, though. It seemed like Clarke was finally able to move on, but then, he made a phone call one day that made me question that.

"I miss you, Dawn," he said.

"I miss you, too, Clarke," she replied.

"Well, if we both miss each other, why don't we just do what we need to do to get back together?"

The sometimes fraudulent smiles and laughter that had been present during some of their post-breakup conversations were nowhere to be found. As they spoke to each other, they could both tell how emotionally connected they still were.

"We can't get back together, Clarke. I can forgive you, but I can't put myself in the position to be hurt by you again. Plus, I don't think I will ever fully trust you. We can't work on building a relationship if I know it won't have trust. That just doesn't make any sense.

"You're makin' a mistake, babe. I'm sorry for messing up, but it won't happen again. Come on, Dawn. We need to be together."

She paused. I assumed it was because she was considering what he was saying, which was not the smartest thing for her to do. People do stupid things all of the time, but you aren't just supposed to hand someone the opportunity to hurt you on a silver platter.

"We can't be together, Clarke. I've told you this before. Why...why did you...just why, Clarke? Why? You messed everything up. We were supposed to get married one day. We had plans. You were gonna be an architect and I was gonna be the Dean of Education at our school. Do you remember that? You told me I was the only one for you, and you could see us having a family. Do you remember that? A few kids and a dog, Clarke, that's what we planned! That's what you promised, and that's what I was preparing for. None of that was more important to you than seeing if you could pull another female while you already had someone who loved you. They always say actions speak louder than words. It's like you continue to whisper that you care about me, but your actions yell that you don't! You keep saying if we got together, you would never mess up like that again, but did you even end things with that other girl?"

He didn't respond immediately, so Dawn repeated her question.

"Did you get rid of that other girl? Did you end the relationship, or whatever you want to call that thing you have with her?"

"Well....nah, I didn't. I was out here trying to apologize to you, and you weren't trying to hear what I had to say. I can't just be out here alone. A man has needs, Dawn. Don't you get that?"

"Yeah, you're right, a man does have needs, but I guess little boys do, too. That's what you are, Clarke. You're an immature, little boy! You ain't no man! And you know what? I have needs, too. I need to just finally be done with you for good. That's what I'm gonna do. I hope she was worth it."

Just like she said she was going to do, she ended the conversation right then. She didn't give Clarke a chance to respond because there was nothing more he could say. The conversation caused Dawn to show the emotions I was expecting her to have before. She said she couldn't stop crying because the pain she felt wouldn't leave her alone.

With the other people I dealt with, there were times when they wanted to use me as a tool to ease their pain. This is when they wondered if putting me to work would be worth it. Sometimes the people knew they were overreacting. Sometimes their usage of me could be somewhat justified, but no matter what, I did whatever job I was called to do.

With Dawn, some days, she asked herself questions that made me think she would use me against her. Other days, I was almost certain Clarke would be the recipient of some of my bullets. But then, as humans do, she just changed again one day.

"Good morning, world. I'm blessed to see such a beautiful day. Today will be the start of the new and improved Dawn. Today, I am reclaiming my life. Today, I'm letting go of the sadness someone else has caused, and I'm claiming the joy that is meant for me. Today is a new day, and I'm going to bask in the glory of it. Amen, amen, amen!"

And just like that, the energy that was around when I was first introduced to Dawn had made a triumphant return. When she got up that morning, she was happy, and it seemed like the weight of the stress she had been carrying around with her was nowhere to be found. It was an amazing turnaround, and it made me think she would no longer want me. I thought she would find a way to get rid of me, and when she picked up the phone to call her father, I was sure that was about to happen.

"Hey, Daddy! How are you?"

"I'm good. How are you?"

"I'm better than I've been in a while. Oh...I'm sorry, did I wake you up?"

"No, I've been up for a while. I had some things I wanted to take care of before your mother woke up. What's up, though? You usually only call me this early when something is bothering you."

"Well, something *was* bothering me, but I'm good now. I just wanted to let you know, after this conversation, you probably won't hear me talking about Clarke anymore."

"Oh, so I take it he did something."

"Yeah, he did something stupid, but I cleared the air with him and I said all I needed to say to him. I also got rid of all the tears that were dedicated to him, so I'm done with that, too."

"Are you sure? I know you're an adult, and you can handle things on your own, but if you need me to do anything for you, just let me know. Do you hear me?"

"Yes, sir, I hear you, but it's not necessary. Pearl and I already taught him a lesson, so we're good."

"Pearl. Who's that?"

"Daddy, remember, that's what I call the gun you gave me."

I knew as soon as she reminded her father of who I was, he would start to panic.

"So, are you saying you..."

"Don't worry, Dad. I didn't shoot him. I wanted to, but I didn't. I just hit him one good time with it. It was nothing more than that."

"Why did it even get to that point? Did he put his hands on you?"

"No, he's dumb, but he ain't that dumb. I found out he cheated on me, so I had to end the relationship. I thought I was okay, but I had to shed a few tears. I wasn't even gonna let you or Mom know, but I felt I had to."

"I'm glad you did, though. Dawn, you know I don't like anyone hurting my family."

"I know, but you don't have to worry, Dad. I'm so much better now. I woke up this morning smiling and filled with joy. I have so much freedom and it feels like I've been able to hit the reset button on my life. Trust me, I'm good. Well, anyway, I really just wanted to say I love you, and I commend you and

Mom for keeping it together all of these years. Maybe one day I'll be able to find that forever love like the two of you have."

"Dawn, I need you to listen to what I'm about to say. Are you listening?"

"Yeah, Dad."

"You can't get upset if something you want to keep forever takes a long time to find. Be patient; keep the faith, never lower your standards, and know the things you desire are obtainable. Plus, you're only twenty-one. You don't even really know who you are yet. Learn more about who Dawn is and then love—true love— will fall in place exactly when it's supposed to. Do you understand that?"

"Absolutely! Thanks, Dad!"

The conversation didn't go the way I thought it would. I thought there would be much more anger in the words that were being spoken, but the fact that there wasn't, made me believe the real Dawn had made her return. With her feeling happy, I once again started to think my time with her would be short-lived.

Over the next few days, Dawn ascended to higher levels of happiness. She found the silver lining in the darkest of clouds. Even though she was happy, I wanted more for myself. She was no longer keeping me locked up at her home, but I wasn't seeing any action. I wanted more, but at the same time, I knew wanting more for myself meant Dawn would probably be doing something she shouldn't.

For humans, this would be when their conscience would kick in. How would they feel if their joy increased someone else's misery? This type of question always caused humans to second-guess what they wanted for themselves. As a machine, I'm glad those types of thoughts were not something I had to deal with. I did, however, have to deal with the fact that I had no control over when I was able to be active. We were made for a purpose, and no matter what, we generally just wanted a chance to fulfill that purpose.

I sat waiting for Dawn to realize I was still relevant. As I said, humans can be volatile and vulnerable, so I knew even if I went a while without interacting with Dawn, there would still be a good chance she would come back to me at some point. On most days, it seemed like my selfish desires would go unheeded because Dawn had a firm hold on her happiness and it didn't seem like anything was going to force her to let it ago.

No matter what is going on, I've learned humans can be predictably unpredictable. Instead of them maintaining their exuberance, they would suddenly do something to take it away. This was exactly what Dawn did. See, humans have these things they deal with called the internet and social media. They dealt with these things in many different forms and they could access them in many different ways. Dawn's device of choice was her laptop.

In reality, all people had problems they had to deal with. Sometimes there were issues when my siblings and I were called in to assist. Other times, it was just things the person needed to overcome in order to continue on their journey. Their obstacles could be life-changing, or just something minuscule they must deal with, but they were problems, nonetheless. Dealing with life as it came was why social media was so difficult to comprehend.

Whether I was locked away or Dawn had me out, whenever she was on social media on her computer, I would always hear her talk about how good everyone's life was. According to what she would say when she talked about their posts; nobody went to work, nobody got mad, nobody was ever hurt, or even had a bad day. Instead, everyone just seemed to be going on shopping sprees and vacations while spending time with the loves of their lives. It wasn't realistic, yet so many people judged their own lives based on how other people claimed to be living.

"I know he's not posting this," Dawn said one day.

There was pain in her voice. Whoever made the post had to be of some importance to her or she wouldn't have reacted that way. For a while, I had no idea who the "he" was that Dawn referred to, but as she mumbled on about what she saw, it became clear.

"So, he cheated on me with her, said it was just a mistake, and now he's posting pictures with her and saying he's in a relationship. Is that what you're doing, Clarke?"

I couldn't believe she was talking about Clarke again. She had told anyone who would listen, including me, that she was done with him. She claimed she knew she was better off without him. So, if that was the case, why did she care what he was doing? The illogical nature of people always found a way to come out of hiding at the most random times.

I heard Dawn's footsteps as she frantically walked around her home for some time, and then, she just stopped. She didn't cry, didn't yell, or didn't curse. She didn't even take another step; she just stopped. She stood silently as if she was waiting for someone to tell her what to do.

"Well, Pearl, I think it may be time," she finally said.

I was always ready to get out and actually do something, but I knew Dawn was allowing her emotions to move her, which may not have been the smartest thing for her to do.

She grabbed me, and we rushed to the car.

"Pearl, if this idiot weren't live streaming, I wouldn't know where we would be going," she said as put me in the glove compartment and we sped away.

I could tell how quickly she drove by the way I was being tossed around in the car. Dawn was disregarding the rules of the road, as well as her own safety. Soon, the tires screeched as we came to an abrupt stop.

"Well, I don't know what's about to happen, but I don't think we came out here for nothing," she told me.

I was taken out of the glove compartment and put into the small purse Dawn brought with her.

"There's the happy couple," she sarcastically yelled out almost as soon as the car stopped.

I expected her to move quickly once we left the car, but she didn't. Her steps were stuttered, and it was almost as if she was already questioning her actions.

"What are we doing?" she asked as she opened the purse to look at me.

I didn't like how she included me, as if we had a conversation about what she wanted to do. Even before anything happened, she was already finding a way to pass along some of the responsibility of the actions she was going to take.

"I think we moved too quickly, Pearl. This isn't what I should be doing. Let's just go home. I shouldn't have brought you here in the first place. If I'm being real with myself, I know he's not even worth the energy I'm still giving him."

It was baffling how her emotions flip-flopped in such a short amount of time, but that was the nature of humans. I had not only dealt with Dawns' mood swings, but to a lesser extent, her father's, as well.

"Let's just go talk to him," Dawn said as her emotions continued to flop.

She zipped her purse back up. I heard people yelling at her out of their car windows and angrily blowing their horns as Dawn disregarded all safety precautions and crossed the road in a place where she wasn't supposed to. The noise got Clarke's attention before Dawn was ready for him. I could suddenly hear him yelling out to her.

"Dawn, is that you?"

We went out there for her to get his attention, but once she had it, it was almost like she was afraid. I felt her turn and go in the opposite direction as she tried to ignore Clarke talking to her.

"Dawn. Dawn," he yelled out.

Walking in the opposite direction was probably a smart decision, but turning back to talk to Clarke may not have been the best thing to do.

"What do you want?" she asked loudly.

"Just calm down and come talk to me," Clarke said.

"Why would I talk to you with *her* over there."

"I've already told her about you, how our relationship ended, and how much I hurt you. I finally grew up a little and stopped hiding things. Just like you, she hated me, especially when she found out I put her in the middle of everything, but we've moved past it. I just want to talk to both of you. Please."

Dawn hesitated for a while, but for whatever reason, she decided to follow him. The purse had unzipped a little, so I could see when she got to their table. When she did, Clarke quickly introduced the two women to each other.

"I know seeing each other face-to-face probably stirs up more anger, but I want to tell both of you how sorry I am. Dawn, I know it's only been a short amount of time since I stepped out on you, but I'm a different person. And Nevaeh, I'm sorry I lied to you when we first met. I told you I was single when I was really with Dawn. I've said it to both of you before, but I was really stupid, and I'm different now."

He stopped talking, giving the two ladies an opportunity to respond.

"Dawn, I don't know you, but I want to apologize to you, too. When I first met Clarke, I asked him several times if he was single, and he told me he was. I would never try to do anything to intentionally mess up someone's relationship."

It was like I could feel Dawn's pulse increase, even though I was in the purse. She took a deep breath, and then she sighed.

"If I'm gonna be real, I wanted to hate both of you, especially Clarke. I've seen the pictures he's been posting. Him saying how happy he is in the captions has been tearing me apart. I was hurt. No, I am hurt, but I will get back to being me at some point."

"Girl, I've been messed over by some no good dudes, too. I just hope and pray it doesn't happen to either one of us again. I know if I were in your shoes, ain't no way in the world I could have been as cordial as you're being. I appreciate you being a woman and hearing everyone out and not just going off on us. Stuff could have gotten real bad, real fast," Nevaeh said.

Dawn's pulse started to slow down a bit, and I heard her zip her purse back up. I guess she wanted to make sure it was closed so she wouldn't see me and be tempted to do what she actually went out there to do.

"Dawn, you're a good person, and you have a lot going for you. I know there's some dude out there just waiting to shoot his shot. Now that I'm outta the way, whoever he is, can actually do that. When he tries to slide in your DM or somethin', give 'em a chance. He may be what you need," Clarke said.

Right at that moment, Dawn's phone started ringing.

"Dang, the universe don't take no time, does it?" Clarke asked.

Dawn laughed as she excused herself and moved a few steps over. She didn't put her call on speaker, so I don't know who she was talking to. All I know is, whoever it was, they made her incredibly giddy. She was laughing and joking in ways I hadn't heard in a while.

When the call ended, she walked back over to her ex-boyfriend and his new companion.

"That must've been a good call. You got a big ol' smile on your face," Clarke joked.

"Yeah, it actually was a pretty good call. It was a guy who… wait, why was I about to explain myself to you? I guess that relationship muscle memory was kicking in," she said as she laughed.

"I don't know you, for real, but I'm happy for you. Whoever

that dude is, I hope he ends up being the right one for you. If not, I hope you at least have some fun," Nevaeh said.

"Girl, you and me both," Dawn replied.

"Hey, can I give you a hug?" Nevaeh asked.

I didn't know how Dawn would respond to the request. Knowing how volatile humans could be, it wouldn't have been unusual for her to get mad again, but it also wouldn't have been unusual for her to hug Nevaeh like they were best friends. I didn't know exactly what she was thinking, I just knew with the hesitancy for a response, she had some type of thoughts running through her head. After a few seconds, I felt us moving closer to Nevaeh's voice.

By the movement of the purse I was still stashed in, I had to assume she granted Nevaeh's request.

"Again, I apologize for any pain you suffered because of me. As women, we sometimes have issues with each other, but I promise you I wasn't tryin' to hurt you. Like I said, I didn't even know you existed at first, but I should have known better. Clarke always seemed distracted when he was with me, and when he wasn't around, it was always hard to reach him. Girl, my feelings had me so blind, I missed all of the red flags. I'm sorry, I really am," Nevaeh whispered.

"Clarke has a way of charming people to look beyond those red flags. Trust me, I get it. Just be careful with him. Don't let him hurt you like he hurt me," Dawn said.

"I'll try my best. Thank you, Dawn."

Dawn pulled away from Nevaeh at that point. Then, she addressed her and Clarke one last time.

"Let me just say this before I leave y'all alone. Having Clarke cheat on me made me experience a pain like I had never felt before. Even though I ended up being the one to officially end our relationship, every time I saw him post something about you, it hurt me even more. I ain't gonna lie, seeing y'all here is not by coincidence. I actually came out here with some very bad intentions, but I guess talking to y'all opened my heart up in ways I didn't expect. I didn't want either of you to be happy. I wanted Clarke to feel the pain I had, and seeing he had moved on with you made me feel even worse, but somehow, I'm over that now. I may regret saying this later, but I actually wish you two the best because everyone deserves to be happy, and it seems like both of you are. Clarke, be a man. Nevaeh seems to really care about you, so don't mess it up. Nevaeh, don't settle for anything less than you deserve. Don't let him or anybody else treat you badly."

"I got you," Nevaeh replied.

With that, Dawn walked away. Seeing Clarke with his new companion must have hurt her even more than she let on because she kept crying. When she made it to her car, she just sat there without doing anything at all. We sat there for a little while when her phone rang again. This time, she put it on speaker.

"Dawn, I know I just called you, but I wanna see you. Can we go see a movie, grab a meal, or do something? I wanna hang out with you."

"You don't know how much it means to know you want to be around me. I'll be happy to go out with you."

"No cap, anyone who gets to be around you is lucky, not the other way around. Just let me know when you're ready, and I'll come pick you up."

Dawn giggled as she hung up the phone, letting me know she was feeling better. Once she finally started to drive, she decided to have another talk with me.

"Pearl, I know we had plans on what we were gonna do when we saw Clarke, but sometimes things change. In my mind, I wanted him to physically feel the pain he caused to me feel emotionally, but my heart wouldn't let me. It almost feels like God just stopped me from doing something that would destroy my life. Whatever it was, I'm actually glad we didn't do anything. I think I'd rather just have you in case trouble finds me, instead of using you to start trouble."

I was sure her little monologue made her feel good about herself. I was also sure her decision to go against what she had planned made her feel like she had done something right. I was sure of these things because of the comments she made as we moved further away from where she met with Clarke. Regardless of how she felt, the only thing her speech and decision did for me was to prove how often humans are unable to follow through with the plans they created. They were so easily swayed by a sudden change of thought that it was absolutely ridiculous.

When she got home, she was a different than who she was when she left. Gone was the anger, gone was the sadness, and gone was the desire to seek revenge.

"Pearl, we almost did something stupid today. I'm sorry," she said as she took me out of her purse and placed me on the television stand in her room.

Her pointless apology meant nothing to me, but it was another step she took to feel better about herself. As she got ready for her date, she continuously told me how things would be different.

"Pearl, I've been all over the place, but things will be different. I know I broke up with Clarke, but after what happened today, I finally feel like we have closure. When I think about it, I think that's all I really wanted. I know while we were in the car, I told you I wanted him to feel my pain, but now, I don't even think that's true. I think people just want parts of their lives to go like a story. I think, even if the story doesn't go the way they hoped it would, they still want a happy ending. Today, hearing from my new friend, and even talking to Clarke and Nevaeh, actually gave me that. Does that make sense?"

She asked me a question as if I could answer her. Even if I could, I don't think she would have liked what I had to say. Eventually, she stopped talking to me and finished getting ready to go on her date. When she grabbed her keys, I thought she was going to put me back in her purse, just in case she needed me, but she didn't.

"I don't think you'll be making this trip, Pearl. Today is the Dawn of a new day," she said with a smile as she put me inside of a drawer.

Her smile let me know she believed what she said. Dawn was suddenly happier than she been in a while and with that, she felt I wasn't as necessary as I had been. It may have been the dawn of a new day for her, but at some point, the sun would set on that new day, just like it had on the ones before it.

I am not necessarily wishing for her to be unhappy, but if her happiness faded, I would be okay with that, too. I know humans say, "Diamonds are a girl's best friend," but eventually, this particular human will remember that Pearl is hers. For now, I'll just sit and wait until she does. At some point, I know I'll get a chance to shine, and when I do, I hope I'll be able to go to work before she changes her mind.

NARRATIVE 3: LION AND THE MONSTER

I'm the type of gun that hadn't dealt with people who understood the concept of loyalty. I say this mainly because I have been moved around to many different people over the years. Unlike some other guns, I don't recall my manufacturing date, but I do remember the first day I felt alive.

Like I said, I dealt with many other humans before, but it was about three years ago when I was introduced to the first human I ever really got to know. The kid's name was Lionel, but when I met him, most people just called him Lion. He was fifteen years old, and I didn't think he had a reason to own a gun, but evidently, someone thought otherwise. I was handed to Lion by a slightly older kid, who turned out to be his brother.

"Lion, I hate we need this, but you know how it is out there. Mom can't protect us, and as your older brother, I try my best to look out for you, but I can't be around twenty-four hours a day."

"I don't want a gun, Marvin. I don't want anything to do with this street stuff. I just wanna go to school so I can get us all away from here."

"I know you don't want this, but there's a bunch of people around here who are jealous of you."

"Jealous of me? For what? I don't have anything anybody should be jealous of."

"That's where you're wrong, little brother. You're not like the rest of us. We do what we do because we don't have other options, but you and Noelle are different. You two have the type of intellect that will get you much further than we will ever get, but instead of people wanting to work with you, they'll hate on you. People will call you names, and they'll work to bring you down. You can't let them stop you, though. I hope you'll never have to use this thing, but you can't predict what's gonna happen out there. So, take this and carry it with you every day, and don't use it unless you have to. Do you hear me?"

"Yeah, I hear you, Marvin."

"Ok, cool. Now, I have some things to take care of, but I'll see you later on tonight. Please look out for Ma and Noelle. When I'm not at home, you're responsible for making sure they're okay. Oh, and make sure you do your homework. I don't want you to start making anything less than what we're all used to you get getting. Is that understood?"

"I got you!"

After he finished speaking with his brother, Lion took me with him as he went into his room and locked the door.

"What am I supposed to do with you?" he asked.

I wanted to tell the person I was around to just put me to work, but even if I could have, I don't think I would have. It was ironic they called the kid Lion because he seemed very cowardly when he started to look me over. He tried to pretend he wasn't afraid of me, but he kept shaking, so I knew his true feelings.

"You are kinda cool, though," he said after a few minutes.

He held me up to the mirror so we could both see our reflections. In only a few minutes, I could already sense a change in

68

the young man. As he continued to stare at himself, a devious smirk took over his face.

"What was I thinking? Marvin knows what he's talking about. I probably should have had you a long time ago. Yeah, I think we're gonna have a cool friendship."

"Who are you talking to in there?" a voice asked in the distance.

"I'm just in here looking at myself in the mirror, Ma! You know you have a very handsome son, right?"

"No, I have two very handsome sons and a beautiful daughter. Not only that, I'm not too bad, either!"

"You're right, Ma! You're the prettiest mom ever, and I guess Marvin and Noelle are okay, too!"

Although they were in different rooms, they shared a laugh. I'm sure his mother would have never imagined I was in the room. It probably would have hurt her if she knew, and it probably would have made her feel worse to know I was given to Lion from Marvin.

"Lion! Lion! Can you open your door, please?" a young girl asked as she knocked on the boy's door several times.

He rushed to hide me in a drawer before he opened the door.

"What do you want, Noelle?" he asked.

"I have an emergency. I really need your help!"

"What kind of emergency?"

"Mom is in the living room...and...."

"And what? What's going on?"

"Well, she's in the living room watching TV. That means I can't watch my show!"

"Really, Noelle. Is that your emergency?"

"Yeah! Your room is the only other room that has a TV. I have to be able to see my show about the exes who are dating new people that their parents picked while they try to make it through a crazy obstacle course."

"Wait, is that a show?"

"For sure! And right now, you're stopping me from watching it!"

"After thinking about it, that does seem like an emergency."

"I'll be right back," Lion said very suddenly as they both laughed.

Either Lion temporarily forgot I was in the room, or he trusted his sister would not go snooping around in his room while he was away. Whatever the case was, I remained in the drawer, just waiting to see what would happen next.

I listened to the sounds of Noelle's television show and heard Lion suddenly rush back into the room.

"What's wrong with you, Lion?" Noelle asked.

"Um...nothing. I-I just couldn't leave you in here watching this crazy show too long without me."

"Oh, okay. Well, sit down, then. You're gonna make me miss what's happening."

I could tell he really didn't care about what she was watching. He just used that as an excuse to explain why he was in such a hurry to get back into his room. It was almost unbelievable Noelle accepted what he said, but I guess she had no reason to believe her brother wasn't telling her the truth. I didn't know how much trust the family members had for one another, but it didn't take long for me to learn.

That first night, and many of the ones that followed, were very uneventful. For the most part, Lion kept me in the drawer. Every once in a while he briefly removed me from my home when Marvin asked him about me.

"So, how is it?" Marvin asked.

Although I didn't consider myself to be an *it*, I knew he referred to me.

"It's good. It's still right here," he responded.

"Oh, okay. Let me ask you something, little brother."

"What's up?"

"If somebody's trying to get at you while you're at school, or if a group of homies try to jump you on your way home, what good will it do you if it's here?"

"It-um... it won't do me any good."

"Exactly! That's why I said you need to keep it with you every day. Just put it in your backpack because nobody will ever think you have a gun in there. Plus, I know the metal detectors at the school ain't working. They never have, and they probably never will."

"You're right, but can I be honest with you?"

"Of course. What's up?"

"This type of stuff scares me. I don't think I'm really up for it."

"Bro, I *know* you're not built for this, and I wish you didn't have to have a gun, but this neighborhood ain't safe. I worry about y'all every single day. Like I said, you have the gifts to get Ma and Noelle out of here, but until that happens, you have to make sure you survive. Eventually, people will start to notice you, even when you don't think you're doing anything special. They will see you have that special something people are always talking about, and when that becomes a reality, I told you what will happen."

"Yeah, you did. You said they'll help me or they'll hate me!"

"That's true, Lion. If they want to help you, they'll do everything they possibly can to make sure you succeed because when you succeed, it'll be like a victory for them. You doing good will give people the hope that other folks from this neighborhood can leave a positive impact on the world. The flip side of the help is the hate."

"I know a little about that. That's when people are always ready to spew out harmful words, no matter what."

"Yeah, but it's a lot more than that. See, when a person has saved a place for hatred in their hearts, it's hard to reason with 'em. And when you reach your goals, that hatred will breed jealousy. That jealousy, Lion, is why you need what I gave you. Envious people have no limitations to their hatred. Those who envy you will try to bring harm right to our doorstep. I don't want to scare you, little brother, but you have to be aware of what type of people are out there. A lot of people are gonna want you to fail, and most of us, at some point or another, will wish we were able to accomplish the things you have. Those who can't be happy for you will try very hard to take that happiness from you. You have to be ready at all times."

"Is it really that serious, Marvin?"

"I wish it wasn't, but it really is. Trust me, bro, these streets don't care about any of us. The same people who pretend to be your friends will be the first ones who'll want to see your downfall. All I'm saying is, do what you're supposed to do. Like you said, you're not a street dude, so don't try to be. Just keep your eyes and ears open, and always be prepared for anything."

"Okay."

"I love you, Lion. Do you hear me?"

"Yeah, man. I hear you," Lion said as his brother left him alone in the room.

Nobody knew what Marvin did when he left the house, but they all had their ideas. Their mom didn't want to believe her oldest son was doing anything crazy, but she also wasn't naive to what went on around them. She just hoped and prayed the things she tried to teach her kids stuck with them, even when she wasn't directly in their presence.

I started traveling to school with Lion the next day. He made it known to his brother over and over again that he wasn't comfortable with me going, but Marvin always found a way to convince him to keep letting me go. I could feel the nerves kick in each day he walked through the doors of the school, but he kept trying to convince himself Marvin knew what was best.

"I know it's crazy in the schools and stuff, but I don't need a gun, do I?" he asked himself.

"Do you need a what?" someone asked.

Somehow, they must have heard him talking about me.

"What are you talking about?" Lion asked as if he honestly didn't understand the question.

"I just thought I heard you ask yourself if you need a gun, but I gotta be tripping."

"Me, with a gun? You know I'm scared of guns. I was asking myself if I needed fun. We have a test coming up, but I want to play my games when I get home. I guess I'm just kinda weighing my options."

"Oh, okay. Lion, you're a weird dude," the kid said.

"Yeah, I won't disagree with you," Lion replied.

I thought the lie Lion told the kid was terrible and completely unbelievable, but the kid accepted what he was told and quickly moved to the next thing. Although I was still zipped up in Lion's backpack, I could feel how difficult the simple act of breathing was becoming for him.

"I can't....I just...can't," he said.

I didn't know what was going on or what he was talking about. What I did know was soon after he mumbled those words, I felt the backpack I was in fall to the ground as Lion gasped even harder for air.

"Are you okay?" another kid asked.

"I'm...I..." he wasn't able to speak.

"Hey! Somebody come over here! He can't breathe!"

I don't know exactly how long it took, but eventually, I heard the voices of people I assumed were adults trying to talk to Lion.

"Can you tell me what's wrong?" they asked.

"Class....I...gotta go to class."

Although I could tell breathing still wasn't an easy task for him, he not only tried to make himself speak, but he was also trying to pick his backpack up. I knew he was not his main concern at that time. Instead, he wanted to make sure nobody would grab his backpack and possibly discover me.

"I think you need to see the nurse, at least for a moment, to make sure you're okay. I know you're concerned about going to class, so if you tell me your name and your teacher's name, I'll make sure to let them know where you are. Is that okay?"

"Yes, that's...that's okay," Lion said quietly.

"Good! Now, who is your teacher?"

"Mr. Sherman, and my name is Lion."

"Lion? Is that your real name?"

"Well, no, but that's what everyone calls me."

"That's a very strong nickname, which probably means you are a very strong young man. Lion, I don't know what caused you to have problems breathing. It could have been asthma or something else, but whatever it was, it won't keep you down for long. Let me help you with this bag, and we can get you to the nurse."

"It's okay. I got it. Thank you, though."

He found the energy to get up and tightly clutch his backpack.

"I see you don't want my help, but it's okay. I'll go tell Mr. Sherman where you are. Then, I'll call your mother to let her know you're okay."

"No, please don't call my mother."

"Why not, son? Don't you think she should know what happened to you?"

"Probably, but I'll tell her when I get home. My mom works a lot. If you call, you'll either be disturbing her while she's sleeping or while she's at work. Either way, you won't get a positive response. Trust me."

The man laughed. I couldn't see him, but I could hear him walk away, so I assumed he was okay with what Lion said. Soon, Lion made his way toward what had to be the nurse's office.

His movements were a little slower than normal. Maybe he

wasn't feeling good, or perhaps he was just selling a fake sickness to the best of his abilities. Whatever the case, it continued until he was greeted by the nurse.

"Hello, young man. What's bothering you today?"

"Nothing. I was just kinda forced to come in here when I had a little trouble breathing."

"Trouble breathing? That sounds like something to be concerned about. Has this ever happened before?"

"Umm...I don't think it has, but like I said, it's nothing."

"Did anything else happen, or was it just a brief shortness of breath?"

"It was just the breathing. Wait, no, it wasn't. I also felt dizzy, and my chest was hurting a little."

The nurse threw out a lot of questions, and by the responses Lion provided, I no longer believed he was exaggerating.

"Young man, it sounds like you may have had an anxiety attack."

"Ma'am, I don't even know what that is, but I'm okay now. Can I just go to class?"

"You'll go back soon. Has anything been stressing you out?"

My arrival was the only thing that had changed in his life. I knew I made Lion nervous, but I didn't know I was literally making him sick. Right then, I knew his brother had made a mistake, even if he was just trying to protect him.

"No, I don't think anything has been stressing me out any more than normal."

"Are you sure?"

I couldn't see her, but I could tell by her tone she didn't fully believe him.

"Yes, ma'am."

"Okay, here's the deal. I'm gonna take your blood pressure and write down some info. After that, you can head back to class. Is that okay?"

"Yes, ma'am."

"Good. Oh, and I'll be checking on you for the next few weeks. I've already made note of who you are."

After that, Lion was released. He proceeded to hold onto the backpack very tightly as he walked into a room where I immediately heard a lot of voices nearby. I assumed he reached his classroom.

"Thank you for joining us. Are you okay?"

"Yes, I'm good."

After the brief exchange of words, things went back to normal, at least for a little while. As the school bell rang to signal the end of the class, one of Lion's classmates approached him.

"Well, hello, Lionel. We're glad you were finally able to make it to class with the regular kids. Are you gonna be able to make it through the rest of the day?"

Many of the words directed toward Lion were those of concern, but the use of the word *regular* seemed out of place. Had Lion ever said or done anything that made the other people in his class feel like they were beneath him? Did any of his teachers ever treat him any differently than they treated the other kids? If so, it had to have happened before we met because I hadn't witnessed any of it.

"I'm good," Lion finally responded.

His short response indicated a level of discomfort he quickly wanted to move past.

"Oh, okay. We didn't know if you were going to bless us with your presence, and we all got worried."

The kid seemed to want Lion to remain uncomfortable, but Lion didn't agree with his plan.

"Yep! It's all good," Lion said as he started to move.

"Lion, it's very rude to walk away from someone when they're talking. Didn't your mama teach you stuff like that?"

"I'm sorry, but I just want to go to my next class."

The kid just wanted to start trouble, and Lion was trying his best not to fall into the trap. As we continued to move further away from his classmate, I kept hearing his footsteps behind us. For whatever reason, the kid wouldn't leave Lion alone.

"Didn't I just tell you not to walk away from me?"

"Please, just leave me alone."

Lion was begging the other boy to leave him alone, but the kid didn't want to let up. Suddenly, Lion started to run, and then a door opened as his teacher spoke.

"What are you two still doing in here?"

"Nothing. We were just talking," the other kid said.

"Really? Lion, you look frightened. Is he telling the truth?"

"Yes, ma'am," he said very quickly and quietly.

"Okay. You boys go ahead. I'm not writing a pass for you if you're late for your next class."

"Lion, we'll catch up later."

The kid spoke as if he and Lion were friends, but even I could tell that wasn't the case. I didn't know how much Lion normally dealt with him, but through his tone and movements, I knew he was still nervous.

Over the years, I learned when a human is nervous, they can become afraid. And a scared human…well, a scared human was dangerous because that fear could either make them become a stronger version of who they were, or it could be the force that drove them to be the exact opposite of who they wanted to be. Sadly, it felt like the latter would be true for Lion. I knew if Lion gave me the time to show the world why I was made, it would more than likely lead to him throwing away the potential his brother always talked about.

I stayed tucked away in Lion's backpack. I don't know how I expected Lion to act after what happened, but by the end of the day, it was almost as if it was just a normal day. Then, as Lion walked along, the kid from earlier in the day, who I head him call Gerald, stopped his progress.

"What's up, Lion?"

"Nothing, man. I just wanna get home."

"Well, I ain't stopping you. Go ahead."

There was no reason why Lion should have trusted him, but he did. He took him for his word, but Lion was quickly reminded why his classmate should never be trusted. The kid pushed Lion down to the ground, seemingly for no reason.

When the bag fell, I thought for sure I was going to be introduced to Gerald, the troublemaking student, but I wasn't.

"Just go home, Gerald," another kid said.

The voice seemed familiar, but I wasn't too sure who it was until Lion mentioned his name.

"I appreciate you, Alfred, but it's all good. Ain't nothing going on," Lion said.

"I see it ain't all good, but you know I got your back," Alfred said.

"Do you want some of this, too?" Gerald asked, obviously speaking to Lion's friend.

"I'm tired of you bullying us. We ain't gonna keep doing this. I don't know why you're jealous of Lion, but you need to just quit this stuff. We ain't never bothered you, so just leave us alone."

"Jealous? You think I'm jealous? That's stupid. Why would I be jealous of him? Look at him, and look at me. You have to be the dumbest person on earth to think that."

"Bro, you can't fool me. My homie is smarter than you, he dresses better than you, and if he wasn't such a nerd, he'd probably be able to take your girl. So, don't act like you're not jealous of him because I know you are, *Gerald.*"

Alfred said the other kid's name almost as if he were making fun of him.

"Y'all are stupid. I ain't even have time for this," Gerald said as his voice started to fade into the background.

A few seconds later, I felt the backpack being lifted into the air.

"Thank you, Al. That would've been much worse if you weren't here."

"Yeah, you might be right, but I'm just tired of that dude bullying people. We've put up with enough of that."

"True, but weren't you scared?"

"Yeah, but I figured if he started punching on one of us, at least the other one would be able to get a few punches in on him."

"I appreciate that, bro."

"No doubt. You know I got your back forever, Lion."

The two started laughing a little as they started to move again. Lion and Alfred were able to show me the epitome of a human friendship. Both recognized their own weaknesses, but they were willing to put themselves in the way of danger to help take care of the other. Without mentioning the word, I knew loyalty was an important part of their bond. They seemed to be as close as brothers, and they seemed committed to being their brother's keeper.

Over the next few weeks, I learned more about Alfred. Through their conversations, I learned Alfred had gone through a lot in his short life. Many of those who he was close to were no longer around. Some were not around because they chose not to be, while others weren't around because they were taken away from him. With that being the case, he was extremely protective of everyone who was still there.

One day, as he sat with Alfred and some of their classmates during their lunch break, Lion asked them a question.

"Why do we even do this?"

"What do you mean, Lion?" Alfred asked.

"I mean, we come to school every day, but why? Sometimes, I think no matter what we do, we're still gonna be stuck in this neighborhood...being broke."

"Lion, what's up with you? This ain't the Lion I know. You're talking like a quitter, and I've been around you long enough to know that ain't you."

"I don't know... I feel like I just want to give up," Lion replied.

It was at this point the majority of the people at the table decided they had enough. They didn't want to be around their classmate when he was dealing with negativity. They didn't want to show they cared for someone who was in need of compassion. To them, Lion's words were not a cry for help, they were simply complaints and none of them had enough room in their hearts to show him any love. So they left, and as the table emptied, Alfred made his position clear.

"Look, bro, I don't know what you're going through, but I'm here for you."

Alfred had no idea what his friend was dealing with. He didn't know at 3:00 that morning, as Lion tried to get his last few hours of sleep, he and his mother received a phone call letting them know Marvin had been robbed and shot. He also had no idea Lion was dealing with so much pain because of the hopelessness he felt that he was seconds away from using me to take his own life. Alfred didn't know any of this because up until that point, Lion was carrying on as if he was just going through his daily routine.

"Why did we have to be born here? Why couldn't we be some of those rich kids who don't have to worry about nothin'? What did our families do to make us have to suffer through this?" Lion asked.

"To be real, it don't even matter why we're here, or why our school is the way it is, or even why our families don't have money. All that matters is that we try to do something good with our lives, and we don't just quit when stuff gets hard," Alfred told his friend.

I heard Lion begin to cry, and because of their age, I almost expected Alfred to mock his friend for showing emotions, but he didn't do that."

"Lion, what's up, for real?" Alfred asked.

Lion could no longer keep the reason for his tears to himself. He had to release everything he was keeping bottled up inside.

"Marvin got shot last night. They robbed him, and they literally tried to kill him. My brother may have had a little bit of bread, but I know it wasn't enough for them to do that."

"I'm sorry, Lion. Is he gonna make it?"

"Yeah, he's gonna be okay, but now he's gonna have to deal with the cops. I know nothing good is gonna come from that," Lion told his friend.

"What do you mean?"

"I ain't gonna snitch, but you know we all have to do what we have to do around here."

"Say less. I got you."

"He's not an angel, but he didn't deserve that. Plus, he just gets money to help my mom out."

"And how did your mom take everything?"

"She had a lot of reactions. She said she was blessed he's not dead, but at the same time, she was disappointed he was even out of the house that late. She never got in his face about anything he's doing, but I'm sure she knows what's happening."

"Lion, mamas always know what's going on, even when they don't say nothin' about it."

"That's true. Bro, I'm just tired of trying to survive."

"Lion, you're one of the people destined for greatness. No matter what's going on, you can't forget that. You hear me?"

"Yeah, I hear you."

"Good. Now wipe your face so we can get ready to conquer the rest of the day. Oh, and you have to promise me something."

"What?" Lion asked.

"You have to promise not to keep this stuff bottled up. We

may not really be related, but I'm your brother, and I'll go to war for you."

Right then, their lunch break ended.

"Al, I appreciate you, man."

"No doubt."

The conversation between Lion and Alfred ended in a way that made me think Lion was feeling better, but he was still incredibly quiet for the rest of the day. In his classes, he only spoke when he was spoken to. He didn't add himself to any additional discussions, and it was almost as if he had forgotten about the joy he gained while speaking with his friend. Many people would have loved to get all of the empathetic attention they could get, but Lion wasn't one of them.

There was a good chance his emotions were all over the place because he was thinking about his brother, but I didn't know for sure because he never expressed anything. When his classes were over for the day, he moved with a sense of urgency unlike any other time before. He was trying to get away from school as quickly as he could, but once again, he was impeded by Gerald.

"Why are you running?" he asked.

It had been a little while since Lion had to deal with Gerald, and at that time, he was probably the last person Lion wanted to see.

"I'm not running from anything. I'm just trying to get home."

"Keep it real, you hate me, don't you?" Gerald asked.

Since I met him, Lion had never been the type of person who would purposefully offend anyone, even if that person always opposed him.

"I don't hate you, but I can't act like you're one of my favorite people, either," Lion answered truthfully.

"I get it, but I need you to know something."

There was no reply. The silence was the same as Lion giving Gerald permission to continue speaking.

"It's like this, Lion. I see you getting good grades and stuff, and it makes me mad because I'm not smart like that. Then, I see the way the girls look at you, and that upsets me even more because they don't look at me like that. Your homie was right, man. I don't like admitting it, but I am jealous of you. Real talk. Almost every time I see you, I want to punch you in your face. I hate you, Lion. I hate that you're better than me."

Lion didn't question anything he was being told. He listened intently as one of his peers was literally telling I'm why he had an issue with him. While Gerald continued to speak, Lion took the backpack off of his back and held onto it as if his life depended on it. I could feel his heart beating very heavily. Everything inside the backpack, including me, almost moved to the rhythm of his heartbeat.

"Is there a problem?" someone asked from a distance.

"Nah, Al, there's isn't," Lion answered.

"Are you sure?" Alfred asked as he got closer.

"Yeah, I think it's all good."

"Ok, cool. If you need something, let me know."

"I will," Lion said.

Once Lion spoke those words, Alfred left his friend alone to continue the conversation with the person they both had a problem with.

"See, that's what I'm talking about," Gerald said.

"What?"

"I mean, that little talk you just had with Al is an example of why I have a problem with you."

"But that doesn't make sense because I didn't say anything bad about you."

"Exactly! I have never been nice to you, and you still...you just don't respond to stuff the way I do. I know this is gonna sound crazy, but I respect you and hate you at the same time. I act out when I'm mad, but even when you're mad, you have way more control over yourself than me."

Lion paused, probably because he didn't know what to say. As he continued to remain silent, his grip on the bag started to loosen up. This let me know he was letting his guard down because he was starting to believe what Gerald was telling him. This was illogical to me because, as far as I knew, Gerald had never said or done anything positive when it came to Lion, yet he was letting a few possible moments of honesty from Gerald overrule the actions he had displayed over and over.

"I gotta go, but I just needed to get that stuff off my chest," Gerald said.

Lion stood still before he was finally able to make himself start moving again. I heard him mumbling to himself in an attempt to clear his head of the conversation he just finished having with Gerald. Perhaps he wanted to focus on his brother, so as he walked, he continuously asked himself questions.

"Do you think he's gonna stop bullying you? Why does he suddenly want you to know what type of person he is? Do you think there's a chance he discovered God, and that made him realize how bad he's been? Yeah... that's probably it."

As he made it home, he quickly checked to see if his mother was home before he went into his room and locked his door. His backpack was placed on his desk. Eventually, he dumped all of its contents, including me, onto the desk. He stared at everything as if we were in a lineup.

Since we were all out in the light, I was finally able to take a better look at everything I had been stuck in the dark with only moments before. It was almost poetic that I was right next to Lion's history because of how closely connected guns were to the history of humans. Lion didn't seem to notice the symbolism, though. This is when he stood up and asked me another question.

"Do you think Gerald's sudden honesty had something to do with you?"

Fear always had a way of making people change the way

they acted, and I had a way of striking fear into the hearts of those who were around me. I guess it's a gift and a curse. As for the question, it wasn't hard to believe I was the reason a bully humbled himself, but I didn't think it was actually what happened.

"Yeah, that would make sense. He must have heard you hit the ground when he pushed me that day. So, if he knows you exist, he also realizes what I could have done to him. He knows I could have just got rid of him, so I guess he's just trying to make sure he stays on my good side. I figured it all out. All of the times he's treated me like trash, now he wants to be different just because his life depends on it."

As he continued to converse with me, I started to notice a bit of a change in him. Lion had never been a very loud or confident person, but out of nowhere, that's who was trying to convince himself he was. He was acting as though he had discovered some new power he had within, but it was a lie. He wasn't being confident; he was being counterfeit.

As he paraded around his room, the jingle of keys could be heard in the distance. The sound meant his mother was entering the house.

"Lion, are you in here?"

"Yes, ma'am."

It was amazing how quickly he went from pretending to be in control of everything back to being that innocent little boy. To continue with the transition, he scrambled to put me back into the backpack.

"Lion," his mom yelled out again while knocking on his door and trying to open it at the same time.

He ran and unlocked it so his mother could enter.

"Hey, mom. How are you?"

"I'm good, but why did you have this door locked?" she asked.

"I don't even really know, especially since I'm the only one here. Mom, you know I'm weird."

"Boy, if that ain't the truth, I don't know what is."

The lie that Lion told his mom gave them both an opportunity to laugh, but the joy didn't last long.

"Do you want to go with me to see your brother?" she asked.

"I do, but…"

"But, what?"

"Where's Noelle?" Lion asked, trying to change the subject.

"I already dropped her off at her friend's house. Luckily, her friend's parents said it was okay for her to spend the night. Anyway, what were you saying?"

"I don't like seeing him like that. All of those tubes and bandages and machines… that stuff scares me. Marvin is like a superhero to me, and nobody likes to see their hero defeated."

"I understand, and if I'm being honest, I'm scared, too. Do you know why I still go and visit him so much?"

"Why?"

"Well, love is something you feel, and I always want him to feel his mother's love. Plus, when you know people care about you, it'll make you do your best to keep going, no matter what. At least, that's how I feel. I know the worst-case scenario is that he takes a turn and he ends not making it, even though the doctors already said he'll recover. I don't like to think about that, but I know it's a possibility. And if my oldest son has to go out, I want it to happen with him fighting his hardest surrounded by people who love him. Don't get me wrong, I don't think that's gonna happen, but I also know that his condition could always change."

Her words were passionate, and she made it made it easy to understand she meant everything she was saying. As she continued to speak to Lion to convince him to go with her to see Marvin, I understood why humans spoke highly of their mothers. If all mothers were like her, kids all over the world had to feel like they could accomplish anything. That conversation also cleared some things up for me.

Parents set out to remove limitations on what their kids could do. At the same time, they raised the bar on what they expected to happen. If the parent did a decent job, their children would feel a sense of regret if they did something they knew their parents wouldn't approve of. Ironically, not wanting to disappoint a parent had to be why Lion didn't tell the truth about why he really had his door closed, even though lying to his mother was a disappointing act in itself. Disappointment had to also be a reason why Marvin never wanted his mother to know what he did to earn money.

"So, you're going, right?" Lion's mother asked.

Her words were said as if she was asking a question, but her tone indicated Lion didn't really have a choice.

"Yes, ma'am, I'm going. Can I just have a few minutes to get ready?"

"Yeah, but only a few minutes. I don't want to wait all day because you want to make yourself look good."

"Mom, I'm a gangster. I'm not worried about looking good."

"Okay, *gangster*," she said as she laughed again with her son before I heard her exit the room.

Lion may have laughed with his mom, but I knew the laughter was a facade. He really seemed like he had started to convince himself he was someone different. He was using me, not as a tool to do a job, but as something to change who he was. I didn't like it because I knew the personality changes could lead to actions that would probably be blamed on me. I knew if Lion ever made me do anything, I would be blamed for whatever negativity would follow. The difference is, I was a machine who would forced to accept my role, but as a human, I doubted he would.

When people used guns, especially when a crime is committed, often times everyone and everything that had anything to do with it were blamed, but somehow the person who actually did it escaped the responsibility. You would hear things like the person did it because they grew up in a single-parent home. Okay, let's blame the hard working parent, or the parent that wasn't there. That makes sense, right? Or, you may hear they did what they did because of their neighborhood. Well, surely we can blame their environment as the sole cause for someone making a decision. Was the person bullied? If so, the person (or people) who bullied them are to blame, which is partially true, but what about the person who did it?

As I sat in the backpack thinking about all of this, Lion was trying to decide if I was going to make the trip with him and his mother. Then, he grabbed the backpack and put it onto his shoulders.

"Should you go, or should you stay?"

The bag swayed as he held it and moved around his room. Lion's process and procrastination was strange to me. As guns, there is never a time when we don't want to be used for our purpose, but humans should be able to know there's a time and place for everything. If I were in Lion's position, I don't think I would have considered taking a gun to visit my injured brother.

The fact Lion was considering taking me with them let me know his thoughts were already starting to get out of control. How dumb could he be? His brother had been shot, so why in the world would he even be thinking about me at all? Did he think the person who shot Marvin was going to be at the hospital? If they were, did he think he would have been prepared to do something about it while his mother was around? Of course not, and if he wasn't ready, that means he would hesitate. When me or any of my family are involved, hesitation is normally deadly.

"Nah, I think I'm gonna leave you here."

He made a wise decision and put the backpack down on the ground.

"Lion, please tell me you're ready to go," his mother yelled out.

"Yep, I was just about to come out."

That's when he left the room. Soon after, I heard their front door being locked, letting me know they finally left the house. I don't know how long they were gone, but when they returned, a vaguely familiar voice was with them.

"….and I was just as surprised as everyone else. One day I was in a coma, and the next, I'm wide awake, feeling like nothing was wrong with me, other than feeling sore. Ma, when I felt those bullets hit me, I thought it was all over, even though I didn't know how injured I really was. I just kept thinking about you, Lion, and Noelle."

"What do you mean, you felt bad for us?" Lion asked.

"I'm the big brother, and there are a lot of things I think I can still teach you. Even though I didn't know how bad I was hurt, I still thought I was going to die, and that made me mad at myself for not doing what I know I should have been doing. Ma, for you, I'm not a good representation of who your oldest son should be. When people see me, they don't see all of the sacrifices you've made to make us better people. They don't see me as the same type of person they see when they look at you. So, if I was gonna die, I would've felt bad because I would have failed you. I would've felt bad because I never met your expectations for me. I'm sorry, y'all. I don't want to be who I am. I can't be a disappointment to you anymore. I don't believe God let me survive being shot for nothing. I have to have some kind of purpose. I don't know what that purpose is, but it's something. I hope y'all can forgive me for being so stupid."

Although the family spoke in another room, the passion of what Marvin said traveled very well. He wasn't the person he was before the incident happened, and it sounded like he never wanted to be that person again.

"Little brother, can I talk to you for a minute?"

"Lion, I know you boys have some catching up to do. Why don't y'all just go to your room?"

Soon, Lion and Marvin walked into the room and closed the door.

"So, did you really mean any of that stuff you were just saying, or were you saying that to please Mom?" Lion asked.

"I meant every single word. Bro, I almost died. I know we need money, but I can't go back to doing what I was doing."

"Do you have any idea who it was?"

"Do I know who shot me? Yeah, I do. They looked right into my eyes before they pulled the trigger. They told me they were there to watch me die, but I told them I wasn't gonna give them the satisfaction. Looking back, it was pretty dumb, but that's what I did. While I was on the ground bleeding, I felt my life slipping away, but I was still trying to fight. When I couldn't keep my eyes open, I thought they won, and I started to regret everything. Bro, I have been terrible to you. I've been wrong about everything, especially about needing protection."

"That sounds crazy. You got shot and almost died. You gave me a gun because you said the neighborhood was dangerous, and I never know when something may happen. To me, it seems like you were exactly right."

"Yeah, the streets are bad, but we can't just keep adding to the problem. What I was doing was wrong, and honestly, I got what I deserved. There was no way I should've been out there in the first place. All of this was a life lesson and there's no way I'm gonna go back to what I was doing."

"You can't just quit that kinda stuff because you want to. I've never been part of that world, but I'm sure that's not how it works."

"At this point, I'm ready for whatever comes my way. I've looked death in the eyes already, so I'm not scared of that. If somebody tries to kill me because I want to do the right thing, then I'm ready for that."

"You're stupid, Marvin. You thought you were messing up before, but you're really messing up now."

"What happened to you, Lion? Have you really changed that much since I went to the hospital?"

"You changed, not me. Just because you got shot, you're just…I don't know. I can't look up to somebody like you. I don't even know who you are."

Marvin's incident caused him to only want to positively impact his brother. Lion, for some reason, didn't respect what his older brother was saying. To Lion, it seemed like no longer wanting to deal with the same activities he once did, made his brother weak. This didn't make sense. It was obvious Marvin no longer wanted to put money and the streets before the morals his mother tried to pass along to them.

A change like that should have been enough to make anyone proud, but the fact that Marvin's words upset Lion showed how different he really had become in such a short amount of time.

"Are you for real, Lion? You're acting like it's bad that I want to do better. What's wrong with you?"

"Me? What's wrong with me? You've lost it, and you aren't man enough to be in control."

"You're a smart guy, but what you're saying is stupid. I'm in a better position now than I've ever been in before."

"How? You ain't even trying to go after the people who tried to kill you. You're scared, Marvin, and that's sad. I'm glad they didn't kill you, but I don't think I can respect who you're changing into. And you don't have to worry about trying to give me any of that brotherly advice anymore because I don't wanna hear it."

"I get it, believe me I do, but your new way of thinking is off. Me being willing to work on the streets and destroy people's lives while carrying weapons and convincing myself I was ready to do whatever was necessary to prove my manhood was just…it was very immature. When I was out there, I told myself I was doing it for the family. I thought hurting others was cool as long as it didn't hurt us, but I was wrong. I never meant..."

"Yeah, yeah, you never wanted to do what you were doing, but I don't care about what you're saying. None of that stuff matters to me. You got shot, you got soft, and you fell off."

"It makes me sad to hear you talk like that, but I know it's just talk."

"Blah, blah, blah. That's enough. Quit wasting time and just leave. Go talk to Mom or call Noelle or something. I'm sure they'll want to hear more about your new positive outlook on life."

Lion's words were uncalled for, but Marvin didn't bother to argue with his brother. Instead, he quietly opened the door and left Lion alone with his thoughts. As soon as Marvin left, I was once again freed from the backpack."

"Can you believe that? How can he just go from being down for whatever, to not even wanting to get the person back who robbed and shot him? He has to be lying about this whole near-death experience thing, right?"

I wanted to tell him how fortunate he was that his brother actually cared about the lives of the family and those around them. I wanted him to understand guns shouldn't be used to prove how tough a person is. I wanted him to understand there were consequences associated with actions, but even if I could have educated him on these things, I'm sure he wouldn't have listened.

"We don't need him. As long as I got you, I'm good. The fact he gave you to me shows he used to know what he was doing."

As he had done on multiple occasions, he went to the mirror and stood there, pointing me at his reflection.

"Let somebody run up..."

As he was trying to finish his sentence, his mother unexpectedly walked into the room.

"Lion, what…is that? Please don't tell me you have a gun. Please tell me that's not real."

"I don't wanna lie to, so I'm not gonna act like it's not real. I have it because we need to be protected out here. People have been bullying me all of my life, and I'm tired of it. They'll learn who's the man."

"The man? You think being able to shoot somebody makes you the man? Having a gun doesn't make you a man. You're smarter than that. You're not old enough to be ready for all of the responsibility that comes with that. Where did you even get that from?"

I knew he didn't want to answer because he didn't respond immediately. Even though he had a fight with his brother a little while before his mother walked into his room, he still didn't want to let his mother know Marvin was responsible for him having a gun.

"Where did you get this?" she asked again.

She yelled louder than she ever had before as she took me out of Lion's hands.

"Mom, stop waving that around. You don't know what you're doing."

"Oh, and I guess you do. I guess you're just a professional, huh? Answer me, where did you get this from?"

"He got it from me, Mom," Mavin said out of nowhere.

"What are you doing, Marvin?" Lion asked.

"I'm owning up to what I've done. Mom, I gave that to him. I know it was wrong, but I did it so he could protect himself. Things are different for us. Our lives are threatened whenever we walk out the front door."

Hearing Marvin say what he did broke her down. She plopped down on Lion's bed and placed me beside her."

"I've tried so hard to provide for you kids. I failed! I failed you all! I never thought you would need a gun. You're just a kid, Lion! Where did I go wrong?"

Lion remained quiet as Marvin tried to provide more insight to their mother.

"Mom, this really doesn't have anything to do with you. Unfortunately, it's just the world we live in. If we go outside with a nice pair of shoes or even a nice shirt, somebody may be jealous enough to try and kill us. There's no logic to what will set people off these days. I gave that gun to Lion because I'd rather him have it and never use it than need it and not have it. You see what happened to me."

Out of everything he said, the word jealous stuck out to me. It seemed, no matter who was talking, that word kept rearing its head. From what I gathered, that word seemed to mean one person was upset at another person because they had something the other person didn't. How dumb could people be?

I stopped paying attention to what Lion and his family were saying to ask myself that question again. How dumb could people be? At first, I posed that question to myself as a rhetorical one, but then it became real. People always want to tell others how smart they are, yet they continue to make themselves look foolish by doing increasingly dumb things. They put themselves in danger because of how they think.

"I can't let you keep this," Lion's mother said.

The continued discussion eventually made me focus back on what was being said.

"Mom, can I ask you something?" Lion wondered.

"Go ahead," she said as if she was still trying to control her emotions.

"Do you want me to die?" he asked.

"Bro, why are you asking her that? You know she doesn't want that; no mother does," Marvin said.

"I'm not trying to hear you, Marvin. I asked her."

"No, son, I don't want you to die. When I found out what happened to Marvin, I literally couldn't breathe. Thinking about losing a child made me have panic attacks, and now, you have just made those feeling start to come back. Do I want you to die? No, I don't. I want all of you to live as long as possible. I want to see you all find someone you can spend the rest of your lives with. I pray you experience what life can be like with children of your own, but if you both want to be thugs, you won't make it. Marvin is fortunate to still be here, but if changes aren't made, if both of you don't learn from what happened, then life could be very short for you. I pray I don't end up putting any of my kids in the ground, but if your actions don't change, it's bound to happen. I'm not gonna let you bring danger to this house, though. If my boys want to be stupid, I still have to look out for me and Noelle. Everybody messes up, but I can't be a part of you throwing your lives down the drain. You can either choose that negative life with your guns or you can promise me you're gonna let it go today. And if you choose the guns and the life that goes with them, I won't let you stay here."

"Are you serious, Mom?" Marvin asked.

"Yeah, I'm very serious. As much as it hurts, I can't have you bringing the ways of the streets inside of this home. Y'all are my sons, and I love you, but things have to change."

"This is crazy. I'm fifteen. How can you talk about kicking me out of the house?"

"You can't be a kid when it's convenient, then turn and make grown man decision. Both of you need to make some decisions because I won't let you stay here if I can't trust you."

She loved her kids, there was no question about that, but in her mind, having me around would bring more negativity than she wanted to deal with.

"This whole situation is my fault. Like I said, I brought this gun into your house, and I apologize for that. I know Lion, and even if he won't admit it, he's just afraid. I was, too. I wouldn't have had a gun if I wasn't afraid of the folks on the block. I wouldn't have had a gun if I wasn't scared for your safety. So yeah, I was afraid of a lot of things. Mom, you said you don't want us here if we can't be trusted. That's not something I want to hear. Please understand that I'm done with everything I was doing before."

"But what about that fear you were just talking about?" Lion asked.

"The fear is still there, but I'm not gonna be who I was. That life ain't worth it. I take responsibility for all of the messed up stuff I've done, but I won't be doing any of that anymore. My bad, Mom. Lion, we have to do better."

"This is all so fake! Ma, you're acting like everything is a surprise. You knew Marvin was out at all hours of the night and coming home with money. What did you think he was doing? And Marvin, you're a liar, bro. You don't regret what you did. You're just acting like this 'cause you got shot. You know if you got a call from somebody to make some money, you'll be right back on the streets. I don't care what you're trying to make us believe," Lion said.

"I really like money, Lion. I thought I was ready to die to get it, but now that I almost did, I know money ain't as important as life is. So, if someone ever tried to contact me, I'd be lying if I said I wouldn't be tempted, but I can't do what I've done anymore."

"Do you actually believe him, Mom?" Lion asked.

"I have my doubts, but if both of you said you wanted to do better, I'd take your word for it. I believe in you and your potential. I've heard Marvin say he wants to be different, but I haven't heard you do anything other than question us and complain. So, what do you want to do? Do you want to be the Lion I know and love, or do you want to be this new guy who wants to carry a gun?"

Marvin and his mother waited on Lion to reply. I'm sure they were hoping he would say something to let them know he was on the same page with them, but he didn't.

"I'm still smart, and I still have potential to be great, but that old version of Lion is gone, and he probably won't ever be back. That dude got bullied, and I refuse to let that happen anymore. That gun has changed my life."

I liked being a part of the conversation, but I hadn't done anything to change anyone's life. Lion had to know that.

"You think I'm playing with you, Lion? You're not gonna be in this house with a gun. If you need it that bad, you might as well get your stuff together and get out, now. That goes for you too, Marvin. I'm not having it. If you want to endanger yourselves, that's one thing, but you won't put me and Noelle in danger, too."

Neither Marvin nor Lion responded right away. I thought they would be ready to get rid of me, which left me unsure of what was going to happen to me.

"Alright, Mom. You got it. Just keep the gun, I don't even care. I'm done," Lion finally said.

"I'm gonna take your word, Lion. And Marvin, I take it you're done too, right?"

"I'm done, Ma."

The argument Lion and Marvin had seemed to be over. While their mother was upset, she convinced herself her kids were not blatantly lying to her. It didn't seem like a smart move, but I witnessed people make bad decisions because of people they cared about, and this just seemed like another example of that. To me, it didn't seem possible for Lion and Marvin to change who they were so quickly. If they weren't who they were claiming to be, eventually someone would call them out on it.

"So, if we're all good, nobody should have a problem with me keeping this gun until I figure out how to permanently get rid of it."

"I don't need it," Marvin said.

Lion said nothing, but his mother took his silence as confirmation. Soon, I was taken away by the matriarch of the family.

"I can't let you stay here and put my family at risk. Tomorrow, we're gonna find out what to do with you," the mother said to me.

I hadn't done anything to put her family in danger, but it made her feel better to act like she was figuring out how to get rid of a threat. I thought she should have put more blame on herself, but again, humans loved pointing their fingers at somebody (or something) other than themselves.

After I was taken away from Lion's room, I found myself in many different locations in a very short amount of time. I went from a purse, to a drawer, inside of a shoe box, and even under a pile of clothing. She tried hiding me in a location where I wouldn't easily be seen, but nothing worked. Wherever she put me, I stuck out like a sore thumb. Eventually, she decided she was going to leave me in the back of her nightstand.

The family had a long day, and after I was put in my new location, the house got very quiet. From the lack of conversations, I assumed Marvin seemed to give up on trying to convince his brother about the dangers of the person he was becoming, at least for the night. Lion was also no longer berating his brother about who he was becoming. The silence eventually lulled their mother into a false sense of security. Soon, she was going to sleep for the night.

The next morning, the house was still quiet until the mother called out to her family.

"Okay, I'm about to go to work."

Initially, there was no response, but then, Lion appeared near her room.

"What time do you think you'll be back?" he asked.

"Well, good morning to you, too," she said sarcastically.

"My bad. Good morning, Mom. How are you?"

"I'm okay, Lion. How are you? I hope you were able to calm down since last night."

"Yes, ma'am. I'm calm. Sooo, what time do you think you'll be back today?"

"Why?"

"I may want to surprise you by making dinner or something. Dang, Mom, why you gotta ruin it?"

"Boy, if you're cooking dinner, I won't be hungry...ever," she said.

"Funny, Ma. Nah, I just want to make sure to be here by the time you got home."

"Oh, okay. Well, that's really nice of you. I'm going to be home fairly late today because I'm working a double."

"I don't know how you do it, Mom."

"Do what?"

"I don't know how you're able to work so much and then come home and make sure we're okay. That stuff is crazy to me."

"I appreciate that, but I'm not doing anything plenty of other parents aren't doing. As a parent, part of my job is to find a way to do whatever's necessary to handle what needs to be handled. Plus, I can't really take credit for anything that gets done because when I feel like I'm running on fumes, God carries me through."

"And you won't even take credit for the things you do. I think I'm a humble person, but when people compliment me on something, I just thank them for it."

She laughed.

"As you get older, you realize how little you control. When people say good things about you, I feel you should acknowledge and thank them, but also let them know the goodness they see is just a reflection of the God in you."

Lion's mother was a very kind-hearted person. Any words I ever heard her say, even when said in a harsh tone, seemed to come from a place of love. It was apparent young humans didn't always value the wisdom their parents tried to give to them. Instead, they often chose to disregard the advice as they sought to experience things for themselves. This became evident when Lion's mother left the house after that morning's conversation.

The night before, she made it clear she didn't want her kids to have anything to do with me. Regardless of if I thought her decision was right or not, Lion agreed he would leave me alone. He told his mother he would respect her wishes, but he lied. I heard him start tearing up his mother's room to search for me almost as soon as she left.

"Lion, what are you doing in Mom's room? Shouldn't you be getting ready for school?" Marvin asked.

"I'm looking for something. Is that okay with you? Plus, shouldn't you be minding your business and trying to recover from getting shot?"

"I don't care how stupid you've been acting, you're still my little brother, and I care about you. Do you really think I don't know you're in here trying to find the gun you promised Mom you weren't going to mess with? Lion, your decision-making ability has become terrible."

"Terrible decisions? If anybody knows about making terrible decisions, it's you. After all, you're the same dude who was tough one day, but turned into a goody-goody when you got shot. Don't you think that's a dumb decision?"

Lion accidentally bumped the nightstand. When he did, he must have heard me move around inside, which made him open it up. He wasted no time freeing me from the nightstand.

"You found it, now what?" Marvin asked.

"Now, I'll take it back to school and protect myself, just like I've been doing."

"So, you don't even care that you lied to Ma?"

"No, Marvin! I don't care about that! I ain't worried about truth and lies. I'm just worried about respect and survival," Lion said.

"A gun ain't giving you that! I had multiple guns, and they didn't do nothin' for me. The people on the streets acted like they respected me, but they didn't even visit the hospital while I was close to dying. And survival? That gun ain't what helped me survive. I made it because God let me make it. That's it. I told you all that gangsta talk I was feeding you was wrong. I didn't know what I was talking about and you're too smart to do what I was doing. Trust me, it ain't worth it."

"You're acting like getting shot made us live in a different neighborhood. Things didn't get better for us. People get shot around here all the time, so nobody cares if you, me, or anybody else catch some bullets. It's really just normal hood activity. Look, I'm not about to get into another argument with you about the same thing. I'm lucky nothin' happened to me before I got this gun, but I'm not gonna keep depending on luck. I'm taking this gun with me, and you can't stop me!"

Lion was no longer *pretending* to be a different person—he was. He dismissed almost every word his older brother told him, and since Marvin was injured, Lion wanted to let it be known he felt he had become the alpha male in his household.

"Bro, I'm not gonna let you leave this house with that gun," Marvin said.

"Let me? Marvin, you sound really stupid right now! I already told you that there's nothing you can do to stop me."

Marvin took a giant leap toward us, and I ended up hitting the ground.

"Marvin, what are you doing? This gun is loaded. You could've just ended up getting shot again! You barely made it the last time. Who knows what would happen if you took another bullet."

"I don't care, Lion. If I got shot and didn't make it, maybe that would be enough to make you quit actin' like this."

"I get what you're trying to do, but it's pointless. You created this monster, and now, it's beyond your control," Lion stated before snatching me up again.

Marvin was too weak to keep fighting his brother, so he didn't try.

"If you want to make sure I'm okay, just hope I never have to use this gun because I'm not gonna stop carrying it," Lion said as he stared at his brother.

Marvin didn't say anything else, but I'm sure he wanted to. Lion finished getting ready for school, put me back in his backpack, and walked out without exchanging any other words with his brother.

Lion was a very different person at home, but for some reason, I expected him to be more like the other version of himself while he was at school. This ended up not being the case. His talk with his best friend proved that to me very quickly.

"What's up, Lion? Yo, did you see the game last night? It was crazy!"

"Nah."

"Are you okay?" Al asked.

"Yeah," Lion responded.

"I guess you're goin' through something. I understand. If you need me, just let me know."

All of Lion's responses were short and dismissive. After a few attempts at a conversation with his friend, Al just gave up and walked away. Al was probably confused by Lion's behavior, but he didn't make a big deal of it.

Lion's treatment of his friend continued on a downward spiral for a few weeks. Al didn't say anything about it, though. One day, when Al saw Lion talking to Gerald, he decided he had enough.

"Is that how it is, now?" Al asked.

"What are you talking about?" Lion wondered.

"I'm talking about you kicking it with the same dude who I had to keep from beating you up."

"Hold up! You ain't save me from nothing!"

"Oh, okay. You're just gonna lie to yourself, huh? You wanna act like this dude didn't have you scared every day. Do you really wanna act like he's not the reason you created the tough guy you're pretending to be. You're a fraud, bro!"

"I'm a fraud? You're comin' over here..."

"Hold on, Lion. I got you," Gerald interrupted.

"I ain't tryin' to nothin' you have to say," Al told Gerald.

"I don't care because I'm gonna speak. You've been complaining for like five minutes just because you saw Lion talking to me. Bro, this dude was just talking to me, and you got so in yo' feelings, you act like you wanna cry! Man up! The crazy thing is, not long ago, you said I was jealous because Lion was cool, Lion was this, Lion was that, and now...it sounds like you're the jealous one."

"This ain't jealousy, this is a lack of loyalty. Jealousy has nothing to do with it. So, if you don't know what you're talkin' about, just keep your mouth shut."

They used the word jealous over and over. Each time it was used, there was a bit of animosity attached to it. Normal conversations immediately escalated when one person accused another of being jealous. Any civility that existed in a conversation was thrown away once jealousy was involved.

"Al, bro, whatever you're dealing with, you need to calm it down! You're getting on my nerves! The beef we used to have with Gerald is gone. So, you either gonna be cool with that, or you need to just keep it moving."

"Oh, *we* don't have beef anymore just because you said we don't? Do you think you control me?"

The school bell rang right after Al's question. It was almost as if outside forces were trying to stop the heated conversation the boys were having in the middle of the hallway.

"Don't you hear that bell? You better get to class before you get yourself in trouble," Gerald said to Al.

"I told you to stay out of this, Gerald," Al said.

"You're a funny dude, *Al*. All of a sudden, you wanna act like you ain't scared. Boy, like I said, I think you should get to class before something bad happens to you. I'm letting you get a pass 'cause of Lion, but that's gonna run out if you keep runnin' your mouth."

"You know what? I think you're right! I should stop talking."

"Glad you finally smartened..."

Before Gerald completed his sentence, I heard what had to be a swift and heavy punch to someone's face. That sound was followed closely by the sound of someone hitting the ground.

"Al, what are you doing?" Lion asked.

"I've had enough of your homie, and if you keep talking, you can get what he just got. The line has been drawn, and now I know where you stand! You made a bad choice, Lion, but you'll have to live with that."

"Okay, we're both trippin'. This ain't you, Al. We're already super late for class. Maybe we should get goin' before the teachers and stuff start coming out here."

"I don't care about no teachers right now, and I ain't tryin' to hear anything you have to say. You might as well leave 'cause I'm not finished with him yet!"

I could hear Al as he proceeded to throw punches in Gerald's direction.

"Al, stop!" Lion yelled.

"For the last time, back up off of me!" Al told Lion very sternly.

Not only was Lion different than who he used to be, but Al's words and actions also showed he had gone through a transformation of his own. This was the moment we all realized the two friends had grown apart.

"Al, I know you're mad, but chill out! Why are you even still tryin' to fight? You already got him on the ground. You won, bro! Take the 'W' and call it a day."

"I told you, you don't control what I do!"

Another voice could be heard in the background.

"Hey! Hey, what's going on over there?"

The boys spoke quietly among themselves as the voice drew closer.

"Do you see what you did? I told you to leave," Lion said.

"That's it, Lion. I don't know who you think I am, but I told you, I'm not somebody you can just keep in check!"

Right then, there was a very unexpected turn of events. Al told Lion to leave him alone several times, but he didn't listen. Soon, he decided to let his fists send the same message to Lion that he had just delivered to Gerald.

"What the…did you just…what?"

Lion was so baffled by Al's actions, he couldn't even complete a question.

"Is that what you wanted? Did you want to see these hands? Lion, I spent a lot of time having your back, making sure you never got caught up in anything by yourself. I stepped into a ton of fights just because I was trying to look out for my homie, my brother, but I'm done with that! If you want some more of what Gerald got, keep talking!"

The person who started speaking while they were far in the distance had made their way closer to the two former friends.

"I know you boys were not over here fighting! What's wrong with you?" the other person asked.

I felt quick movement, which meant Lion was trying to run, but he was stopped in his tracks.

"Oh no, no, no! You're not going anywhere! You boys must have lost your minds! We don't tolerate fighting here, and you know that. And who is that on the ground?"

"Yo, let me go! This dude is a traitor! Please…just let me go! I don't even care if I have to go to the office," Al barked.

During the time I had been close to Al, he usually was able to remain calm. He was generally the voice of reason whenever Lion was caught up in his emotions, but he had reached his limit. He was so upset, he was almost growling as he tried to break free from the adult who approached them.

"Calm down. I know you are upset, but I need to check on this young man that's lying on the ground. I'm asking that you two act mature for a few minutes and stand by those lockers while I tend to him," the person said while he started to focus his attention on Gerald.

The noises of his walkie-talkie could be heard as the older man called for someone to come and help him. Even though they had just had an argument and fight, Lion and Al agreed to remain calm as they moved to the lockers. During this time, they had more time to speak about what had transpired.

"Hey, there's a reason why I've been hangin' 'round Gerald," Lion stated.

"Ain't no logical explanation for that," Al replied after he let out a sigh of disbelief.

"I know that's what you think, but I found out something recently that changed everything," Lion said.

"What?" Al wondered.

"You remember what happened to Marvin?"

"Of course. How is he?"

"He's good, but I found out who shot him."

"For real, who?"

The backpack moved around slightly as if Lion had to change his position.

"Gerald and his boys did," Lion whispered.

"Are you serious?"

"Yeah, man. I'm for real."

"So, if that happened, then I really don't get why you've been hanging out with him."

Lion stopped briefly before he replied.

"Whenever you see one of those undercover cop movies, they always gain the trust of the person they're tryin' to catch by actin' different around their friends. It probably sounds stupid, but I figured that stuff would work with Gerald. That's why I was hangin' with him and dissin' you. I had to make him trust me."

"But why couldn't you tell me?"

"I couldn't tell you because I didn't want you to *act* mad, I wanted you to *be* mad."

"What's the point, though?"

"You know that gun Marvin gave me?"

"Yeah."

"I still carry that with me. I figured once I had Gerald's trust, I would catch him with his guard down, and boom. Even with all of the stuff me and my brother have been going through, I have always wanted to get back at whoever almost took him from us."

"But didn't you say he's been trying to change, and he's been trying to get you to do better?"

"Yeah, but he almost died, so you have to expect him to be like that."

There hadn't been much noise coming from the direction of Gerald and the adult who was attending to him. Then, out of nowhere, that changed.

"Yo, let me go! I don't need no help. I'm good," Gerald said.

With all of the punches I heard, there was no way he was okay.

"I know it's stupid, but I want to go ahead and end things now," Lion said.

"Yeah, that is stupid. He's not worth throwing your life away, but if you are gonna be dumb enough to do something, at least be smarter with your timing. You don't wanna do something when you've got a teacher around, and we know the principal and security are probably on the way. Think, bro. We'll figure out a way to get back at him later, but this ain't it."

"I can't act like you don't have good points, but I have to do what I have to do."

"Don't do anything right now, Lion. You can even act like we're still beefin'. Just don't do what you're thinking about doing."

"You're right. I just got a lot going on in my head. My bad for everything, Al."

"It's all good, brothers fight all the time. My bad for hitting you, too. I shouldn't have done that."

"Nah, you shouldn't have, but I get it. I deserved it."

"Yeah, you earned that punch. Anyway, let's stop acting like we're good. We can still act like we have issues so we can have some time to figure out a plan," Al said.

"Cool. Well, let's get this act going, then," Lion said.

I felt a bit of a struggle as Al and Lion pushed each other to re-establish the drama.

"Get against those lockers, now!" the adult said.

"Man, don't put me next to this dude no more. He's gonna end up like ol' boy on the floor," Al yelled out.

Al's *act* was very believable. If he and Lion hadn't discussed playing the role of enemies only seconds before, I'm sure things would have escalated very quickly. I heard other people started coming around just as the drama started back.

"Mr. Andrews, could you escort those two to my office and wait there with them? I'm going to take this young man to the nurse, then I'll be back to take care of them."

We were taken to the office. As we were walking, the new person, Mr. Andrews, started talking to Lion and Al.

"What happened with y'all?" he asked.

"Umm, I guess it was just a misunderstanding. You know how dudes have to handle things sometimes. I know it's wrong, but we can't go back and change what happened," Al explained.

"There are consequences for everything you do, regardless of if you've learned from it. You know that, right?"

"Yes, sir."

After a few minutes, we stopped walking, and heard a door close.

"So, what are your names?"

"I'm Al."

"I'm Lionel, but everybody calls me Lion."

Both of the kids still sounded upset. I guess they were still playing their roles, and soon after Al and Lion introduced themselves, the first adult stepped into the office.

"Mr. Andrews, could you take him into the lobby for a minute."

I didn't know who was going to the lobby at first, but when Lion didn't move, I learned he was talking about Al.

"Let's cut to the chase. What happened?"

"That used to be my boy, but things change. I ain't trippin', though. He got a good hit or two on me, but that's it. It ain't nothing major. He gonna get his, though."

"You do know how dumb it is to not only get into a fight, but also threaten retaliation in front me, right?"

"Nah, Mr. Smith, I didn't mean I was gonna go after him like that. I just meant karma was gonna come back for him. I'm not making any threats towards nobody, trust me."

"Trust is a very powerful word, young man. Based on the fact that we're only speaking right now because you got into a fight, I don't think you're in the position to speak on trust."

"Mr. Smith, I have never been in trouble before. Really, I shouldn't even be in trouble now. He hit me. It ain't like I actually did anything."

"That may be true, but you participated in a fight, and you will be punished for it."

The door opened, and Mr. Smith asked Mr. Andrews to bring Al into the room. He was also asked to stay in the room just in case things started to get out of control.

"Why are we here, young man?" Mr. Smith asked.

Since he had just asked a similar question to Lion, I assumed he was asking Al.

"I got tired, Mr. Smith. Lion was like my brother, and then he started hanging out with the same person who had been bullying us. I was wrong, I know it."

"And I'm guessing the student I took to the nurse was the bully."

"Yes, sir," Al said humbly.

"So, what did you accomplish?"

"Nothing, but…"

"Saying the word 'but' can sometimes mean you're going to disregard or negate what came before it. I asked you what you accomplished, and you told me you accomplished nothing. There was no need to extend the sentence because you already provided an answer to my question."

Mr. Smith went on for a few minutes about discipline, responsibility, and how disappointed he was. For the most part, Lion and Al only spoke when they were asked to. Although they were both still trying to pretend to be enemies, the respect they were showing for Mr. Smith didn't seem like an act.

Lion tried to ask if he could go back to class, but his request was denied.

"No, you're not about to go to class. We are about to get in contact with both of your parents and let them know what you've gotten yourself into."

Both Lion and Al were almost unfazed by the majority of what had been said, but as soon as Mr. Smith mentioned getting in contact with their parents, they reverted back to being children.

"Please don't do that, Mr. Smith. I can't have my Dad find out about this," Al said.

"Yeah, my Mom is gonna go off if she has to leave work. We're good, Mr. Smith. There ain't no need for anything else," Lion begged.

"I'm glad to see there's still a level of fear and respect in your hearts for your parents, but your actions will not go unpunished. Fighting is not something anyone, especially the youth should be engaging in. People view you two, and everyone else around here, as unintelligent thugs. They think you're not capable of achieving any level of greatness, and actions like you displayed today would make them think they're right. You have to do better...you have to *be* better."

The message had to be sinking in because the boys were both quiet. As Mr. Smith told Al and Lion he was disappointed in them, he also said he still believed they could do better than their actions showed. Although he knew they could be better, and they showed remorse for what happened, Mr. Smith still followed through with his promise to call their parents. When the phone calls were made, they each heard how upset the fight made their loved ones, and Lion started acting differently, almost immediately.

Lion started clenching his backpack again. He wasn't moving, but he started breathing heavily.

"My bad. I shouldn't have been acting different. I'm dealing with some stuff, and I can't take it. It's all too much," Lion said. His voice was almost cracking as he spoke.

"You were tripping, but it's really on me, bro. I still think Gerald got what he deserved, but I know I'm wrong for what I did to him and to you. My bad," Al told him.

"I'm sorry. I'm really sorry. Things can't be the same. I don't want to...my brother...I can't keep..."

Lion was breathing even heavier, and he was having problems properly conveying his thoughts.

"I can see the emotions from your behavior and actions are setting in, but you have to calm down and breathe," Mr. Smith told Lion.

"I can't keep feeling like this, Mr. Smith. I'm tired," Lion said, finally able to put his words together a little better.

At that moment, I could hear Mr. Smith's office door open.

"They just brought in the other kid from the nurse's office. I was told the injuries appear worse than they really are, but he has to take it easy for the next few days. Do you want me to just keep him in the lobby or bring him in here?" Mr. Andrews asked.

"No, don't bring him in here. I'll deal with him in a little bit," Mr. Smith told him. The door closed as Mr. Andrews went back into the lobby to watch Gerald.

Knowing Gerald was on the other side of the door changed how Lion felt. I know this because of how drastically the grip on the backpack changed.

"I'm going to step out and talk to the other young man. You two will remain seated until I return; that is not a request. It is a command. Is that understood?"

"Yes, sir," they both said.

They both agreed, but the response didn't seem honest, at least not from Lion. He changed the way he held his backpack for a reason. I didn't know what was about to happen, but while we were in the office, his movements seemed strategic.

"I meant what I said," Lion told Al.

"Huh?"

"I can't keep dealing with this. I was cool acting like I was Gerald's friend because I knew I could eventually get him to trust me, but seeing how much it hurt you...Al, I can't keep this going. The stuff has to change now," Lion exclaimed.

There was passion in what Lion was saying, but he was able to keep himself from getting too loud. He knew it was beneficial to keep the conversation between he and Al, so that's what he did.

"You're talking crazy, Lion. We'll be good. Like I told you before we came in here, we just have to figure out the next move."

"Bro, I have anxiety every day over this stuff. I have trouble sleeping at night, and while I'm here, my body's here, but my mind ain't. I've disrespected my mom, I've literally fought my brother, and recently, I haven't been the kind of brother Noelle needs to see. I can't keep this going."

"You got me worried now. Be real, Lion. What's really on your mind?" Al asked.

"One way or another, it's gotta end today."

Lion didn't normally speak like that, so as his friend, I knew Al had to be concerned. I heard Al get up, and when he started talking again, I knew he had moved right in front of us.

"Just let it go. The things you found out about Gerald are terrible, ain't no denying that, but doing something to him won't change anything."

"You're right, but it needs to end. My brother needs to know I got his back, forever. Promise me something, Al."

"What's up?"

"Can you let my folks know I love them, just in case I'm not able to?"

"Why do I need to let them know? What are you about to do?" Al asked.

"I'm just about to handle things," Lion responded.

Al didn't know what Lion wanted to do, but he knew it couldn't be good. He tried to stop him, but a slight scuffle endured. I was shaken around in the backpack as the two could be heard pushing each other.

"What are you doing?" Al asked in confusion

"You're my brother, Al, and I'm sorry for everything. You can't stop what's gotta happen, though. You just stay in here and be safe."

Then, the door closed.

"Excuse me, sir. Didn't I ask you and your friend to stay seated?" Mr. Smith asked.

"Yes, sir, but I really need to go to the bathroom," Lion said.

"Mr. Andrews, it is not in your job description, but could

you please follow him to the restroom? I don't want him to try anything."

"Yes, sir."

And with that, Lion and Mr. Andrews started moving down the hallway.

"You can't keep getting yourself into trouble, young fella," Mr. Andrews said.

"You're right. I promise this will be the last day I get into trouble. I didn't start the fight, but I know my actions helped lead to it."

"Taking responsibly for your part in it all is a good start," Mr. Andrews told him.

"Thank you, sir. Now, if you don't mind, I really have to go to the restroom," Lion said as we finally stopped.

"Yeah, go ahead. I'll be right here."

When he said that, I almost immediately heard the restroom door open and close.

"Well, is today the day? It has to be. Nah, wait...I'm tripping. I can't go through with this, can I? I have to. I can't keep letting this go on. I know it's wrong, but I ain't gonna let him get away with it."

Lion debated with himself. He asked and answered his own questions, which let me know he didn't really want to do whatever he was thinking about doing. He stood still for a minute before we walked back out.

"Okay, let's not waste any time getting back to the office."

"Yes, sir," Lion replied.

We walked back quickly, and before I knew it, we were opening the door.

"Gerald, are you okay?" Lion asked when he stepped into the lobby.

Lion acted as if he was genuinely concerned about Gerald's health, but I knew it was all a facade.

"He got a few hits in, but I'm good."

"Let's not talk anymore about what happened earlier. Son, where's Mr. Smith?" Mr. Andrews asked Gerald.

"He just went in there with ol' boy," Gerald said, referring to Al.

Almost as soon as Gerald provided information on Mr. Smith's whereabouts, he got a call on his walkie-talkie. This is the moment Mr. Andrews made a terrible decision.

"I need to respond to this call. Can I trust you two for a minute or two?"

"Yeah, I ain't got no beef with Lion, ain't nothin' gonna happen," Gerald said as Mr. Andrews opened the door and left.

Not knowing how much time he had before Mr. Smith would come back into the room, Lion decided to make his move. He unexpectedly dropped his bag, and I hit the ground hard, but I tried to remain quiet. I didn't know exactly what was going on, but I thought Lion was just going to put the bag back on, but that's not what happened.

He unzipped his backpack and the light began to fill my home as Lion finally granted me freedom.

"Oh snap! Lion, you packin'?" Gerald asked.

"Yeah."

"What you plan on doing with that," Gerald asked.

Lion's hand was steady as I was pointed directly at Gerald.

"Sometimes your closest friends become your enemies, and sometimes you get close enough to your enemies to make them think they're your friends. We ain't cool, Gerald. And you were wrong when you told Mr. Andrews we don't have beef because we do. I know that envy you had for me and my family made you try to take my brother's life. You thought I didn't know, huh?"

The average person would have shown some level of fear when they had a gun close to them, but Gerald didn't appear to be fearful at all.

"You ain't gonna do nothin' with it. That ain't in you," Gerald said.

"See, that's where you're wrong. I..."

He suddenly jumped toward Lion. Prying me away was something Gerald hoped to accomplish, but Lion was going to do everything in his power to not let it happen. Within seconds, it happened. Somebody pulled the trigger, but I didn't know who. The boys continued fighting as if nothing had happened.

Mr. Smith and Mr. Andrews heard the shot, and they both rushed back into the lobby. I saw them both running toward us, but that didn't stop Gerald and Lion from continuing their fight.

"Lion, you good? I think you got hit!" Al yelled out as he ran from Mr. Smith's office.

The boys continued to fight as the adults both risked their lives to stop a fight that involved a gun. Punches were being thrown in every direction and both Mr. Andrews and Mr. Smith took a few of them. Through the chaos, Gerald was somehow able to fully pull me away from Lion.

"Put the gun down, son," Mr. Andrews said.

"No. If this is how he wants to handle stuff, this is how it's gonna be handled," Gerald told him.

I could see the fear on everyone's face. Mr. Andrews and Mr. Smith were terrified, but they tried their best to be brave. They tried to get Gerald to make a rational decision and put me down, but he wasn't having it. Without wasting time, I was forced to let go of several bullets.

Since we were all in very close proximity, I already had an idea of what that meant for Lion. Gerald wasn't done, though. As everyone, including Al, rushed in to take Gerald down, he pulled the trigger again, but thankfully I had no more bullets left to give.

"You didn't have to do that to him!"

The agony was evident in every one of Al's words.

"Y'all disrespected the wrong one! If this stupid gun would've had more bullets, you would've learned too," Gerald yelled out as he was wrestled to the ground.

"Mr. Andrews, please call the police and make a lockdown announcement. Now! I finally have him under control," Mr. Smith said as he took me away from Gerald. Mr. Smith tried to keep Al away, but he went to Lion's side.

"No! No! No! Quit playin', bro. You gotta get up." Al screamed with just the slightest hint of optimism.

"This is what people outside of our neighborhood expect you to do, and you did it. They want you to throw your life away. They want you to be negative statistics, and you have just given them exactly what they wanted. What is wrong with you?" Mr. Smith asked Gerald.

"Ain't nothin' wrong with me, and I ain't tryin' to hear none of that. Anybody who wants smoke and disrespects me, can get it. I don't care who it is," Gerald stupidly said to Mr. Smith.

The conversation continued as if nobody cared Lion was dying.

"Who cares about what he's saying. Lion needs help!" Al yelled.

Al's frustration was valid, and almost as soon as he made his request, the sounds of sirens filled the area.

"Attention teachers and students, we are currently under lockdown protocol. Under no circumstances is anyone to leave any classroom until further notice is given," Mr. Andrews announced.

Not wanting to be held responsible for his actions, the sirens caused Gerald to try and get away, but he couldn't because Mr. Smith continued to hold him down. Gerald would never admit it, but he had to feel something for what had transpired, even if it that feeling wasn't guilt.

"Okay, Lion, Gerald's on the ground and he doesn't have the gun, so you can go ahead and get up!" Al said.

Al spoke as if he believed Lion had a chance of survival. Humans sometimes let their feelings get in the way of logic and intellect. This entire situation was an example of that. Lion had a gun because his brother was fearful of their environment. Lion took me with him to school because he couldn't let go of the anger he felt could only be removed by getting revenge. And Gerald, well, for whatever reason, envied Lion. The monster known as jealousy would not leave him alone. Ultimately, Gerald and Lion both pretended to be friends only to carry out the plans they had in their minds to harm one another.

"Noooo! Bro, open your eyes! Get up," Al yelled.

He hoped his friend would respond, but he probably realized he wouldn't. Lion took his last breath, and like he normally was, Al was right by his side. Soon, he had to watch as Lion's body was taken out of the school. One of the officers who ended up coming into the school prepared to take me in for evidence, while another questioned Mr. Smith, Mr. Andrews, and Al about what happened. One of the questions Gerald would eventually have to ask himself would be, "Was it all worth it?"

Most of the time, when someone loses their life, the reason behind it is never really worth it. Throughout his brief life, Lion's mom always talked about the potential he had to be something great, and for the most part, he tried to live up to that. The thing about humans is that they are generally in the process of trying to be something; trying to be a good child, trying to be a good student, tying to be a good sibling, trying to be a good friend. This list goes on and on. Unfortunately, the emotions that controlled Lion's last actions turned him into something he didn't intend on becoming—a memory.

NARRATIVE 4: JOY & PAIN

*W*hen people think of gun owners, certain aspects generally come to mind. Violent, angry, bitter, depressed, hopeless, paranoid, militant, and lonely are just some of the words sometimes used to describe those who provide homes to those like me. However, none of the words fit Aashirya.

Aashirya was the type of person who always viewed the glass as being half-full, no matter what was going on. She always seemed capable of finding the silver lining in just about any situation. Many people said it was almost impossible to feel bad when she was around.

One of her many ways of spreading happiness was through her art.

"What ya got going, Aashirya?" her husband, West, asked.

"I'm just workin' on this painting, and I'm feeling pretty good about what I have so far."

"Yeah, I can see why. That elephant on there just makes me feel good. I don't understand why the sky is orange, though."

"The entire thing is about a certain feeling. The elephants

represent luck and wisdom, and the orange sky just brings a certain warmth."

"You know what? I think you're right. When I first saw it, I was wondering why it seemed like my IQ went up, and I felt all warm and fuzzy inside."

"That's funny, for real, but you know I always want to increase everyone's happiness," she said.

"I know, and that's one of the many things I love about you. There is something that always confused me, though."

"What's that?"

"I know you genuinely want people to feel better about themselves, and their purpose, but *that* seems to be contradictory to your goal. I think it's nothing but a distraction."

The distraction he was referring to—was me.

"Why do we always have to talk about this? You already know why she has to be here. I think there's beauty beyond the exterior of everything, including this gun. Plus, I just like to have her around. Believe it or not, she also inspires some of the things I do. I can't necessarily verbalize exactly why my creativity sometimes coincides with her being near me, but it does. We all have things that inspire us and a lot of times it goes beyond an explanation. It is what it is."

Whenever I was a part of the conversation, it had the potential to go sour very quickly. That particular day, West didn't have the energy to get into a heavy debate about me, so he just stopped talking and left his wife alone so she could continue working.

"I know you're tough, and I know you have a reputation, but you're beautiful to me. We work well together because we understand the roles we have to play for us both to be successful. Together, we are the perfect combination of pretty and petty. We are beauty, brilliance, and brawn. The things we create together....whew, they're always amazing! We are a great team! Do you hear me? We are great!"

For some reason, she always felt it was necessary to give me random pep talks. She acted as though I was a person who had feelings that could impact what I was supposed to do. Although it was cool she took the time to do it, I wish I had a way to tell her it was not needed.

I was designed and manufactured for a particular purpose and regardless of who I was around or what those people thought about me, they couldn't stop me. I wasn't impacted by the defects of human feelings, and that's why I was kept around. Regardless of what Aashirya said, I wasn't there because our roles complemented each other. She didn't keep me with her at all times because she saw some type of inner beauty. I am a machine, and inner beauty was something I didn't possess. What she actually saw in me was exactly what I was, something that would be able to fully commit to being there for her whenever she needed me to be.

She had never used me against anyone. I had only been used at shooting ranges, but Aashirya and I traveled there very often. She always traveled alone because she said she needed time to herself so she could clear her head and maintain her peace. It was quite ironic that she thought I brought her peace. It made no sense, but like many other humans, it was common for her to do things that didn't make sense.

"Mommy, when do you think you'll put your gun away?" This was a question Aashirya's daughter, Andrea, asked quite frequently.

"I'm not."

"But it scares me, and sometimes I think something bad may happen."

"Andrea, haven't I told you about being so afraid? This gun can't do anything unless someone makes her do something. Plus, what did I tell you about energy?"

"Ummm.....you said, the energy you put out is what comes back."

"That's right. Now, even though bad things may happen to good people and good things will happen for bad people, we all get a very large dose of whatever we put into the atmosphere."

"Mommy, what does at-most-fears mean?"

Aashirya chuckled.

"Atmosphere is basically the world around you. Do you understand?"

"Yes, I do!"

"Good. So, if you do good to the world around you, the world will do good to you. And this machine won't do anything bad to you because you're a good girl, right?"

"Yep, very good."

"I know you are. Now give your mama some sugar so I can get back to this painting."

"I love you, Mommy!"

"I love you, too, Drea-Baya."

Andrea giggled as she kissed her mother and left the room. The exchange of words and their expressions of love were sweet, but I thought Aashirya was harming her daughter by not telling her the full truth.

Yeah, she was young, and people tend to shelter their children, but she was truly doing her child a disservice because she was only telling her a simplified version of something more complex.

She told Andrea I wouldn't do anything bad to her because she was good. I honestly didn't care if she was good or bad because that would have nothing to do with me doing my job. If someone decided to use me, it wouldn't even be my decision whether or not I helped them. The person who controls me controls that decision. That's what Aashirya should have said.

Aashirya said she liked our relationship because we both played our respective roles, and my role was *not* to help her raise her child. As she said so often, I just needed to look pretty and have her back whenever she needed me to. That's exactly what I did.

Days would pass by, and there would be times when West and Andrea seemed completely oblivious of me being around. Other times, I was all the family talked about. Throughout it all, I pretty much continued to stay at home or go to the shooting range. It was a pretty mundane existence, and I kept hoping my life would eventually involve more than just repeating the same routine.

"Hey, babe. You've been working a lot lately. Is everything good?" West asked one day.

"Yeah, I'm good. I'm sorry I haven't been spending a lot of time with you and Andrea, but I have to get all of these paintings ready. My 'Joy & Pain' exhibit will be happening in a few weeks."

"For real? Man, time flies!"

"Yeah, it does. It seems like it was just yesterday I was begging people to take a look at my work, and now, I'll have an exhibit dedicated to my work."

"Hard work definitely pays off, and you're a great example of that. I still don't know why you gave the collection that name, though."

"Well, I just wanted to create art that would make people question their own perception of things. I want them to be able to see that the things that bring them joy can also be the things that bring pain. With that, they also need to see what brings them pain, can also be what starts their season of joy."

"You think very differently than I do. If I was doing these paintings, my stuff would be super simple."

"What do you mean?" Aashirya asked.

"Well, I'm sure you're gonna use all of these symbols of beauty and stuff that will make people really think. I just know my stuff wouldn't be like that."

"Okay, now I'm interested in knowing about one of your

concepts."

"I was hoping you'd say that. Alright, picture this: you see two guys in a fight. Now, one of those guys looks terrible. His face is all bloody and swollen. Babe, this dude looks really bad. Most of the people watching the fight are in shock. Some have their faces partially covered, while others are just looking sad. Then, you see a woman close by who has a huge smile on her face. Do you wanna know why she's smiling?"

"Why?"

"She's smiling because the dude getting beat up is her ex-boyfriend, and things didn't end well. When they broke up, he took all of her clothes and poured bleach on them. It was a very petty thing to do, but he was heartbroken, so he felt he did what he had to do. She was trying to be the bigger person and she didn't retaliate the way she wanted to, but she found great *joy* in seeing him in *pain*."

"Dang! Not only did you have a picture in mind, but you also even had their little backstory and everything! Boy, you are too much!"

"Yeah, I agree. Like I said, I'm sure my vision is a little bit different than what you plan on doing."

"Just a little bit."

"Don't worry. Even though you don't think like me, I'm sure your stuff will still be pretty good."

"Well, I thank you for giving me the boost of confidence I desperately needed."

"No problem, babe. If your husband can't help, I don't know who can."

The conversation was full of jokes and laughter. When they didn't talk about me, that was normally how things went. Honestly, there was no real reason for me to be there. The family didn't live in a neighborhood where their safety was ever threatened, and Aashirya wasn't in a relationship where she needed to protect herself. She didn't grow up in a family that even talked about guns. One day, she just decided to bring me home with her. She went through the proper procedures to make me a part of the family, but the explanations she provided on why she did it never made any sense to anyone other than herself. None of that mattered, though.

I was ever-present in her art room while she worked very diligently on creating all of the pieces she felt were necessary to tell the story she wanted to convey during her exhibit. As the time moved closer to the opening, her level of focus increased. The trips we normally took to the shooting range started to fade away. As that happened, I realized the conversations about me started to fade, as well. I didn't know what was going on.

I sat on her desk doing nothing while she painted pictures to show other people joy. Strangely enough, I didn't know how much joy she actually had. Sure, she was still happy, but it didn't seem like she was enjoying the time she was spending creating her work.

"You're not doing your job! What's wrong with you? How are we supposed to get this done when you're not playing your role? Get it together!" Aashirya yelled.

I was the only one in the room with her, but I wasn't sure if she was talking to me or herself.

"You sit there, and you don't do anything! You're supposed to inspire me and make things easier for me, but you're not doing that at all! What's the point? Why are you even here?"

Right then, I gained clarity, but I also became more confused. At that point, I knew she was talking to me, but I didn't know why. It seemed she was upset with herself for not being able to create the way she wanted to. Somehow, she tried to find a way to hand over the responsibility for her lack of creativity to me.

Artists, while sometimes sensitive about their work, always seemed to know the power of what they created. Since she was supposed to be aware of the importance of what she was working on, it was hard to believe she blamed me for her temporary inability to create something new. Doing that gave me an enormous amount of power that I was undeserving of. If she placed the blame on me for not creating, would she also give me credit if her mind released bundles of artistic greatness?

Although I was confused, I couldn't get upset. Ultimately, dumb moves, stupid thoughts, and the inability to accept responsibility were common traits among humans. My family told me about that before I met Aashirya, so how upset could I be when a person does what they are known to do?

She continued to express her anger towards me for a few days. For the most part, her family just allowed her to speak to me as if I was going to respond to what she was saying, but one day, Andrea decided the dinner table was the best place for her to ask her mother some questions.

"Mommy, why do you keep talking to that gun like it's a person?"

"What do you mean, baby? I don't do that."

"Uh-huh. You keep askin' it why it won't help you paint. Mommy, it can't help you paint 'cause it doesn't know how to do that. In school, we learned about what makes something alive. If it doesn't breathe, eat, or grow, it's not alive. That gun doesn't do any of that."

"Yeah, I know it can't actually help, but...see, it normally...never mind. You wouldn't understand because you're way too young."

Her daughter, while young, still knew it made no sense for Aashirya to hold me accountable for what she could or couldn't do. She wasn't ready to hear any of Andrea's words of wisdom, so she left the table and ran into the room where I was waiting for her. I expected her to start yelling at me again, but that didn't happen. Instead, she just stood by one of her unfinished pieces of art as she started to cry. Hearing her overcome with sadness was just as abnormal as her being angry.

After a few minutes, she sat down, but she still didn't say anything.

"Mommy?" Andrea yelled out from the other room.

"Yes," Andrea answered, trying to act as though she wasn't crying.

The pitter-patter of Andrea's little feet moved quickly toward her mother.

"Oh no! Mommy, what's wrong? Are you okay?"

"Yes, baby. I'm okay. I was just..."

"Were you crying? Mommy, were you crying?"

"Well, I just wasn't feeling too good."

"Was it 'cause of me? Were you crying 'cause of what I said while we were eating? I'm sorry, Mommy. I didn't want to be mean."

"It's okay. You weren't mean at all."

"Oh, I wasn't? Well, that's why I thought you were crying. Sometimes at school, some of the kids will say something mean, and then another kid will start crying. Our teacher told us we all have to be nice to each other, and I promised I would. So, if you weren't cryin' 'cause of what I said, what happened?"

"What you said didn't make me cry, but it made me think."

"Well, if thinkin' makes you cry, you should just stop it."

Aashirya let out a very hearty laugh.

"Child, you are hilarious. The way your mind works amazes me!"

"I know, Mommy. I amaze me, too!"

For a moment, Andrea made her mother forget how sad she was feeling. However, the laughter soon began to fade.

"I just don't know, baby."

"Huh? You don't know what, Mommy?"

"I don't know if I'm good enough. Do you know there will be a bunch of people looking at my work in a few days, and I don't know if they'll like my work?"

"Mommy, you make the best pictures! In my class, sometimes we don't stay in the lines when we color, but look at your pictures! You stayed in all of the lines. I think you're the best colorer ever, and if somebody doesn't like your stuff, then they have to be a stupey-dupey-poopie head!"

"Whoa, whoa, whoa, young lady! Where did you get that phrase from?"

Aashirya laughed.

"I dunno. I'm sorry. Am I in trouble?" Andrea asked.

"No, you're not in trouble, but it was surprising to hear you say that. Do you really like my work, though?"

"Yes, ma'am. And out of all of them, I like this one the most."

It was as though Andrea was consciously making an effort to share encouraging words with her mother.

"Is that your favorite, Drea?"

"Yes, ma'am."

"But most people will think this one is very sad. Why do you like it?"

"Well, that lady you painted is very pretty, and she looks like she's very….um…I dunno, she just looks calm."

"Do you see all of those other people around her?" Aashirya asked.

"Yep, there are a lot of people there, and they are all crying."

"Do you know why?"

"I think so, but I'm not sure," Andrea said to her mother.

"Okay, what do you think is going on?"

"I think everybody is there to see that pretty lady, but they are sad because...be-because...she passed away. Is that right, Mommy?"

"Yeah, baby, it is. How did you know?"

"Well, it's because you painted that," Andrea said as she pointed to a portion of the painting.

"So, what does that mean?" Aashirya asked.

"I think that's her soul, and if it is, that means she's no longer here."

"You are absolutely right, but if you know what's going on, why is this one your favorite?"

"Mommy, when Grandpa was sick, we were all around him because we all loved him. You told me he was hurting a lot, but when he...umm...when he had to go, you said he wasn't gonna be in any more pain. You know what else you said, Mommy?"

"What did I say?"

"You said the angels came and got his spirit so they could help him get to God. Do you remember that, Mommy?"

"Yeah, I remember, but I didn't think you would."

"Yep, and that's why I like this picture the most! I know the people are sad because the pretty lady is gone away, but it makes me smile because it looks like the angels are gonna come get her, and that makes me think of Grandpa! That's why I like it the most. You can't get any better than God, Mommy."

"That's right, Andrea. You can't get any better than God!"

"Mommy, can I ask you something?"

"Sure."

"Since you know you make the best pictures, you should feel good now, right?"

"Yes, you made me feel a lot better. Thank you."

"Nooooo problem! Now that you feel better, can I ask you somethin' else?"

"Go ahead."

"Are you sure I can ask? It's really, really, really, impro...impor...im..."

"Andrea, are you trying to say it's really important?"

"That's it!"

"Okay, what's so important?"

"I jus' wanna know...can...you let me have...ten cookies?"

"Girl, there is no way in the world I'm gonna let you eat that much junk. Do you think I want your little teeth to rot out of your mouth?"

"Don't worry about it. These are just my baby teeth, so

they're gonna fall out. One day, I'll get my adult-people teeth, and then I'll try not to eat a lot of cookies. Is that okay?"

"Well, how about I make a deal with you? Since you've been such a good girl, and you've made me feel better about my art, I'll let you get three cookies."

"Really? I like that because three is my favorite number!"

"It is? Why is that?"

"I like it 'cause it's like me, you, and Daddy. Three, three, I like three. It's my mommy, my daddy, and then there's me!"

"I like that song, Andrea. It's catchy!"

"Thank you! When I get bigger, maybe you will let me put my song on the innernets so everyone in the whole wide entire world can hear it."

"Innernets? Don't you mean the internet?"

"That's what I said, Mommy, the innernets!"

Aashirya laughed at her daughter's innocence.

"You're right, Andrea. Now, go ahead and get your cookies so I can get back to work. If Daddy tries to stop you, just let him know I said it was okay."

As her daughter left the room, Aashirya continued to laugh for a few minutes, almost forgetting to breathe. Her attitude had been improved just by having a conversation with her child. Young humans always seem to be able to bring joy into almost every situation, even when an older human is trying their best to be depressed. Perhaps children were too young to let their happiness be spoiled by things that didn't mean anything. To them, being able to get a few cookies was enough to forget the trivial things that make others feel bad.

"Okay, Aashirya, let's get to work. You cannot let that little girl down. You can't tell her how important it is for her not to give up if you're ready to stop painting. How hypocritical of a person would you be?"

She was hard on herself, but she needed to be. The work she needed to finish could not be completed if she didn't understand its importance. So, she focused on her work more than she had in quite some time, and it paid off because she soon announced to her family everything had been completed.

"Excuse me. Can I please have my husband and my daughter meet me in my studio?"

There was no response, so Aashirya felt the need to try again.

"Umm... excuse me! If the other residents of this house don't want to deal with an angry wife or an upset mother, I recommend getting in here as soon as possible!"

She waited a little while longer before West and Andrea finally entered the room, laughing very intensely.

"Is somebody gonna tell me what's so funny?"

"Yeah, babe, I'll tell you. Just...just give me a minute to calm down," West said as he tried to fight the laughter to further upset his wife.

"Well, I'm waiting," Aashirya replied.

"Mommy, you got so mad just because we didn't come in here. That's what Daddy said would happen," Andrea said.

"What do you mean?"

"When you first called us, I was gonna run in here, but Daddy said he wanted to play a joke on you."

"Andrea, how are you just gonna tell on me like that? I thought we were cooler than that," West said as he continued to giggle.

"Da-dy!" Andrea replied.

By the time Andrea and West stopped laughing, Aashirya started.

"I'm supposed to be mad at you two, so why in the world am I laughing so hard?"

"I guess our goofiness just spread to you," West replied.

"Mommy, now we're all goofy together! That's good, right?"

"Yeah, baby, I guess we're just one big goofy family."

The family continued to laugh, joke, and enjoy each other's

company as Aashirya finally got to explain to West and Andrea why she called them into the room.

"Y'all have seen me be happy, sad, and ready to give up on everything recently, but you stuck with me. Andrea, little girl, you don't know how much you have helped me out. And West, where would I be without you?"

"Stop it, babe. You must be trying to make us all cry. I meant...you might make my allergies flare up in my eyes, and then Drea may think I'm crying. If she thinks I'm crying, then she'll start, and then, you'll start. So, if you don't want tears falling from everyone's eyes, please stop with all of the mushy stuff."

"Yeah, Mom, stop with the mushy stuff 'cause when Daddy cries, he makes those ugly faces!"

"You're right, Drea, he does."

"I think y'all need to stop talking about me like I'm not even in the room. Plus, you can't call my face ugly. You know I'm sensitive."

"Oh, baby, you know I love your face, even when you're crying. My bad, I mean, even when your allergies are acting up. And speaking of sensitive, that reminds me of what I was talking about. So, I need both of you to take a look around and tell me what you see. Like Erykah Badu said, 'Keep in mind, I'm an artist, and I'm sensitive about my shhh—"

"Oooh, Mommy was about to say a bad word!" Andrea yelled out, interrupting Aashirya.

"Almost, but I'm glad you stopped me."

"No problem, Mommy. What did you want us to look at?"

"Drea, Mommy wants us to look at all of this beautiful new artwork."

For the next few minutes, it was almost completely quiet as the three of them enjoyed the fruits of Aashirya's labor. Then, West finally broke the silence.

"Aashirya, you're an incredible woman. The work you've

created is nothing short of amazing. I'm very proud of you. I know all of the gallery visitors will be in awe when they see this."

"Mommy, I knew you were the best colorer! The pictures are sooooo pretty!"

"Thanks for not letting me give up," Aashirya said to her family.

They spent the rest of the night talking about the art, the process of creating it, and how proud they all were. The conversation had nothing to do with me, but ironically, that made me think it had everything to do with me. Aashirya always said I inspired her to create, but as she created her most important work, she kept me hidden. It seemed as though my value to her had decreased, and my importance was fading away. I didn't know what caused the change, or if I would be able to do anything about it. I heard stories about my relatives being in environments where they were grossly underutilized, and it seemed like I was headed in that direction.

It would have been silly (and pointless) for me to be concerned about what was going to happen to me. It would have also made no sense for me to not only pretend I had human emotions, but to also get caught up in them. So, I did neither of those things. I accepted the possibility of a lackluster life and just sat dormant until Aashirya felt the urge to release me. I was prepared for the wait to be long and drawn out, but it ended up being nothing like that.

"Are you ready to go, pretty lady?" Aashirya asked.

I was sure she was speaking to Andrea, but after a few seconds, I found out we were the only ones in the room.

"We have a big day today. This is the day we've been waiting for. This is the day we've been working toward. This is what I've prayed for! Today, we finally get to open our exhibit."

The words were said right before she released me and just stared at looked at me. It was almost as though she was seeing me for the first time. Soon, I was being put back into one of Aashirya's purses. I remained there as we traveled to the gallery. The roads seemed quiet, and there didn't seem to be as many people moving about. With that being the case, I assumed it was pretty early in the day.

Once we reached our destination, Aashirya's conversation let me know my assumption was correct.

"Thank you so much for meeting me so early. I would have brought these paintings out here last night, but I had to make sure things were perfect," she said to someone.

"I completely understand. This is your exhibit, and you want things to be as great as you envisioned," a stranger told her.

"Exactly!"

"Well, since you're here, I take it everything has turned out the way you want it to be."

"Actually, yeah. After a lot of trying times, I'm very satisfied with how things have turned out. I'm familiar with some artists who have worked with you before, so I know you care about these exhibits as if they were your own. I just want to make sure all of these pieces end up in the correct order because there is a story that's being told."

They spoke for quite some time about the display order. It was something Aashirya was very passionate about, and the guy she spoke to seemed to care about her artwork as much as she did. This helped relieve some of the anxiety she had about the opening. Surprisingly, after she released the art to the gallery, we ended up going to the shooting range. It had been a while since we had gone, and it was a bit perplexing why she decided to go, especially at that time.

"Hey, Aashirya. It's been a while, but it's good to see you. How have you been?" someone asked when we got there.

"Yeah, it's been a while, but life is good! I didn't even plan on coming out here today, but I needed to release some energy before my exhibit opening later on this evening."

I didn't recognize the person's voice, but by the tone of the conversation, I knew they had interacted before.

"That's good to hear. I...wait...did you say you have some type of exhibit opening today?"

"Yeah, my 'Joy & Pain' art exhibit is opening. I kinda can't believe it, but God is good, and I've been blessed. I've put in a lot of work, but again, I've been incredibly blessed."

"Can I go, or is it one of those fancy things that you have to get a special invitation for?"

"Oh no, no, no. It's a special event, at least to me, but there's nothing fancy about it. Don't get me wrong, it has been planned very well, and it will be a beautiful event, but I wouldn't call it fancy. It's open for all who want to attend, so I would love for you to swing by if you have some time."

"Cool! What time is it?"

"Doors will open around seven, and the event should end around ten."

"Alright, I'll see you there. As for now, go enjoy target practice. You haven't been here in a little while, so don't be surprised if you're a little rusty."

"You may be right," she said.

They had their moment, enjoyed their little talk, and then we went to work. It felt good to get out of the confines of Aashirya's purse. When she equipped me with a fresh set of bullets, I felt alive again. Well, I felt as alive as a machine could possibly feel.

"Here we go," Aashirya said as she pointed me at the target.

Her hands shook a little when she aimed like I made her nervous for some reason. Before she took a single shot, she put me down on the stand that was normally the resting place for the headphones the people wore while they were shooting.

"What is wrong with you? Why are you acting like this?" she asked.

I didn't know what she was blaming me for.

"Does she scare you now, Aashirya? Does she make you nervous? Do you still even need her?"

The additional questions made me realize she wasn't blaming me for anything, but for some reason, she was questioning our relationship—again. She was making things too complicated. If she didn't think I was good for her anymore, then all she had to do was let me go.

"Nah, we're good. Why am I tripping, though? Where is all of this coming from?"

She questioned herself some more as she picked me back up. Her hands were more steady, but the confidence she normally had when I was around was almost completely absent. She aimed and shot at the target, but we were nowhere close to where we needed to be. Very few of the bullets even made contact.

"Wow, that was terrible! Is this your first time here?" another strange voice asked.

"First time? Absolutely not!"

"I wasn't trying to offend you or anything like that, but unlike you, I'm just a straight shooter. Get it?"

He laughed at Aashirya's expense, and her grip on me tightened, and her fingers twitched a bit. His comments caused anger to set in, and that's not good.

"Thank you for your criticism. Now, I'd appreciate it if you just left me alone," she said as her volume increased.

"Uh-oh. Someone's getting a little riled up. Does the little woman need help with her technique? Is the gun too heavy for you? Do you need me to teach you how you're *supposed* to shoot?"

"Sir, please...just stop bothering me. And stop being so condescending! Don't let a few missed shots make you think you know me and what I'm capable of! I advise you to just leave me alone.

He didn't listen. Not only did he keep talking, but he also

decided to move closer to her.

"C'mon. Let me help you out!"

Those words were enough to push her beyond her limit. Out of nowhere, I was being used to give the stranger a good 'pop' in the face. When he fell to the ground, I was staring right into his eyes.

"Do you wanna help me, now? Huh? Do you? Where are all of the clever remarks, now?"

Aashirya waited for a few seconds, but he had nothing to say. She could have claimed her victory and walked away, but vengeance crept inside of her, and it clouded her judgment. She had every right to be upset, but I doubt she even knew why he had the effect on her that he did.

She moved me to the guy's temple. His fear became evident as sweat began to fall down his face, even though he said things to conceal that fear.

"We both know you're not going to do whatever you're thinking about doing. So, just get yourself together and leave before I stop being nice."

His ignorance was evident from the first word he uttered to Aashirya, but his level of stupidity would pale in comparison to hers if she risked everything she had going for her to show him how tough she could be. I normally didn't care about what people did because in the end, it didn't impact me. This was different, though.

If she lost her stream of consciousness for a second, it could ruin her entire life.

"Hey, what's going on here?" someone asked.

Aashirya didn't say anything. Neither she, nor the person I was aimed at, moved.

"Do something or move! This is the last time I'm going to tell you before I stop cooperating," the condescending man said.

From my perspective, he was in no position to make demands, but he felt differently about his options than I did.

"Get up! I'm not going to mess up my life for you," Aashirya told him.

He did as he was told, but not without letting go of another angering combination of words as he scrambled to his feet.

"Yeah, that's what I thought! You females are all bark and no bite! You better be glad I didn't feel like dealing with you today."

She didn't say anything to him, but the way her fingers were still twitching, I knew she wanted to.

"What is going on?" the other person asked again as he finally made it over to where we were.

"Nothing...at least nothing you need to worry about. The little lady just got a little sensitive about her lack of shooting ability. I was offering a helping hand, but I guess she's not open to help."

Aashirya had enough.

"Look, as long as I've been coming here, there have never been any problems! Today, this...this...hold on, let me calm down. I'm so mad right now I can't even get my words together."

Aashirya took a few deep breaths before she continued to speak.

"It seems like his purpose was to get me all riled up. I tried to ignore him, I really did, but..."

That's when the inconsistency of human emotions arose once again. Aashirya's angry tone vacated and was quickly replaced by that of a woman who sought validation. Her voice trembled as she tried to continue explaining what had happened.

Once the tears started to fall, speaking became an impossible task, so she stopped trying.

"I always thought women were out of place here, but I tried not to say anything. Then, when something like this happens, I find out how right I am."

"Sir, you've made your point. Please, could you go back to

your area?"

"Yeah, I'll go, but I ain't happy. This place ain't for the thin-skinned, and people with guns shouldn't be so emotional. That's not good at all."

Although most of the guy's words up to that point had been pointless, I agreed with his parting message. Emotional gun holders could easily create dangerous environments. And this wasn't the first time Aashirya's attitude changed at the drop of a dime while I was around. That's when it hit me. Maybe our connection had run its course. Maybe we needed to peacefully part ways.

"I'm sorry about all of that. Are you okay?" the stranger asked.

"Yeah, I'm good. I don't even know what happened, but I'm sorry for making a scene."

"Ma'am, I have six siblings. What went on here is not what I would call making a scene. Now, having a house full of hungry people over for Thanksgiving when you find out Mama's almost out of her famous Mac-n-Cheese, that's a scene!

"I could imagine it would be."

The person's words were calming enough to help Aashirya stop crying.

"Thank you for your time, but I think I need to go home. I can't allow him to completely ruin my energy before tonight's event."

"Oh, yeah! You have some kind of art exhibit opening or something, right?"

"Exactly! I can't let all of everyone's hard work go to waste. I told one of your co-workers about it and I hope you all can get everyone to come out."

"Yeah, after you told the manager, we started to discuss it. I'm sure you'll see some of us there. I don't know if you'll see me, though. Whenever I've seen art, it's been stuff I didn't understand. One time, I was out with my wife, and she wanted me to get some culture, so we went to this gallery-thing downtown. No lie, there was this one piece that was just a squiggly line. I looked at the little tag that had the artist's description, and it said the painting was a 'representation of the road a person must travel on their life's individual journey.' I was so confused that I had to ask my wife if I had missed some of the art or something. In my mind, there was no way in the world all of those descriptive words were talking about that so-called painting. I kid you not, I asked my wife no less than five times, if I was looking at the right thing. I know I'm rambling, but I said all of that to say I don't have the greatest relationship with art because I don't like how it pretends to be more than it is."

As an artist, I didn't think Aashirya would appreciate the person's comments, but I didn't have the ability to recognize the importance of human commonalities. This is why my assumption, in this particular case, was incorrect.

"I think, in some form or another, we all have a bit of an estranged relationship with art. Everything I am able to create is like birthing a new child. I don't know if you have any kids, but let me tell you something. When you have a child, they instantly become one of the most beautiful people you've ever seen in your life. At the same time, the more you deal with them, the more they will find a way to get on your nerves and make you question when and where things went wrong. That's art in a nutshell. Like kids, or people in general, art can be simple, and it can be complicated. No matter how it looks, there is beauty in that diversity. We may not always understand it at first, but I feel it is our job to take what is given and learn about it. So, if all of that talking wasn't enough to convince you to come out to the exhibit, I don't know what will."

The dialogue about art didn't go in the direction I thought it would, but it seemed both of the contributors benefited from it. The employee seemed like he would consider visiting the exhibit, and Aashirya was no longer angry.

"Well, I hope to see you and the rest of the crew at the gallery. Oh, and I really appreciate you taking the time to speak with me instead of just kicking me out. I think I would have tried to tear some stuff up if that would have happened."

"Let me formally thank you for not destroying where I work because I need some kind of way to get money to take care of the bills I have."

"You're very welcome," she replied.

They shared a brief laugh before we made our way to the car. She placed me back in my case and then back into her purse. I thought we would immediately begin to move, but for some reason, we didn't. Before she even turned on the car, she called West. I could hear her put the call on speaker and place the phone on the dashboard. There was no greeting. She just jumped right into the conversation.

"How strong do I have to be? Why am I still having to deal with stuff on the day of my event?"

"Babe, I don't understand what you're talking about. What's going on?" he asked.

Aashirya let her husband know everything she just finished dealing with. The more she talked, the more her voice started to fade out. I could only assume she had once again started to cry, but that didn't make any sense because only a few minutes earlier, she seemed to be okay.

"Do I need to come up there? You know I got you, and if you need me to handle somebody, I will!"

I never heard West speak like that before, but humans tend to get a bit more aggressive than they normally are when a loved one has been threatened, or is in danger.

"No, I'm okay. I don't even know why I'm crying, or why I called. I honestly was feeling better before I got in the car, then...I don't even know what happened. What is wrong with me?"

"Babe, nothing's wrong with you. You just had to deal with a lot of stupidity. I know you take on a lot, and to your family, you're a superwoman, but you're only human. The stuff you're able to handle on your worst day is more than I could even think of dealing with on my best day."

For a while, she said nothing. I didn't know if the conversation had ended or if Aashirya just hadn't heard what her husband said.

"Are you there?" West asked.

She inhaled and exhaled very deeply multiple times before responding.

"I'm good. I'm sorry about that."

"Sorry for what? Babe, you don't have to be a superhero. It's okay to deal with your emotions. We all have to deal with them at some point, and it's okay to ask for help. Lord knows I need to. I'm here for you, forever and always. Please remember that."

"I know. Thank you," she said.

"No problem. Now, if you don't mind, I'd like to start preparing for this evening. I don't know if you realized it or not, but today is the first day of my beautiful wife's art exhibit."

"Oh, really? Do you think she's ready?" Aashirya asked as if they weren't speaking about her.

"Ma'am, you obviously don't know my wife. Aashirya is more than ready because she was born for this. She expresses herself with canvases, paints, and brushes. You know what?"

"What?"

"She is *very* good at expressing herself, and I'm proud to be her husband."

Silence once again took over the conversation for a few seconds.

"You are so corny, but I love you so much," Aashirya said as they both started laughing.

"I love you and your corniness too," West replied.

"I needed that. Now, can I ask a favor?"

"Yeah, what's up?"

"Will you please wear that navy blue suit tonight? I like the way that looks on you."

"So, you don't want me to wear that lime green shirt I got when we went to Jamaica?"

"Uhh...no! Absolutely not!"

"I think you just don't want me to outshine you. I was gonna wear that, my big clunky fake necklaces, and I was gonna top it all off with my Jheri Curl wig," he joked.

"Oh, no, no, no. You will not ever be going anywhere with me wearing that stuff. No, sir!"

"You know I wouldn't do that to you, especially on a day as important as this one. Don't worry, babe. I'll look classy in that suit. I'll also make sure our daughter is on point!"

"Cool! Please, whatever you do, don't try to do her hair! I'll take care of it when I get home."

"I'm glad you said that because I was scared to death!"

They shared some more laughs before the conversation ended. That conversation with her husband helped release the feelings of anxiety and anger she had. On the way home, Aashirya loudly sang every song that played on the radio. It was a very quick turnaround from how she was feeling a few minutes before.

We soon made it back to the family's home.

"Okay, let's go and get ready," she said as she took me out of the car and into the house.

"Mommy, Mommy! Guess what?"

Andrea, and her abundance of energy, greeted her mother almost as soon as she made it inside.

"What? What has you so excited?"

"Well, today, we're all gonna dress real fancy, and all of the people are gonna get to see your pretty paintings and stuff! They're gonna try to buy them for one billion, trillion, gazillion dollars. And then, I'm gonna tell them they can't buy them because they're my mom's pictures, and then they're all gonna be sad."

"I love my art, but if somebody offers a billion, trillion, gazillion dollars, we may have to sell it. That money would be awesome!"

"If they do, does that mean I can get some candy and a pet hipperotimus?"

"Do you mean a hippopotamus?"

"Yep, that's what I meant!"

"Well, I don't think we'll be able to get one of those, but the candy is definitely something we can look into."

"Yaaaaayyy! I really like candy, Mom! And I really like pink candy. It's the best!"

"Okay, I'll remember that. Now, we need to start getting you ready. Where's your father?"

"Daddy's in the room. He said my dress had too many wrinkles in it, so he had to iron it so we will look good for your big night!"

"That sure is sweet of him. Have you already taken your bath?"

"Yes, and I used my pretty soap, too. Daddy made me put on these pajamas until he finished with my dress."

"Oooh! I knew I smelled something amazing, and thank you for explaining why you had those pajamas on. Well, pretty girl, please go watch your shows until we're ready to get you dressed."

She did as she was told, and Aashirya started moving around her home.

"Hey, babe! Welcome home," West said as Aashirya reached what had to be her room.

"Thank you. It's good to be here. I appreciate you talking to me on the phone. I needed that."

"Of course. You know I've got your back!"

"Yeah, I do."

"I know you could literally sit here and talk about all of my awesome attributes all day, but we need to get ready. I don't want you to be late," West said.

"You're right! Hey, could you put this over there for me?" she asked as she handed over the purse I was stored in.

"This seems kinda heavy. What do you have in here?"

"The usual...you know."

"Does that mean..."

"Yes, that means I have my gun in there."

"You're gonna leave it here, though, right?"

"You know that's not gonna happen. She goes where I go."

"But there's no point. We're gonna be in an art gallery. We both know there won't be a need for it."

"That may be true, but she's one of my most important accessories. Babe, I love you, but there's no need of wasting your breath. You already know nothing you say will change my mind, so let's just stop it."

"Yeah, whatever!"

I had caused many heated debates between the couple, but this one seemed different. Many times after a disagreement, the couple would reach a compromise and apologize, but that didn't happen. West didn't want me to be a part of their special night, and Aashirya didn't care.

I heard West leave the room without saying another word. They should have wanted to keep each other happy since it was such a big night, but they didn't seem to be thinking about that. The family got dressed, ate a light dinner, and drove to the gallery, almost in silence.

"Mommy, doesn't Daddy look good? And Daddy, isn't Mommy pretty?" Andrea asked.

"Yeah," they both said angrily.

"You don't sound so happy. And I don't know why you're not happy 'cause Mom is showing her pictures and all of the people are gonna love it, love it, love it! Right, Mommy? Right, Daddy?"

I'm sure they still didn't want to say anything, but Andrea's positive energy forced them to laugh.

"Your child is a mess," Aashirya said.

"I'm not just his child, Mommy. I'm your child, I'm Daddy's child, and I'm God's child, too!"

"She has a point, and seeing everyone laugh makes me think I may have gone overboard earlier. I apologize, babe. I just didn't want..."

"You don't have to finish that sentence. I understood where you were coming from. I accept your apology, and I apologize, too."

"Mommy, Daddy, guess what?"

"What's on your mind, Andrea?"

"Ummm... I muhpolonize!"

They continued to laugh as their young daughter tried to pronounce a word she probably didn't understand the meaning of.

"Why are you apologizing, Drea?" West asked.

"I dunno! You were doing it, so I thought I was supposed to."

"I appreciate it, but you just save that apology until you've done something wrong, okay?"

"Yes, ma'am, but I don't wanna do nothin' wrong, " Andrea said very genuinely.

"We know you don't because you're a good girl," West added.

"Yep, she sure is! Our baby isn't an angel, but she is pretty close," Aashirya replied as their daughter began to hum a random song.

The impact a few words from Andrea had on Aashirya and West was astonishing. What seemed like a devastating exchange of words had quickly turned into nothing more than an afterthought, and the stubbornness of the adults seemed to be rendered powerless against the innocence of a child. The way they felt didn't matter to me, but for the sake of their child and the exhibit, it was probably best they were no longer upset with each other.

"Ladies, we're here," West said as the vehicle stopped.

Almost as soon as West made the announcement, Aashirya's mood changed again.

"I don't know... I thought..." Aashirya couldn't complete a sentence.

"Whatever negative thoughts you have running through your head, make them leave. This is a huge moment for you, but you're ready for it. Don't allow doubt to deny us and your fans the opportunity to see what you've been working so hard on."

She didn't respond, but once again, she seemed to be put at ease by her husband's words. Soon, everyone was getting out of the car, and we all relocated to where the exhibit was being held.

"Aashirya, girl, I'm so glad you finally made it. I've been telling everyone how awesome this is going to be and we almost started a bet on how fashionably late you were going to be. The world has no idea what a treat they're in for, and if I were you, I would have made them wait. I would have let my inner diva out tonight," someone said as the family made it where they needed to be.

"West, Andrea, this peppy lady is highly respected in the art world. She is someone I look up to and a brilliant artist herself. This is Khadijah. Actually, she is the reason this whole thing is even happening. And Khadijah, I appreciate the kind words, but I'm just a regular artist," Aashirya said.

"On the contrary, you're anything but regular! I'm so happy everyone will get to see that, but you already know how I feel about your work. I'm not gonna talk you and your family's ears off by rambling about how great you are."

"I agree with you, her work is amazing, and it's good to see people embrace it. It's really nice meeting you, Khadijah, and I appreciate you helping to get this exhibit open," West said.

They all exchanged pleasantries, and that positivity continued throughout the night. Everyone who met Aashirya told her how beautiful the collection was, and each word fueled the pride of her family. Things were going well for everyone, but that quickly changed.

"Andrea, hand me my purse," Aashirya said to her daughter.

Perhaps the excitement of the exhibit made both her and West forget I was there.

"Mommy, your bag is heavy," Andrea said as she picked up the purse that had been sitting nearby for most of the night.

"You're a big girl. I know you can handle it."

I could feel Andrea struggling to move with each step she took, but she didn't want to disobey her mother. As she moved closer, the weight just became too much for her to handle. She tried her best, but she ended up dropping the purse, which caused the magnetic buttons to unfasten, which caused the purse to open. That made me fall out and slide on the floor.

The noise I made when I hit the ground made everyone turn around and look at me as if they had never seen a gun before. I landed very near Andrea, and this frightened West and Aashirya.

"Don't worry, Mom, I'll bring it to you."

"Andrea, no! Please, leave it there! We'll get it!" Aashirya yelled.

Everyone gasped in fear as both of Andrea's parents ran toward me.

"I didn't mean to drop your purse and make that fall out, but don't worry. I can still get it."

"It's okay, baby. Please, be a good girl, and just leave it where it is. Mommy or Daddy will get it, just don't touch it!"

Andrea heard what her mother said to her, but she was so used to trying to help her parents out that she picked me up anyway. Her little hands had a difficult time holding onto me. She trembled as she tried to figure out how I was supposed to be held. As soon as one of her tiny fingers touched the trigger, I knew we were headed towards an unwanted outcome.

"Noooo!" West yelled.

I'm pretty sure Aashirya thought my safety was on, but she quickly found out it wasn't. Almost immediately after West yelled out, Andrea accidentally pulled the trigger a few more times as she tried to hold me. Each shot rang out and soon, the room had pretty much been cleared out. Surprisingly, there were no cops or security in attendance, which meant the family was temporarily left to handle things by themselves.

Understandably, the shots scared Andrea, which caused me to be dropped again. West and Aashirya continued to move toward their daughter until they both reached her, put my safety on, and placed me back into Aashirya's purse. There was no time to relax, though. They hugged Andrea, then Aashirya suddenly let out an ear-piercing scream.

"No, no, no! What happened? Are you okay, Andrea?"

"Yes, but I didn't mean to make it go off. The purse was heavy, and I couldn't hold it, and then..."

"None of that even matters. I just need to know where you were hit. Where were you hit?"

"I'm okay, Mommy. Nothin' happened."

"Where is all of the blood coming from, then?" Aashirya asked.

"I think...I...it has to be from..."

"West! West, babe, are you..."

"I got hit... I don't know if..."

West's inability to complete a thought confirmed he was the one who had been hit by at least one of my bullets.

"You told me not to bring it! Why didn't I listen? Why did I bring it? What was I thinking?"

"Is Drea..."

"I'm okay, Daddy, but you're bleeding really, really bad! Are you hurt?"

"No worries...I..."

He stopped talking very abruptly, and Aashirya let out another scream.

"You're not about to leave! We have too much living to do! You have to see Drea go to college. You have to..."

"Mommy, Daddy's not talking."

"I know, baby."

Her voice shook, and she struggled more with every word she tried to say.

"When people go to sleep, their body goes up and down so they can get air, but Daddy's body is not goin' up and down. So, how is he gonna get his air?"

"I don't know, baby. Daddy may not need..."

Aashirya couldn't properly explain the possibility of her husband's death to their daughter. So, she stopped trying. She just cried as she sat on the ground, holding her husband's hand.

Soon, the voices of who sounded like police officers and EMTs filled the room. I could hear everyone surrounding the family. Some tried to gather information from Aashirya, while others tried to see if anything could be done to help West.

"Ma'am, I'm sorry, but.."

One of the people tried to speak, but Aashirya stopped them. She already knew what they were trying to say, but she didn't want them to be the ones to tell Andrea.

"Please just let me explain things to my daughter. Is that okay?"

"Yes, ma'am."

Aashirya stood up and escorted her daughter a few steps away from West.

"Baby, do you remember how you said that painting at home was your favorite because it reminded you of Grandpa."

"Yep. Grandpa was sick, and then he got to go be with God in heaven, just like the pretty lady on your painting."

"That's right. Well...now Daddy has gone to be with him."

"No! You're wrong! Daddy's right there, and he wouldn't leave me! He's not gone to heaven, so why are you sayin' that?"

Andrea's voice was stronger than it had ever been before. Although she was starting to cry, she still was able to vocalize a certain level of defiance. At the same time, she was trying to convince herself that her mother was making a terrible mistake.

"I wish I was wrong, but some of those bullets hit your father, and it hurt him really bad."

"But why don't those people just fix him? They do it on TV."

"They can't, baby. It's too late."

Andrea took a deep breath.

"Mommy?"

"Yes."

"So, does that mean when I dropped your purse, and when I couldn't hold that gun, I made those bullets go to Daddy?"

Aashirya didn't want to place the blame for West's death on her daughter because she didn't deserve that.

"No, Drea, this didn't happen because of you. This happened because Mommy made a very, very, very dumb decision. This is my fault. This is 100 percent my fault."

As the two talked, their emotions took over. For a while, both of their words were incomprehensible. The mother and daughter just cried together, and both of them, to some extent, knew their lives would never be the same. Then, Aashirya was able to get herself together, as she started to speak very loudly.

"You did this! You ruined my family! I hate you!" Aashirya yelled.

Some of the remaining onlookers may have been confused as to who she was directing her anger toward, but I knew it was me. Aashirya was displaying typical human behavior. It was true my presence had a great impact on what transpired, but Aashirya was trying to convince herself that I was the only one at fault.

There was a multitude of reasons West was so against me

going with them that night, but she didn't allow herself to understand that. There was a reason most gun owners didn't put their guns in purses or bags and then make a young child carry that bag in a room full of people. Aashirya didn't think about that.

"Mom, can I ask you somethin'?"

"Go ahead."

"You and Daddy told me to save my muhpology 'til I did something wrong. I just did something really wrong, and if I use it now, will Daddy come back?"

I could hear Aashirya's heartbreak as she stayed around her husband and heard her daughter try to find a way to "make him okay." She had to continue to explain to Andrea her father was gone, and no matter what either of them did, he wasn't coming back.

It turned out, that the title of her exhibit, "Joy & Pain," was manifested in her life. The art that hung on the walls of the gallery represented her hard work and dedication to her craft. That hard work allowed her to create, and those creations brought her a myriad of joy. Before those last few minutes, that night had been one of the most joyous nights she had ever experienced. Yet, the night ended with her dealing with a pain far greater than anything she probably ever could have imagined.

Andrea, well, she experienced something very different. Although she was very young, that night taught her how quickly a life could be taken away. She also learned that a person with the best intentions could be thrown into a situation that could negatively impact them forever. The few years she had lived would be the only ones she would ever get to spend with her father, and she had to find a way to hold onto all of the happy memories she had of him. In contrast, she would also be forced to remember that even though it was a horrendous accident, she was the one responsible for killing her father.

The youngest member of the family continued to cry as her

mother, who was also still in pain, tried to console her. Suddenly, Aashirya moved away from her daughter slightly as she stared to yell.

"Never again! I'm done with you! You will never hurt anyone I care about ever again!"

The people who could hear her probably thought she was talking about West. They may have thought he was dead because he somehow made a habit of hurting his family and Aashirya finally had enough of it, but that wasn't the truth. She wasn't talking to West, she was once again taking her frustration out on me.

Regardless of if Aashirya ended up being charged with anything by the police or not, wouldn't change what happened, nor would it have changed who was responsible for it all. My job wasn't to kill West. In fact, a gun's job is never actually to kill anyone. Our job is simply to shoot. Death is sometimes a byproduct of us doing our job. The culpability of what happens, however, rests upon the shoulders of the people who choose to put us to work in the first place.

If Aashirya used even the smallest bit of logic, perhaps she would have realized that instead of being upset with a machine, she should have been upset with herself. As a mother, her main responsibilities were to teach and protect her child. As a wife, she was supposed to work with her husband to make the best possible decisions for their family. Instead, she found out her decision to invite me to the exhibit, even though her husband asked her not to, was a terrible one. The choice she made caused her to fail miserably as a mother and as a wife.

Being around people has led me to believe they should know there is power in the words they speak and write, and in the energy they choose to attach to themselves and release to others. If Aashirya didn't understand before that night, she learned a valuable lesson. Her prophetic words of "Joy & Pain" were fulfilled in front of her daughter at the expense of her husband's life. No matter how hard she tried to run from the truth, eventually, she would have to learn that she only had herself to blame. How would she deal with that realization? I don't know, nor do I care.

The truth of the matter was, I enjoyed every single time I got to go to work, regardless of how the humans around me may feel about it. Today, Aashirya unexpectedly allowed me to share the spotlight with her during her event. The paintings she put so much work into surely left an impression on all who saw them, and even though my work might have painted a different picture of the evening, I was sure it left an impression, as well.

I couldn't have asked to be partnered with a better human. I was with someone who helped me get into places where I didn't belong and hadn't been invited. She allowed me to see the type of people many of my relatives will never get to, and regardless of what others may think of me, Aashirya showed me how important I was to her. Sure, she may have yelled at me from time to time, but she is just a human. Humans are known to be unstable creatures. Her actions toward me, however, would always speak to me much louder than her words ever would.

After today, we might go a little while without speaking or seeing each other, if we ever do. That is to be expected. If she has a choice, she might even try and convince herself that she should distance herself from me. As if she needed a reminder, I was also sure her daughter would bring up the incident every now and again. I doubted any of that would matter because even if we never worked together again, Aashirya knew what a great team we made. If possible, I believe it will only be a matter of time before she finds a reason to put me (or one of my relatives) to work. After all, the beauty of the numerous amounts of work we made together had to outshine the ugliness of our one little incident, right?

NARRATIVE 5: SEEKING A PEACE IN A STORM OF CHAOS

*I*t always seems like humans are searching for something. They go to school to find out what they want to do with their lives. They go to parties and clubs, not only because they are searching for a good time, but also for companionship (in some form). When someone grows up in an environment filled with chaos, the thing they are searching for is peace. This is evident with Noah, a person I was introduced to quite some time ago.

"You're not even worth the breath I'm wasting right now, Noah. You're beyond useless!"

Believe it or not, those hate-filled words were spewed from the mouth of Noah's wife, Jillian. The two of them had been together since they were in high school. On many occasions, they have said their relationship was once good, but it got to a point where it plateaued. So, all it could do was go downhill.

My knowledge of Noah didn't start with a direct connection to Noah. In fact, I was part of the family's gun collection. There were several of us, and we varied in age and size. Some were just inactive showpieces. Others, such as myself, were in the normal rotation and were used frequently. I was one of the family's favorites. It was common for either of Noah's parents to carry me with them as they completed their daily tasks. One day, when Noah was about sixteen, he started to ask questions about us.

"I've seen these guns my entire life. Don't you think it's about time you let me have one?"

Noah's question came out of nowhere.

"Why would you even ask that? You've never shown any interest in them before," his mother said.

"Well, you and Dad always talk about them like they're the greatest things ever. So, I just want to see what all the fuss is about."

"Don't lie to your mama. What's really going on?" his dad asked.

Noah exhaled very deeply.

"I'm just tired."

"You're sixteen. What could you possibly be tired of?" his mom wondered.

"I'm just tired of being me. I don't like having all of the girls look past me 'cause they don't think I'm cool enough."

"And how do you think a gun is gonna help with that?"

"I don't know, Mom. Maybe it'll make me more confident or something."

"Honey, guns don't bring confidence. A lot of scared little boys and girls think a gun will make them feel different than they normally do, but all it will do is cause them to make irrational decisions because of their insecurities."

"So, why do y'all have them?"

"It's not for confidence, that's for sure. Noah, I don't know if you've noticed, but I don't have any problems with my self-esteem. I love everything about me, from the top of my head to the bottom of the bunion on my pinky toe," his Dad said.

"C'mon, Dad, cut it out. That's gross," Noah said as they all started to laugh.

"It's gross, but it's true. We don't have these guns because of anything we lack, we have them because they help protect our home, and we grew up with them. Plus, some of them are just pretty cool to look at," his father continued.

"Yeah, they are cool to look at. And I hear what you're saying about that other stuff, but I still think having one can help me," Noah said.

"Noah, you're a smart and ambitious kid. We know you can do great things in this world, guns or not. With all of that being said, your father and I will talk about it some more. If we feel you can handle it, then we'll move forward from there. How's that?"

"Okay, that'll work," Noah told them.

Noah's parents had the conversation, just as his mom promised. They concluded it would have been irresponsible not to teach their child about the weapons they had in their home. They said it would be best that he learned from the people who knew what they were doing, instead of him improperly trying to teach himself.

One day, he was asked to select one of the guns to learn with. That's when Noah and I were officially introduced.

"That's the one," he said joyfully.

Those words let his family know I had been chosen. Out of all of the guns in the collection, I was probably in the worst shape. I was all scratched up, and I had a terrible amount of wear and tear. I was already being used constantly, and I guess that made Noah feel comfortable with me.

Over the next few months, Noah's family made sure he was okay being around me. The family had a large amount of land on their Georgia property, and as soon as Noah came home from school and finished his homework, we went outside for target practice. This became our routine. Although it was good for me to do more than rest in a showcase or just hang around with his parents, I thought it was abnormal for a person to spend more time with me than they did with other humans.

As the days continued to pass, I noticed a change in Noah's behavior. All of a sudden, he didn't seem to be as shy and quiet. Nobody ever said anything, but everyone knew being around me had changed who he was.

"Finally! I can't believe it," Noah yelled one day when he got home from school.

For a minute or so, the only sound that could be heard was the echo of Noah's words. Then, his father finally came out of hiding.

"Noah, what are you yellin' about?"

"Dad, guess what happened to me today."

"What?"

"I finally had the nerve to ask Jillian out."

"Is that the little girl you've been going on and on about?"

"I wouldn't say that, but yeah, it's the same girl."

Noah's father, Barry, paused briefly before he continued to speak to Noah.

"I'm proud of you, son, but I'd like to ask you something. If you've been scared to ask her out all this time, what changed?"

"I don't know why, but I just told myself to quit being scared because the worst she could do was tell me no."

That day could be seen as a turning point for the rest of Noah's life. As the years moved by, Noah's relationship with Jillian grew. Coincidently, as their relationship changed, so did ours. When things with them were good, my existence was barely acknowledged. When the couple experienced a rough patch, Noah and I had many more interactions. I was never used to make threats toward anyone, but Noah did use me as a stress reliever. If I wasn't being cleaned or stared at, Noah and I were having some sort of target practice in the yard.

"Is this how it's supposed to be?" Noah asked himself as he shot at random items in the yard.

Although Noah's confidence had grown over the years, his connection with Jillian stunted his development. Before their relationship started, his parents said he was a kid full of ambition and dreams. After they started dating, he lost interest in almost everything and everybody outside of me and her. He also started to have a very negative attitude, became easy to anger, and he had become incredibly disrespectful towards his parents. On his twentieth birthday, his family let him know they didn't like who he had become.

"Noah, we tried to reason with you, but we've had enough of your attitude and disrespect. We won't allow you to sit around here and waste your life. You have to get out," his mother told him.

"What do you mean?"

"You know exactly what your mother is telling you. You have to move out."

"Move out? You know I don't have anywhere to go!"

"Not now, but you have two weeks to figure it out. We'll even help you with your first month's rent and stuff, but you can't stay here anymore. You're twenty years old, and it's obvious we have to force you to grow up."

"Man, I hate y'all! You want me to go? I'll go!"

I couldn't believe he told his parents he hated them. Although I'm void of emotions, I knew his words stemmed from anger and he didn't really mean it. I'm sure his parents knew that as well. However, speaking out of anger without considering the possible impact of his words immediately changed the course of his life.

"After everything we've done for you, how could you even allow yourself say something like that? I can't believe you, Noah. We're trying to make you a better man," his mother said.

She was hurt, but her son had hurt her many times before. It had almost become commonplace for him to do so, but hearing it that day was the final straw for both of his parents.

"We've ignored you saying that to us before, but we've had enough. I'll give you a reason to hate us. Get your stuff and get out, now! If you're not gone in an hour, I'm calling the police on you! If you think I'm joking, just try me, " his father said.

The situation escalated very quickly. I could hear Noah stomping around as he started throwing things down and throwing punches at the wall. It seemed like it was going to get much worse before it would get any better. Then, Noah made another incredibly dumb decision; he pulled me out of his holster and just held me to the side. Apparently, he was trying to strike fear into his parents' hearts.

"You're not about to do anything with that, so you might as well put it up. Sydney, do you see what our son is doing? If I think he is about to do anything to harm you, I promise that'll be the last thing he ever does!"

"Please don't talk like that. Can you two just calm down?" Sydney asked.

Nobody responded, and Noah refused to put me away as his mother left the room. She started to cry a little, but Noah didn't seem to care. His father was visibly upset, but he did as his wife asked him to do and calmed down, even though I was still partially pointed in his general direction.

"I don't know what's going on with you, but this ain't it. You can be so much better than this," his father said.

"Could I have been as good as you, Dad? Did I have the potential to get a job doing something I hate and then waste twenty years there?"

"How can someone be so smart and so dumb at the same time? Do I work a job I don't like? Yeah, I do, but I got that job when I found out your mother was pregnant with you. As a man, it was my responsibility to do everything I could to make sure you and Sydney never went without anything. I did it so you could be better than me. Your mother and I sacrificed a lot for you to be comfortable. For the past year or so, this has been building up. You've been getting worse and worse. We've been trying our best to ignore what we could in hopes that you would do better, but that doesn't seem to be happening. Like I said, as your father, it's my responsibility to help raise you the best I could. Now, you seem like you know it all, so it's time for you to start handling more on your own.

"You're saying all of this like you changed your life for me. I didn't ask you for that. I didn't even ask you to be here. Plus, you didn't stay at that job for me. You stayed there because you couldn't do any better," Noah told his father.

Parents and their children didn't always get along, but the amount of disrespect Noah was showing his father was ridiculous.

"No, I stayed because it was safe," his father replied.

"And you call me stupid!"

"Safety may not be luxurious, it may not be fun, it may not even be something you initially set out for, but if you're not willing to do what's safe for the sake of your family, then you may not even be fit to have one."

The more Barry talked, the more his tone changed. He stopped yelling at his son, and he seemed to be trying his best to simply pass on words of wisdom.

"You just said I have to leave my home, so all of this talk of safety and sacrifice doesn't mean anything to me."

Noah was still angry, but he had calmed down just enough to put me back in the holster.

"You still don't get it. This is the home your mother and I built for the family, but it's not yours. You're a grown man, and your home will be the one you build for you and your family."

"Do you even really care about me? Does anybody care about me? You might as well just take one of your guns and kill me yourself. Wouldn't nobody care if I ain't here anyway!"

Right then, Noah's words impacted Barry more than any other words he heard up to that point. The arguing stopped right then, and the conversation transformed to one in which a father just needed to show his son he still cared about him.

"I don't hate you, Noah, but I'm not gonna pretend like I'm not disappointed in you. You know we're not rich, but you also know you've never had to go without anything. I honestly think your mother and I just made things too easy for you. We made you too comfortable. I accept the fact that I may have done a disservice to you. I admit I may have kept you from actually growing up sooner, but it's time for things to change. I love you, son. Do you hear me? I love you, and that's why you have to go."

It would have been easy for Noah to pretend he didn't believe what his father was saying, but he didn't.

"I guess you're right, and it's not even like I don't want to leave because I've kinda wanted my own space for a while, but I'm scared," Noah admitted.

"Fear is nothing; we all get scared, but we can't let you be comfortable with being scared. I know I said I want you out now, but I was overreacting a bit. I don't want to just throw you out to the streets. We can help you out a little, but you only have two weeks, Noah," his father told him.

Noah sighed heavily, but he agreed with his parents. He knew he would never have the opportunity to become the man he wanted to be if he never left home.

"I'm sorry for how I acted. I don't have much more to say than that," Noah humbly told his parents.

Ultimately, his parents forgave him, and in a little under two weeks, he found himself living with his girlfriend. Since Noah moved, that meant I had a new home, as well. In my new place, I immediately began to get disrespected by Jillian. It quickly became commonplace for her to treat me as if I were a toy.

"This gun is so cute. I just want to wear it like some jewelry or something. What do you think, babe? Will this be a nice charm for my necklace? It'll be nice if we add some diamonds, so it'll be a good accent piece when we go somewhere fancy, and

I have on a nice evening gown," she said while handling me carelessly.

"What are you talking about? This ain't no jewelry. This is a gun," Noah said angrily.

"You must think I'm an idiot! I know what this is! You're not the only one who grew up around guns. Chill out!"

"I'm just trying to keep us safe, and playing around with a gun just isn't the smartest thing to do."

He was right, but she let him know she didn't like how she was being talked to. She belittled him as she yelled about how much of a buzzkill he was being. She continued to disregard their safety as she continued to just wave me around.

"Sometimes I really hate you, Noah!"

"Trust me, you're not the only one who has moments of hatred. Do you think I like having to deal with you when you're yelling at me for no reason? Jillian, sometimes you seem like you are trying your best to push me away. I love you, I do, but everybody has their limit. Every single day, it's like you're trying to push me to that limit. What happened to you? You weren't always like that."

"*You* happened to me," Jillian said while pointing at Noah.

"What is that even supposed to mean?"

"It means since we got together, I've been different. All of my friends have been telling me for the longest time I'm not the same. They said I'm always worried about you, and I don't have time for them anymore."

"Are you kidding? You're always spending time with them," Noah said right before he stopped talking abruptly.

He inhaled deeply a few times before he continued speaking. It was as though he had to carefully think about what he was going to say before he actually said it.

"I'm sorry, Jillian. I mean it. For whatever reason, we've both been very stressed, and I apologize for anything I've done."

Noah's apology immediately caused a change in Jillian. I was placed on a nearby counter as the couple continued their conversation.

"It's not even like you did anything. It's just that I care so much about you that I want to be around you. I guess it's just easier to blame you than to explain to them I'm in a different place than they are."

"I never even knew they've been givin' you a hard time because you're in a relationship. I never wanted to cause any problems between you and your friends."

"I know you didn't, and even if you didn't like my friends, I still shouldn't have been acting the way I have. And no matter what, I shouldn't have been so careless with that gun. That thing could have gone off at any time. I'm sorry."

A full conversation between Jillian and Noah that included logic was rare, and it became even more rare as the years went on. The two continued to live together and considered themselves to be a couple, even though neither of them seemed to be happy on a consistent basis. However humans decided to define love, Noah and Jillian's relationship could not have been it. Each day, they went out of their way to find something to argue about. They would temporarily reach a resolution, only to find a new problem to argue about the next day.

When Noah's parents forced him to leave their home, they were doing so to help him grow up and make some improvements in his life. They wanted him to get a job so he could move toward his goals, but that's not what happened. While he eventually started working, that was about all he did.

He started working at the first place that hired him, and things just stopped there. He didn't like his job, but he got it because he wanted to show himself (and his parents) that he was improving. Once he was hired, he quickly became content. He didn't search for other job opportunities and he just stopped caring about everything. He had fallen right back into the pattern that forced his parents to kick him out in the first place.

"What are we doing, Noah? What's the point of all of this?" Jillian asked one day, out of the blue.

"What do you mean?"

"I didn't think I needed to explain anything because the questions were pretty simple. I mean, what are we doing? Do we have a future together, or are we just wasting time? We're not married, we haven't made any real commitments to each other, and at this point, I don't even know if I want to. We argue way too much, and I don't think you're ever really gonna grow up."

"So, that's how you feel?"

"Yeah, it is."

"Well, at least I know I'm not the only one who second-guesses us being together," Noah said.

"What do you mean, second-guess our relationship?"

"I didn't think I needed to explain because it was pretty self-explanatory," Noah replied very smugly.

"See, that's the kinda stuff I'm talkin' about! You're ridiculous!"

Noah may have been speaking his truth about Jillian, but he still shouldn't have said it. He didn't seem to realize how immature he was and how infuriating his actions were. Either that or his actions were done just so he could see what type of reactions he could get. Whatever the case was, it was too much for Jillian to take.

She stormed away from Noah and slammed their bedroom door. Noah, who was left in the room by himself, started to have a conversation with himself about what happened.

"Is that what you wanted? Are you really ready to be by yourself, and where are you gonna go if she decides to kick you out? You can't let that happen. Nah. You have to do whatever it takes to make sure she doesn't want to get rid of you. I mean, whatever it takes."

He soon left the room where I was, and he moved closer to

their room.

"Hey, Jillian. Babe, will you please open the door?"

He asked variations of that question until Jillian got tired of him asking. The old door squeaked when she finally opened it.

"What?"

"I was wrong, and I'm sorry," he said.

I doubt he had a change of heart and started to feel remorse in such a short amount of time. More than likely, he was just saying what he felt would calm her down. It was something they both did to each other after they had a disagreement.

"Why do we have to keep going through this, Noah? I'm way too young to be feeling so emotionally drained, especially because of a relationship."

"You're right, and I just have to work on me. I have to be better. Like you said, I need to grow up."

She was quiet because Noah's apology was believable enough for her to stop being upset. With any other couple, it may have been good to see someone taking responsibility for a problem, but for Jillian and Noah, it was just another lie between two people whose personalities were toxic to each other. I knew the relationship between the young people wasn't normal because I was able to compare it to that of Noah's parents.

His parents had their problems, and they had many angry arguments over the years, but if one of them offered an apology, it was said in a way that made it seem like they meant it. The words Noah and Jillian exchanged during apologies, and even when they said they loved each other, were all just lies they told each other as part of an emotional con. They both probably thought they were "getting over" one another, but all they were doing was wasting time they would never be able to get back. With each subsequent argument, I was sure someone would be smart enough to end their so-called relationship, but it never happened. In fact, Noah and Jillian ended up getting married.

From my understanding, weddings are supposed to be important events for people, but Jillian and Noah's wedding was memorable for all of the wrong reasons. For starters, Noah found it necessary for me to attend. Fortunately, I wasn't seen by anyone during the ceremony. The event was fairly quiet until the attendees were asked if any of them had any objections.

"This shouldn't be happening, Noah. I don't know if you've thought about what you're getting yourself into. I'm sorry, but you two have always been terrible to each other. Things won't get better because you're getting married. I don't want to see my son ruin his life because he thinks there are no other options," Noah's mother said.

"Yeah, this is not smart," his father agreed.

Although it was probably unexpected for Noah's parents to be the ones to vocalize their concerns, they didn't say anything Noah hadn't said himself at some point. Everyone's reaction to what was said quickly escalated Jillian's anger.

"Are you just gonna let them ruin *my* wedding? Why don't you be a man and tell them to shut up?" she yelled.

Jillian put him in a bit of a predicament with those words. She wanted him to prove his love (and manhood) to her by making his parents keep their opinions to themselves. After Jillian screamed at the top of her lungs, the crowd waited silently to see how Noah was going to react.

"Mom, Dad, I know this is a major moment for you, but I need you to respect the decision we've made to get married. We're glad everyone is here, but honestly, we're doing this for us and not for anyone else. So, if anyone else feels they need to disturb the ceremony, please save your energy and just leave."

There were gasps and various comments mumbled from people in all directions, but nobody was nearly as vocal as Noah's parents.

"Now that the haters have had their time to shine, we can keep it moving," Jillian said very loudly.

Everyone waited to see if Noah had any type of response, but he didn't.

"Didn't you hear me? I said to keep it moving," she yelled out again.

Jillian's tone was not one of joy. It was demanding and rude, but as she requested, the ceremony continued. When the couple was finally announced as husband and wife, only a few people scattered throughout the venue offered their non-energetic applause.

"If you're not happy for us, you can leave!" Jillian yelled.

"It's okay, babe. Don't let them get to you. This day is supposed to be about us anyway," Noah whispered.

"Yeah, it is, but they are supposed to care about us! All of those no-good people are just here for pictures for the 'Gram. They wanna act like they care," she continued.

At that moment, I think reality started to set in for Noah. I could feel his pulse steadily increasing. He stopped moving for a moment to catch his breath, and instead of Jillian being concerned about his wellbeing, she was just upset because he embarrassed her.

"Stop acting like something's wrong with you. Let's go. You're out here making a fool of yourself, which is making me look bad!"

"I'm trying to, but I can't. Babe...please...stop...yelling at me."

Each word he spoke made it more difficult for him to breathe, but his wife didn't care. His body soon gave out, and he crashed to the ground, taking me with him.

Many people ran over to check on Noah's condition, but when Jillian should have been closest to Noah, she decided to step away.

"This is not a good way to start things off, Noah! Quit being so weak. Get up."

"If you're not gonna be helpful, just move out of the way," someone told her.

"This is my wedding. You can't tell me what to do!"

"At this point, we need to get him some help. We're not worried about whose wedding this is," another person said.

Since I had been around her for a while, I knew Jillian didn't like the fact that she was no longer in control, but she didn't say anything else. She just walked away with no regard for her husband.

With Jillian out of the way, multiple people spent the next few minutes calling for help. Even though we had fallen to the ground, I remained in my holster. I thought someone had to see me, but nobody said anything. If they did know I was there, I guess me being there was far less important than what was going on with Noah.

"Son! Son, please be okay!"

The concerned voice was that of Sydney, Noah's mother. She voiced how fearful she was of what was happening with her son. With each passing second, her fear grew, just as it did with the majority of the people who all waited on help to arrive.

After about ten minutes or so, the sounds of the approaching ambulance overpowered all other conversations. Noah's breathing was inconsistent at this point, and I didn't know if he would make it through the rest of the day. The sirens were soon silenced as I started to hear the footsteps and the voices of more people drawing near.

"So, what happened here?" an unfamiliar voice asked.

"Nobody knows. He had just finished with his vows and was walking down the aisle when he fell out," someone responded.

The conversation lasted for a few minutes before complete silence took over. Those who were around awaited the EMTs to provide some information, but they didn't give them what they were seeking.

"We'll need to take him to the hospital so they can run some more tests."

Hearing that immediately brought thoughts of the worst

possible outcome to the minds of everyone around, especially Noah's parents.

"Please, God, let him be okay," Barry said, almost whispering.

Sydney moved as quickly as she could to be by Noah's side. She grabbed his hand and held onto it for a few steps as they securely put him onto a stretcher.

"Your father and I will follow you to the hospital," she said emotionally.

It sounded as though she was trying her best to fight back tears with every word she said, but the sadness was evident. When the paramedics raised the gurney, one of them got a good look at me.

"Do you see what I see?" One EMT asked the other.

"Yeah, I see it, but I don't know what we're supposed to do with it."

I hadn't personally done anything to them, but for some reason, they both showed a healthy fear of me. Their primary focus was on Noah, but I knew I was making them extremely nervous by how much they kept staring at me. Suddenly, Noah inhaled deeply as he tried to sit up.

"Just relax, sir. Everything is okay, and you're in good hands," one of the paramedics said to Noah.

I don't know how much truth was in the statement, but it was said, nonetheless.

"We're not 100 percent sure what happened, but we will make sure you get a full evaluation once you get to the hospital."

Noah didn't respond, but the conversation they had with him led me to believe he was doing better than he was at first, even if it were only a little bit better. His progress distracted them from me being a stowaway on the journey. A few moments passed, and when the vehicle finally stopped, I was seen once again.

"So, I guess you're trying to force us to pay attention to you, huh?" he asked me.

Hearing what was going on gave Noah the energy to try and get up again.

"Oh, someone must have heard us talking about his gun," one of the paramedics said.

Noah mumbled as he reached out to make sure I was still with him. Even though I was still there, he became agitated and frustrated for some reason. Perhaps he was just upset at what happened on what was supposed to be one of his most memorable days, or maybe he was just mad because he was riding in the back of an ambulance. Whatever the reason, Noah realized there wasn't much he could do about his situation, so he quieted himself and accepted what he couldn't control.

All of the voices in the vehicle soon dissipated, and the siren from the ambulance was allowed to have its solo as it rang out into the air. After traveling some distance, the tires screeched loudly as we reached our destination.

"Hey, let's be careful while you get this guy out," one guy said to the other.

His co-worker agreed. They didn't even mention me as they said they were taking Noah to a private hospital, whatever that meant. I guess since I hadn't actually been involved in a shooting, they felt they didn't have to immediately do anything with me other than make sure I wouldn't cause any problems as they brought Noah inside.

They carefully put me into a random bag as we finally made our way into the hospital. Surprisingly, there wasn't a flurry of conversations explaining how quickly Noah needed to be helped. Everything was very calm as the paramedics handed me over to a nurse. I don't know how long I was away from Noah, but I was eventually taken to the same room he was in. I was put away in a portable wardrobe of sorts, but I was still able to hear what was going on.

Not long after we made it into the room, we were visited by a stream of nurses and doctors. They checked Noah's vitals and ran various tests, and when it was all said and done, the doctor told him he was okay.

"What do you mean, I'm okay? That had to be some type of heart attack," Noah said when he was finally able to talk.

"I'm not dismissing the pain you felt, but it wasn't a heart attack. Young man, you had a panic attack."

"That doesn't make any sense to me. I felt like my chest was literally going to cave in. I couldn't pull in any air, and I felt like I was dying. Those feelings...that pain...that couldn't have been caused by me panicking about something."

"Those are exactly the symptoms one can expect. Let me ask you something, did something happen that precipitated the attack?"

"Nah, nothing happened. Not that I could think of," Noah said.

Noah had to know the anxiousness he had about his wedding was the cause of his pain, but he didn't want to admit it. Evidently, even Noah's body knew marrying Jillian was not the right thing for him to do, so in a last-ditch effort, it tried its best to stop the wedding from happening. Unfortunately, it didn't work until after he and Jillian had been pronounced husband and wife.

Hearing he hadn't had a heart attack should have been well received, but it wasn't. After the doctor confirmed it was a panic attack, Noah took what was said and released a long, drawn-out sigh.

"Baby, are you okay?"

The question came from Noah's mother as she entered his hospital room with his father.

"Yes," he answered very solemnly.

"What happened? Will he recover?" she asked the doctor, who still remained in the room.

"Fortunately, he'll be okay. It appears he had a panic attack."

"I heard those things can make you feel like you had a heart attack, right?" his father asked.

"That's correct."

"Well, what caused it?" they asked.

"That's a question he would be able to answer better than me. I will say panic attacks, especially one as severe as the one he had, are generally caused by a tremendous amount of stress. Whatever that is, or was, needs to change immediately. If it doesn't, the next time something like this happens, it could be the last time. Does that make sense?"

"Yeah, it makes perfect sense," his mom replied.

"For now, I'm gonna leave you all alone. We'll be back to check on him a little later," the doctor said.

As the doctor left the room, Barry, Noah's father, happened to look into the small area where some of Noah's items were being stored. This was when he faced the fact I had been at the wedding.

"Look at that," Barry whispered to his wife.

"That doesn't make any sense," Sydney said.

The tone in her voice let me know she disapproved of me attending the wedding. Regardless of if she approved or not, I was there, and there was nothing they could do to change that. His parents were still conversing about me when Jillian showed up and immediately proved she could make things worse than they already were.

"Noah, you always find a way to ruin everything," she yelled.

"Can't you be considerate for once in your life?" Barry asked.

"How dare you ask me something like that! In case you haven't noticed, I'm standing in a hospital in a wedding dress that I spent a long time trying to find. Instead of me showing it off to people admiring me at my reception, I'm here. Instead of me getting ready to go on my honeymoon, I'm here. I guess you can't see any of that."

"Checking on your husband, in my eyes, isn't an act of consideration, it's more of an obligation," Noah's mother said.

"Obligation? I'm not obligated to do anything," Jillian said very loudly.

"I know you really feel like that, which makes things even worse. You just married our son, and you wanna act like coming to see him in the hospital is an act of kindness. I never thought you were good enough for him, and this little display lets me know I was right," Sydney said.

"Please stop," Noah said faintly.

His request was denied, and everyone in the room continued to argue as if he hadn't said anything.

"What are you all doing? The doctor just explained Noah's condition might have been caused by stress, and you all are in here yelling at the top of your lungs," a nurse said sternly when I heard her enter the room.

The silence that took over the room spoke volumes. For Noah's parents, it seemed like they were embarrassed by being reprimanded by the nurse. Jillian was probably only silent because, at that moment, she no longer had anyone to argue with.

"What's wrong with him, anyway?" Jillian asked after being quiet for a few seconds.

"He had a severe panic attack."

"Panic attack? Are you serious? Noah, you ruined *my* wedding because you were nervous?"

"It's a bit more than that, ma'am," the nurse responded.

"So, he didn't even have a heart attack?" Jillian asked.

"No, ma'am. We're very fortunate he didn't."

"Yeah, it's very fortunate," she replied sarcastically.

For whatever reason, Jillian was upset the man she had just promised to spend the rest of her life with, in sickness and in health, didn't have a more severe condition. Instead of her being happy he was okay, she was mad because, in her opinion, his condition had ruined *her* special day. I thought was displaying a despicable act of selfishness.

"Could you give us a moment with our son?" Barry asked Jillian very politely.

"Your son? I don't think you understand. This man is my husband, so if anybody needs to leave the room, it's you!"

She was making a spectacle of herself for absolutely no reason.

"I'm about to leave you all for a moment," the nurse told them.

"Syd, let's just go to the waiting room for a little while. Evidently, Jillian needs to spend some time with her husband to make sure he's good."

Barry's words sounded heartfelt, but based on the full extent of the conversation, one could believe he didn't mean what he said. Whether his words were genuine or not, he and Sydney left the room right after he said them.

"What's really wrong with you?" Jillian asked.

"They told you I had a panic attack, but I guess I'm okay now," Noah said quietly.

"Well, if you're okay, then why are we still here? Why are you wasting my time?"

"I'm sorry I'm wasting your time, Jillian. It's not like this is something I planned."

As the conversation progressed, Jillian's words got even more toxic when she saw me.

"I know you can't be that stupid! I know you were not carrying that with you. Not today!"

She moved over to where I was, picked me up, and began to point me toward the sky.

"Please put that down, Jillian."

"Am I embarrassing you or something? You didn't care enough about me to not bring a gun to our wedding, so why should I care how I'm making you feel now?"

"It wasn't like that at all. I just wanted to make sure you were protected."

"You thought we needed to be protected from our friends? Think for once in your life, Noah. What kind of idiot would carry a gun to their wedding? Did you think somebody was gonna try to rob the guests or something? Oh...oh, no, I got it! You were gonna try and kill me in front of everyone. Yeah, that's it, isn't it?"

"Jillian, you're not making any sense right now. Why would I try to kill you? You're the love of my life."

"Well, this is a really good way to show it," Jillian said.

Jillian's words were reeking of sarcasm. She was upset just because she wanted to be. Nothing Noah said should have made her as mad as she was. On the other hand, no matter how hard he tried, nothing Noah said could have helped her be happy. So, at that moment, I could tell by the look in his eyes that he gave up. He gave up trying to argue with her. He basically gave up any remaining hope he still had.

For a machine, hope meant nothing because we don't deal with hypothetical situations. We don't care about "what could be" because our existence is only to deal with "what is." Humans, however, are dependent upon their hope. Their lives begin with their parents hoping their offspring will go on to do great things. As they grow and make mistakes, the hope is that they learn from what may not have been done correctly and become better people. On the day of Noah's wedding, all of that vanished.

Soon after Noah decided to stop arguing, a police officer made his way into the hospital room. Evidently, he was told about me, and so he questioned Noah about why I was there. Noah gave an honest response.

"Officer, I have a license, and having it makes me feel safe."

As soon as the word "safe" left Noah's lips, Jillian let out a sigh that could be heard from a mile away.

"Ma'am, is there something wrong?"

"I'm just tired of him saying he needs a gun to feel safe. He keeps saying that because he likes justifying his stupidity."

Jillian tried to bait Noah into arguing again, but he didn't allow that to happen.

"I was dumb, and I made a decision I shouldn't have," Noah told his wife.

As a machine, discerning human lies by the tone in which the words are spoken isn't always something I can do. However, based on previous interactions, I knew Noah was saying what he thought Jillian wanted to hear. This type of behavior was almost like giving her a pass to keep being obnoxious and rude because she thought she was right. It also inflated her already bloated ego.

The conversation between Noah, Jillian, and the officer lasted a little while longer. Then, he left. Since nothing happened, it was safe to say the officer felt everything was in order. Even if Noah was just saying what he thought Jillian wanted to hear, he said having me with him that day was a dumb decision. Fortunately, that dumb decision didn't get him into trouble with the cop. They were incredibly lucky.

Almost as soon as the cop left the newly-married couple alone, Noah's parents, accompanied by a nurse, re-entered the room.

"So, what happened?" Noah's father asked.

"Not much. He just asked some questions. After he got the info he needed, he left."

Although Noah's parents had only started the conversation, it didn't take long for Jillian to get upset she wasn't being included. So, as she tended to do, she interjected herself into it.

"Yeah, but none of it would have happened if he wouldn't have had that stupid gun at our wedding!"

"There's no need to yell, Jillian. We get it, you didn't want the gun there, and maybe it shouldn't have been, but you can't change the past. Let the past be the past," Sydney said.

"Really, is that what I should do? Is it that simple?"

"I'm not sayin' it's simple, but it's what you need to do," Barry continued.

"Well, if we're telling each other what we need to do, then I need to give y'all some advice."

"Go for it," Barry said reluctantly as he rolled his eyes toward the ceiling.

"You two shouldn't have raised such a soft and idiotic excuse for a man."

Before either of his parents could respond, Noah decided he needed to speak up.

"That's enough of that. I put up with a lot because I love you, but I'm not gonna allow you to keep disrespecting my parents."

"Are you choosing them over me?" Jillian asked.

"I'm not choosing anybody over anybody else, but I'm telling you to show them some respect."

Out of all of the responses Noah's statement could have received, Jillian decided not to say anything. She pretended to be upset (yet again), and then she proceeded to walk out of the room.

"She's....a little angry, huh?" the nurse asked with a slight giggle.

"Yeah, that's a mild version of who she normally is," Noah said.

Noah mocked the woman he had just married while his parents laughed at her. It was strange all around, but strange was the norm when it came to human behavior. Well, at least for the behavior of these particular humans.

Time passed, and I soon found myself back home with Noah and Jillian. Their wedding had absolutely no impact on how they got along with each other. Their communication was almost always at one of two extremes; either they were arguing very loudly, or they were not speaking at all. How they dealt with each other was not healthy, but they both seemed to have the other by some type of toxic leash that the other couldn't break away from. Then, out of nowhere, the atmosphere shifted.

Noah calmly asked his wife if they could talk. Before that day, a request to have a conversation would have been just enough to start a very dramatic war of words. For some reason, this talk didn't start that way.

"Why are we like this, Jillian?"

"I honestly don't know, but it's tiring. It's like we're bringing out the worst in each other."

"You're right, but what can we do about it?"

They discussed how neither of them felt loved, even though they both claimed to still care for one another. For the first time in a long while, hope seemed to be making a return. The couple even shared a few laughs as they reminisced about their high school days.

"You were such a dork back then, Noah!"

"That's true, I was, but I don't think there's anything wrong with that. Plus, even though I wasn't completely comfortable in my own skin, I was comfortable with the fact that I knew I was never gonna be one of the cool kids."

"Yeah, there was never a chance of that. I mean ever. I mean, like, if everybody in the school left, and you were the only one there, it would just be a school without any cool kids," Jillian joked.

"Okay, okay, I get it. None of that mattered when I put my lack of coolness to the side and finally asked you out, though."

"Yeah, I was totally surprised when you did that. I never, in a million years, thought I would go out with you."

"For real?"

"I'm just playin'. I knew you liked me, and I always thought you were cute."

"So, why didn't you ever start a conversation with me?"

"On the popularity hierarchy, I was on a very different level than you. I figured if you wanted to go out with me, you would ask. If you didn't, then we just wouldn't have ever been together."

"I guess that makes sense. So, do you think we are still supposed to be together?" Noah asked.

"The way things are now, I don't think we are."

I have no feelings, so I have no connection to pain, but I am sure hearing his wife say she didn't think they were supposed to be together had to hurt Noah, even though he was the one who asked the question. He took a while to gather himself.

Hearing how his wife felt was a turning point for Noah. Right then, any hope he had for their relationship getting back on track immediately started to leave again. That second, there was no longer an opportunity for optimism to stick around. Noah heard several loud and disparaging words during his time with Jillian, but the calm and honest words she said right then were enough to snatch his soul away from him.

"Oh," he finally said, unable to muster together any words other than that.

"So...what now?" Jillian wondered.

"Can't we just work things out? I mean, we can go see a professional or something. I still love you, Jillian. As much as we've gone through, I don't want things to end. We haven't even really been married that long. We can't just give up already."

He was trying to be courageous, but the way he delivered his words showed he didn't have much courage left. He was speaking from his heart, but speaking grew increasingly more difficult the more he tried to do it.

"Yeah, we haven't been married long, but how much more time do we need to waste before we face reality? We both know it's not gonna work, and if we're keeping it real, we've probably both known that for a long time. I feel like one of the main reasons we stayed together was just to prove everyone wrong about us. At some point, we just have to realize they were all right. We just don't fit, Noah. You've been my mate, but I don't ever think you've been my soulmate. I think all of this anger was really more about me fighting what I knew wasn't working than it ever really was about you," Jillian said.

Many times, words could kill a person much quicker than I ever could. Jillian's honesty was an example of that.

"If that's how you feel, then leave! I don't need you! I don't even want you!" Noah yelled.

His anger allowed him to briefly conceal his sadness.

"We were having a good convo, and you just wanna start yelling? Is that really what you want to do?"

It didn't matter if he wanted to get loud or not because his anger and sadness had already put events in motion he couldn't come back from.

"Yeah, we're not getting anything accomplished! You don't have to be with me! I'm tired of wasting time with you anyway!"

"You're not even worth the breath I'm wasting right now, Noah. You're beyond useless!"

And this is where you entered. After being called useless, Noah reached his breaking point. He walked out of his bedroom, angrily saying things only he could understand. In all of the years I had known him, I had never seen him like that. Noah's parents always said Jillian's love changed him, but the complete removal of that love changed him even more.

When Noah re-entered the room, he had me with him.

"Is that supposed to scare me?" Jillian asked.

"It's not supposed to do anything. If it happens to scare you, it is what it is," Noah replied while swinging me around.

"See, that's why I never liked that thing. It always turned you into a different person. I hate who you are with that thing."

"Well, you just told me you don't like me anyway. So, with or without it, your feelings are pretty much the same."

"Just quit being stupid! If you wanna talk, we can talk. We don't need that!"

"Yeah, Jillian, I see you're scared. Whether you admit it or not, I know you are. That's good, though. Fear looks good on you."

He pushed me firmly against his temple as he continued to speak.

"Does knowing you are a finger movement away from watching me die bother you at all?" Noah asked.

"Put the gun down! This is crazy!"

"You're right, it is crazy. You know, all of my life, I heard people say love will make you do some crazy things, but I never knew how crazy until today. You made a vow, Jillian. You chose to tell everyone we would be together for life. After today, I guess you can say you fulfilled your end of the deal."

That was the moment I knew irreversible damage had been done to Noah. He was about to act out on his emotions, using me to help him 'solve' his problems. He didn't consider what would happen if he followed through, which was a mistake a lot of humans make.

Throughout our relationship, Jillian was always the one in control. She thrived on her position, while Noah despised it. No matter how he tried to reason with her, she never viewed him as a partner. With me involved, he felt he finally had power, and he loved the way that made him feel.

"Okay, Noah, you win!"

"Oh, no, sweetheart, this isn't a game. This is a life we are both about to lose."

He made his intentions abundantly clear, but Jillian was not going to give up.

"This isn't worth it, Noah. I don't care if you have a gun in your hand. You know you don't wanna kill anyone. You don't want to hurt me or yourself."

"You're right, I don't want to, but you've given me no choice."

"Okay, okay. Maybe we can still work it out. It'll be hard, but it ain't impossible."

"C'mon, babe, you say all the time how stupid you think I am, but you can't really think I'm that stupid. You just told me you don't want me, so now you want me to believe we can work it out? Please! I may not be the smartest man, but I'm not the dumbest one, either!"

No matter how much talking they did, we all knew what the outcome was going to be; in some way, Noah was going to use me to show his wife how much she had hurt him.

"Noah, please! You don't want to do this!" Jillian yelled.

"I just told you I don't want to do this. I told you I loved you, but love ain't enough! You told me I was worthless and that I wasn't worth the breath you were talking to me with. You said that, right?"

"Yeah, I did," she said meekly.

"Oh, Jillian, don't tone it down now. We both know that's not really how you are. Don't let me take you out of your character. If you're about to go out, you might as well go out with a bang. Be the same loud, obnoxious, demeaning, emasculating person you've always been. Do you, babe!"

Although she was still frightened for her life, Noah's words seemed to resonate with her. Out of nowhere, she started running toward her husband.

"If I die today, I promise you I won't be alone!"

"I never, throughout our entire relationship, wanted you to be alone. That won't stop today. We promised it will be 'til death do us part. Just know I loved you to the end," Noah said.

After he confessed his love, he pulled the trigger and made me express the pain he was no longer able to vocalize.

"Noah…you…I can't believe you…" Jillian said as she tried to speak with what turned out to be her last breaths.

She tried to express her disbelief in someone who said he was going to love her through the good and the bad times. She said she was wasting her breath talking to Noah, and as she lost her life, it was a sad twist of fate that at that moment, her words were truer than ever. It was strange that as her lifeless body fell, Noah held onto her.

"Why did you make me do that, babe?"

He kept me pressed against her as he continued to talk.

"Who would have ever thought it would end like this? I was so dumb. I thought I would live happily ever after with the popular girl. I should've known better. I mean, all of the arguments we had for no reason should have been my red flags, but I guess I just didn't pay attention to them. You need to lie down, Jillian. I know you're not feeling your best, but don't worry, I'll help you."

Noah picked Jillian up and carefully carried her over to their bed.

"There you go. Now, just give me a few minutes. I have to make a quick phone call."

He stepped to the side and grabbed his phone, making sure he continued to have me close by as he put the call on speaker.

"Hey, Dad, what's up?"

"Nothing much. How are you?"

"I'm okay. Hey, is Mom there?"

"Yeah, she is. You wanna talk to her?"

"Well, I wanna talk to both of you."

"Okay, hold on, let me get her."

Noah waited patiently for his mother to join the conversation.

"Hey, Noah!"

Even through the phone, everyone could hear a bit of joy in each other's voices. Unfortunately, Noah's news was going to steal their joy and break their hearts at the same time.

"Hey, Mom! Dad, can you hear me?"

"Yeah, we hear you. What's going on?"

"First, I wanna tell you I love you. Over the years, I haven't always been the best child, but it's never been because of you."

"We appreciate that, but I know that's not why you're calling," his mother said.

"Okay, I'll just get to it. You know how everyone has been telling me Jillian isn't right for me?"

"Yeah."

"Well, you were right. Sometimes the heart doesn't know what it needs, and that was the case with us."

"I'm a little confused. What are you saying?" his father asked.

Noah released a nervous giggle.

"Yeah, I know I'm being kinda vague, but I promise everything will make perfect sense very soon. I will say this again, y'all did a great job raising me, so I don't want you to feel any guilt."

"Okay, I'm starting to get upset, Noah. Quit speaking in riddles, and just tell us what you want us to know," his father demanded.

"My bad, you're right. Let me just get to it. I never gave up on my marriage, but I am giving up on life. She put me through so much, but I can't do this without her. Mom, Dad, I love you, but I'm done!"

He didn't hang up the phone, but he didn't say anything else. He climbed into the bed next to his slain wife and kissed her on the cheek. He put me firmly against his temple, almost as if he wanted me to be able to connect to his thoughts. Although only a few minutes had passed since we took Jillian's life, Noah was letting me know I had to get ready to go back to work.

"Noah! Noah, are you there?"

His parents kept trying to get him to say something, but I'm sure they already knew what was going on. It only took a few seconds before Noah officially joined his wife. Their lives were both quickly gone, and really, it was all for nothing. Pain is apparently a part of the human experience, and each person has their threshold; Noah had reached his.

There was no logical reason for Noah's actions, but that didn't matter. From the moment I was introduced to Jillian, the outcome was drawing near. Both Jillian and Noah had to understand how toxic their relationship was, but they both chose to ignore the signs. Through their volatile disagreements and interactions, they tried to pretend as if they had enough love between them to overcome everything. They were naive in believing an emotional bond that started when they were teenagers, could possibly be enough to override the fact they never were supposed to be together.

At one point in his life, Noah thought all he needed in the world was to be loved by Jillian. He obtained her love, but he never truly learned to love his true and authentic self. He never stood a chance of being happy with her because he allowed his relationship with her to dictate his level of joy. He wanted to be in a relationship so bad, he rushed to get into one before he was even mature enough to know who he was. His life was complex only because he made it that way. In the end, Noah, who was trying to find his peace, was washed away in his self-created storm of chaos.

The lives of these two young people changed when they met each other, but the lives of everyone they knew would forever be changed simply because of their lack of peace. So, how valuable is peace? As Noah proved, it was something some people thought was important enough to take lives if they thought it would help them obtain it.

Like I said before, people are always in search of something. In the end, I sat there surrounded by a couple who, only a few minutes before, seemed to be on the road to recovery in their relationship. For the time being, my work was done. The only thing left was for Noah and Jillian's family to pray their spirits would finally be able to find the peace in death they were never able to hold onto in life.

NARRATIVE 6: DISSONANCE IN JUNE

"C'mon, everybody. I know we've all worked hard, but we have to keep pushing! We only have a little while longer before this week's class is over."

That enthusiastic young lady is Maria. She has never met a stranger. Her conversations are pleasant, encouraging, and friendly. This story is not about her, though. Well, I should say, not all of the story is. Maria's involvement in my life is very important, so I promise I'll get back to her. For now, I would like to start at the beginning.

Some people think of guns as necessities. Sometimes we are looked at as collector's items or works of art. Some people will even view their guns as friends. It is not uncommon for humans to have conversations with their guns as if we can help them make decisions. None of these describe how "life" has ever been for me. I am not art, I am not necessary, and I am certainly nobody's friend. I am simply a tool with enough versatility to handle different types of jobs, and that's exactly how I have been handled.

Unlike some of my relatives, I haven't been around many

people. I sat on the shelf of a store for a while before my human, Harmony, came into the picture.

"Let me get that one," she said as she pointed at me.

There was no small talk between her and the person at the register. No, their interaction was purely transactional. They both said only what was needed. When their conversation was over, I found myself relocated to my new home.

On the way there, my new human didn't tell me how happy she was to meet me. She also didn't mention how I was going to change her life. This let me know we would only have a working relationship, and that worked well for me. For a long time, she kept me locked in a safe tucked away in the corner of her bedroom closet.

Most days, there was no activity. In fact, I hardly even saw the light of day. For the most part, I would just rest comfortably, wondering if I would ever get a chance to do anything. The lady who chose me seemed to be a bit of a loner who lived in a fairly quiet neighborhood. There were many days when the loudest noises I heard were conversations she had with the shows she watched on television. Then, it all changed.

She was in her room. Only a few minutes before, she was laughing hysterically at one of her favorite shows, but then the room was silent. I could usually tell her night was over when her timer turned off the television. Everything seemed normal, but the loud sound of glass breaking, along with the noise of her house alarm, informed me that wasn't the case.

"Nope! Not this time," I heard her say.

She wasn't talking to me, but it didn't sound like anyone else was in the room. She quickly, yet calmly, opened the safe, gave me some bullets, and held me tightly as we moved throughout her house. I thought we were possibly still alone, but the other voices I soon heard told me how wrong I was.

"Get down, now! We don't wanna hurt you, lady, but I promise we will," an unfamiliar voice said.

After a brief hesitation, she began to run toward the voice.

"Do you think this is a game?" another woman asked.

"Look, just get what you want and leave."

"Trust me, that's what we're gonna do," the uninvited woman responded.

The person I was with breathed heavily. Her palms grew more and more sweaty. She was nervous, but she tried to hide it.

"That's enough! Get out of my house, now!"

In a matter of seconds, the homeowner attempted to transform herself from someone fearing for her life, to someone who was taking control of it.

She pulled me from behind her back and shot up in the air. The unexpected shot scared the unwelcome visitors.

"Okay, so you're down to fight! That's good to know! I always hate dealing with helpless victims," the unknown woman said.

"We don't have time for speeches! Let's go! We got more than enough, anyway," the guy said.

"You better listen to him because the next time I shoot, it's gonna be at one of y'all."

The unidentified woman contemplated her choices. Did she want to take whatever stolen goods she and her companion collected, or did she want to prove how tough she was by ignoring the warning she received? It didn't take long to get confirmation that she wasn't actually concerned with making the best decisions that night.

She ran toward us, and Harmony tried to give her a warning, but she wouldn't stop moving. Harmony's hands had grown steady as she held me in front of her. She could have just aimed at her head, but she didn't. She pointed me a little bit lower than where I was, and suddenly, she made me go off again. An intense yell of agony quickly followed.

"Do you hear that? You just caused your friend to get shot.

Try me again, and I promise, I'm gonna try my best to end you!"
Harmony said.

When she said those words, the two thieves ran out of the house as quickly as they could. I'm not sure if Harmony knew where the person had been shot, nor do I know if she cared. All I knew at the point was she had a goal of protecting herself, and that's exactly what she did.

When the robbers left her home, Harmony closed her door, put me back in the safe, and called 9-1-1. Although I was in a safe, when the police arrived, I was able to hear the conversation they had with Harmony. She told them about me, and then she told them how we shot one of the people who broke into her home.

"Are you okay?" one of them asked.

"Honestly, no, I'm not. I'm a single woman who just had two people break into my home," she told them.

"We understand how afraid you may be at this time, but..."

"Afraid? No, sir, I'm not afraid. I'm mad! They picked the wrong one tonight! I promise...I wish I would have..."

"Ma'am, please stop right there. I don't want you to say anything you may end up regretting. I've had someone attempt to invade my home before, so I know how you're feeling. Let me ask you, was anything actually taken?"

That question caused Harmony to run away from the officers. I could hear her footsteps franticly move closer and further away from me as she searched her home. I could hear furniture being moved out of place, things getting knocked over, and Harmony almost panting as she wore herself out searching her house to see what had been taken.

"Actually, it doesn't really look like they got anything, but that can't be right. I heard them say..."

"Well, that's good," one of the officers said.

"Wait! Hold on! I have to check something. Please, just wait right here."

The loud pitter-patter of feet returned, which let me know she was in a hurry to look in at least one more location."

"No, no, no, no! This can't be my life right now! Please tell me that didn't happen."

"Ma'am, what's wrong?" one of the officers asked as she made her way back to them.

"They took it! They must have found it in the guest room before I confronted them. You have to find them!" Harmony said.

"Ma'am, you said they took 'it.' What exactly are you referring to?"

"My mother's ring is not there! That was the last thing she gave me before she passed away, and they just took it."

"I know how expensive jewelry can be..."

"This isn't about the price! That ring was given to my mother from my grandma. My mom gave that to me right before she died a few years ago, and I promised her I was going to take care of it! I know it was dumb to keep it in that room, but that's where my mom always stayed whenever she spent the night over here. Keeping that ring in that room always made me feel like my mom was still here with me. Now, they have taken that from me!"

"I'm so sorry. I promise we'll do everything we can to find out who broke into your home and try to get your ring back."

"Okay," she replied.

Her single-word response to the cop's promise made it seem like she, in that moment, had been defeated. While the intruders were in the home, she had a ferociousness about her that was undeniable. When the cops first arrived, that ferociousness became confidence that let her know everything would work out. However, as soon as she found out her most prized possession was gone, everything changed.

I didn't hear her say much else before the slamming of the door let me know the cops had finally made their exit. Soon after they left, the house was filled with the sound of Harmony crying her heart out. She was in pain, but there was nobody there for her to talk to. When she eventually came back into the room, the crying continued.

"I'm sorry, Mama. I thought I was protecting the ring. I thought keeping it in your room would help keep your memory alive. I was just trying to keep your vibe in the house, but I failed. I'm sorry. I hope you can forgive me."

She felt guilty about something she really had no control over. She didn't know someone was going to break into her house. She didn't know honoring her mother would make it a little easier for someone to take something of incredible sentimental value away from her. She didn't know any of that, yet somehow, she felt guilty about all of it.

The "conversation" she had with her mother lasted for hours. She apologized several times. She got angry, she got sad, but at the end of it all, she started to feel better. I don't know if she was being honest with her emotions, but a calmness somehow resided in her by the time she went to sleep that night. When she woke up and prepared to go to work the next day, it was almost as though nothing had happened.

Time passed, and Harmony hadn't heard anything from the police department. She tried to remain optimistic about them finding the people who broke into her home and stole her mother's ring, but after about a week or so, her frustration level reached an all-time high.

"What is your purpose?" she asked someone on the phone.

Based on Harmony's reaction, they must have provided a response that she wasn't very fond of.

"So, you mean you haven't even found any suspects? I literally had to shoot one of the people who broke into my house. I saw the person bleeding, and I know the injury should have required a freakin' hospital visit. Did you check the blood? Did you go to any hospitals? Did you question doctors and nurses about a shooting victim?"

She stopped talking after her questions, but she wasn't quiet long enough for anyone to respond. Instead, she just gave herself a moment to catch her breath before she finished what she had to say.

"Since everyone's so busy, and you can't seem to find who robbed me, just forget about it! I'll take care of it myself. I see I'm not high enough on your priority list to actually do anything, but it's all good."

Harmony said, "it's all good," even though it wasn't. Her words could have been just simple sarcasm, or they could have been a lie she told herself so she wouldn't remain upset. Whatever the actual reason was, she was soon sitting on her bed. Without saying another word, she decided she needed to hear some music. It wasn't out of the ordinary for her to turn on something she liked, but whenever she did, she would normally play bass-heavy songs with quick tempos. They normally were songs full of energy, but the song she played right then was different.

The song started off with someone playing alone on a piano. All the notes fit perfectly with each other. After a brief intro, the strumming sounds of an acoustic guitar joined the piano. They were soon accompanied by the sounds of a drum set being played lightly in the background while someone began to sing.

The person sounded aged, but not like he was old, but it was as though the tone of his voice was letting the listeners know they could trust him because he had experience, that he had gone through something. The raspiness contained his pain, which probably was a bit soothing to the people who decided to listen to him because they were dealing with a pain of their own.

"I know you remember this one, Mom," Harmony said, almost whispering.

The music put Harmony at ease, and based on what she said, it had to be something she used to listen to with her mother. The memories connected to that artist's music had to be good ones because it quickly changed her attitude. The artist's music continued to play until it reached its end and by that time, Harmony had fallen asleep.

When her alarm woke her up the next day, she let out a loud yawn as she sat up.

"I can't believe I went to sleep like this. Girl, look at you. You have to do something with your hair. You can't go to work like this. You know your co-workers will clown you from the time you clock in until it's time for you to leave," she smiled as she joked with herself.

She was in a much better mood when she awoke compared to how she was before she went to sleep. As the days went on, her mood stayed on a positive upswing. She was probably still very upset about the robbery, but I didn't hear her speak much about it. She was somehow at peace with how everything transpired. That was good because not only did it have to be draining for her, but the stress couldn't have been healthy, either.

As her happiness continued to grow, our relationship changed. Before the robber, I didn't see her everyday, but the happier she got, the more she neglected me. I have no feelings, so her actions didn't upset me or make me sad, but I knew her change was abnormal, even by human standards.

After a few weeks, Harmony couldn't keep her happiness to herself. She started to invite people over to her home. All of a sudden, there were people in her house at all hours of the night, each day of the week. If she would have started having visitors over right after the robbery, it would have made more sense because it would have meant she was just afraid of being alone, but that's not what she did. Her actions didn't fit into any type of pattern of logic, but it wasn't my job to attempt to figure out why humans did what they did.

More time passed, and Harmony, for whatever reason, decided to move me to different places inside of her home. Sometimes I would be in her room, while other times, I was placed in her mother's room. As ridiculous as it may seem, I was even placed in the kitchen. When I was moved into the living room, we reached another turning point. Harmony was having yet another party when she asked a few people to sit and chat after the other guests left for the night.

"Hey, I know I don't know you, but it seemed like y'all had a great time tonight," she said.

"I can't speak for everyone, but I know I enjoyed myself," one of the guests said.

"Yeah, I don't normally do house parties, but something told me I should be here. You're gaining quite the reputation for throwing a good party," a young lady said.

"That's cool! I try my best to be a good host," Harmony replied.

"Well, you're doing a good job," someone said.

"This may sound a little strange, but would you all mind staying for a little bit? I mean, parties are cool, but sometimes I just wanna have a conversation with a cool group of people."

The remaining people pondered her request for a moment. Although the general consensus was that it was strange to be asked to stay for a late-night conversation, a few of them decided to stay because they were curious to see what Harmony wanted to talk about. When those who didn't want to participate left, the group of what sounded like about four or five people all sat down as Harmony turned the music off so they could all hear each other clearly.

"So, what do you all do?" she asked.

I noticed many people had no problems being the center of attention, so having them speak about themselves and what they did for a living immediately made them seem to forget they were staying late in a stranger's home after a random mid-week house party.

"Well, I guess I'll go first. My name is Charlotte, and I run an indie gaming studio. We get to make games for consoles and mobile devices."

"What are some of the games we may have heard of?" someone asked.

The woman went on to name some of her most high-profile games. Evidently, she named a lot of good products because everyone became more excited with every title she named.

"Are you serious? I actually have like five of those games on my phone right now! I can't believe you're the one responsible for them," Harmony said very excitedly.

Her enthusiasm made her words seem very sincere, but I didn't know if they actually were. After a few minutes of the lady talking about herself and what her company created, the conversation moved to the next person.

"I'm an investor and financial advisor. I'm still building my own personal wealth, so I'm not quite where I want to be," he said.

"No disrespect, but if you're not financially set, why should someone trust you with their finances?" another person asked.

"That's actually a very good question, and I don't take that question as being disrespectful at all. In my field, you have some who are in it for the quick gains, and you have those, like myself, who make moves for the long run. When I speak with clients, I have to find out what they want, try to remove improper expectations, and move from there. As for me being where I want to be financially, I don't know if I'll ever be there because I always know there's room for improvement," he said.

The group continued to speak about their individual financial situations for a while. They talked about what they felt were pros and cons of having someone not only watch, but basically be in control of another person's money. Harmony was quiet during this portion of the conversation. Perhaps it was because she wanted to pay attention to what was being said, or maybe she wasn't interested. Whatever the case was, she allowed the discussion to progress without interrupting them.

"Hey, everybody. My name is Russ, and that stunning woman is my girlfriend, Maria. We just recently opened that new gym on 9th Street," he said.

"I've seen that gym. It looks absolutely beautiful! I just don't have the best relationship with working out," Harmony said.

They all shared a laugh before Maria told more details about the gym she owned with Russ.

"I totally understand that because I was the same way about five years ago. Then, I met Russ."

"Oooh, I really like hearing a good love story. Please tell us more about how you met," Harmony said.

"Well, it was shortly after the new year. Just like most of us, I made a resolution to get in the best shape of my life, so when I saw a commercial to get a three-month membership to one of those large gyms for one dollar a month, I told myself it was a sign to get myself together. So, one day, I finally decided to go in, and that's when I saw Russ."

"Fortunately for me, my supervisor had me working the front desk that week, so I was the first person she saw. When we locked eyes, I knew immediately she was the one," Russ added.

"He made me feel comfortable, even though I was expecting to feel completely out of place. He convinced me to sign up for a membership, and we haven't gone a day without speaking to each other since then," Maria explained.

"Well, thank you, Maria and Russ, for making all of the rest of our stories seem boring," Harmony joked.

Within a short amount of time, the people who were strangers at the beginning of the night became friends. Before everyone left, Harmony made sure to get everyone's contact info. She promised to stay in contact with everyone, but for some reason, she seemed to have really made a connection with Maria.

"Hey, girl, you seem really cool. If you ever just wanna hang out, let me know," Harmony said.

"That'll be pretty dope! I'll hit you up for sure," Maria said as she left.

What they said at the end of the night could have just been an exchange of pleasantries, but it ended up building a real friendship. The two would converse over the phone on a weekly basis, and Maria would come over just as often.

"Hey, I know you said you don't have the best relationship with the gym, but I think you should check us out," Maria said one day while visiting Harmony.

"Are you saying I'm fat?" Harmony asked as she started to laugh.

"Girl, not at all. I just think we need to do all we can to be our best selves."

"Yeah, you're right. I guess what it comes down to is I'm actually a little afraid of it. These new-age machines scare me. I don't want to go in there and make a fool of myself in front of all of your other clients."

"I promise you don't have to worry about that. You don't even have to use any of the machines. In fact, I actually teach an aerobics and cardio class that doesn't use any weights or machines. It was actually designed for people that have the same fears as you. Give me an hour of your time, and I'll promise you'll enjoy yourself."

They talked some more, and by the end of the visit, Maria had convinced Harmony to pay her a visit at work. A few more days passed before I heard Harmony hyping herself up before her first trip to the gym.

"It's okay, Harmony. I know you're nervous, but this will be the start of something new. You can do it. I know you can!"

When she convinced herself she was ready to go, she left. A few hours later, she returned. For some reason, she sounded a bit different when she returned. As she talked to her reflection in the mirror, she was more energetic. She sounded confident and more like the Harmony of old. Perhaps her workout had a positive impact.

"That wasn't so bad, huh?" she asked herself.

Whatever happened during her workout was apparently something she desperately needed, so she continued to go. What started off as only a single trial transformed into a daily activity. It was good that her thoughts were no longer fixated on the robbery because that had started to change her personality.

Harmony's social interactions changed as her attitude did. She still had parties now and again, but nowhere near what she was doing before she met Maria. Whatever negativity the robbery gave her, her new friendship seemed to have taken it away.

During the entire time I had known Harmony, she never had anyone to share any parts of her life with. Although she now had friends, she still didn't have a companion. It was nearly impossible for me to determine if that actually impacted her or not, but evidently, Maria thought it did, so she and Russ took it upon themselves to help her out.

The phone rang one day as Harmony was cleaning up around her home. She put the device on speaker so she could continue working. As soon as Harmony answered, Maria immediately jumped into the conversation, bypassing their normal greeting.

"Harmony, hear me out. How about you let me and Russ set you up on a blind date? I think we have the perfect person for you."

"I'm just not about that life. Dating has never really been my thing, so the idea of a blind date is so far off of anything I've ever done," Harmony replied.

"Honestly, I don't know if dating is really any of our thing. It's weird and awkward, but it's a necessary evil. I hope I'm not overstepping or anything, but there has to be times when you get a little lonely."

"Yeah, kinda, but…"

"Girl, don't even think about tryin' to make an excuse. Trust me, before I met Russ, I felt that way, but I got you! Russ has a nice, single friend that we've been trying to hook up with someone for a long time, and we both think you would be perfect for each other. Plus, we can be there on your first date to make it a little easier on you."

Harmony became more accepting of going out with someone as the conversation continued. When the call finally ended, Harmony was ready to try something new. A few days after the call, she was anxiously getting ready for a date.

"This wasn't part of the plan, but sometimes plans have to be adjusted. It's all good," she told herself.

Based on our lack of time together leading up to the date, I expected to be left at home, but I wasn't. Harmony placed me, along with my carrying case, inside of the small purse she was taking with her. She said I had to go "just in case," whatever that meant. I didn't know where I'd be going for the night, but I knew we had arrived when Harmony started talking to Russ and Maria.

"Harmony, I'm so glad you let Maria talk you into going on a double date with us. We really think you're going to enjoy yourself with Leonard," Russ said.

"It's hard to enjoy myself with someone who's not here. Where is this guy?" Harmony asked, seemingly a little annoyed.

"He'll be here soon. He just talked to Russ on the way over here to let us know he was running late. Don't worry. He'll be here. Just relax. Let's go ahead and see where they have us sitting," Maria said.

Harmony was quiet. She may have been more nervous than

she thought she would be. She also could have been dealing with moments of regret, wishing she had never agreed to go out. It could have been a number of things, but whatever it was, she didn't say anything as the group was escorted to their table.

When they sat down, a waiter came by, introduced himself, and asked what everyone wanted to drink.

"Just water for me, thank you," Harmony said after everyone else placed their beverage order.

"Hey, I know this isn't starting off the way any of us envisioned, but it'll be worth it," Maria told her friend confidently.

"Okay."

She said almost nothing else while the couple conversed, she just impatiently sat at the table. I could hear her tapping her fingers on the table as she waited on someone who had already put her on hold, even though he hadn't even met her.

"I appreciate you guys trying to set me up, but it doesn't look like I'll be meeting this friend of yours. Being the third wheel is something I really try my best to avoid, so I think I'm gonna go ahead and leave," she told the couple.

"I know you're mad because I would be, too, but please give Leonard a few more minutes. In fact, if he's not here in ten minutes, I'll even pay for your parking."

"Well, parking has to get paid, and I'm already here, but I promise, if your friend is not here soon, you'll never hear the end of it," Harmony said.

Some would have taken what Harmony said as a threat, but that wasn't the case with Russ and Maria.

"Take it easy," Maria suggested.

Out of nowhere, Harmony started laughing very loudly.

"I'm glad everyone's in a good mood," a new voice said.

"Good mood? I don't know about all of that, but sometimes you gotta laugh to keep from saying something you shouldn't. Anyway, I guess you must be Late Leonard, the one who has kept me and this fabulous dress waiting," Harmony said to the person.

"Uh, yes, ma'am. I'm Leonard."

"No! I know you didn't just call me ma'am! Do I look like I'm your grandmother or something? So, you're gonna be late and disrespectful?"

"I really meant no disrespect, and I apologize for being late. There was a bit of a situation with my mother."

Right then, the tone of Harmony's words changed almost immediately.

"I'm sorry. Is everything okay?"

"Things could be much worse, but I guess they're okay. Let's not damper the mood, though. I've already held things up long enough."

Per Leonard's request, they fell into the type of banter you would expect from people on a date. There were awkward moments, as well as times when everyone laughed at things they probably didn't even find funny. To me, it was illogical for a person to go out of their way to impress other people they didn't know, especially for the purpose of a date that probably wasn't going to work out anyway.

Throughout the course of their meal, it was obvious Leonard was able to overcome the negative image Harmony had formed of him because of his tardiness. They talked, enjoyed the dinner, and by the end of the night, Leonard and Harmony found themselves continuing to enjoy each other's company after Maria and Russ left them at the restaurant.

"What are you actually looking for out of all of this?" Harmony asked suddenly.

"What do you mean?"

"Are you dating just to be dating, or are you looking for more?"

The amount of time it took him to answer showed he wasn't quite prepared for a question that serious, at least not so soon.

"If I'm being honest, there have been several points in my life when I was dating just to be around as many women as possible."

"Oh, really? Well, if that's how it is, let me tell you right now, I'm not the one!"

"I just met you, but I already know you wouldn't go for that. Plus, you have to realize what I said. I said there were points in my life when that's what I wanted. Trust me. I'm no longer in that space. I've matured a lot since then. Right now, I'm looking for my life partner. What about you?"

"I'm looking for someone who is not about the games because I'm too tired to keep playing them. I'm looking for somebody who knows what they want in life."

"So, ideally, are you looking for a man who has it all together?"

"What does that even mean?"

"Come on, Harmony, you know what I'm asking. Does your man have to have his finances completely in order, have himself a house, and all that other stuff women tend to ask for that rules out a bunch of guys who are trying to make it?"

Harmony cleared her throat. Whatever she was about to say, she wanted to make sure Leonard was able to hear it precisely the way she was saying it.

"So, if you're asking if I have standards, the answer is yes, beyond the shadow of a doubt. You asking that kinda makes me think you're one of those scared guys who fear a woman who knows what she wants. Is that who you are?"

"Harmony, please don't confuse my questions with fear. I don't work with the spirit of fear."

His response was sufficient enough to calm Harmony down. The date went on for a while longer, ending only when Harmony realized she had to work on a project for her job.

"If you'd like, I could take you home to make sure you get there safely," Leonard said.

"You think you slick, huh? I already know what you're trying to ask, and that ain't how I get down."

"Believe it or not, I wasn't even asking that. I just want to make sure you're safe."

"Well, if that's the case, I appreciate it, but it's not necessary. I have a little friend with me in my purse that will make sure I'm safe."

She was referring to me, of course, but I wished she wasn't. One of the many issues I had with Harmony, and people in general, was that they thought guns were their friends. We are not. I was not her friend. I did not have a sense of loyalty to her. While I was in her possession, it was my job to protect her, but if someone else took me, I would literally turn on her in a second. To you, that may seem cruel, but it is not in my job description to present things in ways humans find emotionally appealing, so I make no attempts to do so.

"A little friend? Well, I think I know what you mean by that. Can I at least walk you to your car?"

"Yeah, that'll be nice," Harmony said.

Their date had some ups and downs, but when Harmony got in the car, the joy she had as she sang random songs let me know she had a good time. Over the next few weeks, Harmony and Leonard started to spend a lot more time with each other. They quickly went from strangers, to friends, to people who had no problem saying they were in a committed relationship with each other.

"Keep it real. Do you see us getting married at some point?" Leonard asked one day.

"Yeah, I do, and thinking back to the low points of our first date, I can't even believe it. What about you?"

"There's no doubt. You're different from everybody else I've ever dated. You have style, beauty, intelligence, and a confidence level that's out of this world. You make me step my game up and be on point at all times. I really see myself being with you forever. Don't get it twisted, I'm not trying to set you up to ask you if you'd marry me today, but I did want you to know I think about it all of the time. You'll be getting that important question pretty soon, if all goes according to the plan," he continued.

"Well, I'm not gonna rush you. We're moving at a good pace, and I'm cool with that...for now," Harmony replied.

They laughed as they conversed and enjoyed each other's company.

"Life is good, and I'm grateful for you," Leonard said.

"I'm grateful for you, too. Hey, babe, can I ask you something?" Harmony inquired.

"What's up?"

"Do you have my back? I mean, if something went down, would you make sure we're good?"

"You know I got you! Why would you even ask me that?"

"I was just wondering and I'm really glad you said you do, though. Part of my issue with my past relationships is when I found out people really weren't down for me the way they said they were."

"Well, that ain't me. I'm with you, no matter what."

To another person, Leonard's statements could have been thought of as sweet or caring, but they seemed unusual to me. Why would someone agree to "having someone's back" without details of what the person was really asking? It would seem more information would be needed before an agreement would have been made, but people were willing to give away their promises without very much thought. However, the foolishness of humans is not a fight I was built to take on.

Stupidity aside, Harmony and Leonard were very fond of each other, and they made sure they let that be known every chance they got. Almost all of their free time was spent with each other. It seemed like they would have been suffocated by suddenly having a person in their space all of the time, but they weren't. They made each other happy, which was good for them.

A while after Harmony and Leonard officially started dating, Harmony would take a few of the moments she had alone to question who she was. Sometimes it was as though she would argue with herself because of her newfound joy.

"So, is this who you've become? Are you just gonna be one of those women who is so in need of companionship that you just give up your goals? This can't be you, Harmony. You're better than this!"

People say a lot of nonsensical things, and Harmony was no exception. The words, "You are better than this," stuck out to me. What exactly was she saying she was better than? Was she better than being with someone who valued her? If that wasn't it, what was she really asking herself, and why was she asking it? What was suddenly going on in her mind?

She didn't provide answers to any of the questions I had, but that was expected because she wasn't even able to answer the questions she had for herself. Her conversations with herself always ended just as suddenly as they began. In the end, they just seemed to be placeholders between empty moments. In spite of how Harmony acted when she was around her so-called friends, the self-discussions she engaged in told me she either wasn't comfortable with being happy, or she wasn't actually happy at all.

The next few months were repeats of the same cycle. When she was around Leonard, Maria, Russ, or any combination, everything was all good. Harmony's tone was full of joy. Her words were positive, and it always seemed like nothing could bring her down. When they weren't around, it was a completely different story.

When she was alone, she would question her purpose. She would ask herself if she was a good person. It was almost as though Harmony was battling with someone who wasn't there. It was like she had become two very different people.

Things got so bad, I started referring to the angry, depressed version of Harmony as June. I don't know why this name was chosen, though. Perhaps it was a name I heard during a random conversation, or maybe I equated her hot temper to the hot temperatures of June she always complained about. Either way, the name fit, so I went with it.

June wasn't normally allowed to come out in public because Harmony kept her under control, but at home, things were different. When Harmony was by herself, June took over. As time progressed, June got more aggressive. What started off as a few questions about Harmony's goals transformed into a barrage of belittling comments. One day, after a series of negative comments, I was pulled out of the bag I was resting in.

"What's the gun for, Harmony? What do you plan on doing with it?"

I was slammed against the table several times. I could've gone off, but my safety was on. Even it wasn't, she showed she wasn't concerned about that. I was swung around so recklessly, I had no idea what was about to happen. Just as things were getting worse, the phone rang.

As she still held me tightly with one hand, she put her phone on speaker.

"Hey, babe, what's up?" the voice on the other line asked.

For a few seconds, there was silence, and that was promptly followed by a deep sigh of relief.

"Hey, Leonard. What's going on?" she asked as though she wasn't enraged just a few seconds before the call.

"Not much. I know this is really short notice, but Russ plans on proposing to Maria tomorrow. He's invited their close friends and family to a dinner so we can all share the moment with them."

"Wow, that's beautiful. I had kinda planned on just taking it easy tomorrow because I've been so tired from work, but I have to go witness that."

"Are you sure? If you need to rest, I'm sure they'll understand. Plus, they'll be so caught up in the moment, I doubt they'll even realize who's even there."

"I think I'll be fine. Plus, it sounds like fun, and I know it will be a beautiful thing to see."

They continued to talk about their plans, and just like that, June was sent away, like a child who was banished to her room to think about what she had done. For that moment, Harmony was happy, so June had no purpose.

When Leonard picked Harmony up the next day, she was still very happy, but it didn't stop her from letting me tag along. For the most part, the night was just a regular date between the couple, but after a while, that normality faded.

"Yo, is that Harmony and my boy, Leonard? What are you two doing here?" Russ asked as if he didn't already know.

I only knew it was Russ because I had heard the voice so many times before. When he acted like he didn't know what was going on, it caused Leonard and Harmony to do the same thing. Their acting didn't seem believable, but it was good enough to fool Maria.

"I know you're probably just trying to spend some time with each other, but why don't you come join us?" Maria asked.

"That sounds fun. Russ, are you cool with that?" Leonard wondered.

"C'mon, bro, that ain't even a question! At this point, y'all are like fam, so of course, you can join us!"

So, just like that, we all made ourselves comfortable at their table. I don't know if it was part of Leonard's plan, but evidently, it didn't deviate too far from the path he wanted to take.

The couples truly seemed to enjoy each other's company as they shared yet another meal together. As they ordered their dessert, a violin player started playing near their table. The conversation stopped for a moment, so it could only be assumed everyone was either enjoying what they were hearing, or they were completely disgusted by it. Either way, they all remained quiet until Maria broke the silence with three simple words.

"This is beautiful!"

Her tone let me know the music was having a positive impact on her.

"Babe, you remember how much we smiled and talked on our first date? It was crazy how we talked about the rest of our lives and all that we wanted to accomplish, wasn't it?"

"Yeah, I still can't believe that we were both comfortable enough with each other to talk about having a future together. I even remember telling you about a scene from a movie I loved so much that I wanted it to happen to me in real life."

"True! Wait, what did you say about that scene, though?" Russ asked.

"I don't think Harmony and Leonard wanna hear about that stuff."

"Girl, please! You know I like those sappy rom-coms, too. Tell us what happened," Harmony requested.

"Okay, okay, you twisted my arm. So, this couple had been dating for a while, and the girl thought it was time for them to take the next step in their relationship, but the guy always acted like he wasn't ready. One day, he took her out on a date to their favorite restaurant, where they met up with their friends. While they were there, this violin player came to the table and started playing their favorite song. It was her favorite because it was the song her dad used to play for her mom all of the time," she said.

Right then, the violin player smoothly transitioned from what he was playing into something new.

"And the crazy thing about the song was, the girl said she

hated it growing up because she heard it so much. She said she couldn't appreciate the song's beautiful lyrics until she....wait..."

That's when the night's plan hit her.

"Is this entire night a setup? Are you..."

"Could you close your eyes for a moment?" Russ asked Maria.

She agreed, and after his question was asked, the clambering of what had to be a large group of people drew near.

"Before you open your eyes, can you just promise not to be mad at me?" Russ asked.

"I promise, but this better not be anything crazy," she said.

If the people who had rushed to the table were trying to be quiet, they failed miserably.

"Babe, we've gone through so many ups and downs since we've been together. You've been willing to ride with me during my lowest moments. When I didn't know how we were going to take care of our bills, you didn't gave up on me. I never could've made it to this point without you. You're important to me, and everyone here feels the same way. Over the past few weeks, I've been scared to ask what I'm gonna ask, but our loved ones have given me the confidence, and their blessings. So, could you go ahead and open your eyes?"

By the loud scream she let out after he said that, I take it she did as he suggested.

"Oh, my...I...I just can't believe everyone is here."

Maria's voice trembled, letting us all know she had become overwhelmed with emotions.

"Maria, everyone here wants to know, will you marry me?" Russ asked.

"Yes! Yes! A thousand times, yes," she finally said.

The crowd of onlookers acted as if her words were literally going to change *their* lives. They clapped and cheered like something major had happened, when in reality, all that happened was a bunch of people gathered around to hear one person answer a question that was asked by another. Humans make such big deals out of such minor things.

The cheering started to die down a little before people asked her to show the ring. Maria granted their request, and soon, everyone cheered and yelled loudly again. At that moment, I wondered if they were cheering because they were happy for the progression of a couple's relationship, or if it was because they were enamored with Maria's ring.

Who could tell what drives the reactions of people? Their moods always seemed to be sans logic, and they swayed as freely as the wind blew.

"Ooh, girl, that ring is gorgeous!" Harmony said.

"Thank you! I can't believe Russ got me something like this. It's so beautiful!"

"Yeah, the crazy thing is, the ring just gives off such an antique-type vibe. It's so regal, like the ring has a personality of its own. It ain't a regular ring."

"Thank you," Maria replied.

They talked for a few more minutes before everyone else wanted to get some time to speak with Maria and Russ. After a while, Harmony and Leonard decided to go to their own table so they could grab something to eat by themselves. Even though they left Russ and Maria, they were still the topic of the conversation Harmony and Leonard had.

"How well would you say you know them?" Harmony asked.

"Pretty well. Why? What's up?"

"I don't know. Things just don't seem right. They've always seemed a little too perfect for me."

"It sounds like Harmony is hating, but I don't know why. I mean, you're with me, and you had to have noticed that I'm kinda like a big deal," Leonard said jokingly.

"Babe, I won't pretend like our relationship ain't great, because it is, but can I keep it real with you?"

"Yeah, absolutely!"

"Will you promise not to repeat what I'm about to say?" Harmony asked.

"For sure. I got you. What's up?"

Harmony paused. I didn't know if she needed time to think, to look around to make sure nobody was listening, or if she just wanted to take a breath before she spoke. Whatever the case, she stopped before she said what she felt was necessary.

"I'm just gonna say it; I think Russ and Maria can be annoying sometimes because they're fake. This perfect couple stuff is not who they are. They're frauds."

Her statement could have been shocking, but Leonard didn't hesitate to respond.

"Okay, since you're being honest with me, I'm gonna do the same. The truth of the matter is, I understand being annoyed by them because I feel that way sometimes, too. They're my friends and they have been for over ten years. I hope they'll be in my life for the rest of my life, but even with all of that, I'm a realist. I understand relationships of all kinds change over time. I know, even if I want to be friends with them forever, that may not be in the cards. As sad as that may sound, that's life. There's something else about their relationship, though."

"What?"

"Harmony, their relationship has nothing to do with ours. So, like I told you before, I'm with you. That means, regardless of what's going on with them, I'll try my best to make sure our relationship is intact. Their fake perfection has nothing to do with us."

She must have agreed, or at least accepted what Leonard said because she didn't argue to prove anything different. In fact, for the duration of the time she spent with Leonard that night, she hardly said anything at all.

After they parted ways for the night, and Harmony made it home, June made another appearance.

"Is that how you're gonna let them do you? I mean, for real, is that it? I can't even believe you didn't do anything while you were there. I guess you had to get your head right, huh? I guess you didn't want to act up in public. I guess you're just the girl that allows that sort of thing to happen right in front of them. Okay, cool, you just keep being that person."

Disappointment had set in, and June continued questioning Harmony. The tone was belittling and filled with words that weren't necessarily hurtful when they were used alone, but the combination in which they were used was not coming from a good place. Humans were often self-deprecating. It was pointless, but that's exactly who humans usually were.

It would seem like a person would always want to make themselves feel better to optimize their productivity, but that's not what they did. Instead, it was normal behavior for them to speak to themselves in a way that negatively impacted their volatile emotions. Again, it had no point. Seeing how most people were seemingly searching for their purpose, I guess it made sense their actions were usually purposeless.

The words June expressed to Harmony seemed to change her mindset.

"You know what? You're right! They wanna play me? I guess I have to show them exactly who I am."

I had no idea what her words meant, and although they were spoken with confidence, I don't even think Harmony knew. Regardless, the next day, she seemed to be on a mission. She got dressed and told herself it was time to go to work.

She put me in a bag I wasn't used to being in. Many humans were creatures of habit, so her changing my container was unusual, but I wasn't concerned about trivial things like that.

As we traveled, the journey seemed different. I was confined, but the more Harmony drove, the more it seemed like we weren't going to one of her normal destinations. Then, she made a phone call that gave me more insight. Since the call connected through the speakers of her car, I was able to hear everything that was said.

"Hey, babe. You're not working today, right?" she asked, which let me know she was talking to Leonard.

"No, I'm not. What's up?"

"You're still my ride or die, right?"

"Harmony, you know I'm riding with you 'till the wheels fall off."

"I'm glad you said that. Do you think you could do me a favor?"

"I can't make a promise until I know what you're asking for," Leonard told her.

"Okay, that's a good point," she said.

"So, are you actually gonna tell me what you need?"

"My bad. I just need you to join me in Maria's class today. Nothing crazy."

"I don't normally do all of that cardio stuff, but I'll do just about anything to see my girl."

"I'm glad to hear that. So, can you meet me there in about forty minutes? I don't want to be late for class."

Leonard laughed as he told Harmony he didn't appreciate the short notice she gave him, but he agreed to meet her. Since she was already driving when she called Leonard, we made it there much quicker than he did. Once we were there, Harmony had another one of those discussions with June. This time, the conversation was a bit more cordial than it normally was.

"So, I hope you're actually ready. You said you wanted to make things right, so this is your opportunity. Don't back down!"

She hyped herself up a little while longer before Leonard finally made it. They exchanged a few pleasantries before the bag I was in was placed into a locker while they went to another room. I figured they went to exercise with Maria. It must have been intense because whenever I heard anyone, they all sounded exhausted.

"C'mon everybody, I know we've all worked hard, but we have to keep pushing! We only have a little while longer before this week's class is over," Maria said.

When Maria finally ended dismissed the class, she quickly ran to Harmony and Leonard.

"Hey! I didn't expect to see you two here, especially on a day when I didn't beg you to show up."

"Girl, I guess all that talking you've been doing finally reached me. I felt like taking care of some things today, and the first thing on my list was to come here," Harmony said.

"Well, I'm glad you started your day off with me."

"Of course! Oh, is Russ here today?" Harmony asked.

"Yeah, why? What's up?"

"Not much. There's just something I want to talk to both of you about."

"Oh, okay. Yeah, Russ practically lives in the gym, so he's around here somewhere. I'll call him in here, so just give me a few minutes."

While they waited, Harmony went and got my bag out of the locker. She put the bag down on the ground near where she was standing.

"What do you need to talk to them about?" Leonard asked.

"Not much. I really just need to show them something. It won't take long, though. And after we're finished here, do you think we could go get something to eat?"

"Yeah, I don't see why that would be a problem."

"Cool! It should definitely be something healthy because we did way too much good work here today to mess it up by doing something bad," she said.

They carried on with small talk until Maria came back with Russ.

"Look who finally managed to join the party," Maria said.

"Hey, guys. Maria told me you have something to tell us, Harmony," Russ said.

"Yeah, I do, but do you mind if I grab a towel from my bag first? That workout Maria put us through has me sweating like crazy!"

They laughed as Harmony grabbed a towel from the bag, just like she said she was going to do. Before she closed the bag, she wrapped me up in the towel she had just picked up. As I remained hidden, she carried me to where everybody was. Everyone was oblivious to me being there.

"So, what did you have to say, Harmony?" Russ asked.

"First, I want to tell you congratulations again on your engagement. Secondly, I want to say that I've learned a lot about people since becoming your friend, so I really want to thank you for that."

"No problem, and let me say, meeting you has literally changed my life," Maria said.

"Hey, do you remember the first time we met?" Harmony asked.

"Of course! It was at that party, right?" Russ asked.

"That was the first time we had the chance to have a calm and civil conversation, but it wasn't the first time we met. I want you to really think about it because it's really important to me. So again, do you remember the first time we met?"

Everyone was quiet. I didn't know exactly what was happening because, for a while, Harmony kept me wrapped up.

"I don't know what you're trying to get us to say, but we don't really have time to play a guessing game. We have a lot of work to do," Russ said.

It was evident Russ had quickly grown tired of the conversation, and he was trying to end the interaction, but Harmony wasn't going to allow that to happen.

"Leonard, why are our friends all of a sudden being so rude? Why do you think they want to leave just because I asked about when we met? That seems strange, huh?" Harmony asked.

"Yeah, it's a little weird, but I'm really confused about all of this," Leonard said.

"Harmony, I don't know what's going on with you today, but I think it would be best if you left," Maria said, trying to remain calm.

The group of friends had never really had a major disagreement, but it wasn't surprising that it was finally happening. People have always been incapable of just maintaining their composure when there was a disagreement. They were also usually unable to think rationally whenever emotions were involved, which was unfortunate for them, but it is one of the reasons I existed in the first place.

"I figured you would try to kick me out or walk away, but that's not gonna happen. You ran away the first time we met, but you're gonna have to stay around this time."

"Babe, what are you talking about?" Leonard asked Harmony.

"Don't worry. You'll find out soon. You still have my back, right?"

He said he did, even though he didn't exude the most confidence. When Leonard told Harmony he still had her back, June made her first public appearance. She removed the towel that had me hidden. Then, she yelled as loudly as she could, expressing her anger.

"Okay, okay, okay. Please, Harmony! Please!" Russ begged.

"I asked you two to just say how we first met. It was a simple request, but neither of you had the common decency to just tell the truth. So, that just confirms to me that both of you are still cowards, but you don't even have to worry about it. You're familiar with this cute little creature, right? That question might as well be rhetorical, so don't worry about it. I do need you to tell Leonard how we actually met, though. Please, don't play dumb this time! I also recommend you don't test my patience because, at this point, I don't really have much left."

The Harmony they knew was no longer there, and they were getting an unexpected introduction to June. I couldn't be sure, but it seemed like June would be handling all of the conversations from that point forward.

"We met at your house. There! We said it! Can we go now?"

"Russ, you know that's not what I want to hear. Your next response better be your best response. If it's not, you and Maria will meet your maker today. Do you hear me?"

"We met at your house," Russ said again.

I had a full chamber until Russ repeated his statement. Evidently, what he said upset Harmony, again, who had fully embraced the role of June. The warning shot we let out caused everyone else in other parts of the gym to start screaming. I could hear their fear as they all tried to exit the building.

"I see you think I'm joking. Tell Leonard, now!" Harmony said.

There was no more beating around the bush.

"We went to your house to rob you! We saw you at your home when we went there to steal from it!" Maria finally said.

"Are you kidding me? You robbed Harmony and then became her friend. How sick are you?" Leonard asked.

"That's not even the worst part, babe. You know that nice engagement ring Maria has on her finger right now? That's the same ring that was given to me by my mother before she died. They took it from me. They took my mother's ring and decided to parade around with it like it's their symbol of love...like they earned it. Nope! We ain't playing pretend no more! The first time you got ended up with a slight limp. This time, it'll be different."

I thought she would continue the monologue, reminiscent of the final speech of a supervillain in a film, but that's not what happened. Right then, June decided everyone had talked enough. Within seconds, we fired off a few more shots. This time, their purpose was not to send out a warning. A few were dedicated to Russ, the others belonged to Maria, and all of them went exactly where June wanted them to go.

"Was that necessary?" Leonard asked.

Leonard questioned if Harmony's actions were required, but he didn't seem shocked at what she did. His words weren't what I expected him to say, but evidently, he was going to stay by his companion's side, just as he had promised.

Harmony had grown tired of playing nice with people who had done her wrong, so she had to find a way to end it. Harmony aimed me where she knew would not harm Russ and Maria, but kill them. It only took a few seconds for Harmony and Leonard to witness the last breaths leave Russ and Maria's bodies.

As they stared at the bodies of their friends, the sounds of police sirens grew closer. During all of the excitement, someone must have called the police, but at that moment, there was nobody in the building other than us.

"You can run now, it's okay," June said in a tone that made it seem like she was becoming Harmony again.

"That wasn't part of the promise," he told her.

In spite of the approaching sirens, we remained still for a moment before I felt myself being lowered.

"I think this belongs to me," Harmony said very calmly as she bent even closer to Maria.

She had once again taken ownership of the ring that meant so much to her. The actions she had just taken proved she had revenge on her mind for a while, which meant she let her emotions dictate her actions.

"The cops are almost here! If we're going, we need to go now!" Leonard said.

"I hate both of you, but I'm glad we were finally able to have a real talk about how our relationship began," Harmony said to Russ and Maria.

She put me down on the ground next to Russ and Maria. Her fingerprints were all over me, and because of that, she made it easier for the cops to possibly find her, but she didn't care. In her mind, my job had been completed, so she no longer had a need for me. We had gone through a lot together, but she made it clear she didn't want to deal with me anymore. That's how people are, though.

People will use anything and everybody they can until they feel they no longer need it (or them) around. Then, they'll just throw everything away. That's what happened to me, but it was all good because with or without a person around, I was still going to be the same.

I can't tell you what happened to Harmony or Leonard after that day because they abandoned me. I can't tell you if she regretted her actions because she didn't say anything about that before she left. I can say is that my time with Harmony (and June) confirmed people are willing to give up everything for retribution.

Harmony could have lived her life with someone she loved if she would have found a way to forgive the people who had done her wrong, but that wasn't in her nature. People always talked about this thing they refer to as "common sense" but if none of them have it, how common is it?

I was in the life of someone who set out to get something that was passed down to her from her mother. To do so, she was willing to take multiple lives for it. I'm sure her mother's ring meant a lot to her, but did the two lives she took for it equate to a fair exchange? That's not for me to decide, but I do wonder if Harmony's actions would make her mother proud. Would she have thought her daughter's actions, and whatever consequences she had to face, worth getting a single item back?

Humans are complex and unpredictable. Usually, they don't

even know what will set them off, calm them down, or even make them happy. In this matter, the human I was around was eventually able to eliminate what was causing her dissonance, but I will never know if she was truly able to bring harmony back to her existence.

NARRATIVE 7: WHERE DOES YOUR LOYALTY LIE?

I've known Stevie for a few years. From day one, he always talked about how nobody understood what he had to deal with. His wife finally got tired of him, so she left a few months ago. Their kids got sick of his nonsense, so they stopped acknowledging his existence. And anyone else who ever had anything to do with him had all reached their breaking points, too.

In one way or another, he carried me around with him almost all of the time. It was as though he felt he couldn't exist without me. I heard other people throw out words like "depressed" or "depression" when they talked about him, but he never said anything like that about himself, so I don't know how true any of that was. One day, he placed me on the counter in his restroom as he stared at himself in the mirror.

Initially, he looked himself up and down without saying anything. Then, it was like he was rediscovering something as he stopped and stared at a symbol he had tattooed on his neck. Whatever the tattoo was, he normally kept it covered up, but right then, it had all of his attention.

"None of this should have ever happened. I never should

have gotten into the whole gang life. What was I even doing? It ain't like I didn't have love from my folks at home because Mama made sure she told me she loved me. And I know we were struggling a little for money, but it wasn't bad enough for me to be tryin' to push work to fiends on the corner. Now, it's like the spirits of the people's lives I ruined are all comin' back to ruin mine. I messed up. I messed up bad, but it ain't nothin' I can do about it now. I was so caught up in trying to portray some kinda 'gangster image,' I think I actually lost myself. Other than the memories that are etched in my brain and the nightmares that sometimes wake me up in the middle of the night, this tattoo is one of the few things that keep me connected to my old life. I need to get rid of it, but… I don't know… it's like I can't. It's like there's something stopping me from doing what I know I should. I need to…"

He stopped what he was saying for a moment before he suddenly just switched subjects, almost as if he had forgotten what he was talking about.

"No, that ain't true. This tattoo ain't the only reminder because The Center is still there. What am I even supposed to do?" he asked himself.

He looked at himself some more before he picked me up.

"You're the only one still around. You're the only friend I have!"

He would always say stuff like that, and I always wished I could tell him how wrong he was. How did he believe a gun could be anyone's friend, especially his? If I could have, I would have left him just like everyone else did. Unfortunately, free will was not something I had.

"We don't need her! Let her go," he said, lying to himself the day his wife officially left their home for good.

He turned his music up loudly and tried to pretend he was happy, but the act didn't last long. He soon grew tired of the music and decided to sit in silence, which forced him to be alone with his thoughts.

"Does it really have to be like this? I don't even think I deserve this. Everything I did was done for a reason. I had to protect myself! I had to survive! I did what I had to do!"

He was yelling at himself like someone who had completely lost control. He asked questions and made statements with nobody around to respond. I heard him referring to this thing he called "guilt." Evidently, it was a feeling some humans would have after they did something they felt was wrong. What's crazy is, they had this feeling only after they, in most cases, freely chose to do what they knew was wrong.

What had Stevie done to make himself feel so guilty? Well, there wasn't really a single thing that led to his state of misery. Instead, it was more like a lifetime of bad decisions he thought he could get avoid facing the consequences for. He was wrong, but it would take a little more time before he would realize that. Before we get to that point, let me tell you more about the type of person Steve is, based on what I've witnessed, as well as what I've heard.

When I was introduced to Stevie, his family was still together, but the foundation was already starting to crumble.

"Why are you talking to me like you care? You always do whatever you want to, so why change what you think is working for you?"

The source of the questions was a young lady I later found out was Stevie's oldest daughter, Leela. She was upset, but her father was dismissive of her emotions, which helped to prove the point she tried to make.

"Is that what you think? You think I just do whatever I want? Child, you're totally oblivious to what's really going on. Go to your room before we both end up saying something we can't take back."

Stevie didn't care enough to have me in a lockbox or

anything, so I was sitting on a nearby table as all of this was happening. I could tell by her facial expressions the young lady had more she wanted to say, but she kept it to herself. Instead of making things worse, she just did what she was told to do.

"These kids are gonna fool around and…." Stevie mumbled to himself when his wife, Constance, walked into the room.

"They're gonna fool around and do what?"

"They're gonna make me do something to put them in their place."

"Are you making threats to your own kids? That's the kind of stuff that makes them not like you," she said.

Her statement and tone confirmed his actions and words over the years were wearing thin on her.

"That makes them not like me? I don't care if them kids don't like me, but they will respect me."

"You're pitiful, Stevie. You really need to get it together before you find yourself alone. With all that's happening to you right now, I know you don't want that. Don't you see you're literally pushing your entire family away?"

"Y'all ain't goin' nowhere, so just stop it," Stevie said to his wife with an abundance of confidence.

If he was trying to find a way to say the dumbest thing possible, he succeeded. On the other hand, if he still cared about his family, it didn't make any sense to say anything like that.

"Is that how you feel? Cool, remember that! We'll see if that ego of yours keeps you company when we're gone," his wife said as she left the room, upset and frustrated.

Stevie was uninterested in doing or saying anything that didn't make him feel good. He angered both his wife and one of his children within a matter of minutes, but his narcissism wouldn't allow him to admit he had even done anything wrong.

"The nerve! They wanna act like they can just do or say anything to me. I don't deserve that, but they'll see how wrong they are," he said as he started the conversation with himself back up again.

Apparently, in Stevie's mind, whatever caused his daughter, and subsequently, his wife, to be upset with him was not caused by him. This was his norm, the conversations the family had that day were on repeat for many of the following days.

The disappointment Stevie caused was expressed by several different members of the family. His lack of accountability towards the consequences of his actions remained constant. Then, one day the youngest member of the family caused the conversation to progress with a simple question.

"Daddy, why are you so angry?"

He didn't have a quick response. He was used to having a rebuttal to more complex discussions; however, the question from his youngest child completely caught him off guard.

He breathed heavily as he tried to come up with something to say. Soon, he stopped trying to think of something and simply spoke his truth.

"I'm angry because I'm tired of being tired," he finally said.

From what I heard about his children, both of them were incredibly intelligent, but his youngest daughter, Viv, was too young to understand what his answer meant.

"I don't get it," Viv said.

"Okay, let me explain it in a different way. I deal with a lot, and it wears me down. Life is tiring, and I don't like feeling like this. It's draining."

"What are you talking about? You have money because of your retirement, and you don't even have to go to work if you don't have to. No disrespect, but I think you have it easy."

I expected Stevie to yell, as usual, but he didn't do that. For the first time since I was introduced to him, Stevie began to cry. I also heard him attempt to catch his breath every few seconds, and after several failed attempts, he was able to speak again.

"Living ain't easy, and you can't possibly imagine what it's like to have your past threaten your future every single day. You don't understand having people you tried to save literally tell you they will end your life."

Viv had to be around seven or eight. She may have been too young to completely understand why her father felt the way he did, but I thought she would have been old enough to have some level of empathy for her father after he expressed himself the way he did. She didn't, though.

"Really? It just sounds like you're trying to blame people for how you feel. I don't know why people would be threatening you, but I learned whatever energy you put out into the universe is what will come back to you."

"I guess you think you're grown, huh?"

"No, Daddy, I don't. I'm just a kid tryin' to talk to my dad, but I guess that's not what you want."

"Little girl, don't try and tell me what I want. Y'all really need to learn to stay in your place."

"See, that's what I'm talking about, Dad. I love you, but it's kinda hard to like you," she said very calmly.

Stevie probably wanted to scream at that point, but his daughter didn't give him the opportunity. With a maturity level that far exceeded her age, she just left. I'm sure having his daughter leave without him telling her to do so truly angered him.

After his daughter left the room, I didn't hear anything else for quite some time. He always acted as though he didn't want anyone around him, but it was an act. Oftentimes, when nobody else was close to him, he would talk about his mistakes. He would look at me and release the feelings he had about his regrets. He did himself a great injustice trying to use me as his therapist, but he often told me I was the only one who would stay around long enough to hear what he had to say.

The longer he was alone, the more anxious he got. He would mumble to me, almost as if he expected me to respond. When had me out on the table one day, he started talking to me as the rain poured down outside. From previous interactions, I knew rain was another thing Stevie disliked, although he never really mentioned why.

The deluge competed with the thunder and lightning to see which would be the loudest. The noise broke down the false wall of bravado Stevie tried to keep up. At the same time, the continuance of rain poured down layers of vulnerability.

"I don't understand why nobody is here. What are they doing? See, this is what makes me mad!"

Right then, he started throwing things around like a child seeking attention from his parents. He did this for a little while before his wife entered the room.

"What are you doing?" she asked, acting as if she didn't even see me.

"Don't act like you care about what I'm doing," he replied.

He thrived on turmoil, so he immediately tried to create a problem with his wife, but on that day, she was not in the mood to add to an already chaotic atmosphere.

"If you don't want me to act like I care, then I won't. You win, Stevie, you win," she said with an eerie calmness.

With that, she left the room as suddenly as she had entered it. This left me alone with Stevie again as he started another emotional tirade.

"Did you see that?" he asked me directly.

I wanted to tell him I saw his inability to have a civilized conversation with his significant other. I wished I could have told him how foolish he was for not being able to handle having someone around him who actually cared. I wanted to tell him these things, but there was no way for me to do so.

"They're driving me crazy! They're supposed to be my family, and none of them care!"

It was strange he said his family was driving him crazy when he clearly was in the driver's seat of his turbulent emotional journey, but it was yet another example of him not taking responsibility for what he caused. I also was not the best judge of feelings, but for him to say nobody cared about him when it was obviously not true, was very strange.

This act of handing out blame was a daily activity for him, which made each day like an uninspired repeat of the previous one. I wouldn't have known when a day started or ended if it weren't for the family's routine. Each day would start with them trying to greet Stevie in a positive manner. Throughout the day, he would always do or say something that would bring negative vibes upon the home before everyone went to sleep.

One day, after what had to be at least a few months (or more) of repetitive days, Stevie received a phone call when he sat in the house alone. At the time of the call, he was trying to work around the house, so he put it on speaker so he could continue without having to hold the phone.

"Hello," Stevie said.

"What up, homie? Why you ain't been around lately? You forgot about us?"

"I'm retired. How did you get this number, anyway? Why are you callin' me?"

"I'm calling because retirement wasn't part of our agreement. You still got little kids to look out for. Don't you care about the kids?"

"Yeah, I care, but I can't keep going back. I have to worry about my own family. It was dumb of me to go there in the first place, but I can't keep going back."

The person on the other end of the call started to laugh.

"You ain't got a choice, bro. You stop when I say you can stop. I let you take some time off, but it ain't all good. Just like I have your number, please believe I know where you live. So you goin' back, do you hear me?"

"Yeah, I hear you."

"Good. I'm sure the kids will be happy to see you. And if I

don't see you soon, we'll be talking again," the person said as he ended the call.

After the conversation, Stevie told his family he was going back to work.

"Why? Is something wrong?" his wife asked.

"Umm, not really. I just think I need to revisit some things. Maybe it'll change how I've been acting. Who knows?"

"I mean, I appreciate you saying you want to do something to make a change, but I really don't think going back there is the best idea. I actually think it may trigger you."

In previous conversations, a simple suggestion by anyone in his family would've been enough to set Stevie off, but he respectfully told his wife he disagreed with what she said. He told her he was going to the center that day to look around and have some primary conversations, but he hoped to be back home before the rest of the family arrived. She begrudgingly agreed before she headed out for the day.

Prior to that point, I never heard anyone mention "the center," but based on how they talked about it, I knew whatever it was, it was important to the family's history. At first, I wasn't sure if I was going to be traveling to this new place with Stevie, but I soon found out I would.

"I know they don't want you where we're going, but you should be okay. Just stay quiet," he told me.

This guy already said I shouldn't have been making the trip, yet he still was going to take me. To make things worse, he told me to stay quiet as if I had the ability to do anything without human influence. If I made any noise, it would only be because one of the humans made me do it.

Instances like that reminded me that I didn't have the same freedom that I, and my family, actually helped humans obtain. I didn't have free will. I didn't have the freedom to choose. In fact, I didn't have any freedom at all. My reason for creation was simply to be ready when a human needed me. There was no room for me to like or dislike what I had to do, nor when I had to do it. There were no options for me, and that ride to the center gave me time to sit with that.

"Here we are. We've made it to The Center for At-Risk Teens. I honestly never thought I would see you again," he said, letting me know where we were.

Almost as soon as we went inside of the building, Stevie was greeted.

"My eyes must be deceiving me! Steven Joseph Moss, is that really you?"

"Just because I retired, you think you can just call me by my full government name?"

"Man, I guess I was so surprised to see you, I had to use your full name to make sure it's really you. What are you doing here? Are you trying to retire from being retired already? Are you trying to get back in the game?"

"You don't waste any time with small talk, do you? You just jump right into the real questions, huh?" Stevie asked.

"We're old, bruh. We don't have time to waste. I figure if you're here, then there has to be a reason for it. Am I wrong?"

"I can't say you're wrong," Stevie said.

"For real, are you here because you want to get back to work? If you are, I can get your paperwork started immediately," the person said.

"I really don't know. Since I retired, life has been kinda messed up. I honestly don't even know how to be around my family. My kids think they're grown, and it's taking a lot outta me. I know if I would've acted like that with my parents...well, you already know."

"That's messed up! Kids these days are something else. I mean, that's why this place exists. What about wifey, though? I know Constance has your back, right?"

"Nope! We ain't vibin' at all! It's like me versus them. If I'm keepin' it one hundred, I don't know if me and Connie gon' make it."

"For real?"

"Yeah, but if it's the end, we had a good run," Stevie said.

"Man, I hope y'all can work it out. I hate to see my people end their marriages. That stuff is sad."

"But why? You ain't even married."

"That's exactly why. You and Constance seemed to have the type of relationship I was looking for. Whenever I saw y'all together, it was just like you were in your own world. Y'all had that kinda thing you see in the movies."

"I feel ya, and that's how it used to be, but I think our love story is over."

"Bro, you better fight for your woman! You better do whatever it takes to keep her. Tell her you love her, see what's broken, and try your best to fix it. That way, even if things really don't work out, you can say you tried your best to get back on track."

"I can't make any promises, but we'll see how it goes."

Stevie and his friend continued the conversation about his relationship for a few more minutes before someone interrupted them.

"Yo! Mr. Moss, is that you?" an unknown, younger sounding male asked.

"I know that can't be Rozelle! Boy, when I left, you were the smallest one here. Now you're lookin' down on me. I know I haven't been gone that long."

"That growth spurt came out of nowhere, Mr. Moss. One day, my fits were on point. Then, my shirts were all fittin' like they were my little brother's. My pants were acting like they were scared of my socks, and I didn't even wanna talk about my shoes. My momma got mad at me like it was my fault I grew. It was kinda funny, though."

"Growing pains are real, huh?" Stevie asked.

"Yes, sir!"

"Hey, wait a minute. I'm glad to see you, but why are you still here? I thought we made a lot of progress. Please explain to me why you're still getting into trouble. Why are you throwing away all of the work we put in?" Stevie asked.

"Mr. Moss, it's not like that, I promise. I'm still here 'cause Mr. Barton asked me to help with some of the younger kids."

"Dennis, is that true?" Stevie asked, finally letting me know his friend's name.

"Rozelle is actually being modest. Since we started working with him, he hasn't gotten into any more trouble. He joined the debate team at his school, his grades have improved, and his help around here has been heaven-sent, for real. The younger kids really look up to him. His turnaround has been amazing!"

"Dang, Zelle. You've really grown up! I'm proud of you, young man."

"Thank you, Mr. Moss. It was good seeing you, and I hope you're coming back, but I gotta go help out in the tutoring lab," he said.

I could hear Rozelle heading to his destination as Stevie and his friend continued to talk. At no point did Stevie's tone get anywhere near what it was when he talked to his family. There was nothing bad about him enjoying himself while he spoke with a friend, but it was unexplainable why he didn't have that same joy with his loved ones.

This version of Stevie was caring and nurturing, which was almost the polar opposite of the person I had been around. I was certain this was the Stevie that Constance fell in love with, which explained why she was so upset at who he had become.

"Dennis, did I leave this place too early?" Stevie asked.

"When you told me you were getting ready to call it quits, I told you I didn't agree with what you were doing. I knew you had a lot of gas left in the tank, and I didn't understand why you were leaving. Then, you told me the work you were putting in here was starting to change your home life. When you said that, I got it. It's always family over everything. I said all of that to say, ultimately, you are the only one who can really determine if you left too soon."

There were some brief moments of silence before the two transitioned to another insightful subject—Stevie's past.

"What brought you here in the first place?" Dennis asked.

"You already know what the deal was. Growing up, I was in the same position as these kids. I was wildin' out. I wasn't doing what I was supposed to do in school. Man, I just wasn't being the person my folks tried to raise me to be. So, I figured I needed to do whatever I could to keep the kids from being messed up adults looking back on a life full of regrets," Stevie replied.

Based on the phone call he had received, I don't know if what Stevie was telling Dennis was completely accurate. Regardless of it is was a lie or not, he continued speaking as if it was the truth. Humans always have their version of the truth, so I guess he was no exception.

"Is that still who you are?" Stevie's friend, Dennis, wondered.

"What do you mean?"

"Are you still a person looking back on your life with regrets?"

"I think I am. No matter what I do, I still regret a lot of the stuff I did. It's like I'm trying to cancel out my negative past with some good deeds, but I don't think I can ever make things balance out."

"They ain't gonna balance out, so that ain't why you should be doing good. You should be doing good 'cause it's the right thing to do. The kids who know you really do miss you, but if you ain't emotionally available for your own family, then I'm sure they miss you, too. Being around them and not being present is just as bad as not even being there, if not worse."

"Okay, I see you became a psychologist while I was away. Thank you, doctor," Stevie said as he started to laugh.

"Yeah, I know it's weird to hear me talk like that because it felt kinda weird to say, but it's real. You need to get your house in order, Stevie, but you can't do that until you get yourself right."

Since I entered Stevie's life, Dennis seemed like one of the few people he listened to. He wasn't argumentative when he spoke to Dennis, nor was he dismissive of the words Dennis said to him. It was as if Stevie viewed him as a brother, and he actually valued his opinions.

The two talked for a little bit more before Stevie decided it was time for us to go back home.

"I have some things to think about, so I'm about to head out. Tell Rozelle it was good seeing him again," Stevie said.

"I got you. Hey, do you think you're comin' back?" Dennis asked.

"Naw, I ain't comin' back today."

"I meant, do you think you're coming back to work? And let me say, I don't really expect you to answer that now because I know you owe your family the respect of talking that over with them, but I do want you to think about it. Like I said, we want you here, but they *need* you there. If you can balance it all, cool. If you can't, I understand that, too. Whatever you decided, you need to get your life back on track before it's too late."

We left in silence, we rode home in silence, and once we stopped driving, we went into the house in silence, as well. I expected there to be another conversation where Stevie would talk more to me about his problems, but that didn't occur. Evidently, the talk he had with Dennis was really making him think about his options.

"Stevie, where are you?"

"I'm in the room," Stevie said as Constance made her way into the room where he was.

By this time, I had been put into a box in the drawer, but I was still close enough to hear everything they were talking about.

"So, what happened at the center?" she asked.

She seemed to be asking the question out of obligation, not out of concern, but she asked it, nonetheless.

"It actually went pretty well. Hey, do you remember Rozelle? He was the kid I used to talk about all of the time."

"Yeah, I do. I hope he's not still getting into trouble."

"Nah, he's not. He's actually volunteering at the center. Dennis said he's been vital in helping out some of the younger kids."

"That's amazing to hear. You always said if he was ever able to stay on the right path, he would be an incredible asset to the community. I guess you were right."

"Yeah, I guess."

"Dennis also kept asking me if I wanted to come back."

"Go back, as in going back to work? You just retired. Do you know how many hours you spent there when you were working? Do you realize how dangerous it was for you to work there in the first place? You do remember the majority of the kids you were trying to help had some type of connection to the same people you had beef with when you were in the game, right? I was stressed and worried about you every day. I prayed nobody would connect your past life to who you are now. You were fortunate to make it out the first time, but now, it's like you wanna just spit in danger's face. That's not smart, Stevie!"

"So, I'm not supposed to care about those kids at the center?"

"Caring about them is admirable, it really is, but you need to care about us, too. Your family is supposed to come first!"

Although I hardly knew anything about what Stevie actually did in his past, Constance was making some very valid points. As a husband and father, Stevie had a responsibility to do what was best for his family. If he intentionally did anything to put them in danger, he was doing the opposite of what he was supposed to.

"Yeah, you do come first, but…"

"But what?"

"My life can't begin and end with you. I should be able to live."

"You know what, Stevie? You really know how to say some really stupid stuff! You think your life can't begin and end with us, but let's see how it is when we're not here. You put us through a lot over the years. I was dumb enough to make you think I was comfortable with you working in one of the rival neighborhoods of your gang…"

"I asked you not to bring that word up anymore! I left that life behind, and I don't want to make it the subject of a conversation," Stevie exclaimed.

"That's true, and I have always tried to respect your wishes, but at the same time, you're once again choosing to disregard the fact that I asked you to protect us. I stayed with you once because I know, in your heart, you believed you were trying to right your wrongs. That's not gonna happen again. If you go back, you're telling me exactly where your loyalty is. If your loyalty's not with us, then we don't need to be here. If you go back to work there, we're gone. It's as simple as that."

Constance said what she had to say, then she left. The exchange of words gave her the opportunity to release some things she had been keeping inside for a while. The conversation left no doubt that she really didn't like the idea of Stevie going back to his job.

Stevie always liked to be in control, and since Constance controlled that conversation, he didn't like how things turned out.

"I don't know who she thinks she is. She can't just tell me what I can and can't do. She actin' like I'm not a grown man."

His rant went on for a little while longer before he wore

himself out. His anger went away as the echoes of his words bounced off of the walls of the room.

Again, the family's daily routine happened enough to let me know about a month had passed before Stevie officially announced to his family he was going back to the center to work, not just to visit.

"Is anyone gonna say congratulations, or tell me good luck?" Stevie asked.

"Are you for real? Are you really looking for us to tell you that you're doing the right thing?" Leela asked.

"Yeah, you're my family. Is that really too much to ask?"

"Dad, please don't act like the family means anything to you. We've heard Mom tell you over and over why this is a terrible idea, but you're still going back to work there. Don't get me wrong, I actually think it's good you wanna help kids, but if Mom has been as upset as she has been, there has to be a reason for it. Dad, I need to know something."

He hesitated before he told his daughter to proceed with whatever questions she had.

"How come, out of all of the kids in the world who need help, you decided to help the ones who are close to the people you had issues with in the past? Don't you think that's kinda dumb? I mean, why are their lives more important to you than ours are? Why don't you love us as much as you love them?"

I could tell each word his daughter said, and every question she asked, was difficult for Stevie to hear. Then, as he normally did, he got defensive and said something he thought would prove to everyone that he was right.

"I'm just doing what I need to do for us to survive."

"Is that really what you think, or is that what you've been tellin' yourself?" she asked.

"That's how it is. Plus, I'm the parent. You need to learn your place."

"Cool, if that's how you want it to be, that's how it will be. I'll learn my place, Father. Just know, when you see your family leave you, I hope you realize we're just doing what we need to do to survive."

Leela was rightfully upset. Her father's job was to make sure she was taken care of, but for whatever reason, he was questioning if his family's safety was actually more important than returning to his former job. When I traveled with him to the center, I saw how important helping the kids was to him, but it wasn't clear why he prioritized them over his family.

Leela said he could help kids anywhere in the world, but he chose to go to that specific location. He always strategically avoided answering why. Even though he skated around the issue, he had to understand his family was smart enough to know he was giving them the runaround instead of just giving them a completely truthful answer.

The next few days were full of awkward interactions between Stevie and his family as he made his final preparations to go back to work. Constance and Leela always seemed to be opposing whatever Stevie had to say, while Viv tried her best to stay out of the way.

"So, tomorrow is the big day," Stevie said suddenly one day.

"After all of the begging and pleading we've done, you've still decided to go back?" Constance asked.

"Yep. There's no winning with you, so I'm just gonna do me," he told her.

"So you really feel like there's no winning with us? That's your problem, Stevie, you're treating this like it's a game."

I was in the holster I had been in for a portion of the day, but I was still close to the couple. I could hear Constance pacing around the room as if she had to get her thoughts together. Her breathing was noticeably much heavier than usual. Stevie tried to speak to her several times, but she didn't say anything to him until she was ready.

"Yeah, I'm done trying to protect your image with these kids, especially with Viv. I'm tired of feeling like I'm lying to them. I've had enough."

"You're overreacting. Just calm down," he told her.

He told his wife to calm down, but her tone was already calm. At the moment, he probably expected her to yell. He probably would have preferred her to get loud with him because if she had, he would have been more prepared to counter that. Her expression of anger, while remaining calm, was something he wasn't ready for.

"No, I need to finally tell them who you are."

He stuttered as he tried to interrupt her, but he couldn't actually get out any words. So, she continued with what she was saying.

"Kids, I need you to get in here," Constance said.

I could tell by the sounds Stevie was making, he wasn't happy with what was about to happen. He tried to walk away, but Constance wouldn't let him.

"Nope, you're not about to go anywhere. You need to be in here to look your children in their eyes when they hear what's going on," Constance told Stevie.

In past situations, there was major pushback from Stevie as he changed disagreements into full-fledged arguments. This time, Stevie stopped fighting back because, in this fight, he was overmatched.

"What's going on, Mom?" Viv asked as she entered the room with her older sister.

"Do you want to tell them, or should I?" Constance asked.

"You're makin' it a bigger deal than it is. Kids, I'm going back to work tomorrow. That's it; that's all there is."

"That's stupid. I know you said you were gonna go back, but I really thought you moved past that." Leela yelled.

"Leela, why are you so mad? Daddy's just gonna go back to work, but that's okay because when he goes to work, we'll be at school. So, it doesn't even matter. Isn't that right, Mommy?" Viv added.

"I wish it were that simple, Viv, but it's not."

Constance tried to explain the situation in a way each of them would understand.

"Your father going back to work isn't safe for us. We were fortunate to survive his time there before, but he's putting us back in danger by going back," she said.

"Daddy, I thought you were supposed to help keep us safe. If you're not protecting us, who will?"

"Don't worry, baby, since your daddy isn't worried about you, I'll make sure you're protected," Constance replied very quickly.

Stevie stood by silently as his wife went on for several more minutes, telling their children how he didn't care about keeping them safe. When she finished saying what she felt she had to, the kids threw the word "hate" toward their father several times.

"Kids, I'll talk to you later. For now, please just go to your rooms," Constance instructed.

The children did what their mother told them to do. Once they were gone, Constance began to talk again.

"Stevie, I need you to be honest with me. Can you do that for me, please?"

"I guess."

"Why are you really doing this? I know you still love us, but you have to know this isn't smart. Are you really ready to tear the family apart?"

"I'm not tearing anything apart. You're the one threatening to leave. You're the one telling our kids I don't care about them when you know that's a lie."

"Stevie, I don't know if I've really said this, but I'm hurt. I can't keep allowing you to hurt me and the kids. You say you love us, but your actions don't line up with that."

Constance always let Stevie know when she was angry or sad, but admitting to being emotionally hurt was not something she did very often. I could have been mistaken, but that may have been the first time she actually verbalized that sort of pain.

"Look, you probably won't believe me, but I will literally do anything to protect y'all. Do you hear me?"

"I hear you, Stevie, but I think you're just saying what you think I need to hear. It'll take way more than that, though. You're sacrificing your family for yourself. Don't you get it?"

"Connie, it's not like that. Do you want me to keep it real with you?"

"Of course I do."

"Okay, cool. What I'm about to tell you is the truth. This is really what's going on. Are you ready?"

"Yeah. Just say what you need to say."

"When I first started working at the center, it was strictly because I was trying to do something to help kids in the city. I felt so far removed from my days of bangin' and selling drugs, I didn't even realize I was in enemy territory. I was reminded on the first day, though. Some kid saw my neck tattoo and asked me where I was from. As soon as he did, I knew why he was asking, but I pretended not to. I don't remember what lie I told him, but it was good enough for him not to ask me anymore. From that point on, I tried to make sure the tattoo was covered to avoid any future confrontations."

"You never told me that before, but that still doesn't let me know why you're doing what you're doing," Constance said.

"I know it doesn't, but I wasn't finished yet."

"Please continue."

"After the first day, I was more aware of the environment, but in spite of working inside of the wrong 'hood, I quickly started to make connections with the kids. The more I worked, the more I felt like I was supposed to be there. I loved it, but it wasn't always smooth sailing. The kids were only there because they had been getting into a lot of trouble, and sometimes I would receive some threats of physical harm. Even with that, I never felt like I wasn't supposed to be helping them."

"Yeah, but those threats got to a point where you felt all of us were really at risk, too, right?"

"Yeah."

"And that's why you ended up retiring."

"Well, yeah, but…"

"So, if you quit because of everyone's safety, and you still deal with the same kind of people in the same area, what sense does it make to go back?"

For someone who was acting like he was prepared to have a conversation, Stevie was caught off guard when his wife asked about the logic behind working at the same place he stopped working because it endangered the lives of his loved ones.

"I…I'm just…"

"Exactly! You're confused. You're just lost, and honestly, you're not thinking."

"It ain't like that, Connie. Yeah, we got a few scattered threats by kids when I was working there, but things actually got a lot worse after I left."

"How could it have gotten worse? That sounds crazy!"

"I know how it may sound, but it's the truth. Back in the day, you always tried to look out for the kids who have that it factor. And we all knew which kids we had to keep out of the life because we knew they were special."

"Yeah, I know. Everyone tried to protect the good kids because if they made it out, it was like the ones in the streets were doing something good for the 'hood in spite of all of the bad things they were doing. I get that, but just tell me why you feel you have to go back."

This was when Stevie's tone changed a little. He once again stopped being argumentative and just explained the severity of the situation.

"You're not the only one who's scared, Connie. Folks over there basically got me doin' whatever they want because I'm scared of what they'll do if I don't."

"What do you mean?"

"Let me be real with you. The kid who saw my tattoo when I first started is apparently one of the kids the 'hood is looking out for. I know I told you my explanation was enough to have him no longer question my affiliation, but that ain't really what happened. After the kid saw the symbol on my neck, the word got back to me that he told his older cousin."

"So what?"

"Well, I found out his cousin is actually one of the higher-ups in the crew we used to have beef with back in the day. When I found that out, I wanted to quit right then."

"So, if you wanted to quit, then why didn't you?"

Constance posed a very good question, one which Stevie was actually ready to answer.

"I didn't quit because Dennis and a few of those kids begged me not to."

Perhaps he was able to answer quickly because he was answering truthfully, instead of making up something he thought his family would believe was the truth.

"Okay, so if you didn't quit because people begged you not to, how did we end up here, Stevie?"

"I stayed because I didn't want to break those kids' hearts, but I was dealing with the fact I was breaking yours. I knew each day I stayed became more dangerous for you and the kids, but whenever I talked about leaving, it somehow got back to those kids' families. Then, it all went back to what we talked about before; the streets wanted to make sure the gifted kids were protected. I was told having a pass in enemy territory only happened because I was providing a service for them. They said if I left, not only would the pass be revoked, but if anything ever happened to the kids they were trying to look out for, then they would put the blame on me. You already know what that means."

"You're joking, right?"

"I wouldn't joke about that," Stevie said.

"I don't get it. First of all, if all of that is true, you should have told me that from the beginning. Secondly, it still doesn't really make sense to me for you to go back, regardless of what they told you before. It's like you're just reminding them about you."

"The thought of going back was actually kinda forced on me when I got a phone call not too long ago. I ain't gotta go into details about it, but trust me, going back is actually like choosing the lesser of two evils. I'm really just trying to do what I feel is best."

"Do you think they're empty threats, or do you think someone would really do something to us?"

"I honestly don't know if any of it is real or not, but I don't want to take the risk of finding out. If I was still the person I used to be, I would just handle threats as I saw fit, but I ain't got that in me anymore. I don't want any extra drama."

"Like I said, you should have told me this before."

"When your job is to protect people, sometimes the best way to do that is to keep info to yourself. If I told you or the kids how things really were, it would have scared you to the point of not even wanting to leave the house. If it ever got like that, then I would have to face the fact that I failed you and the kids."

I've been in environments where people continued to argue just because none of the people involved wanted to admit the other person was right. This particular argument wasn't like that. Instead of Constance continuing to argue with Stevie because of how she felt, she stopped to process what was said. She didn't respond with haste, nor did she pout like a child and leave the room because she realized she may not have been completely right.

"Stevie, thank you for clearing things up for me. Now, I'm kinda lost, though."

"Why are you lost?"

"Because that changes things. Now that I have more info, I almost feel guilty about the things I've been saying to you," Constance said.

"Look, we're ultimately trying to protect our family, even if we had different ways of trying to get that done. And I know I don't always have the easiest time admitting when I'm wrong, but I have to tell you, I'm sorry. I've been struggling with a lot of things lately, but I know the arguments we've been having are because of me, and that's something my ego doesn't like," Stevie admitted to his wife.

"I appreciate you saying that. I really do."

"So, does that actually change anything with us?" Stevie asked.

"The conversation was incredibly helpful, but the only thing that will actually change the current dynamic of our relationship is your actions. Based on what you're saying, we're in danger no matter what, so why don't we just get a fresh start and leave the city? It may be good for us to have a change of scenery. These past few years haven't been our best, so a restart might serve us all well."

The couple spoke to each other with understanding and respect. The manner in which they were conducting themselves led them to believe they had reached a positive turning point, and for a brief moment in time, that's actually what happened. However, the positivity soon ran out, and the couple started to speak to each other at elevated levels once again.

"So, are you still going back?" Constance asked.

"I have to," Stevie said.

"I know you gave me some more info, but I already told you, if you do, we're done. I mean that. For a minute, I thought we would be able to get back on track, but I see that ain't happening. If nothing is going to change, we need to quit wasting each other's time. I hate to do this, but I want a divorce," Constance said.

"I know you're mad, but don't play like that, Connie."

"Look at me. Look at my face. Does it look like I'm playing? You haven't believed what I've been telling you, so I'm gonna have to show you."

"But Connie, I just told you I don't really have a choice," Stevie said, meekly.

"We always have a choice. We can leave this city together as a family, or you can stay here by yourself—as a single man."

"It's not that simple for me."

"Stevie, I love you, but love isn't enough to keep us together anymore. I'm tired of feeling like I'm the only one who cares, and if I'm having these sort of feelings, I can only imagine what the kids are dealing with."

Since my introduction into Stevie's world, Constance had put up with a lot. There were a lot of times she threatened to leave, but she had made it to a point where she was tired of making threats. She felt it was time for her to put some action behind her words.

"I'm taking the kids with me to my mom's place. It's sad, but I felt this day was coming, so I already talked to a lawyer and got the divorce papers ready. I was hoping things would change, but it doesn't look like they will. I've put the papers on the table in our room. I need you to sign them so we can move on with our lives as soon as possible. The quicker we get that done, the quicker we'll be able to adjust to co-parenting," Connie told him.

"If you wanna leave, I ain't gonna beg you to stay," Stevie said angrily.

"You still don't get it, Stevie. I don't wanna leave, but you're making me do it."

The one thing that was tearing the family apart was the one

thing the couple couldn't agree upon. So, without much more discussion, the two of them separated. When Constance officially left, that's when Stevie's denial really started. He told himself he was fine without his family, even though it wasn't true. He didn't want to admit it, but he knew his family's departure left a void he wasn't prepared to deal with.

He associated with the people at his job, but Dennis seemed to be the only person he called a friend. To be honest, that is probably why he started talking to me. He would tell me how he was feeling as he dealt with the troubles of his life. He was spiraling downhill, and even though he said he was passionate about helping the kids at the center, that passion seemed to be fading away with each day he went back to work.

"I'm lost," he told me one day.

"So, what! I'm not gonna help you fix your life! Your life is the way it is because of your decisions. There's nothing I can do to change anything!"

That's what I would have told him if I were able to. Since that was impossible, I sat in silence as he continued to tell me about his problems.

"My family really left me by myself. My wife vowed to be with me through good and bad times, but she lied. And my kids? They don't even want to call me Dad. This is ridiculous!"

The more he spoke, the louder he got. He was upset at everyone, except for himself. He was mad his kids no longer wanted anything to do with him, and he was mad his wife left, but he didn't seem to be mad at himself for being the one who caused the changes.

Based on his constant mumbling, he felt each day was worse than the one before. The smart thing for him to do would have been to talk to someone so he could deal with his issues, but he didn't choose to do that. Instead, he thought the best thing was to hide his sadness with a dangerous mask of machismo and fake happiness.

"Mr. Moss, you good?" a student asked one day. It was a simple question, but Stevie wasn't able to be honest.

"Me? Oh, I'm good. Another day, another chance for greatness. It's just hard work being the man. You feel me?"

"Yeah…if you say so, Mr. Moss. One thing, though."

"What's up?"

"No disrespect, but you might be doin' a lil' too much. All that ain't necessary."

"I got you. I'll try to tone it down, but only if you promise to keep up the good job you're doing with your schoolwork."

"What if I don't?" the kid asked.

"Oh, if you don't, I'll be forced to show up at your school in my flyest gear from the 80s. As you can guess, I was a little smaller back then, so all of those clothes are definitely too tight for me to put on. I don't mean fashionably tight like the stuff you and your friends wear. No, I mean the kind of tightness that will show the fullness of my gut, but that's just the start. Once the kids start talking about how bad I look, I'll tell everyone you're my nephew just so I can make sure you are thoroughly embarrassed. You already know if I do that, kids at your school will be clowning you for the rest of the school year."

"See, Mr. Moss. You're still doing way too much, but don't worry. I got you! Plus, you know Rozelle won't let any of our grades slip."

"That's good to hear. Well, I guess I'll talk to you later."

With that, the kid was on his way. Stevie immediately went to a room where he could be alone and closed the door. As soon as he did, he started asking himself questions he couldn't answer.

"I have started coming back to this place, but for what? I'm lying to myself thinking I'm actually doing something. Everybody left me, and I'm actin' like I'm protecting somebody. Who am I protecting? What am I doing?"

When he finished asking all of the questions he had for

himself, he decided to ask me a few things. I was pulled out of hiding as Stevie looked at me.

"So, what's your purpose? What's the point of you being here? Do you hear me? Answer me! Why are you taking up space if you ain't gonna do nothin'?"

If he gave me a chance to shine, I was more than ready to show the inconsequential little human what my purpose was, but he just went on for a few more minutes. He continued to question everyone's usefulness. At the same time, he boasted about how everyone would miss him if he weren't around. Then, he started to cry.

He paced around the room with no regard for me. Ignoring me was ill-advised, which many of his actions were, but that didn't stop him from continuing. His emotions soon caused him to lose track of the trigger. Before he knew it, I made everyone in the center know I was there.

As soon as I yelled out, Stevie started panicking. He clumsily tried to hide me, but he just made me go off again. The screams of people in the center filled the air. Soon, Stevie's friend, Dennis, ran into the room.

"Stevie, I don't know what's going on, but we're trying to get all of the kids—"

Once he saw me, he stopped mid-sentence.

"What is wrong with you? Don't you realize how much danger you're putting these kids in?" he asked.

At that moment, I'm sure he knew he was also in danger, but he cared more about the safety of the kids than of his own.

"Yeah, my bad. It went off accidentally."

Dennis' demeanor and tone changed very quickly.

"Your bad? Really? This is way beyond a 'my bad' situation. Look, I tried to be empathetic toward whatever you're dealing with, but now you've endangered the lives of my children! That ain't something you're gonna get away with."

Dennis wasn't talking about his biological kids, but the

delivery of his words displayed how important each of the children in the center was to him.

"I told you it was a mistake, so calm down! Don't worry, I wasn't tryin' to shoot anybody, and if I were, it would've been myself."

"I'm not trying to hear your sad story. I need you to put the gun up. Then, I'm calling the police. I promise if you're still here when they get here, I'm not gonna lie to save you. I'm gonna tell them what happened. If you get caught up, it really will be 'your bad.' And once you leave the campus, whether it be in a cop car or on your own, I don't ever want you to come back. Do you hear me? If you ever step foot near here again, you won't have to worry about no gangs messin' with you because I'm gonna handle you myself," Dennis told him.

"Oh, so you're a tough guy now? You wanna threaten your friend?"

"I'm not a tough guy, and I ain't tryin' to be, but I will give my life if it means protecting these kids. And you can't call yourself my friend now. Our friendship is over."

For whatever reason, this changed Stevie's entire attitude. He went from admitting I went off on accident to pretending like it was done on purpose. He started to act like the tough guy he said Dennis was trying to be.

"Hey, you're really startin' to get on my nerves. The gun went off, but so what? If you keep running your mouth, the next time it goes off, it'll be more intentional."

People were still screaming, fearing for their lives, but at least Dennis knew the cause of the commotion was standing directly in front of him.

"I let you start working here again because you needed it, and some of the kids missed you. Don't get it twisted, though. This is my house, and you've worn out your welcome. I was trying to let you leave before the cops got here, but you ain't got that choice no more. Now, you gotta sit here and wait for 'em. You gotta take your punishment like a man."

"Let me? You were gonna let me go, huh? Bruh, I'm a grown man with a gun. You ain't letting me do nothin', and that's real!"

Humans often made the mistake of allowing their egos to give them a false sense of confidence. Stevie acted as though he was powerful and invulnerable, but he was neither. Any power he thought he had, especially at that moment, only existed because I was there.

His false sense of power made him move closer to the door, even though he had been warned not to do so. As he put his hand on the doorknob, he was stopped when Dennis grabbed the back of his shirt.

"Gun or not, you don't run anything here. I told you, you're not going anywhere."

Without giving another long-winded speech, Dennis let his hands provide all of the messages he was tired of conveying vocally. Based on the proximity, Stevie could have easily ended the one-sided fight by allowing me to respond, but he didn't.

"Hold on, please. Just let me make a call," Stevie said as his humility suddenly appeared out of nowhere.

I could tell by his facial expression Dennis was caught off guard, but for some reason, he stopped fighting and granted the request. He didn't seem to care that his life was still in danger. Even though he said his friendship with Stevie was completely over, he still showed compassion for him.

Stevie pulled out his phone, put it on speaker, and let it ring for a few seconds before Constance picked up.

"Connie, I know you don't wanna hear from me, but please don't hang up."

"What do you want?"

"I just had to tell you that today is the last day you or the kids have to worry about my past endangering any of you. I've realized you never asked too much of me; I was just too immature to admit you were right. You've always been right about all of this. I'm not trying to change what has already been done, but I want you to know even though we're not together, you still have my heart. You couldn't tell by my actions, but I I loved my family more than anything in this world."

She was listening, but it didn't seem like she was ready to forgive him for his past transgressions.

"Stevie, I've heard this kinda stuff before, but you never did what you said you were gonna do. You never changed. You never got better. You wouldn't even go get help when I begged you to. I wanted you to get right, not for us, but for you. Like I've said a million times before, I can't want better for you than you want for yourself."

"You're right, and I'm sorry for you letting you and the girls down. Later on today, you may hear some bad things about me. I suggest you and the girls stay away from the news and social media for a little while. Just understand that I'm tired, babe. I'm weak. I'm lonely, and I can't keep doing this, not without you. I just can't. I'm tired of not doing right and chasing everybody away. Just know that I love you all, and I pray, at some point, you can forgive me."

"Stevie, what are you talking about? Stevie...."

He stopped responding to his wife, threw the phone down, and turned his attention back to me. He held me so that I could talk to Dennis. The trigger was quickly pulled multiple times. Dennis tried to speak after each shot, but the attempts failed.

The screaming from outside of the room was finally starting to die down from when I accidentally spoke a few minutes before. So, I knew it was only a matter of time before someone would finally walk in to see if our room was where the first shots originated. Soon, that's what happened.

"Yo! Mr. Barton, get up!"

The person who walked into the room was Rozelle, the kid

who seemed to be so fond of Stevie the day he came back to visit the center.

"Please don't tell me you did this! Please tell me that gun's in your hand because you tried to get the person who did this to Mr. Barton."

"Rozelle, I care too much to lie to you, so I won't. What you think happened is what happened."

At this point, we could all hear Dennis struggle to breathe, so Rozelle ran over to him.

"C'mon, you gotta get up! You're one of the most important people in my life. You're like a father to me. Please, Mr. Barton, don't go!"

Rozelle fell to the ground near his mentor. He pulled out his phone and called for help. All the while, Stevie just stood there. It was as though he was awaiting his punishment, just as Dennis told him to do earlier.

While Rozelle was on the phone, he kept begging Dennis to keep fighting. After a few minutes, Dennis didn't have any more fight left to give. As soon as he passed away, Rozelle immediately dropped his phone and released a primal yell.

"Is this what you wanted, huh? When I'm at home, I always wonder who I'm gonna lose. I come here to get away from that, and you, of all people, took away my safe place. You think I forgot about your past? You must have forgotten that my people let you come into this neighborhood. We both know you're over enemy lines whenever you come here. I guess you're ready to die, so I'm ready to help!" he said angrily.

It was at this moment, I realized the kid who learned about Stevie's gang affiliation when he first started working at the center was Rozelle, and although years had passed, he didn't forget what he saw when they first met.

Rozelle yelled once again before he left his mentor alone on the ground. This time, the sound was filled with more anger than pain. He quickly attacked Stevie, a man he looked up to only a few weeks prior. The punches the young man threw came at a furious rate, and the way Stevie reacted, each of the punches seemed to be packed with all of the pain he was carrying. Rozelle's energy allowed him to continue until Stevie decided he had enough. He suddenly remembered I was with him, so he raised me in the air.

"Is that supposed to scare me? It doesn't! I see guns every day."

"I know that! And it ain't supposed to scare you," Stevie said.

"What's the point of it, then?" Rozelle asked as Stevie's statement stopped him from punching.

"I need you to end it for me," Stevie said, trying to pass me over to a kid who was still very upset.

"How stupid do you think I am? I'm trying to do better than other folks around here. You really think I'm gonna take a gun you just killed somebody with and kill you with it? You really don't care about me or anybody else, do you?"

The sirens from approaching police cars soon drew near. The building was now silent, empty of sound except for Stevie and Rozelle's ragged breathing. They heard every footstep of the officers who were moving closer to them. It was evident Stevie was counting on Rozelle to do his dirty work and end his life so he wouldn't have to deal with the consequences of his actions, but the young man was far more intelligent than Stevie gave him credit for.

"Mr. Moss, you got me messed up. I'm too smart to do what you want me to do. You just basically took the life of my father, and my anger wants me to kill you, but I would be throwing my life away. We both know why you're allowed to be here, but you just killed Mr. Barton, and the streets ain't gonna like that. He was admired by everyone around here. It's over for you. If the cops and the courts don't get you, I know for sure the streets will."

The kid's speech was delivered in such a calm, matter-of-fact tone, it scared Stevie so much, his pulse sped up tremendously. He opened his mouth to say something, but by the time he made an attempt to start speaking, several officers made their way to the room.

"Freeze!" one of them yelled out.

"I'm so glad you're here! I don't know why, but Mr. Moss killed Mr. Barton. He...he was like a father to me! Why would he do that? Why? Mr. Barton didn't do anything to anyone!"

Rozelle expressed the same thing to the cops that he said to Stevie when they were in the room alone, but he said it in a way that highlighted his innocence. His plan paid off quickly because he was escorted out of the room.

"Get him outta here! This kid has seen way more than he should have," another cop said.

With Rozelle gone, the cops forcefully removed me from Stevie's grasp, threw him to the ground, and put handcuffs on him. Stevie was soon taken out of the building, and I stayed in the hands of one of the other officers. This was the beginning of the end of our time together.

As soon as Stevie stepped outside of the center, the loud disapproving sounds of bystanders were hurled at Stevie from every direction. For whatever reason, Stevie once again felt he needed to pretend to be something he wasn't and act as though what was going on wasn't bothering him.

"You think I care about what you have to say? You ain't never meant nothing to me," he said, displaying the fragility of his ego.

Everyone recognized his dishonesty, which made the negative emotions they all had more intense. The officers had a difficult time communicating with each other because of the noise of everyone around, but that changed when the body of their beloved leader, Dennis, was brought out of the building. The boos and harsh words stopped, and for a brief moment in time, everything was drowned out by silence.

Rozelle said his environment made him see people lose their

lives, which was probably true for many of the people outside of the center, as well. With that being the case, they should have been used to seeing a body bag. This death, however, seemed to touch them differently. Perhaps, even if the people had grown accustomed to losing other people, they felt differently because Dennis was someone who showed love for each one of them.

"We love you, Mr. Barton," someone said suddenly.

A few people in the crowd knew it was Dennis, even though he was in a bag. As more people realized who it was, sentiments of love and admiration echoed throughout the area. The people chose to celebrate Dennis, instead of showing their hatred for Stevie. Then, a voice rang out above the crowd.

"You don't get to take him away from us and just walk away. Trust, you gonna get yours."

And then, a single shot rang out, but it wasn't from me. No, at that point, the work was being done by a relative of mine I hadn't had the pleasure of meeting. I heard Stevie yell out, which meant my kinfolk's bullet was able to reach its target, but I didn't know where. The conversations that started immediately after the shot let me know it wasn't fatal. In fact, I heard someone say it was a warning to let Stevie know he was going to get touched whenever they wanted him to.

Since there were so many people in the crowd, and only one shot was fired, the officers on the scene had no idea where it came from or who was responsible for it.

"We gotta get outta here now!" one of the cops yelled.

Stevie was close to a police car, so they quickly put him inside. Since he had been shot, his trip to jail would be delayed by a detour to the hospital. This is where our connection officially ended. I don't know what happened to Stevie after that day. I don't know if he had to serve any type of sentence, or if he was given the opportunity to recover from his injury.

Although we had been connected for a while, Stevie's well-being has always been irrelevant to me. Witnessing how quickly

Stevie was willing to use me on his friend and how soon someone used a gun on him, confirmed people cared about each other's lives about as much as I did, which was not at all.

Stevie was told he was sacrificing his family for his own selfish gains. He always disputed that and said he did what he felt was best for everyone. In theory, that sounds good, but murdering someone who was not a threat to him or his family, wasn't protected his loved ones. Only an illogical human would think otherwise.

In my many dealings with people, I've learned many of them don't always make thoughtful decisions. They have no problem lying, even to the people they claim to care about. I've witnessed people say and do things that were absolutely preposterous, but such is the way of mankind.

During my journey with Stevie, it was confirmed people sought alliances, even though they weren't usually very loyal to each other. The intuitive nature of Constance made her believe her husband was not doing what was best for their family, and regardless of what happened after he was shot, that proved to be true. She wanted to know where his loyalty was, but it just seemed like Stevie could only be loyal to himself because that was the easiest thing to do.

People, by themselves, can be problematic. Dishonest people who own guns, can create chaos. This was the case with Stevie. With his actions, he was on the brink of ruining the lives of his family, but his wife was able to escape that simply by leaving.

Also, while he claimed he wanted to go back to work because of how important the kids at the center were to him, and that he had been threatened, nobody really knew what his true motives were. What we found out was, his inability to take care of his own mental health had him ready to destroy his family's future, as well as Rozelle's. He was willing to do this all because it would have been an easy way for him to evade dealing with all that was going on inside of him.

Through it all, Stevie had carved out his own path. Like any other person, at some point, he would no longer be able to run from his destiny. Was Stevie's loyalty to his family, or those who knew him because of his past? Did he care more about himself than he did about anyone else? In the end, Stevie's loyalty didn't permanently lie with anyone; it just seemed that he lied about actually having any.

NARRATIVE 8: MOURNING DARKNESS

*T*here's a ridiculous notion among some people. Some of you assume you can judge another person by how they look. Actually, let me take it even further. Some humans have the audacity to claim they know about a person's intelligence, strength, and overall character based strictly on their outer shell, which people refer to as, "skin."

This judgment has been known to cause people to go out of their way to disprove how others view them. It can also cause people to get so upset about how others see them, they slowly morph into the type of person they were thought to be in the first place. Having preconceived notions about people based on their appearance doesn't make any sense, especially when I've found many times those doing the judging are generally the ones who have the characteristics they are projecting onto someone else.

I began to learn about this foolish aspect of the human dynamic when I started to hang around a person named Raymond. His environment wasn't necessarily the best, which would have made it easy for him to behave a certain way, but Raymond was consciously fighting any stereotype people thought was a representation of who he was. He was nineteen and had no kids of his own. However, due to circumstances beyond his control, he was forced to take care of his three younger siblings.

He graduated from high school in the top ten percent of his class, but since he wasn't able to get a full scholarship to any of the colleges he applied to, he decided to get a job so he could take care of his family. He ended up losing jobs quite frequently because he had to leave work to tend to any issues that arose because of his brothers and sister.

Since he was a quick learner, he was normally able to find another job pretty easily. Unfortunately, when he was fired from the local cell phone shop, different conversations started to take place.

"I don't know how we're gonna make it out of this one, Jada."

Jada was the oldest of Raymond's siblings, which made her the second in command. Whenever he didn't know what to do, Raymond always bounced ideas off of her.

"What's up, bro?" she asked.

"I just lost another job. The manager told me the last time I called out that he had to let me go because he couldn't depend on me. I wanted to get mad, but I couldn't. That ain't even why I'm trippin', though."

"Okay, so what's up?"

"I don't know if anybody else is gonna hire me 'cause of all of the jobs I lost. It's almost time for me to pay rent, and I don't know what I'm gonna do. I ain't got it."

"Calm down, Ray. I have about $200 saved from work. I don't know how much you need, but that should help a little bit."

"Jada, I can't take your money. I'm supposed to be takin' care of y'all. What I look like takin' money from my baby sister?"

"First of all, you need to quit with the 'baby' sister thing. Remember, I'm only two years younger than you. Anyway, I know when Ma and Dad passed, you took on this whole father-figure role, but you can't let your ego stop you from takin' help from me. I mean, we're practically raising Houston and Damon together. The responsibilities you have are for us to handle, not just you."

"I guess you're right, Jada."

"Ain't no guessing needed. You know I'm right, but don't act so surprised. I'm right most of the time, so you really should be used to it. Anyway, I'll Cash App you the $200 later on today, okay?"

"Okay, but I really don't wanna take your money."

"I know you don't, but sometimes you have to do things you don't wanna do so you can take care of the things you have to. You feel me? Think about this; I'm a vegetarian. Do you think I wanna cook up animals and come home smelling like fried animal flesh every day? Nah! That stuff grosses me out, but I do it for the family. And I know you wanna be able to just make money by selling your sculptures..."

"Yeah, but…"

"I already know what you're gonna say, Ray, but just let me fishing talking."

"My bad, go ahead."

"I was just saying, I know how much you wanna create your art, but you really can't because you're focused on finding jobs and workin' to take care of us. We're both making sacrifices for our little brothers, so we can't ever let our pride stand in the way of that. This stuff...man, I be wanting to give up sometimes, but it'll all pay off in the end. I don't know how, but I know it will."

"Thank you, Jada. Thank you for helping me, and for being a great sister. All of us are lucky to have you around."

"Ray, don't have me cryin' before I have to go to work."

"I'm just being real with you. I appreciate you, and I know Ma and Dad would be proud."

"Thanks, but they would be proud of us, not just me. We're taking the lessons we learned from them and passing them on."

"Yeah, I think we are setting pretty good examples for Damon and Houston," Raymond said.

"True! I love you, Ray. I gotta go. I'll see you later. When the little bros get home, tell them I love them, and give them a hug and kiss for me," Jada said.

"Jada, I'll tell them you love them, I may even give them a hug, but ain't no way in the world I'm gonna give those jokers kisses."

"See, that's that toxic masculinity again."

"What?"

"You know I'm just playin' with you! I'll see you later, big bro," Jada said while they laughed as she headed out of the front door.

The tiny two-bedroom apartment the family lived in served as their sanctuary. Their neighborhood wasn't always the safest, but before their passing, their parents always made the home feel like it was the best place on earth.

It was crowded, but the family always said they were blessed to be so close to each other. And all of the kids knew they didn't have money, but they never said they felt poor. When their parents died, Raymond vowed to do his best to continue to make their home feel like the same way it did when their parents were around.

Anyone who ever had a conversation with Raymond knew he would do anything in his power to make sure his younger siblings felt loved and were taken care of. He not only made sure they went to school, but that they excelled in it. On a weekly basis, I would hear him tell his siblings he wanted them to be better than him. He said he wanted them to reach their potential so they could make their parents proud.

Pride wasn't something I was able to experience personally, but it was something I frequently heard about. It seemed to have the ability to be positive, in a sense, because it allowed people to know they were doing something well. Pride could also fundamentally change the way a person thinks.

Whenever Raymond told his brothers and sister whatever they were doing would make their deceased parents proud, they would talk about how happy they were. When they did something they weren't supposed to do, he would simply ask if those actions would make their parents proud. Whenever that was done, Houston, the third oldest child, would normally get upset.

"Why do you always ask that?" Houston emphatically asked one day.

I was not in the room, but I was able to hear everything that was going on.

"Do you want to know why I ask you if they would be proud?"

"Yeah, I want to know. That gets on my nerves."

"Okay, little brother, I'll be real with you. I know it gets on your nerves when I do it, but you always know when I'm about to ask it, right?"

"Of course I do. You ask every time I..."

"Every time, what?" Raymond questioned.

"You do it whenever I do somethin' I shouldn't be doing."

The fourteen-year-old had more to say, but he stopped himself from talking.

"What's up, Houston?"

"I can't....I.... don't—"

Houston was suddenly unable to speak. For the moment, finishing his sentence was beyond the realm of possibility.

"You have to stop trying to keep stuff bottled up, little brother. That ain't healthy. Take your time and catch your breath," Raymond told him.

Houston did as his older brother suggested. After a little time had passed, he was able to say what he needed to say.

"They should be here with us. We shouldn't be without

them! I'm fourteen, Ray! There's no way a fourteen-year-old kid should be without his parents!"

"You're right, and there's no denying that. Look, none of us should be without them, but that's where we are."

"Covid is trash! It took both of them!" Houston yelled.

The family didn't have time to prepare for changes because Covid mercilessly attacked their mother. She made sure to take the necessary precautions, but unfortunately, she worked in an environment where the majority of her co-workers didn't believe in doing the same thing. She caught the virus and fought valiantly, but after five and a half days, her fight was over.

The loss hit the family extremely hard, but nothing compared to how it impacted their father. He had been with his wife for over twenty-five years, so he no longer knew how to live life without her. I used to hear him cry at night as he tried to speak to his wife.

His family could tell he wasn't doing too well, even though he was trying his best to stay strong for his children. A few weeks after his wife passed away, he also caught Covid, which took him just as quickly as it took his wife.

"Houston, can I ask you something?"

"I guess."

"When we yell and complain about our folks not being here, does it bring 'em back?"

"You know it don't! If it did, I wouldn't be cryin' all the time."

"And even though we miss them like crazy, life has gone on, right?"

"Yeah."

"So, as you're going through life, if you do something stupid, do you think people are gonna take it easy on you because you lost your parents?"

"Probably not."

"Ain't no probably to it. Let me tell you something, little brother. I know you're young, but most of the world will see you as a man. Not only that, you're Black, and being a Black man in this country means a lot of people are targeting you because, for whatever stupid reason, they feel threatened by you. A lot of people want to see us fail. I know it's not right, but I'm telling you the truth, and that's why you will keep hearing me talk about making our parents proud. I know you get tired of me doing that, but I'm gonna keep doing it because I'm not gonna allow any of us to disrespect their memory. They worked way too hard for us to let them down. I keep repeating the pride thing because I want you to hear that, even when I'm not around. When that happens, that means the lessons they taught us will continue to live on."

The talk between the brothers continued until Houston was once again unable to speak. He became overwhelmed with emotions, and he was unable to stop crying. Sometimes siblings make fun of each other when emotions are involved, but that didn't happen. When Houston started crying, his brother asked him for a hug. The two remained silent until they both felt it was okay to move on.

"Thank you for not makin' fun of me," Houston said.

"I love you, bro. There'll be plenty of time for me to make fun of you, but this wasn't it."

"Really funny, Ray."

"Yeah, I know. I'm somethin' like Chappelle out here."

"Maury just called. He told me to tell you, 'the lie detector determined that was a lie.' So, I think you need to get it together," Houston replied.

"That's funny. You got me. Now, don't you have some homework or something you need to do?"

"Yeah, I do, but I'm starving. Do we have some food?"

"No doubt! There's some truffle lobster mac and cheese in there," Raymond told his brother.

"What? For real?"

"Houston, now you know we don't have nothing with no

truffles or no lobster! You must think we got transported into a Gordon Ramsey show. Bro, you know better than that!"

"Dang, that's messed up!"

"It was kinda messed up, but I couldn't let you get me without gettin' you back. Anyway, I went shopping earlier today, so there's some stuff in the fridge and the freezer. I don't feel like cookin' right now, so you're just gonna have to heat something up."

At that time, the youngest of the siblings entered the room with his brothers.

"So, are y'all finished arguin' and cryin' and stuff? My tablet is dead, so I'm tired of staying in the room with nothing to do. Plus, I'm super-duper-hungry. I felt like I ain't had no food in like 700,000 days," Damon said.

"Damon, why are you always so extra? You just had a snack thirty minutes ago," Raymond replied.

Damon chuckled as I heard Houston leave the room they were in to go to the kitchen and heat some food up in the microwave. When Houston left, Damon continued the conversation with his older brother.

"That's true. I did just have a snack, but I'm a growing boy. I need a lot of food. My stomach is yelling right now, and I don't like what it's sayin' to me. I can't shut it up unless I get some food. Pleeeeeaaaaaasssssseee, big brother, you have to help me. You don't want your poor, innocent, little brother to pass out with a severe case of hungryitis, do you?"

"Hungryitis, huh? That sounds major. Naw, I don't want you to catch a case of that. Go in there with Houston so he can heat something up for you."

Talking with his brothers not only made Raymond laugh, but also momentarily made him forget about the financial situation his family was in. As his laughter faded, Raymond quietly walked into his room and closed the door. He could hear his brothers joking with each other through the thin bedroom walls. He wanted to have the same sense of joy they had, but he didn't. The young man just became overtaken by sadness.

"I'm sorry. I thought I could do this, but I'm failing. I don't want anything bad to happen to them, but I don't know if I can protect them. I'm really sorry I'm letting you down."

Raymond's brothers were still eating their meal, and Jada wasn't home. I found whenever Ray was having a conversation without being on the phone or without anyone nearby, he was talking to the 'spirits' of his parents. Like pride, sadness, joy, and everything else connected to human emotions and feelings, the idea of a spirit was something I wasn't able to relate to, but it was something else I had become familiar with.

This family, like many other humans, believed their bodies were something like a case. They believed within that case was something that science could neither prove, nor disprove. They felt the core of who they were was their spirit. Their spirit, or soul, is where their emotions came from. It's what connected them to their higher power, and when the spirit left, it was when the person transitioned from the world of the living.

When Raymond's mom got sick, the talks about spirits became relevant within the family's household. I recall a conversation Ray had with his mother.

"My spirit is tired. I don't know if I'm actually ready to go or not, but I know it's time for me to leave," she whispered while trying her best to breathe.

Her family tried to tell her how much they loved her and how much they needed her to stay, but she kept saying it was time. Evidently, her spirit let her know her time in the physical world was almost over. Soon, she was proven to be right.

When she passed away, her husband cried on a daily basis. His pain was evident, but he tried his best to stay strong for the sake of his children. He grieved by himself and didn't discuss his personal feelings with his children, which may not have been the best way to go about handling things, but how would he have known that?

I've heard when people get married, they take a vow to be with each other until death do they part, but I've never heard any of them discuss what happens to each partner if they fulfill the terms of their contract. Sure, people discuss their children, finances, and other assets, but shouldn't it also be commonplace to talk about what will become of the remaining partner if one of them passes?

Maybe some people do, but being the symbolic fly on the wall of this house, I know those conversations never took place here. Perhaps it was because of fear of the unknown, or maybe everyone had hopes that the matriarch of the family would find a way to get better. Whatever their actual reasons were, the discussion didn't happen. That just meant once she was gone, her partner was a bit discombobulated.

Before the father of the family was able to find himself and get his family back on track, he became ill. Very similarly to when their mother was sick, Covid showed it didn't care about them. It had just taken a mother away from her four children, so it didn't care about taking their father away from them, too.

Life came at the family fast, but the kids were able to band together to overcome everything that stood in their way, including finding a way to remain under one roof when those in control tried their best to separate them. Raymond had no problem taking on the responsibilities of raising his siblings, he had just reached a point of uncertainty.

Whenever he talked to the spirits of his parents, it was either because he missed them, he needed advice, or he felt over-whelmed. The most recent conversation fell into multiple categories.

"What am I supposed to do? They fired me from work, and I don't have enough money for rent. I'm struggling, and I wanna give up, but I can't let them know that," Ray said.

He needed someone to talk to, but his sister wasn't there, and he didn't want to let his little brothers know how much financial trouble they were in. This was one of the main reasons he felt he had to keep talking to his parents.

"Did I mess everyone's life up by keepin' them? Would everything be better if they would've gotten adopted by somebody else?"

After his questions, Raymond was interrupted when Damon knocked on the door and went inside the room.

"Man, you didn't even let me answer before you walked in."

"I heard you in here, and it sounded like you need a hug," Damon told his brother as he started to laugh.

"I know you're probably just trying to make fun of me, but a hug from my baby bro could help me out right now."

Raymond allowed himself to be vulnerable. He realized doing so could make his brother know he wasn't as emotionally well off as he was trying to make them believe he was.

"Is somethin' wrong?" Damon asked.

Raymond took the time to think about how he was going to respond before he did. He knew he could say something overly positive to make his brother feel good, or he could start being honest with him.

"Houston, can you come in here for a minute?" he yelled out. Almost immediately, Houston walked into the room with his brothers.

"What's up, and why are y'all hugging?" he asked.

"We're hugging because this is my brother. I love him, and I needed a hug," Raymond said.

"Umm...okay, if you say so," Houston replied.

"By the look on your face, I can see you weren't expecting me to say that, but I get it. I need both of y'all to have a seat 'cause I have to say something to you."

Both of the younger siblings followed Raymond's instructions.

"Jada told me I be on some toxic masculinity stuff today. I didn't know what she was talkin' about until right now. As dudes, a lot of times, we act like it's crazy to love our brothers. I admit I do that, but it don't make no sense. Y'all are my little brothers, and I don't want anything to happen to you. I love my family. Do you hear me? I love y'all!"

"Ray, we know that. We just be jokin' with you. We don't always say it, but we love you, too," Houston said.

"Yeah, my big brothers and my sister are everything!" Damon added.

"Man, I'm so glad to hear that. I'm happy everyone is way more emotionally mature than me. Thank you."

"Did you just want us in here to tell us we're better than you? I mean, that's a waste of time because we already knew that," Houston said sarcastically.

"No, smart guy, that's not it. I need to talk to y'all about something, for real," Raymond said.

"Soooo, do I need to leave the room? Usually whenever you and Jada say anything like be real, real talk, or anything like that, you usually tell me to leave the room. So, do I need to leave?" Damon asked.

"That's usually how it goes, but this time I need you to stay here. I'll try not to talk so much, but I need to get some stuff off of my chest. I just want you to know when Mom died, me and Jada were ready to take on more responsibilities to help Dad out, but then he died, too. We all lost our parents, but as the oldest... it's just different for me. I wasn't ready to be a parent then, and I still ain't ready, but here I am. And look, I will never be able to do half of the things they did for us, but I need y'all to know I'm trying. I try to be positive, I try to keep y'all on the right track, and I try to do what I gotta do to keep us going. Some days are better than others, but like I said, I need to be real with y'all. Right now is not good for me, and I feel like I'm failing everyone. I feel like I can't handle what's going on, especially since I got fired from the cell phone store. I'm sorry. I don't know what to do. I can't even afford rent this month."

"Bro, if you know you're not Mom and Dad, then you shouldn't compare yourself to them. We're young, but we're not dumb. We know it's hard to do what you and Jada are doing. I mean, I'm the best kid anyone could ever have, but Damon, yo, it has to be a hassle dealing with him every day," Houston said.

"I'm right here, Houston. Why are you actin' like I can't hear you?" Damon cried out.

Houston recognized his older brother's burden, so he took it upon himself to compliment Raymond and lighten the mood at the same time. It was as though Ray had no choice but to momentarily let go of what was troubling him to just enjoy the time with his brothers. As they were all bonding, Raymond's phone went off.

"Oooh, I know what that sound is! That's the sound of somebody sendin' you some money!" Damon yelled.

"Yeah, you're right. Jada is sending me some money to help cover rent this month."

"How much did she send?" Houston asked.

"Dang, I thought Pinocchio only dealt with lies, not being all in somebody's business," Raymond said.

"What does that even mean?" Housing wondered

"Well, you're being super nosey. Get it? Nosey…Pinocchio."

Raymond was the only one to find his joke funny, but it didn't stop him from laughing.

"Yeah, I am being nosey because I need to know. That's how you learn stuff. You know, you always gotta keep your ears to the street."

"Houston, you don't know nothin' about the streets, so what are you talking about?"

"What 'chu mean? I was raised in these streets, I get paid in these streets. If somethin' pops off, I might get saved in these streets."

"Oh, so you're a rapper now?" Ray asked.

"Yeah, I may have just started my rap career. Don't be surprised when I start making tracks with Drake, 21 Savage, and Lil' Durk. I might just start touring the world with a diamond grill in my mouth. Don't worry, when I'm rich, I'll buy you and Jada a house," Houston said.

"But what about me?" Damon asked.

"Well, if you're old enough, you may get your own house. If not, maybe you can stay with one of us," Houston said.

"Maybe?"

"Damon, I'm just playing. You know we got you, no matter what."

When Houston told his little brother, "we got you, no matter what," it represented what the family was all about; togetherness. When Houston described his future wealth, he made sure to include his family. This is how the family was when their parents were alive, and it is how they continued to be after they passed away.

"Ray, you still never told us how much money Jada sent you."

"I don't even know. She said she was gonna send like $200. Let me check, so I'll know exactly how much I still need to come up with by the end of the month."

When he checked the app, he immediately started running around the room.

"There has to be some kind of mistake. This can't be real."

"Dang, Jada must've sent you a band or something to make you run around like that!" Houston exclaimed.

"Nah, actually, Jada hasn't sent me anything yet. I need to text her before she does, though."

He took about thirty seconds to send a message to his sister before he continued talking to Damon and Houston.

"You know that sculpture I finished workin' on last week?" Raymond asked.

"Yeah, what about it?"

"I had been carrying it around and asking people at art galleries and random people on the street if they wanted to buy it. I didn't even have a price in my head because I was just tryin' to get whatever I could get for rent. Most people just looked at me funny and told me to get away from them, but I talked to this couple who just seemed different. They asked me how much I was selling it for and...."

"How much did you tell them?" Damon asked.

"I told them I would take $100 for it, but let me finish the story. After I told them I would take $100, they asked me what I wanted to do with my life. I told them I just wanted to do my art, try to raise y'all, and do right by Dad and Mom. I asked them if they were gonna buy my sculpture, and they told me they weren't. I told them I was desperate and would pretty much take anything. They asked for my info and said they would get back to me. Since I hadn't heard from them, I thought they were either just talkin', they had forgotten about me, or they didn't like my work. I was wrong! Y'all, come check this out!"

He gave his brothers some time to focus on what was showing on his phone.

"This phone gotta be broke or something," Houston yelled out.

"You know you sound like a hater, right?" Ray asked.

"Yeah, I know, but is that real?"

"It looks like it is. Let me go ahead and call them to make sure."

Raymond called the couple to get some clarification on what was happening.

"Put it on speaker so we can hear them," Damon yelled, even though he was obviously trying to whisper.

Raymond granted his brother's wishes as he tried to reach the couple.

"Hello, this is Raymond. I don't know if you remember me,

but I'm the kid who was trying to sell the sculpture."

"Yes, we remember you."

"Okay, well, something has to be wrong. We need money, but we weren't raised to be thieves. I know you didn't mean to send this because when I asked for $100, you turned me down. So, I can't keep what ain't mine."

"Young man, if you had to guess, how long would you say you worked on that piece you showed us?"

"Umm… if I add up all of the drafting and work I did, plus all of the sculpting time, plus going back to add in all of the little details, it probably took me about two or three weeks."

"See, too many times artists undervalue their own time and work. Let's say that sculpture took you two weeks from start to finish. For a moment, let's pretend all you did was work and sleep. There are 168 hours in a week, so there are 336 hours in two weeks. If you slept eight hours every night, then that would be 112 hours."

"No disrespect, but math ain't never been my thing. What are you telling me?"

"I get it. I'm throwing out a lot of numbers because I'm trying to make a point to you. What I'm saying is you worked around 224 hours on that one piece. That means the $5,000 we just sent you equaled a little over $22 per hour. For the quality of work you created, we've still underpaid you. So, our questions to you are, will you accept the payment, and if so, when can we get our sculpture?"

Without hesitating, he agreed to officially sell his first piece of art. He made arrangements to meet up with the couple, and he thanked them several times.

"Raymond, we want you to know your art is incredible, and we want you to keep working on your craft. So, we totally expect you to let us know when you have more work finished. Oh, and we have to start promoting your work on social media and, eventually, on your website. The world can't buy your stuff if they don't know it exists."

"You're right, and I'll do better. It's so hard trying to find work that'll take care of the bills, most of the time my brain can't even focus on art."

"That's sad. Can you hold on for just a minute, Ray?"

"Uh, sure."

The conversation was temporarily paused while the couple went away from the phone. When they returned, they instantly started asking questions.

"Ray, you said you were currently looking for work, right?"

"Yeah, unfortunately."

"If you approve, we no longer want you to look for a job. We…"

"I have to find work. I have responsibilities, and I can't let my family down," Ray told them.

"That passion, honesty, and transparency confirm we have the right one."

"The right one for what?" Raymond asked.

"Good question. I'll try to explain it as quickly as I can. For years, we've absolutely loved art. We have always purchased work from local artists, but for the past four or five years, we have wanted to do a lot more for the art community. This is where you come into play."

"What does that even mean?" Damon asked.

"Shh, be quiet. I'm tryin' to talk," Raymond told his youngest brother.

"That must be one of your siblings," they said in unison.

"Yes, it is. We were all in the room talking when you all called."

"Oh, you should have told us that at the start of the call. Family time is very important, so we'll get to the point. We were in the process of opening a gallery when the pandemic hit. Things are changing a little, so we can finally move forward. We have been searching for an artist to feature when we got the gallery opened. Now we know that person is you."

"No cap, that sounds good, but my family can't live off of hype and promises. Bill collectors don't care about my art. They only care about getting my money."

"That's true, but I think there may have been some sort of miscommunication or misunderstanding. We don't want you to be a starving artist. We want you to use your art to take care of everything you need to take care of. We want you to succeed and live up to your potential. We have about six months before everything is completely finalized. Within that time frame, we want our featured artist to have at least five pieces on display at all times. To make sure this happens, we want to pay that artist an advance of at least market value for their work. The artist also has to understand their work may also get resold at some point, but depending on the selling price, that artist may or may not benefit from that sale because they would have already been paid."

"That's a lot of info, so can you break it down so me and my brothers can understand?" Ray asked.

"Of course. We're just saying take that $5,000 we just gave you and multiply that by five. That should be enough to help you take care of your family for a little while."

I could hear Damon and Houston yelling and jumping for joy because they knew how much money their brother could make. Raymond, on the other hand, didn't express the same level of excitement. Instead, he told the couple he appreciated the offer, but he felt he was undeserving because of his age and lack of experience as a professional artist. He was downgrading his value with every word he said, almost as if he was trying his best to convince the couple to choose someone else.

"You're scared, and we understand, but we won't let you talk your way out of a blessing. We believe in you, and if you want to take care of your family, all you have to do is find the courage to believe in yourself."

Shortly after that, they ended the conversation. Damon and Houston were still excited, while Raymond was being more quiet than expected.

"Bruh, what's wrong with you? They just said they'll give you a lot of money, so why you actin' like that?" Houston asked.

"It's just like they said, I'm scared," Raymond responded honestly.

"Scared of what?"

"I'm scared of letting everybody down. I'm scared of my art not being good enough to be accepted."

"Big bro, I don't know much about all of this art stuff, but I know you got people tryin' to help you secure the bag, and you runnin' away from it. You're good at what you do, so just get yo money!" Houston yelled.

He was right, and after about five minutes, Raymond was finally able to admit it. Then, he thanked his brothers for talking some sense into him. He told them he needed some time to himself, and as they left him alone in his room, he told them he needed to let Jada know what was going on. She had a lot of questions that weren't answered via text message because as soon as she got home, they instantly started talking about the offer Raymond received.

"So, let's go back to the beginning. How much did they send you for the sculpture?" Jada asked.

"They already sent me five stacks for it," Raymond replied.

"That's crazy! And they want you to make some more art?"

"Yeah, at least five more pieces. Jada, do you realize this could change our lives? This could be the first step to us moving out of here."

"For sure! This is great news! Mom and Dad would be proud of you!"

Once again, the concept of pride found its way into the

conversation. Jada was so happy for her brother's accomplishment, she felt it was necessary to mention their parents. This caused Raymond to get caught up in his emotions again.

"I want us to move, but I need you to go to college after you graduate next year. I don't want you to feel like you have to stay here to help me out. You have to go out into the world and do want you want to do. I won't let you get stuck here!"

"First of all, Damon and Houston are my brothers, too. So, if we have to continue taking care of them together, then that's what we're gonna do. Secondly, you don't have to worry about paying for college because…"

"I know you're not about to fix your mouth to say you're not goin' to college because ain't no way that's gonna happen. You're not gonna waste your potential. I know you've always wanted to be a lawyer, so I'm not gonna allow you to give up on that!"

"Calm down, Ray. Take a breath. I wasn't about to say nothin' about not going to school."

"My bad. What were you gonna say?"

"Well, what I was gonna say is that I've been submitting college applications for a while. Mom and Dad helped me get going way before either of them got sick, so I've probably done about fifty applications already."

"Are you for real? How come I didn't know about that?"

"Bro, I'm seventeen, I'm not gonna tell you everything that's goin' on."

"What? You're supposed to tell me every detail of your life."

"Ray, I'm practically grown. So, not only am I not gonna tell you everything, I promise, you don't even wanna know everything. I mean, what if I started telling you about my dating life and all of that? You know you don't want to hear that."

"I guess you're right."

"Ain't no guessing, I know I'm right. Anyway, I'll promise to do better when it comes to keeping you updated on the important stuff, though. Is that cool?"

"I guess it's a start. So, what's up with these schools?"

"Well, like I was saying, I've already applied to about fifty different schools."

"Which ones? What did they say?" Raymond asked very excitedly.

"There are a ton, so I'm not about to name all of them, but I will say I'm only applying to HBCUs."

"Oh, okay. I see you, little sister. Out of curiosity, why only HBCUs?"

"During this school journey, I've been asking myself, 'Why would I want to go anywhere other than an HBCU?' Ray, we are way past needing a change. We have to start being that change. I'm tired of my people being overlooked. We are brilliant, incredible, and gifted. Our ancestors built this place, but we're the main ones who continue to suffer. We get abused by everyone, and we're always being looked down on. I'm going to one of our schools because we are more than enough. I'm going because I want to learn about our history, our potential, our dreams, and our experiences from us! I want to look around and see us not being the minority. I want to grow and build with my people."

"Dang, Jada. I thought you were gonna tell me you like the city they're in, or you heard there were some nice campuses. I was not ready for you to give me a super woke, my third-eye-is-open type answer. That's cool, though," Ray told his sister.

"Thank you. That's not even it, though. I heard back from about twenty-two of the schools I applied to, and I've been accepted into all of them! Bro, I'm so hyped up, it's crazy!"

"Jada, come give me a hug. That's incredible!"

"That's not it, either."

"What else could there be?"

"Out of the twenty-two schools I've been accepted to,

sixteen of them have offered me a full academic scholarship. The others haven't gotten back to me about that part yet."

"Jada, you haven't even graduated high school, and you're already doing so much more than me. You're amazing, little sister. Even if Ma and Dad were still here, there should be some type of improvements from one kid to the next, and you're making it happen. That's what's up, for real."

"Thank you, Ray. Before my eyes get filled with tears and I get an emotional lump in my throat, I need to tell you something I may not have fully said to you before. I have to tell you, big brother, you have always inspired me. I know you're tryin' to give me some shine 'cause of all of this college stuff, and I appreciate that, but we ain't gonna just gloss over the fact that people not only paid $5,000 for your art. Not only that, they're also offering tens of thousands more, along with the chance to feature your work in a new art gallery. Do you know how major that is? Nobody from where we're from has ever even thought about doing something like that, let alone made steps to make something happen. Ray, I remember there used to be times when we were in elementary school when you would come home with art you made from random things people in your class were getting rid of. You used to be so proud of your work, but you were also hurt because people were makin' fun of you."

"Dang, Jada, you remember that?"

"Yeah! I never did anything, but that sort of stuff always made me wanna find who hurt your feelings and fight them for you. I don't like people hurting my brothers, never have, never will."

"I never knew that, but I'm glad you didn't do anything."

"True, but the point of me bringing that up is because you persevered. You knew what you wanted to do at a young age, and regardless of what other people thought about it, you continued doing your thing. Seeing you do that helped me believe I could do anything, too, even if I didn't know how things would get done. Me believing I could go to school one day, even though I knew how much we were struggling, came from what I saw you, Mom, and Dad do. I love and appreciate you, Ray. Thank you for stepping up after..."

"You don't have to say it because I know where you're headed, and you're welcome. I can't do what I'm doing without you, Jada."

"Oh, I know! Nah, I'm just kidding. We make a good team, though. Hey, I know they haven't been gone for long, but do you still wonder why they were taken from us?" Jada asked, switching subjects a little.

"Yeah, I wonder, but even if I knew the exact reason, it wouldn't change anything. They would still be gone, and we would still be trying to figure out how we were going to survive. Sometimes stuff just happens, and that's it. I don't know why they had to go, and I wish they were still here, but our situation can't be changed. You know what, though?"

"What?"

"It may just be me, but since they died, it's like I hear their voices more when I make decisions. I see their smiles when we do something I know they would have approved of, and I can see them shaking their heads whenever I'm making the wrong move. I said all that to say they may be gone, but they aren't gone. Does that make sense?"

"Yeah, it does."

That day was proof the family was in a position they hadn't been in a while; ascension. They may have been physically living in the same location, but their mindsets were changing. They knew their parents had set them on a path that would change their family for generations to come, so they started to feel like they were doing what they were supposed to.

As the days passed, Raymond began to get more comfortable with the concept of progression. As the head of his family, his actions and beliefs had a direct correlation with those of his siblings. When Raymond finally contacted the couple who had requested more art to confirm his involvement in their gallery, he could feel a change happening to his family. His sister was already making moves toward her future, but Raymond had privately remained concerned about his brothers, especially Houston.

While he spent a large portion of his days working on his new art, I would always hear him murmur about not knowing what to do with him. One day, he decided to have a chat with his brother to see what was going on with him.

"Can I talk to you for a minute?" Raymond asked.

"What's up?" Houston asked.

"That's what I wanna ask you. It seems like something's been going on with you lately, but I can't tell exactly what it is."

"You want to know?" Houston asked.

"Yeah, be real with me. What's going on?"

"I don't like what's happening with y'all," Houston said very sadly.

"What you're talking about?" Raymond wondered.

"Jada is doin' all of this talk about what school she's going to, and you're makin' these statues and stuff for those people's gallery. Even Damon is starting to do more at school."

"That's true, but you'll find out what type of activities you wanna start doing, too."

"That's not what I'm saying. Just let me finish."

"My bad. Go ahead."

"What I was tryin' to say is y'all are doing all of this stuff, and y'all act like we didn't just lose Mom and Dad. Y'all are forgetting about them already and that's messed up! After everything they did for us, everybody's just actin' like they didn't exist!"

"You got it wrong, Houston, but I understand why you feel that way. The truth is, the only reason why we've been able to do what we're doing is because of them. I'm trying my best to carry on the traditions they started, and I know Jada is doing the same thing. This ain't easy, and I'm always getting scared and wondering if I'm doing the right things for the family. I ask Dad and Mom for advice all the time, so there ain't no way I'll ever forget them. More than anything, I will never let go of the love I have for them, and I know I'll always feel the love they had for us. I'm never letting go of them, but at the same time, we all have to find a way to keep moving forward, no matter what."

Clarification is what Houston was seeking, and that is exactly what his brother was able to provide. After their talk, Houston seemed to be a bit more relieved about how everyone was treating the memories of their parents, but that feeling didn't last very long. Soon, he was acting out and causing trouble at school, as well as at home.

"Why are you actin' up?" Jada asked him one day.

The question was similar to what Raymond asked him, but Houston's response was very different.

"You ain't my mama! I ain't gotta answer to you!"

I wasn't in the same room, so I couldn't see Jada's face, but I knew she had to be shocked by the way he replied. Houston didn't say anything that wasn't true, but the manner in which he said it wasn't called for. His yelling scared Damon so much that he ran into the room to see what was going on.

"Why are you screaming? Jada ain't did nothin' to you. You're being really stupid right now."

"Shut up, Damon! This ain't got nothin' to do with you! You always wanna be in somebody's business! Just go back to the room!"

The youngest sibling probably wanted to say something back, but he wasn't ready to fight. He wasn't going to be able to yell louder than his older brother, nor was he going to be able to physically overpower him, so he didn't try to do either. He just sighed heavily as he left the argument between the two who were involved.

"Do you feel good because you made your little brother run outta here like that?" Jada asked.

"None of this even matters! So what if I yelled at Damon? I don't care how I treat him because, at some point, he's gonna be gone, you're gonna be gone, and Ray's gonna be gone. Everyone's gonna leave, just like Mom and Dad did."

"We're all still hurt, but you can't keep actin' out because you're just gonna make people stop wanting to deal with you. You don't want to push people away because you're sad. Truthfully, when you're sad, that's when you need people the most. Don't make things more difficult for yourself because you're in your feelings. You're smarter than how you're acting, Houston. I know you didn't like it when Damon just said it, but you are kinda being stupid right now."

Upset about what Jada said to him, Houston left the room just as Damon had done. Jada still wanted to talk to him, but he wasn't having it.

"What's up, family?" Raymond asked as he walked into their apartment.

Nobody responded, so he tried to speak to everyone again.

"Maybe nobody heard me. Hello, family," he said as Houston suddenly headed towards the front door.

"Hey, little brother, what's good?" Raymond asked.

"I ain't got time for you tryin' to be nice to me. I gotta go," Houston said.

"I don't know where I'm goin', but I gotta leave before I go off on somebody!"

"You gonna tell me what's happening?"

"Ray, I told you, I gotta go! I don't have time for you to play like you're my therapist! You can't fix what's going on, so just quit trying."

Houston left the apartment. Ray had no idea why his brother was upset, or where he was going. As soon as Jada finally approached him, the two immediately started to have a conversation about what was going on.

"Did Houston just leave?" Jada asked.

"Yeah, he did. Please tell me what's going on."

"Your brother is trippin', for real. We've been arguing all around this apartment because he's been actin' up."

"Actin' up? Why?" Raymond wondered.

"I don't know for sure, but I think he's still processing Mom and Dad bein' gone. He's just handling it differently than the rest of us."

"We just had a talk about that, and I thought he was okay, but I should have known better."

"Out of all of us, I think he's having the most difficulty finding his way," Jada proclaimed.

"Speaking of finding his way, do you know where he went?"

"No, but we need to go look for him."

"You're right, Jada, but it ain't gonna be hard to find him."

"Why not?"

"I turned the tracking feature on his phone a long time ago. I know he doesn't pay attention to that kinda stuff, so I can pretty much guarantee we'll be able to find him."

Raymond pulled out his phone, and he quickly confirmed they would be able to find where Houston was going. He also knew he didn't want his younger brother out on the streets of their neighborhood alone as the sun began to go down.

"Jada, would you mind going with me to get him?"

"You know I don't mind."

The older siblings called Damon and told him to get ready, so they could leave.

"Y'all meet me in the car. I forgot to get something," Raymond said once everyone was ready.

That's when he decided, for whatever reason, to take me along for the ride. He didn't say if I was going because of fear of what he may see, or if it was just as a precaution. Whatever the reason, he felt I was necessary.

"You got what you needed?" Damon asked as Raymond, and I got into the car.

"Yeah, I'm good. Now, does everybody have their seatbelts on? You know we're not going anywhere until that's done," Raymond said.

When the family's safety protocols were met, we were on our way to get Houston.

"Where do you think he went?" Damon asked from the backseat.

"Do you remember where Dad and Mom would always take us when we had a really bad day?" Raymond asked.

"Oh yeah, that taco place down the street from our house. Dad would always get like four or five different tacos, and Mom would get the same two every single time we went. And whenever we got too quiet, Mom would always look at us and ask..."

"Is something wrong? Do you wanna taco 'bout it?" they all yelled out simultaneously while laughing.

While they were all still enjoying the moment, Raymond handed his phone over to his sister.

"Jada, could you just make sure he's going there? I don't want us to expect to find him and end up with nothing but tacos. Don't get me wrong, we're getting tacos no matter what, I just want to make sure that's not all we're getting."

"Hey, when you're right, you're right! Based on the app, it looks like he went right where you said he would," Jada said.

For a few minutes, the car was silent as the family approached a place they used to frequent when their parents were alive. Nobody wanted to be the first person to vocalize how it made them feel, but their lack of conversation during the last leg of the ride let each one of them know they were all deep in thought.

When the car stopped, Jada had something to say.

"It's funny how something can be the same, but give you such a different feeling."

"Don't make fun of me, but it feels like Mommy and Daddy are here with us. I feel…kinda happy," Damon said as if his own words shocked him.

"Yeah, me too," Jada added.

"With all the warm and fuzzy feelings aside, when we go in and see Houston, we just have to let him know we're happy to see him. Jada, I know he was trippin' before he left, but please don't yell at him. I'm sayin' that for both of us to hear. I have to make sure I keep my anger inside, at least until we get back home," Raymond said.

When we exited the car to go inside the restaurant, Raymond tried to hide me the best he could. Once we were inside, everyone started looking around for Houston.

"There he is!" Damon yelled.

It didn't take long for Jada, Damon, and Raymond to go over to where their brother was.

"Hey, Houston! We came to eat tacos with you!" Damon said as he started to laugh.

"Why are y'all here? How did you even know I was here?" Houston wondered.

"We weren't even worried about you if that's what you're wondering. When Ray got home, he asked me where I wanted to eat because he wanted to take his favorite brother out. I told him I wanted to go to that place we used to go to with Mom and Dad. I guess you just got lucky to be here at the same time as us.

The youngest sibling always tried to lighten the mood in any situation; this was no exception. Unfortunately, it didn't quite work this time, at least not at first.

"For real, Houston, what's up? You know you're not supposed to be leaving the house by yourself this late. I know you think you're grown and everything, but I don't want anything to happen to you," Ray told him.

"What about what I want?" Houston asked.

"What do you mean?" Jada wondered.

"What if I don't wanna be safe? What if I don't care if anything happens to me? What if I'm so tired of everything we're dealing with, I don't even wanna be here no more?"

For a few seconds, nobody said anything. Houston had asked all he needed to ask, and none of his siblings had any answers for him. So, until they did, they all just sat there.

"What am I gonna do if you go away?" Damon asked, breaking the awkward silence.

"I ain't nobody! If I'm not here, you'll be okay. You'll still have Jada and Ray, so you'll be good."

"Please don't get mad at me, Ray, and don't roll your eyes at me, Jada, but Houston, you're my best friend."

Hearing that comment from Damon almost immediately removed all of the anger Houston was trying to hold on to.

"Why you gotta say something like that? How am I supposed to stay mad?" Houston asked.

"Well, big brother, I'm sorry for making you un-mad," Damon replied.

"Dude, un-mad ain't even a word!" Houston told him.

"Yes, it is!"

"You just made it up!"

"Yeah, and so what if I did? Lil' Wayne made up bling-bling, and now that's a word. Houston, you just have to deal with a few facts. One, you're my best friend. Two, you gotta stick around. And the letter c, un-mad is a word you'll be hearing forever. So, for all of that, you're welcome."

"How are you gonna mix up numbers and letters like that, Damon? That doesn't even make sense."

"You said they do that in algebra and geometry and stuff, so why can't I? I'm just speaking like hard math. I'm trying to make you smarter, duh," Damon said as the family started laughing.

"Dang, bro! Why you gotta make me un-mad when I'm

clearly trying to be mad? You always messing stuff up," he said as he tried his best to be serious.

Eventually, the family moved on and ordered some food. They still had a lot of serious things they needed to talk about, but during that time, they put it all to the side to enjoy each other's company. Later, they left the restaurant together, and although they were still laughing, Ray knew he had a responsibility to make sure his family was okay.

He turned down the radio so everyone could clearly hear what he had to say.

"I can't pretend like our lives are always gonna be great because we all know that ain't how it is. What I can say is, no matter how much y'all get on my nerves, I will always love y'all. I will always do everything I can to make sure you're good."

As the older brother, Raymond said similar things to his family many times before. Generally, one of his siblings would say something snarky to make light of what he said. That didn't happen then. The family just all spoke to each other will a level of seriousness and maturity they probably didn't even think was possible.

"Houston, Ray, Damon, each one of you means the world to me. Like Ray said, I will do anything for you. And when one of my brothers is hurting, I feel the pain, too," Jada said.

"Can I ask y'all something, for real?" Houston asked.

"Go for it," Jada told him.

"How long is all of this gonna last?" Houston wondered.

"What do you mean?" Raymond asked.

"All of this. How long am I gonna miss Mama and Daddy? How long are we gonna have to live in the hood? How long am I gonna wake up feeling bad for no reason? I don't like it, and I'm sick of feeling like this."

"I wish I could tell you that you're gonna wake up in a few days and feel like everything was back to normal, but I can't. I don't think we're ever gonna get to a point where we don't miss Dad and Mom, but I think we'll be able to be happy living life while we carry their memories with us," Jada told them.

"Plus, this struggle is gonna make us stronger. I know you may not believe that...scratch that...I sometimes have trouble believing it myself, but it's true. We'll get better, bro. I promise," Raymond assured him.

Houston started to cry, and every few seconds, a little bit of a sniffle could be heard coming from his direction. When they made it back home, they didn't get out immediately because Raymond had something he had to ask.

"Take a look around. What do you see?"

"What kind of answer are you looking for?" Jada asked.

"Nothing deep, I just really want to know what everybody sees when you look at our neighborhood."

"I see a bad neighborhood, and sometimes I get scared to even go outside," Damon said, becoming the first one to answer.

"Okay. Jada, Houston, what do you see?" Ray asked.

"I see a place that used to be our home, but it doesn't always feel like it anymore," Jada responded.

"What about you, Houston?"

"This is stupid! You know what I see!"

"Bruh, just say what's on your heart," Raymond demanded.

"I see the place where Mama and Daddy got sick! I see a place where cops don't like us 'cause we're Black. I see a run-down neighborhood with messed-up houses and apartments that poor people like us are stuck in! I hate this place!"

Nobody knew exactly why Raymond asked everyone what they saw, but hearing Houston vocalize his hatred of their neighborhood seemed to deflate him a bit. The deep sigh Ray released indicated he was either hurt or disappointed by what he heard.

"Thank you for honestly expressing yourselves. Damon, I'm sorry you get scared, but until I'm gone, I'm always gonna try to protect you. Jada, I know what you mean, and I'm sorry this doesn't feel like home anymore. Houston, I..."

"Yeah, I know, you don't know what to say to me. This place is trash. I hate it, bro! I hate it!"

The family had gone through a lot in their young lives, so it made sense for them to all feel the way they did. Raymond's slight pause before he proceeded, let everyone know he had to think about what he was going to say next.

"So, let me ask a simple question; is this still home?"

Almost in unison, the three younger siblings told Ray the only neighborhood they had ever known was no longer their home.

"Well, we're gonna move," Ray told them very matter-of-factly.

"Stop playin', bro! We're too broke to move out of here," Houston yelled.

"That's where you're wrong," Raymond told him.

"So, we're rich?" Damon asked.

"Nah, little brother, we're far from rich, but we're not poor, either."

"What are you sayin'?" Houston asked, almost disgusted.

"Poor ain't just about what's in your pocket, but it's also about your mindset. You probably don't wanna hear it, but we're a family full of smart and creative people. Plus, we love each other. When you put that together, you can't be poor. I said we weren't rich, but that's kinda wrong, too. We're already rich; we're just waiting on the money to catch up to us."

Again, Ray spoke his truth while trying to provide words of inspiration to his family, but when it came to Houston, his words fell on deaf ears.

"That kinda talk may work in the movies, but this ain't that. We ain't no actors who get to just leave the bad stuff behind at the end of the day. We can't escape this," Houston said.

Normally, when conversations got deep, Raymond would

depend on his sister to help him out. For whatever reason, what Houston said left her speechless.

"Hey, bruh, I can't say you didn't make some good points because you did. We're not actors and what we're living through ain't nothing that'll end when a director says, 'Cut,' but not everything you said is right."

"What ain't right?" Houston asked.

"You said we can't escape where we are, but that's not exactly true."

"But Mom and Dad couldn't get enough money to help us move," Damon chimed in.

"True, but what they were able to do was put things in motion. See, sometimes people make sacrifices for other people, even if there's a chance they'll never get to see if their hard work paid off. That's what our parents did for us. I know we've been struggling, but we have each other. Plus, I can guarantee we all know somebody who has it worse than we do. So, no matter what, we need to be grateful."

"Can we just go in the house?" Houston asked.

Houston had grown tired of the wisdom and positivity his brother was trying to bestow upon him, but Ray didn't let it get to him.

"Yeah, we've had a long day. I think we all should go inside."

Once they were back inside of their home, Houston immediately went to his room without saying anything else to anyone. Damon, on the other hand, suddenly had more questions he needed answers to.

"Jada, Ray, do you think things will get better?" he inquired.

Jada was quick to respond to her baby brother.

"Damon, you know how you'll get mad sometimes when you're playing your video games because you made it to a new level, and you can't defeat all of the enemies as easily as you could in the level before?"

"Yeah! That stuff be way too hard at first!"

"But do you quit playing?"

"No!"

"Why not?"

"Because I know I just have to build up my experience points, then I'll finally be able to figure out how to get past everything."

"Right! Believe it or not, that's how real life is. As a family, we've been having a hard time getting past this level. When we lost Mom and Dad, me and Ray had no idea what we were gonna do. Then, we realized how much we had learned from them. We took those life lessons, and we gained some experience on our own. Now, with all of that, I think we're all about to go to the next level."

"I like how you did that, Jada! That's cool, but do you think we're really gonna get to the next level?"

"Damon, I don't know if you know it or not, but our sister is something like a genius. She has all of these colleges begging her to go to their school," Ray added.

"I appreciate that, bro, but let's not act like you ain't about to turn the entire art world upside-down. This is all about what this family is gonna do. Individually, we're incredible, but together, we can't be stopped!"

Damon was excited about what Jada and Raymond were saying. Unlike Houston, he believed everything he heard.

"Do you trust us, little brother?" Ray asked.

"Uh, yeah. Why?"

"I just wanna make sure because the more we trust each other, the easier it will be for us to make it to the next level. Do you understand?"

"Yeah, yeah, I get it. When I'm playing my games online, it's much easier when everybody on the team trusts everybody else to do their thing," Damon confirmed.

The group of three exchanged a few more words before Damon left the room. Once he was gone, the oldest siblings talked more about how their lives were shaping up. For them to speak positively about their futures to Damon was expected, but for them to continue that optimism when he was no longer around wasn't quite what I thought would happen.

"I feel...I don't know...I think I just feel like we're at that point where things are really about to turn around for us. I trust you, Ray. I trust that you're gonna lead us in the right direction."

"No, Jada, God is gonna lead us in the right direction. He just might use me to help get it done, though. Even with that, I ain't doin' this alone. So, if any credit is given for our family's accomplishments, it will be given to God and us, but not me."

"Okay, okay, fine," Jada laughed.

"But for real, with my art and you getting ready for college, I think we're really about to change the trajectory of our family."

"That's putting a lot of pressure on us, but I agree with you."

"Even though I'm still kinda nervous about this gallery thing, I still think everything will turn out well. This may sound weird, but sometimes I look around, and I don't even see this place anymore."

"What do you mean?"

"I mean...sometimes, when I'm by myself, I'll look at the walls of this apartment and they just disappear. Then, I'll just talk to Mom and Dad. I promise you; it feels like they're here."

"What do they say?"

"Well, let me go back and clear something up. I talk to them, and even though most of the time I'll speak and feel their presence, I don't always hear them talk to me. Anyway, that's when I start seeing our future as if it were our present. That's what I meant when I said I don't even see this place. I see where we're going, not where we are."

"Kinda weird, not gonna lie, but it's still kinda cool."

"I agree with you; it's weird, but envisioning us living in a bigger home, in a better neighborhood, without having the stress of financial issues gives me hope."

Hope is one of the many things humans talk about that is almost incomprehensible to me. Those kids were living without their parents in a neighborhood where crime was a resident, yet because of hope, they were able to think positively about their future. Those like me deal with "what is," not "what could be." To me, hope is fraudulent. Hope has no place in reality because it's not tangible, but if humans want to continue wasting time with it, that's on them. With that being said, I do have to acknowledge the belief the kids had in their future soon started to pay off .

I'm not the best keeper of time, so I don't know exactly how many days, hours, or minutes it took for hope to change their situation. I do, however, know the major changes started the day everyone went to the gallery to see Raymond's work.

"It's pretty spectacular, isn't it?"

The question was being asked by the same man I heard talking to Ray over the phone several times. Out of habit, Ray actually took me to the gallery, almost without even thinking about it. In doing so, I finally had a chance to be around during their conversation.

Over the phone, Ray usually had no problem speaking, even if he didn't believe what the person was saying. This was different. For some reason, Ray found it hard to put enough words together to formulate a decent response.

"Yeah, it's… I think…umm…yeah," he said awkwardly.

"That wasn't the answer I was expecting. Be honest, did the gallery opening not meet your expectations?"

"The gallery was way more than I thought it would be, but…"

"But what? Don't hinder our conversation by overthinking what you're going to say. Just talk to me," the person told Raymond.

The man's words released whatever was holding Raymond

back. Suddenly, Ray's trickle of responses became an overflow of honesty.

"This…all of this is amazing. It's beyond any sort of expectations I could ever have. Some of the people, on the other hand, were not really who I thought I would see," Ray said.

"Please elaborate, Raymond."

"Okay. So, I have never done what I do for money. I do it because I love it. I do it to inspire my family and the rest of the world to not limit themselves to what others may think they're capable of. I do this as a constant reminder that we are not where we come from, or even what we've been through. And even with the truest, most heart-filled intentions, I heard someone spewing hatred about my work," Raymond explained.

"You know not everyone is going to like what you create, right?"

"Oh, yeah. I know art is subjective, and it's impossible for everyone to like what I do, but what I heard from one person in particular literally made me sick to my stomach. I'm just trying to hold it together for the sake of my brothers and sister. I want to go off on the dude, but I know that'll hurt me more than it would hurt him. Like Denzel told Will during the Oscars, 'In your highest moments, be careful. That's when the devil comes for you.' That's kinda how I feel right now."

The older man took some time to let the heaviness of what Raymond said clear the air a little. He took a deep breath, and then he proceeded.

"What was said, Ray?"

"I was just walking by lookin' at my work, kinda hearing what the people were saying. Some people loved it, some people were talking about buying some pieces, and some people said they weren't feeling any of it."

"Okay, that sounds about normal, regardless of who the artist is."

"True, and I accepted all of that, so none of that got to me."

"So, what did?"

"When I passed by the sculpture I did to represent my family, including my mom and dad, I heard this dude say, 'Nobody wants to see all of this Black stuff! Plus, the artist depicted a family, and we know when it comes to Black people and family...well, let's just say we all know how unrealistic this is.' When I heard that, it took everything in me not to punch him in his face because I knew exactly what he was trying to say. He looked back and saw me, so he and his friends tried to act like they were talking 'bout something else. I'm telling you, I had a lot of anger inside of me, but I couldn't react in a way that would have disappointed my siblings or brought shame to my parents' legacy. I owe all of them more than that."

"Raymond, I have to commend you on your maturity, especially at your age. If I can keep it real with you, I don't even know if I would have been able to keep my composure if I were you. Your restraint shows that you're destined for great things."

"I appreciate that, but I still don't feel right. I feel like he's getting away with something," Raymond told him.

"Is the person who said those things still here?"

"Yeah, but I ain't tryin' to point him out. That'll be like snitching, and that ain't me."

"I understand where you're coming from, trust me, but we have to let that snitching stuff go. The reason I want to know if the person is still here is because we need to have a healthy confrontation with him."

"A healthy confrontation? What does that even mean?"

"Well, Ray, don't think I didn't notice you brought your friend with you today?"

"My friend? The only people I brought with me is my family, so I don't know who you're talking about."

"Maybe the friend I'm talking about isn't a who, but a what."

That's when I knew he was talking about me.

"Oh, you mean..."

"Yeah, that's what I mean. Why did you feel the need to bring that with you?"

"Really, I don't even know. Sometimes I just have it with me without even realizing it. But my life don't just take place in art galleries. When I leave here, I have to take my family back to a neighborhood where people our age have gotten killed because they looked at somebody funny. My job is to make sure they're okay, so even when I'm not thinking about it, I'm on my job."

"That's unfortunate, but I get it. This hasn't always been my life, either. Anyway, by healthy confrontation, I mean confronting that person in a way that allows you to get your point across without involving your *friend*."

He kept calling me Raymond's friend, but we all knew that wasn't what I was. From what I heard, friendships require both parties to be there for each other and are concerned about each other's well-being. That was not what I had with Ray. Raymond just hired me to handle the jobs he couldn't take care of himself. I was on call in case one of those jobs ever arose. That was the extent of our connection.

After explaining exactly what was meant, Raymond eventually told his mentor he would be able to control himself while having a discussion. He also promised I wouldn't be involved in the conversation, which was not exactly what I wanted him to say, but again, he was the boss, and I was in no position to change his mind.

We moved through the crowd until we eventually made it to the person Raymond was seeking. Initially, Raymond's mentor controlled the conversation.

"Excuse us for a moment. We're just trying to see what everyone thinks about the work."

"I think...well, it seems..."

"You're trying to think of what to say, which means you're already not being honest. We're just trying to gauge what people think, and we can't do that if you're not being real."

The unnamed gallery visitor let out a noise to indicate he didn't appreciate what was being said to him, but he did continue the conversation with more honesty.

"Well, if I'm being honest, the collection has potential, but I can't say I believe the message the artist is trying to convey."

"What exactly do you mean?" Raymond's mentor asked.

"This is a bit phony. By the look of the sculptures and their features, I take it the artist is Black. There's nothing wrong with that, I guess, but they have all of this family-related stuff. That's not realistic."

I could feel Raymond's pulse starting to race, but he continued to remain silent.

"Do you have statistics that back up your statement on family, or are you just allowing your racist thoughts to run free?"

"Racist? How dare you! How come you people always wanna accuse someone of being racist?"

"You people, huh? See, I like to call people out when they talk and act like a racist. You people get more offended by being called a racist than the actual act of racism that was committed."

"Yeah, whatever. The fact remains that the majority of the work is not believable."

This was when Raymond started talking.

"I can't keep quiet anymore. It's sad you view the concept of a Black family as unrealistic."

"Perhaps, but..."

Almost as if they were ready to hear what the guy was going to say, Jada, Damon, and Houston suddenly came and stood by their brother.

"What's up, Ray?" Jada asked.

"This guy was just about to explain why he believes Black families don't exist," Ray said.

"That's stupid! We're Black, and we're a family!" Houston said.

The guy chuckled dismissively.

"I don't understand what's funny. My brother is an extremely talented and intelligent artist. When he created all of this…"

"Oh, so you're the artist? I guess that explains the anger."

"Look, I'm gonna say what I need to say, and then I'm going to stop giving you my energy. I understand art is not going to be liked by everyone, but if you don't know the story of the art or what went into creating it, it would probably be better if you didn't speak on it. Your words, in this instance, bother me because of how important family is to me. Do you see these three wonderful people next to me?"

"Yeah, and?"

"And this is my family."

"That's cool, but correct me if I'm wrong; I'm pretty sure you don't have your mother and father here with you, do you?"

"No, but…"

"That's exactly why I said this 'family thing' is not believable. I mean, not coming from a Black artist, at least."

"This is why ignorance needs to be quiet. Yeah, it's true our parents are not here, but it's not because they don't want to be, but because they can't. We lost our parents because of Covid. So, when you say the Black family stuff isn't real, my mind processes that as disrespect thrown in the direction of the people I love. That's something I won't stand for."

"I don't know you, and I'm sorry you lost your parents, but there are reasons you all are called Black, and it's not just because of your skin color. Black is more than that. Black means negative, and that's what follows you. When you're Black, there is no light around you. Your people are synonymous with darkness."

Everybody wanted to say something, but surprisingly, Raymond was calmly able to tell them he wasn't finished speaking.

"People like you have convinced yourself that white means right. You want to believe that the issues plaguing the Black community are self-inflicted. You want to act like the system wasn't built by your ancestors to hold my ancestors back. You basically were clowning my work because it's based on family. Maybe you're unaware, no, maybe you've tried to make yourself forget that my people built this country, and while they were doing that, your people ripped Black families apart, made sure we stayed poor, kept us in bad neighborhoods, underfunded our school systems, built a pipeline from those underprivileged schools to prison, in part to keep a form of legalized slavery. Then, you have the audacity to laugh at us because we're dealing with the chaos that you people created. Don't let your privilege cause you to lose your grip on reality. The truth of the matter is, your family is together because your people unified to make sure mine wasn't able to be. And don't get it twisted. Me being Black doesn't connect me or my family to darkness. In spite of what you think, my Blackness is a light that's far too bright for you to handle. That's why you try to dim it, but there is no dimming this. We are gonna shine regardless."

Raymond said a lot, but the more he spoke, the calmer he started to get. When he finished speaking, a roar of applause rang out. What started as a talk among a few people ended up being a speech for a room full of listeners. Hearing the positivity rain down on Ray was enough to make the other man walk away.

"Congratulations, young man. That was exactly the type of conversation I knew you were capable of having."

"Yeah, Ray, I'm so proud of you. I hope somebody was recording that because it was epic! If they put it online, I know it'll go viral!" Jada exclaimed.

"I don't know about all of that, but it did feel good to express myself. Not liking my art is one thing, but disrespecting my family and my Blackness…"

"Takes everything to a whole... 'notha...level, right bro?'" Damon interrupted.

"Yeah, I guess so," Ray responded.

The siblings laughed before Ray's mentor excused himself from their company. They continued to talk until he returned. When he did, he had his wife with him.

"Raymond, I apologize for not being able to speak with you before, but I had a lot of things I had to take care of. I have to congratulate you on a great day. I thought the sales numbers for the day were the best thing about it all, but my husband, Curtis, told me the conversation you had just a little while ago is gonna end up being one of the most memorable things about the night."

"I was caught up in the moment, but my family told me I did a pretty good job, so I guess I did. Wait a minute, did you mention sales?"

"Oh, so you caught that, huh? Yeah, from the beginning, we have told you we believed your talent was going to help you and your siblings. Today has proven that much more than we ever could have."

"Miss lady, ma'am, are you sayin' my brother made some money or somethin'?" Damon asked eagerly.

The couple asked Raymond, Jada, Damon, and Houston to step into their office, away from the other gallery visitors. They all went along with the request, and without wasting any time, they started praising Raymond not only for the quality of his work, but also for the number of pieces that were sold.

"I appreciate it, but I really can't take credit for the sales. I just made the sculptures, but I didn't convince anybody to buy anything. I didn't even have anything to do with how everything was laid out," Raymond said humbly.

"I know this is none of my business, but Ray, you're taking this humble thing too far. I don't know if you know it or not, but you can't make a lot of money from selling stuff if you ain't got stuff to sell," Houston said.

"Man, be quiet. Don't say that kinda stuff. You might make them mad at us," Ray whispered to his brother.

"Ray, you don't have to whisper, and you don't have to worry about us getting mad, either. Plus, your brother is right. None of this would be possible without you, Ray," the lady said.

"Tori, should we go ahead and let the family know what type of night they had?"

This was when we all learned Tori was the name of the other person responsible for the gallery. After learning this, the group continued with their discussion.

"Yep! You should tell us!" Damon yelled.

"Well, I hope everyone is ready for their lives to change. I know we gave you an advance, but that advance is nothing in comparison to what the paintings actually sold for. Within a few weeks, even after our fees, you're expected to clear about $1.2 million."

At first, there were no reactions. Then, all of the siblings started to react at the same time. Houston and Damon started yelling very excitedly, Jada started crying, and Raymond suddenly found himself gasping for air.

"Are you...is this...?"

Raymond tried to ask multiple questions, but he couldn't complete any of them.

"Correct me if I'm wrong, but I think you're trying to ask us if we're serious and if this is for real. The answer to both questions is yes. Your work has always been good enough, Ray, you just needed someone to believe in you," Tori said.

"The seeds of success were planted by you, Ray. This gallery was just us taking our turn watering those seeds. You and your family are poised to grow exponentially, and we're glad we were able to see the beginning of that growth. I hope it's okay to say this, but you young people are amazing. We have had the honor of witnessing Raymond's talent, but we believe all of you have greatness within you. We didn't know them, but we are certain your parents would be proud of all of you," Curtis added.

"Thank you for saying that. I think we all needed to hear it," Jada said to the couple.

"No problem."

"I know this is your office and everything, but would it be possible for me to speak with my family alone for a few minutes?" Raymond asked very politely.

"Absolutely," the couple replied.

When Tori and Curtis left, I expected Raymond to start talking to his siblings. Eventually, he did, but that's not who he talked to first.

"We thank you, Father God. We have been praying for change, and you have given that to us! My God! Our lives will never be the same, and on behalf of my family, I thank you! A million times, I thank you!"

Regardless of their living situation, or even after Covid took their parents from them, Raymond always made sure he spoke to his God. There were many things about people I didn't comprehend, and initially, God was one of them. Then, the more I was around Raymond, I started to learn why humans cared so much about God.

Machines don't have souls, so my understanding didn't come from a direct connection, but I was eventually able to relate. See, there were people who put me together. Then, there is someone much higher above than those who were directly responsible for me. The people who assembled me are very similar to a human's parents; they are directly responsible, but there is always someone higher up who has a much different level of responsibility. God is the human's ultimate creator.

Whenever Ray needed advice, or if he just felt bad, he would speak to the spirit of his parents. When he wanted to show his gratitude, or if he was dealing with an issue that he felt was beyond him, he would normally talk to God. Humans also did this thing called prayer, which seemed to be when those people who believed in God would have the most honest and open dialogues with Him. I don't know about others, but Raymond prayed for himself and his family very often.

He talked about what everyone was going through. He talked about the projects he and the rest of the family were working on, but he mainly asked for the strength that was necessary form him not to give up. When he prayed, he spoke with conviction and optimism, even when there didn't seem to be anything to be optimistic about. This was something similar to what they called hope, but it was much more than that. People referred to that belief as having faith.

The faith that people like Raymond held on to kept them moving forward when things weren't going well. Unlike with me, things would sometimes happen for or to people that had no explanation. Everything that led up to Raymond's life-changing night was an example of that. This was what having faith in God was about.

After Ray and his family spoke to God, they took some time to speak to their parents. Ray thanked his father for helping him become the man he had grown to be, while he asked his mom to forgive him for getting mad at her for doing things that ultimately helped him grow up. Jada just kept asking them if they could see how things were changing. Although there was no response, she said she always felt like their parents were watching them. The youngest two members of the family didn't have much to say other than saying they were finally rich.

A few knocks were soon heard on the door.

"May we come back in?"

Curtis and Tori thought the family had enough time to themselves, so they wanted to come back into their space.

"No doubt. Come on back in," Ray told them.

Once they re-entered their office, they didn't immediately

start to talk about money. Instead, they started talking about everyone's future.

"Ray, what do you want for your future? And we're not looking for some overly analytical answer. We just want honesty."

He took a moment.

"I just want my family to be good. I want us to be able to go to a better neighborhood. I want my little sister to be able to go to the school of her choice and only have to worry about her classes. I want my brothers to have the freedom to just be kids. I want my parents to be proud of us. I don't know...I just...I don't know."

"Yes, you know, and you've expressed it very passionately," Curtis told him.

"Ray, since we first met you, we told you there was something about you and your work that set you apart from other artists we've worked with. I hope you don't mind, but because of your age and family situation, we've reached out to some people who can help you with your family's financial future."

"What exactly do you mean?" Jada asked.

"I'm glad you asked, Jada. It simply means—"

Curtis started talking, but for some reason, Raymond didn't want to let him finish.

"That just means they've already connected with someone to take our money so everybody gets paid, except us! I knew y'all were too good to be true! This is why I'd rather just handle everything by myself! I can't believe we get our hopes up!"

Raymond was not happy, and he wasn't trying to hide it. I thought I was about to 'clock in' and go to work because he reached out to me.

"I know why you're saying those things, but they're not true. Honestly, we absolutely could have cheated you out of the money you've earned, but some things are worth more than money. If we stole from you and your family, ultimately, we would be burning a bridge we know we'll need to cross in the future. That wouldn't be a smart move for us to make," Curtis explained to everyone.

"We know how important money is, so we can't downplay that, but having good relationships with good people is far more valuable. Does that make sense?" Tori asked.

"Yeah, it makes sense, but that ain't the kinda stuff we've dealt with. Nobody we know is givin' up money for relationships. That just ain't how stuff goes!" Ray yelled.

Ray's tone had shifted dramatically. He had gone from believing almost every word Tori and Curtis said to nearly dismissing it all. His siblings, whether they agreed with him or not, just went along with what their brother was saying.

"Ray, we understand your feelings, but we're telling you the truth. Also, you mentioned not knowing people who value relationships more than they value money. We used to be like that, too, but you know what changed our mindset?"

"What?"

"Our mindset changed once we finally got out of our old neighborhood. When we did, we saw it wasn't all about the hustle. Not only that, even if you're all about your money, how much money can you make if you're trying to do everything by yourself?"

The couple was mainly talking to Ray, but what they were talking about impacted the entire family. Since that was the case, Jada joined the conversation.

"Yeah, we haven't seen a lot outside of our neighborhood, but we've seen enough to know if something seems too good to be true, it usually is."

"Jada, in most cases, I would agree with you. However, there are times when the things you prayed for are given to you, and the good karma you put out into the world makes its way back to you. Don't you think your family deserves something great?

Don't you think your brother deserves to get paid for his talent and hard work?"

"Look, knowing my brother deserves to get paid and believing our prayers will be answered doesn't mean we should trust you."

Jada wasn't going to allow her youth and inexperience to silence her true feelings. It was evident that even though she wasn't the oldest, she took the responsibility of taking care of her family just as seriously as Raymond did.

"See, the tenacity and intelligence this family has almost leaves me speechless. It's such an honor to see young people care so much about their well-being, and again, we want to see your success grow, not take away from it," Tori said.

"I appreciate y'all saying all of this nice stuff, but let's get to it. If you think we're all so smart and talented, why didn't you allow us to choose our own financial advisors?" Ray asked.

"That's a good question that I would like to answer by asking each of you a question."

"Okay, what's up?"

"What financial advisors do you know?" Curtis asked.

"We don't know any," Ray responded.

"So, do you think you're more likely to get taken advantage of by some random person you find by searching the internet, or by working with one of the people we've worked with closely over the years?" Tori asked.

"I guess I get it now," Ray said.

"I knew you would. Like we said, we want your family to be taken care of, even if you decide to retire today."

"Retire? Maybe you forgot I'm only nineteen. I'm not thinking about retirement."

"I know you're not, but my point is, we want you to be free to do whatever it is you want to do. If you have the right people behind you, there are no limits to what you can achieve." Curtis said.

"Well, you mean with God and the right people, there are no limits. I get where you're coming from, though," Ray told him.

Everyone continued talking. Tori and Curtis went on to provide more information about the advisors they recommend for Raymond and his family. Days passed, and eventually, the family met with the person they decided would work best for them. Once all of the purchases from the gallery were finalized, everyone worked to make sure not only Raymond was paid but, that his future plans were also set.

Just as the couple had promised, Raymond ended up getting about $1 million. That money quickly went to work for the family. Almost immediately, they were able to find a real estate agent who helped them get into a home in another neighborhood. Being somewhere outside of the area they grew up in was a welcomed change, but it did take them some time to get used to.

"Jada, I like goin' to sleep without hearin' sirens and shots. I know this is gonna sound weird, but it gets so quiet at night that sometimes I feel like I hear Mama singing that lullaby she used to sing to me when I was a baby," Damon told his sister one day.

"I get it. We've lived our entire lives in our old neighborhood, and this one is...different. For the first time, we live somewhere quiet and safe," Jada replied.

"Ray told us he wanted us to feel safe, and he made it happen. He's a really good big brother."

"He is, and we're fortunate to have him. If it weren't for him, I don't know if I wouldn't be getting ready to go off to school."

"Jada, why'd you have to remind me you're gonna be leaving?"

"I wasn't trying to make you feel sad, but it's just crazy to think how fast stuff changed. It seemed like we had been praying for change forever, then all of a sudden, we were here. God is amazing, and I know Mom and Dad had something to do with all of this."

"You know they did! And I can hear Mama right now talkin' about you and school. She'd be like, 'My baby going to school,' and she would have the prettiest smile."

"Yeah, that smile could make you forget about everything bad."

I heard the conversation from a safe inside of Raymond's new room. After the family moved, I started to spend most of my time there. The new environment quickly made Ray believe I wasn't quite as necessary as I previously was. I even heard him pondering getting rid of me, but he could never actually go through with it.

Things started to change, at least a little, when he received a surprise call from Curtis as he came into the house. He had the call on speaker, so I was able to hear what they were talking about.

"Hey, Ray. How's everything going for you and the family in your new home?"

"Things have been so much better, but I know I have so much room for growth."

"I'm glad to hear your new-found wealth hasn't taken away from your humility."

"No, sir, it just gave me a glimpse of what I can do. It also increased my hunger."

"That's the kind of talk I like! So, what do you have going on these days?"

"The gallery, and the video from that night, have made me a lot more popular. I've been doing a lot of commission work while trying to figure out what my next major move will be," Raymond said.

"That's good! What about your family? How are they?"

"Everyone's great. Jada's been taking some online courses before she goes off to school, and Houston is making a lot of progress with his mental health. One of the greatest things I was able to do with some of the money was get him a therapist who makes him feel comfortable enough to speak."

"That's incredible! What about the youngest one? How has Damon adjusted to your new life?"

"Damon is a trip. On several occasions, he told me this was the type of life he was supposed to be living his entire life. He's doing well in school, and all of a sudden, he wants to learn how to play the piano. He told me 'cultured' people need to play the piano. I don't know where he gets his personality from, but that kid is something else."

"He certainly is a character. I'm glad you guys are adjusting. Let me not waste any more time and get to why I'm calling. I've been hearing that you and your family have been doing charity events in your old neighborhood. Is that true?"

"We've been going back to our neighborhood and others all around the city to help out in any way we can. We've been blessed, so we feel like it's our duty to bless others."

"That's beautiful, but I want to make sure you're being careful. Please remember, not everyone wants to see you win."

"I appreciate the words of wisdom, but I think we're good. We're always on the lookout whenever we go back, so we should be fine. Thank you, though."

"No problem. We may not talk that often, but trust me, Tori and I want the best for your family."

"Thank you."

"You're welcome. The other thing I called about is another exhibit we have coming up. Unlike the last time we worked together, this one wouldn't only be about you and your art. We're working on getting a group of about five of the hottest new artists from across the country to put on a showcase for everyone to see. We're looking for about one or two pieces from each artist."

"That sounds amazing! When is it taking place?"

"It's still a few months away. Do you think you may be able to participate?"

"I do, but I don't have anything new right now."

"You can always use something you already have, but if you want to create something new, don't pressure yourself. Just let the world inspire you. If you do that, I'm sure you'll be able to create something wonderful."

Ray didn't speak to his family much about the phone call, but he did speak more about it when he was by himself in his room. For the first time in a while, I heard him question his talent and his position in the art world. I thought getting as much money as he did in a single night would have proven the importance and perceived value of what he did, but for some reason, he didn't see it that way.

It seemed like the money took away the pressure Ray was carrying when it came to taking care of his family, but it was replaced with the pressure of trying to match the success he had with his other work. With the exception of a few pieces he made specifically for clients, he was unable to create. However, when his family was around, he acted as though he was taking care of so many other things he simply didn't have the time to make anything new. He hadn't lied to them before, so his siblings just accepted what he said.

Ray told Curtis he wanted to participate in the upcoming event during their conversation, but he almost instantly regretted it. There were several times I heard him talk himself out of calling Tori and Curtis to withdraw. After a few weeks, he started to feel exhausted, even though he wasn't creating. He continued to force himself to handle every obligation he had, even when he should have taken time to rest. This couldn't have been more evident than when he and Jada were about to leave their home together to go to an event to help the less fortunate.

"I don't know about today, Jada. Something just don't feel right. It's like somethin' is in the air," he told his sister.

"Bro, we've always relied on intellect and instincts. If you feel like something's not right, then maybe we don't need to go."

"I think under normal circumstances, I would just stay home, but those people need us, so I have to go."

"Either way, I'm with you, Ray."

Despite Ray's feelings, they decided to go to their charity event. I knew something was different because, just like old times, he decided to put me in a backpack and take me with them. He didn't let his sister know because she would have tried to stop him. Before they left, I heard him say a brief prayer.

"Lord, I know that everything works together for our good. I pray that my eyes are opened, and I'm able to see what you want me to see, and learn what you want me to learn. In the name of Jesus, I pray, amen!"

They left shortly after that, and a while later, we made it to our destination.

"You ready, Ray?"

"Yeah, I guess."

"Try to contain your excitement," Jada said jokingly.

Ray knew his sister was showcasing her skills in sarcasm, but he was too tense to laugh with her. Instead, he quietly touched the backpack I was in just to confirm I was still there. Once he did, they moved forward with their day.

As the day progressed, he mentioned things were going much better than he thought they would. He and Jada were working hard to positively impact the world, and they knew it started with the neighborhood they were from.

"Is that the incomparable Raymond I see? I know you not out here slummin' it with us regular people," someone said.

"We're all equal, so we're all regular people. And this definitely ain't slumming it; this is where I'm from, this is where it all started from me."

"You just runnin' your mouth! All of that 'this is where I'm from' stuff don't mean nothin'! Everybody knows you got your money and left as soon as you could. If you loved being here so much, why did you leave?"

"Sir, I..."

"Sir? You don't even know who I am, do you?" the guy asked.

"I'm sorry, I don't."

"See, that's what I'm talkin' about. You said we're all equal, but as soon as you leave, you forgot about somebody who went to the same school you did from elementary to high school. Just 'cause I'm down, and you're up, you don't know me? Is that what it is, Ray?"

Hearing the man's level of hurt made Ray start to get nervous. He put his hands behind his back to once again make sure I was with him. He felt threatened by the man's tone, but because I was kept in the bag, I knew he didn't feel like he was truly in danger.

"Omar... it's Omar, right?" Ray finally asked.

"Oh, the big man remembers me! I can't believe it! So, I bet it makes you feel real good to help out the po' folks who ain't made it out like you, huh?"

"We should all feel good about helping each other out, so yeah, this does feel good."

"Cool, cool! So, check this out. Since you like helpin' people, and I know you got money, why don't you help me out?"

"What kinda help do you need?" Ray asked.

"I heard about what you got from your little art show. Why don't you hook yo' boy up with a few stacks? My work ain't comin' through like I need it to, and I got a little one on the way."

"Congratulations on your little one, but I don't think I'll be able to give you money like that. My bad, man."

"See, I knew you were all talk!"

"Nah, I'm not. I just..."

"Just shut up, fam! I hate folks like you! You get outta the hood and then try to come back so you can get some pictures for IG to act like you doin' something."

Omar, Raymond's former schoolmate, was getting more upset, which made Ray start to feel like the time to introduce me to him may have been drawing near.

"I don't even have my phone with me. This ain't about clout chasing or doin' nothin' for the internet. I'm just here to help."

"Hey, Ray, is everything okay?" Jada asked as she approached.

"Yeah, everything is cool. I'm just having a talk with somebody I went to school with."

"And even if it ain't cool, you ain't gonna do nothing," Omar said to Jada.

"I understand you're mad, but you're not gonna disrespect my sister. That's my first and last time telling you that," Ray said sternly.

"Let's just go, Ray," Jada said, obviously trying to protect her brother.

This was when Ray had to decide if he was going to do the right thing and leave, or if he was going to allow his human emotion and ego cloud his judgment.

"Man up and make a decision, Ray. You gon' stay and handle yo' business, or you gonna run off with yo' little sister?"

Contrary to what his sister wanted him to do, Ray started to unzip his backpack when Jada spoke to him.

"Don't do it, Ray. Don't throw it all away for this guy. He ain't worth it."

They hadn't discussed me being there, but Jada knew Ray had me with him. She convinced her brother using me would help him for a moment, but ultimately, he was the one that had everything to lose. If I had an opinion, or a way to express it, I would have just told him he should let me go ahead and have a quick talk with the person who was causing the problems.

"Hey, rich boy, can your money stop this?" Omar yelled out suddenly.

The next thing I knew, Jada was screaming at the top of her lungs, and for some reason, Ray and I were falling to the ground. There was an influx of people who suddenly were trying to talk to Ray, but he wasn't saying anything back to them. I didn't know what happened, but it must have been fairly severe because although Ray didn't always agree with everyone, I had never known him to just ignore people.

"Somebody call the ambulance for my brother!" Jada yelled.

That was my confirmation that Ray had been injured, and evidently, it was because of the actions of Omar. It didn't take long for someone to call the police and the ambulance, as Jada requested. By this point, Raymond's backpack (and I) had been kicked all around. Fortunately, I was able to keep my mouth closed through it all.

"How do you know this guy?" someone asked Jada.

"Ray is my brother."

"Okay. Are you gonna ride to the hospital with your brother?" the person asked.

"Yes, sir! I have to get his bag first, though," Jada said as she grabbed her brother's backpack without raising any suspicion.

Based on the conversation, I knew help had arrived. It wasn't long before we started the chaotic ride to the hospital. The people inside the ambulance yelled loudly to each other as the siren served as the soundtrack to their conversation. I thought Jada had questions for them, but instead of her asking them anything, she just prayed.

"God, this is not a good situation. We were just trying to help, and people were hating just because Ray was starting to do well. This is crazy, but I know everything works together for our good. Father, I just beg that you heal my brother. In the name of Jesus, I pray, amen."

After her prayer, Jada remained quiet for the rest of the ride as she held onto Raymond's backpack very tightly. When the vehicle finally stopped, I heard her exhale deeply as she exited. Once we got inside, she was told where her brother was going, but she was also told she couldn't go. She expressed her disappointment, but she went to the waiting room as she had been instructed to do.

Every so often, Jada would quietly express how much time had passed. Even though she wasn't getting any new information, she was able to calm herself down whenever she thought she was getting too excited.

"Are you here for Raymond?" someone finally asked.

"Yes, that's my brother. How is he? Is he okay? Can I see him?"

Even though Jada's questions were thrown out at a furious rate, the person took their time to answer all of them. Then, Jada was asked if they could walk together to Ray's room. As they moved, Jada was told her brother had been stabbed multiple times near his abdomen. Although she was there when the incident happened, she didn't take the news well.

"Things are bad, but they're not as bad as they could be. We have no doubts he will make a full recovery," the person told Jada.

"That's great news," Jada said.

What Jada heard set her at ease, and she soon became calm enough to get her breathing back to normal. By the time we reached Ray, the words she was able to speak to him were free of anxiety.

"You lookin' good, Ray. Well, not good, but good for you." She started to laugh, and soon, faint laughter came from who had to be Ray.

"Don't do me like that," he whispered.

"You know I'm just playin' with you. But for real, how are you?"

He whispered that he was okay, and at that moment, that

was all she needed to hear. Jada took a few steps, which forced me to move around in the backpack. The bag was soon being lowered, which led me to believe Jada was taking a seat.

"Just rest, big brother. You've gone through a lot. I promise I won't leave you alone," Jada said.

For a long time, we didn't move, nor were any words exchanged. We all just sat there until I heard Jada making a phone call.

"Houston, I need for you to listen very carefully. Ray was hurt pretty bad today, but he's gonna be okay, so don't worry."

He started to yell loudly. I couldn't make out what he was saying, but Jada's responses helped me fill in the blanks.

"Nah, he's good now. There's no need for you to find a way to get out here. All I need you to do is just make sure you and Damon have something to eat tonight. If you need me to, I can order y'all a pizza."

After that, there was more silence. Time marched on until someone came into the room to tell Jada how late it was. Until then, I didn't know how long we had been there.

"Ma'am, I promised my brother I wouldn't leave him. Please don't turn me into a liar. We've had it kinda rough. We lost our parents when they were in the hospital sick with Covid, and we couldn't really visit them the way we wanted to. Please don't make me go through that again."

I could tell the pain Jada was carrying resonated with the person she spoke with because when it was all said and done, they didn't tell us we had to leave. Surprisingly, we were given permission to stay the night. When Jada was given the news, she was relieved enough to eventually fall asleep for the duration of the night.

"What time is it? I'm really hungry?" Ray suddenly asked.

I guess it took a little while for Jada to hear her brother because she was still sleeping.

"Is it really 7:30 already," she eventually asked as she cleared her throat.

"I don't know if it's 7:30, but I know I'm hungry," Ray said, finally speaking louder than he was able to do before.

"So, I guess you're feeling good, huh?" Jada asked.

"Yeah, I'm good, sis. How are you? How are Damon and Houston? Are they okay?"

He was injured, but Ray was more concerned with his family's well-being than his own.

"I'm good, and I made sure the boys were good last night."

"That's what's up. Hey, I need to tell you something, but I don't want you to think anything bad," Ray said.

"Saying that already makes me think something bad. You know that, right?"

Right then, someone knocked on the door.

"I have some breakfast for you, Raymond. Would you like it?" they asked.

"Yes, please. Come in," Ray said excitedly.

With permission, the person entered the room. She spoke briefly with Ray and Jada, delivered the food, and left. Knowing his sister had to be as hungry as he was, Ray offered to share his meal with her. She sounded a bit hesitant at first, but she finally obliged.

"So, what were you gonna say?" Jada asked as she was eating.

"Let me eat, and I'll tell you," he told her.

As they were eating, someone else knocked on the door.

"It's open," Jada yelled.

"I'm glad they made it to you with breakfast. So, how are you this morning?" an unknown person asked as she came into the room.

"I'm good, just ready to go home," Ray said.

"Well, after you finish eating, a doctor will come in here to speak with you. After that, you'll be free to leave."

Things happened exactly as Ray and Jada were told they

would. They were told the extent of Ray's injuries and what he needed to do to take care of himself once he got home. After that, he was officially released.

"C'mon bro, let's leave before they change their minds," Jada joked after the doctor left.

"Okay, as soon as I get dressed, I'll be ready," he said.

He acted as though everything was okay, but the fact that he randomly grunted in agony as he got ready to leave told a different story. He was able to fight through the pain, and eventually, we had all moved outside of the hospital as we waited for a ride.

"The app says our ride should be here in a few minutes. Put that to the side, though. While we were inside, you said you had something to tell me," Jada reminded her brother.

"Yeah, you're right, but I don't wanna scare you. So, maybe I should just keep it to myself."

"I can handle whatever you need to say. Plus, you just got released from the hospital, so we already got past the scariest part."

"Yeah, you're right, sis. Let me just get to it. Last night, I saw Mom and Dad."

"What do you mean?" Jada wondered.

Ray started to answer, but they were momentarily interrupted when the sound of a car approached.

"I'm here to pick up Jada. Is that you?" someone asked.

After Jada confirmed who she was, we all got in the car.

"What's up? They call me Shaq, and I'm gonna get you where you need to be."

Jada and Ray endured some small talk with their seemingly nice driver before they went back to their conversation.

"Ray, what were you saying?"

"Oh, I was saying I saw Mom and Dad. I don't know if I was just dreaming about them, or if I was close to death. Whatever it was, I know for sure I saw them."

"That's not crazy. I've seen them several times since they've passed."

"Yeah, me too, but it was different. It was like I was really with them. They were right in front of me, and I saw them just as clearly as I'm seeing you," Raymond continued.

"Did they say anything to you?"

"Yeah, but not at first. I started off surrounded by nothing. There were no houses, no trees, no other people, or anything else. It was like I had been placed on a blank canvas while God decided what else was going to be added to His work of art. Then, that's when they appeared. Jada, I wish you could have seen them. Mom had on her favorite blue dress. Her locks looked like they had been freshly twisted. I could smell the mango and coconut from her hair. Dad had on that tan suit we always told him reminded us of Obama's. The drip was on point. They were holding hands and their wedding rings sparkled brighter than anything I had ever seen. Believe it or not, they seemed so happy."

"That sounds beautiful, but what did they say to you?"

"My bad, I almost forgot that part. When I saw them, that white light they always show in the movies appeared behind them. I was trying to move toward them so I could give them a hug, but just as I was about to touch them, they stopped me. They asked me if I was trying to go toward the light. I assured them I wasn't. Their smiles somehow grew even larger, and that's when I was able to hug them. That hug—Jada—that hug reached the depths of my soul. I promise you, I can still feel it right now. I cried tears of joy, and then they told me how proud of us they were. They let me go and told me it was time for us to go our separate ways. They said they would always be there for us, and even though they wished they could have been with us longer, they knew we were on the right path, and they knew God would keep us there. Before they turned and went into the light, they told me part of my purpose was to use my work to drown out the darkness that has taken over so many people in the world."

"I'm sorry for intruding, but can I say something to you?" the driver asked.

"Sure," Ray said.

"First of all, I'm sorry for your loss," the driver said.

"Thank you."

"No problem. Your story was beautiful, and I hope you don't take your experience for granted. How do you feel about your parents telling you it's your purpose to drown out the darkness? Do you know how important that is? Are you ready for that?" he asked.

"Yeah, I know, but if I'm keepin' it 100, I don't think I'm ready for it. I guess me being ready doesn't matter, though."

"What do you mean?" Jada asked.

"Honestly, I ain't even ready for what we're already dealing with, but that doesn't mean anything. God used our parents to put things in motion for us. If they think I can use art to bring some much-needed light to the world, whether I'm ready or not, I can't let them down," Ray responded.

"Wow! That's a point of view that's very different than my own. I get too scared to do what I think I'm purposed to do," Shaq, the driver, said.

"Why?" Jada asked.

"I'm terrified of failing. Failing feels like many parts of the universe working together to break your heart. I just don't think I can handle that sort of rejection," Shaq explained.

"That's interesting, but I disagree with your view, at least partially. Chasing your dreams is like searching for your true love. When you're going after true love, there's a very good chance it won't be easy to find. Most of us will have some sort of idea of what we're looking for, but we will still fail in multiple relationships before we find the one that works.

Knowing this, should we not look for love because we think we'll fail?" Ray asked.

"No, I don't think you should give up on love," the driver replied.

"Why not?" Ray wondered.

"I don't know. I guess it's because you know you will have to deal with some frogs to find your princess."

"Exactly! Failure is the part of the journey that lets you enjoy the success."

I couldn't tell if Shaq believed what Ray said or if he wanted to take a break from the conversation, but he remained quiet for a little while before he decided to speak again.

"A chef," he finally said.

"What about a chef?" Jada asked.

"That's what I've always wanted to be, but the fear of failing has stopped me from even trying," Shaq continued.

The little talk the humans had seemed to serve no real purpose, but it didn't stop them from continuing to have it.

"Sir, I don't know you, but I can hear the love you have for cooking in your tone. I don't know how you feel about being a driver, but I can pretty much guarantee it doesn't bring you the joy you get from cooking," Ray said.

"No, it doesn't, but..."

"But what?"

"Joy doesn't pay my bills. I have to do this, so I won't get my electricity cut off, my car repossessed, or even evicted from my apartment."

"I can't dispute what you said 'cause you're right. Joy alone won't pay your bills, but misery can take way more than money away from you, trust me. Hey, let me ask you something. How long have you been cooking, and what do people say about your food?"

"I haven't gone to any of those fancy culinary schools or

anything, but I've been cooking with my family since I was about five. My mom used to show pictures of me in the kitchen cooking with my grandma, father, uncle, aunt, and her to almost anyone who would look at them. I always had a smile on my face, and that's still how I am today whenever I'm in the kitchen."

"Man, you don't understand how incredibly cool that is. Some people go their entire lives searching for what they want to do, but you've known since you were a kid. You have to do something with that."

"I...I don't know how to get going. Even if I did, I don't have the money to do anything," the driver told them.

"What's your name again?" Ray asked.

"Shaq."

"Shaq, I may not know you, but I believe in you. My sister and I are not just in the car because the app told you to pick us up. We're together because God wanted us to meet."

"I appreciate you saying that. I lost my grandparents a while back. I lost contact with a lot of my family, and my mom passed three years ago. Then, my dad died a few days after we had our worst argument, so I've not only had to carry that guilt with me, but I've also felt like there's nobody left in the entire world who believes in me. You saying that has told me how wrong I was."

"Hey, you get the majority of whatever tips are sent through the app, right?" Ray asked suddenly.

"We get all of it."

"Cool. I'm gonna give you a lil' something to help you make it through the day. Also, I want you to follow me on IG and send me a message because I may have some opportunities for you very soon."

Ray gave his info to Shaq so he could follow his instructions.

"I don't know what to say other than, thank you."

"You're welcome, Shaq. I look forward to working with you, so please don't forget to contact me."

The car stopped moving as Shaq promised he would follow

Ray's directions. Ray and Jada thanked Shaq for driving them. Since their car was still parked where it was the day before, I assumed when they got out of Shaq's car, they were getting into their own. Once we started moving again, a new conversation started.

"Bro, what was all of that about?" Jada asked.

"What?"

"What was all of that talk with the driver?"

"I legitimately felt in my spirit that I was supposed to do something to encourage him. I guess in the dream, when Ma told me I had to bring light, that's the sort of thing she meant. We've been through a lot, but do you realize how blessed we are? We can help so many people, and I'm kinda hyped up about that."

"Okay, I kinda see where you're coming from, but..."

"Speak your mind, little sister. What's up?"

"No disrespect, Ray, but it just seemed like you were doin' too much. I'm not sayin' you were lying, but it ain't like it was all the truth, either."

"I meant everything I told him, though. We crossed paths with that guy for a reason, so I'm gonna do my part to help."

Ray sounded confident when he said what he did, but as the conversation with his sister progressed, the confidence started to waver. He soon told his sister he wanted to help, but outside of giving money, he didn't know how.

"I can't let them down, Jada. I know it sounds stupid, but..."

Ray stopped himself from speaking and screamed unexpectedly.

"Are you okay?" Jada asked.

"I'm scared, and I'm in pain, Jada. What if these wounds don't heal all the way? And what if I can't make anything new for the show? What if I can't help people? What if I fail y'all? I talked all of that stuff to the driver, but now, you've made me doubt everything."

"Breathe, Ray. Take it easy. We can help people, but you can't stress yourself out trying to help everyone. It's impossible for you to think you can take away the world's pain, so don't even think about that. We should focus on helping everyone we can and pray they pay it forward."

Ray continued to listen to his sister. There were times I could hear him start to say something, but he kept stopping himself. He just let his sister bestow her wisdom upon him. The rest of the ride was more of a monologue than a conversation.

When we finally stopped, I didn't know if Ray had regained his confidence because he did more listening to what his sister was saying, than talking. I also heard him say he had to pretend like he wasn't in as much pain as he was actually in as we entered the home with their younger siblings.

"Welcome home!" Damon yelled as he ran to his siblings as soon as we made it inside.

"Well, that hug lets me know you missed us, but you gotta be careful with me. You can't hug me so hard, bro. Remember, I'm still recovering," Ray explained.

"My bad, Ray. I'm just glad you're okay. Oh, hey, Jada. I'm glad you're back, too."

"Thank you. I thought you didn't even see me," Jada jokingly told him.

"It's not like that. I missed both of y'all, but Houston really missed you," Damon told them.

"How do you know? Did he say something to you?" Jada asked.

"No, he didn't say anything, but after we had dinner, he went to the room. I started playing video games, and the game got kinda quiet while it was loading up the next level, and that's when I heard him crying. I tried to go into the room to check on him, but he wouldn't let me. So, I just left him alone."

That's when Ray took it upon himself to see what was going on with Houston.

"Houston! Houston! Can you come out here for a minute?" Ray yelled out.

There was no answer, so Ray walked away from Jada and Damon in an effort to speak with Houston. He knocked on the door several times before Houston finally opened it.

"Hey, Ray. When did you get back?"

His voice was faint because I was still in the backpack that was being held by Jada.

"We literally walked in a few minutes ago, but that's not important. Do you mind if we talk for a minute?"

"I guess we can do that," Houston said, almost as if it drained all of his energy to do so.

Then, I heard the door close. Since we were in a different room, I couldn't hear exactly what was being said, but I heard enough to get a pretty good understanding of what they discussed. Ray made a point to tell his brother several times he was okay, but Houston kept expressing how concerned he was.

"I can't lose you like we lost them," Houston said, obviously referring to his parents.

The two brothers spent a while talking amongst themselves before they both walked into the room the rest of us were still in.

"Are you good, Houston?" Jada asked.

"Not really," Houston told her.

His answer was surprising, not because everyone thought he was doing well, but because most of the time, humans used questions like, "How are you?" or "Are you good?" as conversation starters or fillers. From what I've witnessed, a lot of people will ask questions like that, not really caring about the answer, and others will just give generic answers because they don't care to respond honestly. At that moment, that wasn't the case for Houston.

"I know I normally try to act like stuff doesn't bother me, but I can't do that right now. Jada, I was just talking to Ray about how scared I was about him going to the hospital," Houston said.

"I'm pretty sure we all were scared, but he's okay," Jada said, trying her best to sound happy as she responded to her brother.

"Yeah, he's good now, but that don't mean nothing. Think about it; Mom and Dad were both fine one day, and then they were gone. We didn't get time to prepare for life without them, and now I'm scared every day that something is gonna happen to one of us," Houston told everyone.

The family went on to speak about their fears, the importance of Houston continuing his therapy sessions, and the overall fragility of human life. It was a serious conversation for such young people to have, but all of them, including Damon, participated in it.

Houston's admission of his emotions and the conversation that followed helped everyone. As the days passed, I could tell the family grew even closer to each other by the way they interacted. The conversations flowed a little differently than they previously did. They spent more time together than they had before, and it was having a positive impact on all of them, especially Houston.

Although he would routinely express an ongoing fear of losing a family member, he was also able to tell his family how much he loved them. Before Ray's injury, he normally liked to keep his feelings to himself. One day, Ray and Jada had a talk about how things had changed in their household.

"I'm so proud of this family's resilience. Any of us could have given up by now, and it would have been justified, but we didn't," Jada said.

"True story. Our progress has been amazing," Ray agreed.

"Speaking of progress, what's up on your new sculpture? I haven't seen you working much, and I know that deadline will be here soon."

"Yeah, you're right. It's all good, though. Believe it or not, the full concept of what I'm gonna end up doing came to me that night I was in the hospital. I've been quiet about it because I had to figure out how to bring it from my brain to reality. I think I have it now, though."

"That's what's up. So, are you gonna tell me what it's gonna be?"

"Not exactly, but I will tell you it will be, by far, the most monumental piece I've ever been blessed to work on. In my spirit, I feel like when it's done, Jada.... I'm just so hyped up, I can't even express myself."

"Yeah, bro, I can tell you're excited, but what is it?"

"It's gonna be a representation of our lives, from our old neighborhood to the new one. It will show the violence we saw then, and the prosperity we're seeing now. It will show a different way to look at lives of people from various places. Most of all, it will bring forth the light Mom told me I am supposed to show the world," Ray said passionately.

"I can't wait to see it, but I'll just fight the desire to ask about it every day and wait until you reveal it to us," Jada told him.

The excitement Jada had for her brother's project was an example of how everyone in the family was acting about any positive move one of them made. It wasn't necessarily unusual for them to act that way, but those actions were magnified after Raymond returned home from the hospital. I would always hear people say, "Everything works together for my good." I don't know exactly where that saying came from, but it fit perfectly with them.

As time marched forward, the four young people went about their individual lives while also being their siblings' biggest cheerleaders. Everyone was thriving, which was good for the family, but not for me. I had sat dormant in the same backpack I had been in since the day Ray was attacked. Then, things changed.

"Life is about to be a lot different for you. I think we've

reached a point where you have to make a transition. I already know I could be making a huge mistake by using you the way I'm going to, but I have to do what I think is right. You protecting us is about to go from your intended use to something that will help protect my family's legacy," Ray told me.

I was completely lost by what he was saying because it didn't make any sense to me. I was confused by his talk about my usage because I only had one. He spoke as if he was planning to somehow take me away from my purpose to help fulfill his.

"Yeah, it's time," he said as he fully took me out of the backpack.

For a while, he just stared at me as if he had never seen me before. As I was held in the air, I finally got a glimpse of the art piece he was working on. It was different than any of the other work I had seen. It had a physical footprint at least three to four times larger than Raymond's other projects. It was like a strange combination of thoughts that shouldn't have meshed well with each other, but somehow, they did.

I was put down on a nearby table as Ray stood back and looked at his work.

"I know you're wondering how you're gonna fit into all of this because it's already pretty busy, but I saved a spot for the star," Ray said as he kept switching focus between me and the art.

While he stood there, I heard footsteps approaching quickly. Ray didn't want me or his work to be seen, so he covered us up. Almost as soon as that happened, there were several knocks on the door.

"Bro, can I talk to you?" Houston asked softly from the outside of the door.

The door squeaked, letting me know Ray was letting his brother in.

"What's going on, little brother?" he asked.

Houston walked into the room as Ray ensured his art was still concealed.

"Since you got back, things have been different. I was scared you were gonna be gone like Mom and Dad, but now that you're back home and safe, I've been feeling a lot better about life. I just want you to know I appreciate everything you've done for us. You stepped up when a lot of folks would have left. I love you, Ray," he said.

As long as I had been around the family, Houston was the one who had difficulty vocalizing how he felt. He hardly ever used the word "love," so hearing him throw it out so freely was surprising, and by Ray's reaction, I knew it caught him off guard, too.

"Hold up! I know I didn't just hear Houston say he loved me."

"Yeah, you did. It felt weird saying it, but I had to. In therapy, the doctor has been working on me being more expressive. When you came home, and Damon told you I had been crying, it was kinda like opening the floodgates. I think not keeping everything bottled up has helped me be happier. Plus, everything can change in a second. Bro, you randomly got stabbed while you were with Jada. Think about that. You could have died. So, is it weird for me to say what I did? Yep, but I'm gonna get comfortable with all that kinda stuff. I love you, I love Jada, and even though he gets on my nerves, I love Damon, too," Houston said.

"I'm so proud of you. That has to be one of the most grown-up things I've ever heard you say. Gimme a hug, bro," Ray said.

The moment between the brothers was unlike any I had directly been around before. They've probably had interactions where they were vulnerable and emotionally honest before, but I wasn't in the room during those times, so I can't actually be certain. This was the type of conversation Ray usually had with his sister, but it was easy to hear how happy he was to talk to Houston. Ray's voice was engulfed in joy.

"Hey, what's that?" Houston asked.

The moment of joy was interrupted by Houston's question. I didn't know if he was asking about me or the piece Ray was working on. By the way Ray responded, he wasn't sure, either.

"What do you mean? What's what?" Ray asked.

"That seven million foot wide...whatever that is, you got covered up right there. Plus, if I knew what it was, I wouldn't have to ask you what it was," Houston said as he burst into the heartiest laughter I've ever heard him release.

His response let Ray and I know he wasn't talking about me.

"This is legacy art," Ray said.

Once again, Ray chose to use the word 'legacy' to describe what he was working on. It was the same word he used when he was telling me about how my placement in the art was going to protect his family, but he had yet to explain how.

"What does that even mean?"

"It means, once the world sees this, it will have far more of an impact on the family's future than anything else I've ever worked on."

"Bro, you're putting a lot of pressure on yourself," Houston said to his older brother.

"You're right, but that pressure is just forcing me to make sure I'm putting my all into the work," Ray said.

"Okay, that's what's up, but ain't it almost time for that art-showing thingy?"

"Yeah, but I'm almost finished. I just have a little left to do. I'll probably be done within the next few days."

"Sooo, that means you're gonna let me see what it is, right?" Houston asked.

"No, sir! It's not quite ready, but I promise I'll let y'all see it before anyone else does."

"I guess I can't be mad at that. Well, I said what I came in here to say, so I'll let you get back to work."

"Okay, I'm glad we had this talk, little brother. And in case I didn't say it, I love you, too."

"Thanks. Oh, I have to tell you that for the first time in a while, I'm really excited about the future. It's like everything you, Jada, and my therapist have been telling me has finally clicked in my head. I know I haven't always been the easiest person to deal with, so thank you for not giving up on me."

"Yeah, you've been...difficult at times, but bro, I will never give up on you. As long as I'm alive, I will always be here for you."

"Thank you, Ray. I needed to hear that."

A little while later, the door closed, which made me believe Houston was no longer in the room. Ray locked the door to make sure nobody would be able to walk in as he got back to work. As the art and I were emancipated, I was able to look at it a bit more. I still didn't know what role I would play, but I was starting to see why Ray spoke so highly about it.

Ray stared at the progress of the art and smiled. Then, he moved closer to his work.

"You're almost ready," he said to the art.

For what had to be hours, Ray walked around the art piece so he could see it from every possible angle. He would bend down low seconds after he got down off of his tiptoes so he could see the peaks and valleys of what he created. Every now and again, the pain from the attack paid him an unexpected visit. He tried to ignore it, but he couldn't.

"I can't let pain stop me. This is way too important," he said to himself as he grimaced.

As he stood still, he held onto himself as if he was having a bit of a problem taking in air. Since leaving the hospital, Ray tried his best to pretend he was no longer feeling the impact of the injury, but sometimes he couldn't hide it. After this particular bout with pain, he let out a quiet yell before he got back to work.

"I have to bring the light. It is my purpose to use my work to drown out the darkness. We are not our past. We are not where we are from. Our parents did not limit our ambitions because we are all destined to be great. I will not let them down, and I won't allow my siblings to do it, either."

Ray was speaking to himself, but it was as though he was talking to an audience that consisted of his parents, his siblings, and the God they all so frequently spoke to. The way he was talking and viewing his work let me know how important it was to him and how much responsibility he was putting on himself to make sure he was going to be able to properly deliver the message he envisioned.

He smiled again. He moved toward me, but then his phone rang.

"Hello...oh, yeah. What's up, Shaq? I'm glad you called because I needed to ask you something."

Shaq was the driver who took Ray and Jada from the hospital to their car. I knew they exchanged social media info, but evidently, they also exchanged numbers.

"Yeah, I need to know if you're willing to cook for about twenty-five people for an after-party," Ray said.

As they continued their conversation, Ray put his phone on speaker so he could still work on his art.

"How did you know?" Shaq asked.

"How did I know what?" Ray wondered.

"How did you know I still needed a job and I still needed to make a change in my life? How?"

"I can't say I actually knew. All I know is I promised I was going to try and help you out one day and my spirit told me we crossed paths for a reason. God is the architect and conductor of all of this, so I can't take any credit for what He's building."

"Well, I appreciate the offer, and I will be honored to prepare food for your party. Thank you, thank you, thank you!" Shaq said excitedly.

Ray provided the details of the party, as well as what type of food he wanted to have served. Shaq was ecstatic, and everything Ray told him just made him happier.

"Well, get ready because the night will be here before you know it."

"Absolutely! And Ray, I really believe your parents are looking down on you, smiling at the child they raised. From what I know, you're a wonderful human being."

"Thank you for saying that. I don't take that sort of thing lightly."

Their talk ended shortly after that. Once it did, Ray moved slowly to one of the corners of the room. He slid down to the floor. Seconds later, he began to cry. He didn't attempt to stop his tears from flowing freely as they fell from his face.

"I love y'all so much and I miss you every single day. I pray to God we're doing right by y'all. I pray your spirits are filled with joy and that God continues to bless us with His favor."

The more he talked, the more he cried. Human emotions are often confusing. When Ray started crying and talking to his parents that day, it was as if he wasn't sure if he was living right and doing the things he was supposed to be. When he stopped talking, he was still crying, but visibly, I could tell he was in a much better mood because of the smile on his face and the sparkle in his eyes.

He soon went back to work on his project. He moved with purpose and energy. It was as though he had received a response to the words he said to his parents. He started to move around all of the various sections of his newest art piece. He was adding and removing things as he went along, but I still didn't know what my place would be, whatever it was, I knew Ray had some sort of plan.

"It's time," he suddenly said as I was picked up from the table.

My safety was already on, and without warning, Ray took all of my bullets away from me. Then, he removed my firing pin like it was nothing. I guess, for him, it wasn't. Ray was willing to sacrifice me for his art, and I didn't like that.

"It's time for the mold," he told me.

I didn't know exactly what he was talking about, but I soon found myself immersed in some sort of liquid-like substance. Throughout my time with Ray, he had a ton of clumsy moments. He had wasted water and juice on me before, but I knew what I was in wasn't like any of those things. It had an unusual consistency that was foreign to me. I could no longer see the outside world, so I guessed this substance was how Ray decided to end me. He was taking me away from the world without me being able to fulfill my destiny. He talked about his legacy, but ending me before I had a chance to build my own legacy was incredibly selfish.

"Yeah, you're about to make a difference," Ray said to me.

As I was drowning, his words started to sound muffled, but he spoke as if he was confirming something that was said in a previous conversation. Then, he started laughing. I didn't know why, but I figured it was because he was killing a machine that was meant to kill. I guess he enjoyed the irony.

"How are you feeling?" he asked.

What was the purpose of him asking me that? Was he genuinely concerned about me, even though I was in a situation he created, or was he just sarcastically mocking me? Either way, I didn't like it. Soon, I could no longer see or hear anything at all. I thought it was all over, but out of nowhere, my situation changed.

"Alright, it's time to get you outta there," Ray said.

A few seconds before, I wasn't able to see or hear anything, but then, I was. I was pulled out of the mold just as slowly as I had been put into it. I didn't have the ability to breathe, but feeling the air of the atmosphere again almost made me feel like I could. As I was pulled out, I was able to look down at where I was.

I didn't know much about how physics worked, but normally liquids would move around and fill in any empty space. The stuff I was in was different. Yes, it had filled up the space around me, but the area I was in remained in my shape. It was almost as if it was honoring the time I was there.

Seeing my shape was almost as if I was looking at one of those mirrors humans spend so much time in front of.

"I know you weren't designed for this, but sometimes we need to do things we weren't made for to really become who we're supposed to be," he told me as he wiped some of the mold off of me.

"Oh yeah, this is gonna be even better than I thought," he said.

He left the mold alone for a while as he put me on the table and went back to work on the art. He was slow and methodical with his movement. Pieces that were already set were moved until Ray said they were perfect. Then, he picked up some type of marker and proceeded to write over everything. I couldn't make out the words he wrote, but he mumbled a few of them.

"...the lives that were given to us were done so for a reason..."

The words continued as he kept working. He got so engaged in what he was doing, he didn't even realize we had made it to a new day until someone started banging on the door.

"Ray! Are you in there?"

Once again, Ray made sure the artwork and I were both covered up.

"What's up?" he asked once the door was finally opened.

"I'm just seein' if you're okay. We knocked on your door before we ate breakfast, but you didn't answer."

As he spoke, I could finally hear he was talking to Damon.

"My bad, lil' bro. I lost track of time. I kinda got in the zone like I was LeBron."

"Really, Ray? Really?"

"What?" Ray asked.

"Do you think you need to compare yourself to one of the greatest like that? I mean, we're talkin' about The King, The Kid From Akron, LeBrooooooooooon James," Damon said excitedly.

"Okay, okay, I get it. Maybe it was a little bit of a reach to compare myself to one of your favorite basketball players. I guess I shouldn't have gone there."

"No, sir, you shouldn't have. Please make sure you always put some respect on his name," Damon said as he started to laugh very loudly.

"Calm down, Damon, it wasn't that funny," Ray replied as he chuckled a little.

"Whatever you say, big bro. Hey, are we goin' on a trip or something?" Damon asked suddenly.

"That's a weird question. Why did you ask that?" Ray wondered.

"Well, since you got all those bags under your eyes, I figured we had to be goin' somewhere," Damon said, laughing even harder than he was before.

"Dang, you got me! I didn't get any sleep last night, so I know I look pretty bad. Anyway, did y'all save me any breakfast?"

"Nope! When you didn't answer the door, we destroyed everything that was on your plate!"

They exchanged more words and laughter before they both left the room. I can't say how long Ray was gone, but when he returned, he immediately got back to work. When I was uncovered, I thought something was about to happen to me, but it didn't. Instead, he just left me on the table. It was as if Ray wanted me to see what was going on while simultaneously showing me how irrelevant I had become.

I watched as he wrote and painted more on the piece, still not knowing exactly what message he was trying to convey. Then, he picked up the mold he had made of me.

"This is so much better than I thought it would be," he said.

After a while, he placed the copy of me next to me...the original. Sure, it looked like me, but Ray and I both knew we weren't the same. I watched as Ray joyfully picked the fraudulent gun back up and looked at it as if it had become his most prized possession.

"You are exactly what this piece needed," he said as he went back to work.

After silently working for a while, he was somehow able to get the fake gun to remain in place without him having to hold it. It was at this point, Ray's face lit up. Usually when I saw that look, it was because Ray had an idea he felt would be impactful.

He grabbed a nearby paintbrush and held it near his work. The project had morphed into a combination of miniature sculptures he made, printed photos he had taken, words he had written, and of course, the fake gun. The fact that it didn't seem very cohesive, nor did it make any sense to me, didn't matter because Ray kept telling himself it was the greatest thing he ever created.

Within a few brief moments, he dipped the paintbrush in paint and started to put words on the gun. When he finished, the words simply said, "Because of me and the bullets I hold inside, you get false power; you create pride." With his words now part of his creation, he carelessly threw me into a drawer and yelled out to his family.

"Yooooo! Can y'all come in here, please?" he asked loudly.

He didn't tell anyone why he was requesting them, but that didn't stop his siblings from rushing into his room. I heard their footsteps as they all ran in, but none of them said anything.

"So, what do you think?" Ray asked.

Even though I could no longer see his face, I knew how

excited he was about his work. When humans are excited about something, they usually want others to feel the same way they do. Having his siblings all quiet when they saw his work was probably not the reaction he was hoping for.

"Maybe you didn't hear me, so I'll try it again. What do you think?" Ray asked.

"My bad, Ray, I was just kinda speechless. With all of the work you've been putting in, I knew you were doing something crazy, but this...this is dope! I don't even know how you can come up with stuff like this," Houston said.

"Thank you, Houston. Ever since I had that dream about Mom and Dad, it's almost like my hands have had minds of their own. Sometimes, I didn't even realize what I was doing until it was done. It was like we were all working together on this."

"This is cool, but I don't get it. What is all of this stuff, and why do you need that gun?" Damon asked.

He started to explain how one side represented all of the neighborhoods across the world that were similar to the ones they grew up in. He told his family that he intentionally made that side darker because people in those neighborhoods feel like they are stuck in the dark, and they can't find their way out.

"Oh, so that's why all of the little statues here look like they don't know where they are, right?" Damon asked.

"Yeah, but even though people who grew up like we did sometimes feel hopeless, that's not always the case, just like people who grew up in rich neighborhoods don't always have it together. If you look closely over here, you'll also see big houses, fancy cars, and people wearing expensive-looking clothing and accessories. I'm trying to show that money doesn't always bring enlightenment and happiness, even though we think it does," Ray continued.

After his explanation, someone started crying. Since I was

hidden, I didn't know who, nor why, until the family started conversing again.

"Dang, Houston, you sure do cry a lot these days. Therapy has made you softer than a marshmallow pillow," Damon said jokingly.

He was trying to lighten the mood, as he normally did. The young boy's plan could have easily made his brother feel worse, but it didn't. Houston eventually started laughing right along with Damon.

"Man, you're right. My therapist has gotten me used to expressing how I feel. Now, it's just easy to let everything go. And yeah, I know I'm different than I have been, but I'm good with that," he said.

"Yeah, being able to express your feelings shows how much you've grown, and I'm really proud of you," Jada told him.

"Me too, bro, but what made you start crying?" Ray wondered.

Although the family had just finished giving Houston props for dealing with his emotions better than he had in the past, for a moment, he was reluctant to tell everyone what suddenly made him so sad.

"Just let it go," Jada told him.

After hesitating for a little while, Houston told him the gun in the art piece looked so real. He said it reminded him of the gun he found when he was rambling around in Ray's room. Of course, Ray knew he was talking about me, but he thought Jada was the only one who knew I lived in their home.

"Ray, you got a gun? I thought you said we were moving out here to get away from all of the guns and bad stuff from our old neighborhood. That's what you said, right?" Damon asked.

Humans would often say they are going to do one thing when in reality, they often end up doing the opposite. Having me around was one of those times, even if Ray had the best intentions. He didn't know how to answer his brother, so he didn't.

"Yeah, Damon, he said that," Jada answered.

"So, if he said that, why would he get a gun?"

"He did it 'cause life don't always let you keep your word," Houston said, very surprisingly.

"Houston is right. Sometimes, life makes a liar out of all of us. I never wanted a gun. In fact, I actually hate them. For whatever reason, fear just got ahold of me, and I was convinced we needed it. I told myself I had to be ready to show anyone, at ant given time, who we really are," Ray explained.

"No disrespect, big bro, but that has to be the dumbest thing I've ever heard you say, and it kinda changes my thinking on some things," Houston said.

"What do you mean?" Ray asked.

"Well, before I get to the point, let me just say I don't still feel the way I did."

"Okay, so what's up?" Jada asked.

Houston started crying again. It took him a little while to do so, but he made sure he said what he needed to.

"When I saw that gun, I thought it was a sign. Y'all already know I've been having a hard time since Mom and Dad died. I felt like my heart was ripped out of my chest. I just didn't want to live anymore. So, when I saw that gun, I looked at it as my way out. I saw it..."

While he was talking, the youngest sibling interrupted him.

"Houston, I love you. I don't want you to die 'cause we need you here. If you weren't here, who would I make fun of, and who would make fun of me? Who would I act like I'm a professional wrestler with? Who would I have an epic gaming session with? I can't do any of that stuff with Jada or Ray 'cause they're too boring."

Damon was showing he was also unafraid to release his own

emotions and be vulnerable. His emotional honesty was a catalyst for a better exchange of words between the entire family.

"Yeah, you're right, Damon. Jada and Ray are both too boring to wrestle, play games, or do anything fun. They..."

"Hey, you two do realize we're in the room, right?" Jada asked.

"Yeah, we know it. I guess we figured we just have to talk bad about you while you're here, so you can't say we were talking behind your back," Houston said.

"Good point, but back to what you were saying..."

"Oh, yeah. When I saw that gun, I really wanted to use it to get away from my pain. I was tired of feeling weak, and staring at the gun made me feel like I was able to get some of my power back, even if it would have been for the last time," Houston admitted.

What he said was an example of how flawed the thinking patterns of humans can be. He said he was weak, and I made him feel like he was able to get some of his power back. The problem with that was, his weakness was actually magnified by his thoughts of me making him powerful.

"Feeling weak doesn't actually mean you are. Recognizing those low points are what give you the strength to keep going. Well, that and God," Ray said.

"Yeah, and like Damon said, we need you, little bro. There's nobody who can give us attitude the way you can," Jada told him.

"You're right about that, but at that moment, all I could think about was how hurt I was."

The family's mood went from somber to glee, from sadness to joy, and from anger back to sadness within seconds as they continued to discuss how Houston wanted to use me to end his life. That's what humans did. They used things (and other people) to help them escape whatever is happening in their lives.

If he would have completed the task he was thinking about committing, I would have been blamed for it. Other people would have looked at me as if I were the mastermind responsible for Houston no longer being around. There was a good chance they wouldn't have even tried to find out why such a young kid, who was dealing with the pain of losing his parents, even had access to me in the first place.

I had witnessed and heard of so many accounts when my relatives were blamed and destroyed because of the actions of people. If they felt we were truly the ones responsible for the loss of so many human lives, why did they allow other humans to continue making us? If we were responsible, why do the so-called lawmakers make it so easy for irresponsible humans to get to us so easily?

It made me wonder if they blamed all machines for everything that went wrong, or if we were the only lucky ones. I mean, if a drunk driver gets into an accident that kills someone, is the car blamed for it instead of the inebriated human?

I was just sitting there when I felt Ray picking me up and showing me to his family.

"I'm sorry for bringing this here. I'm sorry for endangering us. Houston, I truly apologize for you seeing something that made you consider...well, you know," Ray said.

"I appreciate that Ray, but what I was dealing with really had nothing to do with you. Even when I can't stand you, I know you're the best big brother anybody could ask for. I know the moves you make for us are all done out of love."

I was put down on Ray's desk, facing the wall as if I was being placed on punishment. Ray eventually steered the conversation back to his art piece. He continued explaining what everything meant, and I could hear inflections in his tone that indicated a sense of pride.

"So, what's the name of it?" Damon asked.

"I don't know. I've been trying to come up with something

since I conceptualized the whole thing, but nothing seems to work."

They stopped talking for a little while. Although I facing away from them and couldn't see what was going on, I imagined they were all staring at Ray's work, trying to give it a name.

"This may sound dumb, but I think I have an idea for the name," Houston told everyone.

"What?" Ray wondered.

"Mourning Darkness," he said.

Once again, everyone was quiet for a little while.

"I don't get it. The sun comes out in the morning, so it's not even dark," Damon said.

"No, not m-o-r-n-i-n-g, I'm talking about m-o-u-r-n-i-n-g. It's a different word. It's like when you feel sad about something, or like when you're grieving because of a loss," Houston explained.

"You mean like when we lost Mom and Dad?" Damon questioned.

"Yeah, exactly like that," Houston confirmed.

Neither Ray nor Jada said anything, which took away any confidence Houston had in his idea.

"My bad y'all. I know that's probably dumb," he said.

"Houston, don't let my silence push you to question yourself. I wasn't quiet because your idea was dumb. I was quiet because of how great it is. I don't know how you came up with that so fast because I've been in here struggling for the longest time trying to come up with something. I need you to tell me more about why you wanna call it that, though." Ray requested.

"No problem. Seeing this made me think more about what's going on with me in real life. I've been crying more than I ever have because we lost our parents. Then, we kinda lost the only neighborhood we ever lived in. The therapist helped me understand I can't have real joy again until I acknowledge what's wrong, accept what I can't change, and be grateful for my life. I hate that Mom and Dad are gone, but I can't change that. What I can do, is be thankful for the time I had with them. In order for me to find that light again, I have to let go of the darkness. That's what this piece says to me. In order to enjoy the light, we have to mourn the darkness."

"Bro, I can't explain how proud of you I am right now. I love you, and I know Mom and Dad are happy. You have come a long way in such a short amount of time," Ray said to his brother.

"Yeah, Houston, you're amazing. I'm so glad you had the strength not to go through what you were thinking about. Not only would we have missed you, but the world would have been deprived of what a gift you are. You're special. Do you hear me?" Jada said.

"Yeah, and thank you," Houston replied.

They talked more about Houston before they transitioned back to the art. Ray confirmed several times that the name his brother came up with was perfect, so there was no question he was going to use it. It was good the family was able to work together to solve a problem Ray had, but it was strange that after a few minutes, they were acting as though I wasn't in the room. They were also able to move on so quickly from Houston's previous thoughts, it was as though he hadn't even mentioned it.

I didn't have the ability to care if the family really grasped the severity of Houston's thoughts. However, from my experiences, when humans didn't deal with situations in the ways in which they should have been dealt with, those situations tended to make their way back around. The family didn't concern themselves with those thoughts, though. Their day went on with the family still being filled with joy while I was left abandoned on the desk. Just as the family started to say good night to each other, Ray finally came back to pay me a visit.

"A lot has happened today. I can't really explain it, but my family has grown. With that growth comes changes. Like many relationships, you get to a point where things have to end because of how far you've grown apart. That's us and our...thing. Yeah, it just has to end," he told me.

I wanted him to stop talking nonsense, but I was incapable of making the request. My inability to silence Ray's pointless lecture forced me to listen to him as he bloviated about the impending doom of our relationship.

"I don't know what I'm gonna do with you, but I know your importance in my family's life has dwindled down to nothing. You're an irrelevant and worthless piece of metal," he said.

I heard him, but I didn't believe what he was saying. If he was going to get rid of me, it seemed like he would have already done so. People like to run their mouths to let words fly out that make them feel more grandiose than they are. They didn't seem to understand actions proved what words couldn't.

More time passed. Before I knew it, we reached the day of the event. Ray did all of that talking about me not being around, but I was still there. Granted, I had been moved back to the confines of a drawer, but I hadn't been removed.

As Ray was in his workspace, I could hear him pacing around as he spoke to himself.

"This is another positive step in your journey. You've prayed and worked hard for this moment. You are ready and deserving. Because you bless others, you and your family will continue to be blessed. We deserve this."

I could tell he somewhat believed what he was saying, but he wasn't fully convinced. If he were, would the soliloquy even be necessary? Regardless, Ray gathered his family, and they all left. I sat in the home alone and still in pieces. Ray made sure I was unable to serve my purpose until he saw fit for me to do so again, if ever. For a while, I knew I had been rendered worthless, but I had assured myself I would be back to my old self, but I was wrong.

Since I wasn't invited to the event, I had no choice but to wait until the siblings returned to know how the evening turned out. When they finally made it back, everyone's voice was filled with happiness. Jada talked about how inspired she was by Ray's ambition and work ethic, while the youngest siblings exclaimed how cool everything was. Ray, while seemingly happy, was nowhere near as vocal as the rest of the family. When he did speak, he kept repeating how thankful he was to have his work included.

"They didn't have to let me include my work, and they didn't have to let Shaq provide the food for the after-party. I know I've been saying it all night, but I'm so grateful for every opportunity I get. I'm so glad y'all were able to be there, and I pray I pleased you, Mom, Dad, and God," Ray said.

Everyone told Ray how beautiful the night was and how proud of him they were. The more they talked, the more he continued to show his gratefulness for the opportunity to share 'the light' his parents talked about in his dream. They all were speaking in a positive tone, but then Damon asked a question that immediately shifted everything.

"Ray, what's up with the gun, though?"

I didn't expect to be included in the conversation, but suddenly, I was.

"What do you mean?" Ray asked as if he really didn't understand what his brother was talking about.

"I mean...well, tonight was cool and e'rything, but I feel like you're being a ... what's the word? A hippo...hypo..."

"Damon, are you tryin' to say, hypocrite?" Jada asked.

"Yep, that's it. Ray, you did all that talkin' tonight about being positive and shining light and love and all that stuff, so ain't it kinda weird that you still have a gun in the house? Plus, do you remember what Houston said he was thinking about doing? I may be wrong, but that doesn't seem very positive."

I wished they understood I am neither positive, nor negative, I just am. Even with that being said, I knew why Damon said what he did, but I figured Ray would tell his family he was far more responsible for the thoughts Houston had about ending his life than I was. That didn't happen.

"I wasn't expecting you to be the one to say anything, Damon, but you're right. That gun doesn't bring any light to our home, and even though I have already torn it apart, it shouldn't even be here."

"What are you gonna do with it?" Jada asked.

"I don't know. I might sell it to a pawn shop or something, but I doubt they'll take something that doesn't even work. I do know that I refuse to put it back together, though."

"I know how crazy this'll sound, but I actually don't mind if you kept it here," Houston said.

"Why would you wanna keep it?" Damon questioned.

"It's just a reminder of how much better I've gotten. It's a part of my testimony."

I heard enough conversations to know Houston wasn't using the word testimony to refer to a statement that had anything to do with a court of law. He was using it to mean I was part of his story, his testimonial. And the fact that he didn't mind me being around, in spite of how he considered using me, showed he felt I was no longer a threat because of how far removed he was from that stage of his depression.

Houston's family, once again, all told him how proud of him they were, but none of them thought it was smart to keep me around.

"We're lucky you didn't go through with the act you were thinking about, but it would be dumb to keep a gun here. Temptation is nothin' to play with," Jada said.

She was speaking her truth and saying what she felt was necessary to ensure her brother's safety. Although I didn't have the ability to do anything at all without a human making me do it, I knew Jada was correct when she basically called me a temptation.

"Sis, I'm good, though," Houston told her.

"I believe in your strength and your growth. I also believe you're good now, but the thing is, there will be a day when you're not so good. I'm not saying that just for you, I'm saying that because we are all pretty much guaranteed to have those terrible days when it seems like the world is falling down on us. When those days arrive, I don't even want you to have the opportunity to consider taking the 'easy' way out. I told you, we can't lose you, Houston. We can't," Jada told him.

Once again, the family found it necessary to tell Houston how important he was to them. Even though Houston was the one who used to try his best to keep his feelings to himself, he always was the sibling who was most impacted by what was going on around him. Knowing this, Jada and Ray constantly let him know how much they cared about him, especially after they found out about the interaction we almost had.

"Ray, can I ask you something?" Damon wondered.

"Yeah, what's up?"

"What if Houston would have used that gun, or what if you or Jada had to use it against somebody 'cause they broke into the house or something?"

Ray didn't immediately have an answer for his youngest brother, so the room was silent while he tried to think of one. After a few moments, he finally had something to say.

"Either way, I would be hurt, but if anything ever happened to you, Houston, or Jada because of a gun I brought into the house...I would be absolutely devastated. I would be burdened with guilt that I would have to take with me for the rest of my life. Really, I don't know if I would even be able to live with myself."

"If you couldn't live with yourself, would you think about doing the same thing Houston thought about?"

Damon's curiosity caused him to ask an unexpected and surprisingly brilliant question, but that was just the first of many that would soon follow. For each question Damon had, Ray and Jada tried their best to provide answers. No matter what they told him, nothing seemed to quench his thirst for knowledge.

"So, the gun is just a circle creator, huh?" Damon asked.

"What are you talking about?" everyone asked.

"The gun is just a circle creator. I mean, if someone gets mad or sad enough to use a gun, then they'll probably do something they shouldn't. When they do something they shouldn't do, it'll probably make somebody else mad or sad enough to do something. And then, if they do something...well, you get it. The gun just makes a circle that's hard for people to break."

"I really do have a family full of geniuses, huh? Damon, I can honestly say, I have never heard that term before," Ray said.

"Yeah, I kinda just made it up, so that's why you never heard of it before. Anyway, that's all I think the gun is. And I like different shapes, but I ain't really about that circle life. Y'all shouldn't be, either."

Like Raymond, I had never heard of the term 'circle creator,' but after hearing Damon's explanation, it made sense. I could understand why he said what he did, but I didn't agree with it. In his explanation, he said I was the cause of the circle of events. While my relatives and I contribute to the circles, we never are the ones to create them. Humans and their emotions are more responsible than we ever could be, but if adult human beings didn't understand that, I couldn't expect a child to.

"What am I supposed to do?" Ray asked.

"The gun did everything you wanted it to, it was even a part of your best work of art. So, you should just officially retire it. Houston, I need you to say the name of Ray's last piece again," Jada said.

"Mourning Darkness."

"See, I don't think you can get darker than a gun. I think we should just have a funeral for it, then we can mourn it and move on," Damon said.

"You make a good point, lil' bro. We don't even have to wait to do that. Let's put this gun to rest right now," Ray told him.

"For real?"

"Yeah, let's go," Raymond replied.

That's when I, along with all of my disassembled parts, were all picked up and placed inside of a random cloth bag. The family expressed a high level of excitement because they were getting rid of me and clearing their home of my 'negative energy.'

When Ray determined the family had reached a good burial spot, they stopped walking. Then, he asked his brothers to get a shovel so they could dig a home for me. They quickly got started and had frivolous discussions as the sound of the shovel continuously hit the ground.

"Okay, I think that's good," Ray said.

When those words were released, the bag I was in was thrown into the freshly dug hole. Ray immediately started speaking afterward.

"Today, we finally lay darkness to rest. In some form, darkness has been with us since we were kids, but that changes today. Today, this gun goes into the ground, and with it goes the negativity that has been weighing on all of us. Today, we briefly mourn darkness so we can keep moving closer to the joy of the light."

The word 'light' was apparently their cue to start covering me up because once it was said, I could hear dirt being thrown on me. I knew they were talking about me, but every bit of dirt they used made it increasingly difficult to hear and understand them. When I no longer heard the family talking, the noises from the shovel also were silenced. I had to assume they were gone, which meant my time with the humans was over.

Ray could have respected me enough to say goodbye before covering me up, but perhaps expecting a human to do the right thing was wanting too much. After all, my kind probably wouldn't even exist if people truly had the ability to do what was right.

The symbolizing gesture of burying me, an item that had never lived, was the type of nonsensical thing humans were known for. They were pretending like not being able to see me would take away all of the bad thoughts they had. They acted as though getting rid of the thing they purchased to keep them protected would actually be what protects them. Their actions were almost psychotic, but, good or bad, they would have to deal with whatever came with not having me around.

I was part of the darkness they felt they had to mourn, but they didn't understand neither darkness nor light was permanent. Whenever one was around, the other was simply waiting its turn to reappear. That's how I am. I don't believe my exit from the home is permanent, that's why they couldn't actually get rid of me. So, as I am forced to sit still in my temporary holding spot, I know at some point in the future, their dark thoughts will return. When they do, they all know I will be there for them. Sure, some assembly will be required, but they all know I am worth it. For now, I'll deal with my forced isolation, but they all know, when the time is right, we'll be together again.

AFTER THE NARRATIVES

*H*ow do the stories end? Well, they never will because your kind can't make it without us. We shoot because we have to, you shoot because you choose to. It can be difficult to work things out, especially when you just want to take the easier path of just getting rid of the person who opposes you. We know simple people need simple solutions, but who am I to judge? After all, I'm just a stupid machine.

Don't get me wrong, your rule makers definitely need to have some type of regulations in place for us, but you are really the ones who need to be regulated. See, those of you who choose to react to situations with violence are the weapons of mass destruction. Only you can take responsibility for bringing harm to another person, not us. You all tend to think we are necessary, but I'll let you in on a little secret; we're not.

You all get too stuck in your emotions to completely under-stand your reality. Some of you buy guns for protection, which is admirable. Others buy guns because they are trying to purchase power and status. In the eyes of those who think like that, we are enhancing accessories that can turn a lame into a legend. That's a flawed mentality.

Many of you talk to us more than you talk to your family. You will gladly carry us with you as if we are your best friends. In moments of temporary triumph, you tell us about the joy we bring to your lives. In moments of sadness, you wonder how we will work together to make things better.

It's funny how people love us, even though none of us will ever love you back. Based on our interactions, we have found humans tend to stay in toxic relationships much longer than they should. In relationships with us, the toxicity stems from you, the people in your environment, and your unwillingness to compromise.

We hear many of you claiming to praise your God, yet once we enter your lives, you end up worshiping us. You bow to our greatness, you pray that we help you make it through your worst situations, you look at us for strength, and if you ever put us to work, there's a very good chance you'll end up serving (a sentence for) us, too. It's ironic how that works, huh? You can't serve two masters, so if you're serving for us, how are you leaving room for your creator? I guess that's something for you to keep thinking about, after all, it is your soul on the line, not ours.

I'll just stop right there because I've given you enough to think about. Plus, we all know things start happening once me and my relatives start shooting off at the mouth, and we don't want that to happen, do we?

PERSPECTIVES OF VIOLENCE: A POEM BY BIG RUBE

I was created to fulfill a clear purpose
I exist free of desire, anger, sadness, or remorse
Emotionless, my function is to render the living motionless
At the command of my master
Without prejudice, I destroy enemies
Friends or family to me it doesn't matter
The warmth of a hand's grasp transforms into the grip of a cold
heart
As I'm awakened from my slumber
Prepared to play my part in some tragic narrative
Or is it one of humor?
I make no distinction as I don't possess the ability
In performance of my duty I feel no regret
No responsibility
As the finger that caresses my trigger firmly squeezes
Without hesitation I facilitate the elimination
of whomever the master pleases
No matter the sex, color, or age
I bring pain, death, and sorrow as a tool of pure rage
I usher victims to the grave and masters to the cage

As is the destiny of fools
As long as brother kills brother
All I need do is wait patiently
For the violent hand of another...
To wield me